BUZZELLI
COLLECTED WORKS VOLUME 3

The REVOLT of the WRETCHED

by
Guido Buzzelli

"Resurrection" Script by
Guido Buzzelli &
Grazia de Stefani

*"A Star for Ganymede"
Script by*
Giorgo Dell'Arti

Translated by
Jamie Richards

FLOATING WORLD COMICS

Failed Revolutions and Forever Wars

Valerio Stivè

THE BOOK YOU ARE HOLDING in your hands contains a piece of comics history. In 1965, Guido Buzzelli, a painter and comic artist based in Rome, set out to make what we would today call a graphic novel. He would create it without the support of a publisher and with no intention to make a series out of it; two requirements that were de facto for Italian comics of the time. It's difficult to imagine what a forward-thinking idea this was. The concept of independent comics did not exist in Italy (nor the rest of Europe) in the early sixties. Writing and drawing a long-form story from a place of self-expression was trememdously unique when comics were considered a commercial product and always commissioned by a publisher. By doing so, Buzzelli laid a foundation for generations of auteur comic artists to come.

Buzzelli completed *The Revolt of the Wretched* in early 1967, and it is now considered to be the first graphic novel produced in Italy, even coming before Hugo Pratt's *The Ballad of the Salt Sea*. Corto Maltese's first adventure was serialized in short chapters between 1967 and 1969, while *The Revolt of the Wretched* was published in 1967 as a standalone piece — more of a graphic novel than Pratt's, which is part of an ongoing saga with the same main character.

The Revolt of the Wretched had a troubled editorial history. After being rejected by numerous publishers, the comic debuted at the 1967 Salone Internazionale dei Comics (the predecessor to the Lucca Comics & Games festival). It was published in the Lucca Comics Almanacco, with a print run of just 200 copies. It was only in 1970 that the story reached a wider audience when an entire issue of the short-lived comics magazine *Psyco* reprinted it.

It was thanks to French comic artist and renowned editor Georges Wolinski, that Buzzelli found a wider audience, first in France and belatedly in Italy. Wolinski discovered *The Revolt of the Wretched* in the pages of *Psyco* at a newsstand kiosk while honeymooning in Naples, Italy. As editor of the legendary French magazine *Charlie*, Wolinski published *Revolt* in the December 1970 issue. That breakthrough success allowed Buzzelli to publish many other stories in France and opened doors in his native Italy, in magazines such as *Linus*, *Alter Alter*, and *Comic Art*.

In *The Revolt Of The Wretched* the reader experiences Buzzelli at his purest and rawest form. With his painterly and unrestrained style, Buzzelli was one of the most unique artists in the Italian and European comics scene. As a painter first and foremost, his techniques were deeply rooted in the Italian tradition, especially in the late Renaissance art of Caravaggio. His work was also strongly influenced by Goya, particularly in his depiction of violence and brutality.

The works of Buzzelli can be separated into two themes: grappling with his own demons; and exploring his political and social critiques. *The Revolt of the Wretched* primarily falls into this latter category. Like his suqsequent works, *The Labyrinth* and *HP* (two stories published in Volumes 1 & 2 of this Collected Works series), *Revolt* constructs a desperate and disillusioned allegory of our evermore polarized society. It foretells the political upheaval of

1968, and the disillusionment that followed. "*The Revolt of the Wretched* is a failed revolution," Buzzelli stated in an interview with ANAFI (Amici del Fumetto) from the 2002 edition of *The Labyrinth* by Grifo Edizioni.

Another recurring feature in Buzzelli's independent comics is his subversive and playful use of genre. He often employed the genre of science fiction, but with a surreal or postmodern twist. The stories in this volume are a peculiar kind of science fiction that take inspiration from Alex Raymond's *Flash Gordon*, and add a hallucinatory element. Stories like *Resurrection*, *A Star For Ganymede*, and *Zasafir* are visionary trips not only into space, but also into unknown worlds laden with psychological metaphor. The main characters — and the reader as well — are abruptly catapulted into distorted versions of our reality, finding themselves astounded, disarmed, and helpless.

In the case of *Zasafir*, the characters are not just lost in space, they are left with with no resolution at all. The first volume was published between 1980 and 1981 in the seminal Italian magazine *Alter Alter*. It was originally 39 pages in black & white, with one color episode. The story was later expanded and partially reworked both in color and text for the French market. *L'Echo des Savanes* magazine reprinted it between 1984 and 1985, and the publisher Albin Michel collected it in a single volume.

The second volume of *Zasafir* was never completed. The unfinished work appears in this book, and has only recently seen the light of day, thanks to Coconino Press' Italian edition of Buzzelli's works published in 2022. That volume's *The Incomplete Zasafir* contained a rediscovered annotation by Buzzelli himself, outlining his work in progress:

> "Leo's series of adventures (a personal, nostalgic, slightly ironic evocation of the world that fascinated me as a child: Flash Gordon, Ming, the planet Mongo...) will enact the age-old battle between good and evil (Zasafir and Atesm) on the planet Zarau, a metaphorical adaptation of our Earthly world. This fantasy is punctuated with conversations between father on Earth and son in space that juxtapose the disappointments of the older generation against the hopes of the next, and also give the story a rhythmic cadence. All this on a single, highly-readable level, with a tone more reminiscent of fairy tales than science fiction while still using clearly futuristic imagery."

The key to understanding Buzzelli's visions is satire; a cruel, bitter, and disenchanted satire addressed to the modern world and modern man. Along with Buzzelli's characters, readers are often left with no explanation to understand the circumstances and worlds in which they find themselves. Endings are open and unresolved. Buzzelli's stories need to be seen as a rupture, a breach that opens a door to the unreal, posing questions and dilemmas.

Ultimately, the revolution is a failed revolution, the battles between good and evil do not see an end. Buzzelli leaves us with questions unanswered. His art boldly provokes us, scornfully disturbs us. These are the things that make him a great artist and one that is still relevant today.

The Revolt of the Wretched

(1967)

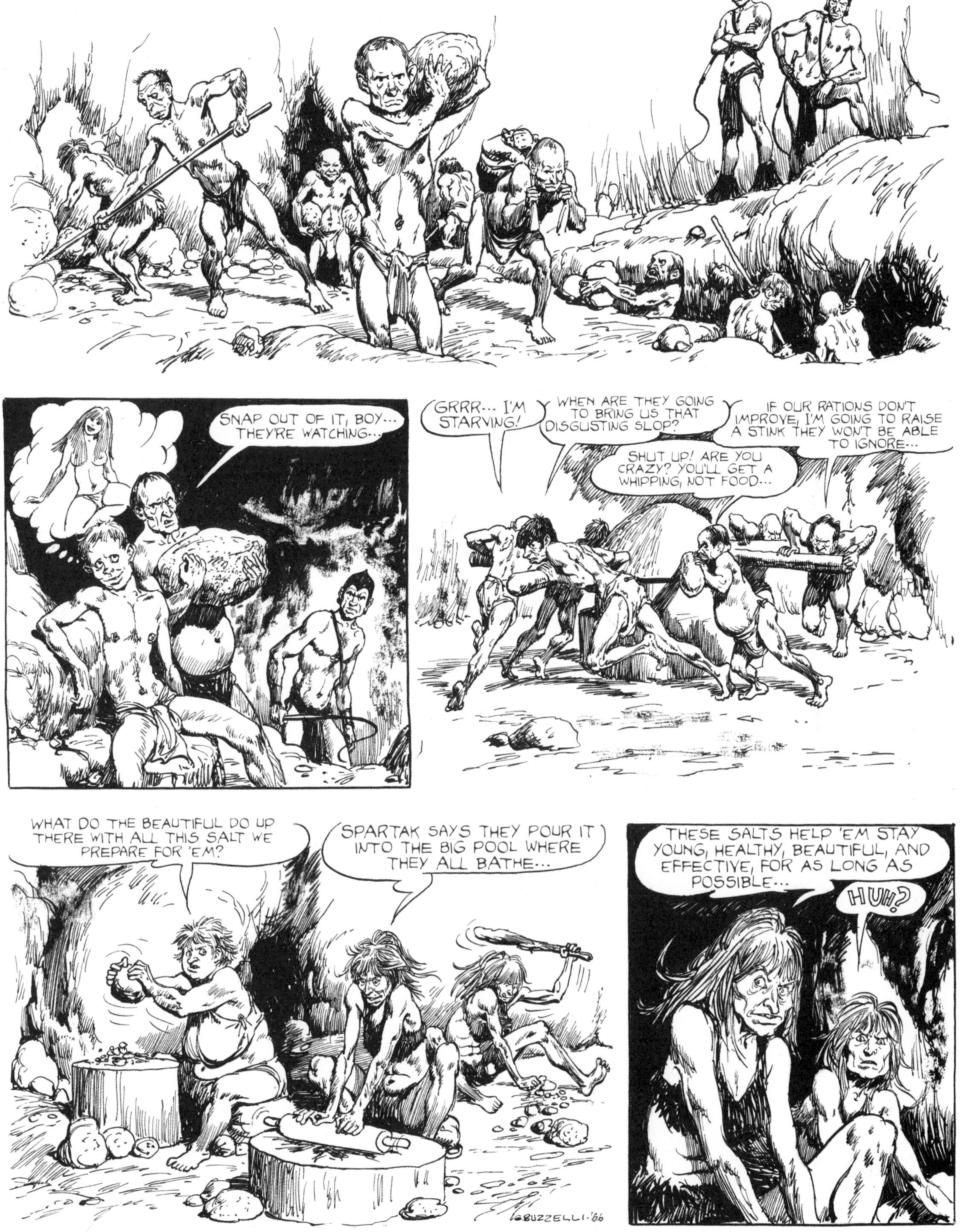
SNAP OUT OF IT, BOY... THEY'RE WATCHING...
GRRR... I'M STARVING!
WHEN ARE THEY GOING TO BRING US THAT DISGUSTING SLOP?
IF OUR RATIONS DON'T IMPROVE, I'M GOING TO RAISE A STINK THEY WON'T BE ABLE TO IGNORE...
SHUT UP! ARE YOU CRAZY? YOU'LL GET A WHIPPING, NOT FOOD...
WHAT DO THE BEAUTIFUL DO UP THERE WITH ALL THIS SALT WE PREPARE FOR 'EM?
SPARTAK SAYS THEY POUR IT INTO THE BIG POOL WHERE THEY ALL BATHE...
THESE SALTS HELP 'EM STAY YOUNG, HEALTHY, BEAUTIFUL, AND EFFECTIVE, FOR AS LONG AS POSSIBLE...
HUH?
G.BUZZELLI-'66

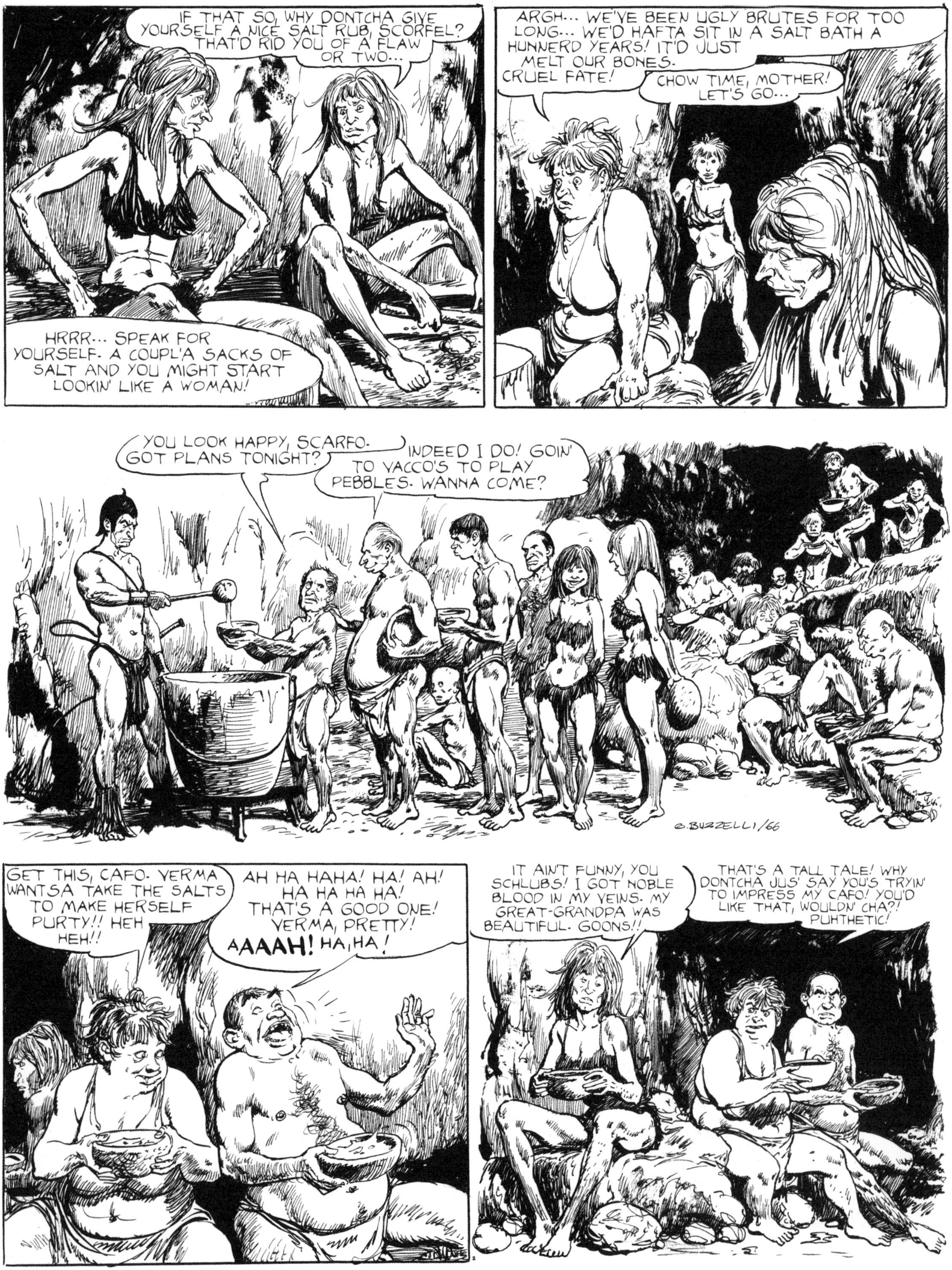
IF THAT SO, WHY DONTCHA GIVE YOURSELF A NICE SALT RUB, SCORFEL? THAT'D RID YOU OF A FLAW OR TWO...
HRRR... SPEAK FOR YOURSELF- A COUPL'A SACKS OF SALT AND YOU MIGHT START LOOKIN' LIKE A WOMAN!
ARGH... WE'VE BEEN UGLY BRUTES FOR TOO LONG... WE'D HAFTA SIT IN A SALT BATH A HUNNERD YEARS! IT'D JUST MELT OUR BONES- CRUEL FATE!
CHOW TIME, MOTHER! LET'S GO...
YOU LOOK HAPPY, SCARFO- GOT PLANS TONIGHT?
INDEED I DO! GOIN' TO VACCO'S TO PLAY PEBBLES- WANNA COME?
G. BUZZELLI/66
GET THIS, CAFO- VERMA WANTSA TAKE THE SALTS TO MAKE HERSELF PURTY!! HEH HEH!!
AH HA HAHA! HA! AH! HA HA HA HA! THAT'S A GOOD ONE! VERMA, PRETTY! AAAAH! HA, HA!
IT AIN'T FUNNY, YOU SCHLUBS! I GOT NOBLE BLOOD IN MY VEINS- MY GREAT-GRANDPA WAS BEAUTIFUL- GOONS!!
THAT'S A TALL TALE! WHY DONTCHA JUS' SAY YOU'S TRYIN' TO IMPRESS MY CAFO! YOU'D LIKE THAT, WOULDN' CHA?! PUHTHETIC!

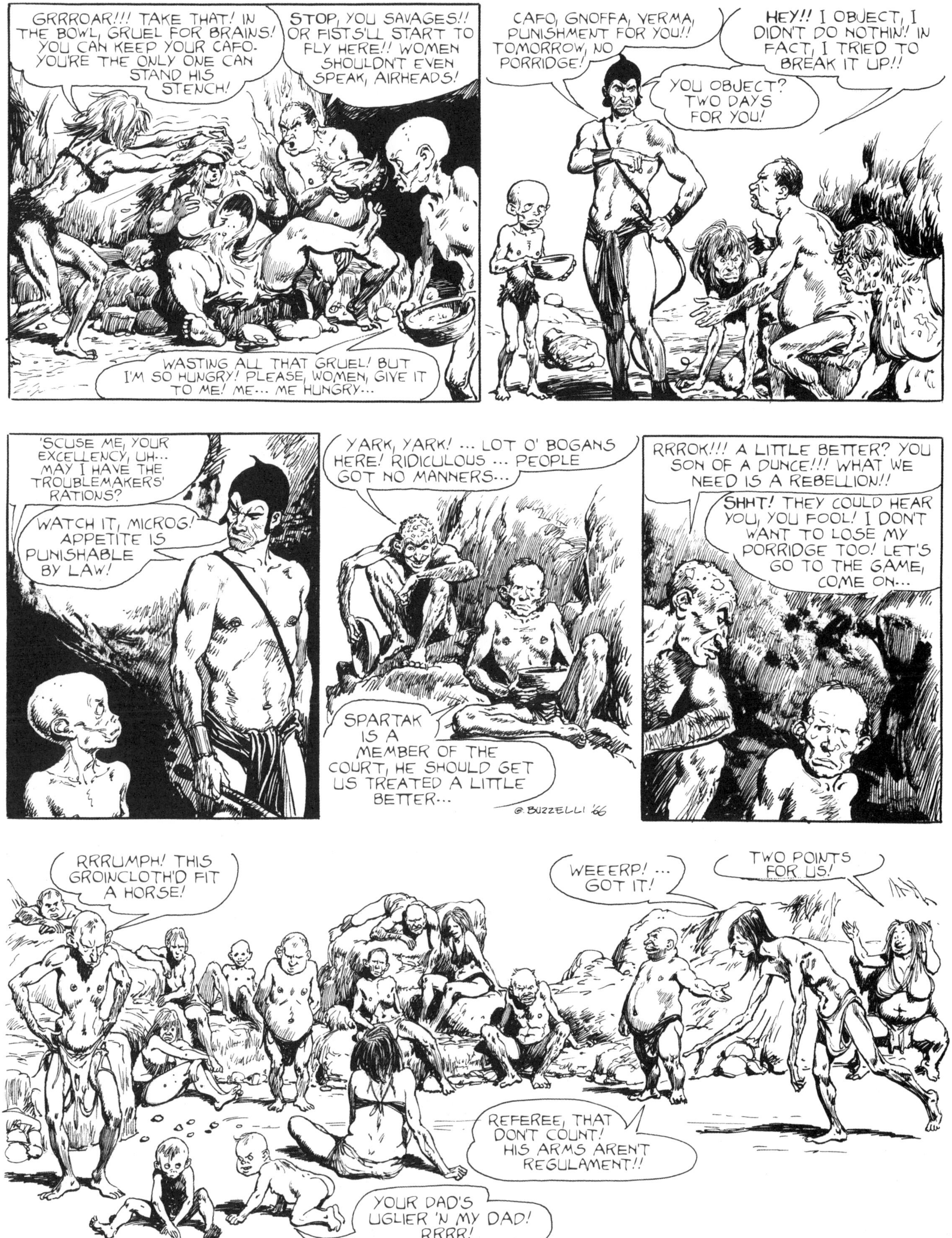
GRRROAR!!! TAKE THAT! IN THE BOWL, GRUEL FOR BRAINS! YOU CAN KEEP YOUR CAFO- YOU'RE THE ONLY ONE CAN STAND HIS STENCH!
STOP, YOU SAVAGES!! OR FISTS'LL START TO FLY HERE!! WOMEN SHOULDN'T EVEN SPEAK, AIRHEADS!
WASTING ALL THAT GRUEL! BUT I'M SO HUNGRY! PLEASE, WOMEN, GIVE IT TO ME! ME... ME HUNGRY...
CAFO, GNOFFA, VERMA, PUNISHMENT FOR YOU!! TOMORROW, NO PORRIDGE!
HEY!! I OBJECT, I DIDN'T DO NOTHIN'! IN FACT, I TRIED TO BREAK IT UP!!
YOU OBJECT? TWO DAYS FOR YOU!
'SCUSE ME, YOUR EXCELLENCY, UH... MAY I HAVE THE TROUBLEMAKERS' RATIONS?
WATCH IT, MICROG! APPETITE IS PUNISHABLE BY LAW!
YARK, YARK! ... LOT O' BOGANS HERE! RIDICULOUS ... PEOPLE GOT NO MANNERS...
SPARTAK IS A MEMBER OF THE COURT, HE SHOULD GET US TREATED A LITTLE BETTER...
G. BUZZELLI '66
RRROK!!! A LITTLE BETTER? YOU SON OF A DUNCE!!! WHAT WE NEED IS A REBELLION!!
SHHT! THEY COULD HEAR YOU, YOU FOOL! I DON'T WANT TO LOSE MY PORRIDGE TOO! LET'S GO TO THE GAME, COME ON...
RRRUMPH! THIS GROINCLOTH'D FIT A HORSE!
WEEERP! ... GOT IT!
TWO POINTS FOR US!
REFEREE, THAT DON'T COUNT! HIS ARMS AREN'T REGULAMENT!!
YOUR DAD'S UGLIER 'N MY DAD! RRRR!

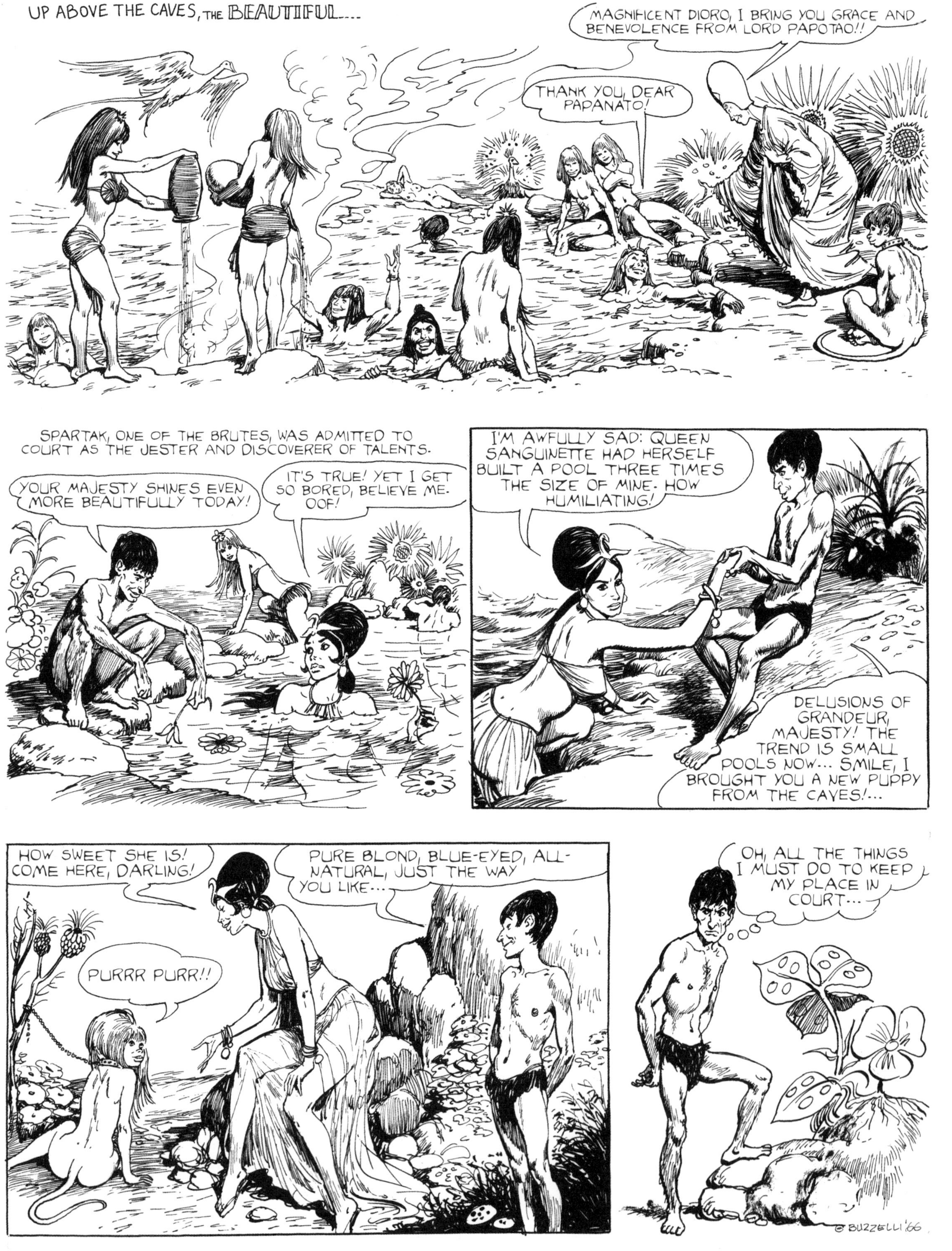
UP ABOVE THE CAVES, THE BEAUTIFUL....
MAGNIFICENT DIORO, I BRING YOU GRACE AND BENEVOLENCE FROM LORD PAPOTAO!!
THANK YOU, DEAR PAPANATO!
SPARTAK, ONE OF THE BRUTES, WAS ADMITTED TO COURT AS THE JESTER AND DISCOVERER OF TALENTS.
YOUR MAJESTY SHINES EVEN MORE BEAUTIFULLY TODAY!
IT'S TRUE! YET I GET SO BORED, BELIEVE ME. OOF!
I'M AWFULLY SAD: QUEEN SANGUINETTE HAD HERSELF BUILT A POOL THREE TIMES THE SIZE OF MINE. HOW HUMILIATING!
DELUSIONS OF GRANDEUR, MAJESTY! THE TREND IS SMALL POOLS NOW... SMILE, I BROUGHT YOU A NEW PUPPY FROM THE CAVES!...
HOW SWEET SHE IS! COME HERE, DARLING!
PURE BLOND, BLUE-EYED, ALL-NATURAL, JUST THE WAY YOU LIKE...
PURRR PURR!!
OH, ALL THE THINGS I MUST DO TO KEEP MY PLACE IN COURT...
© BUZZELLI '66

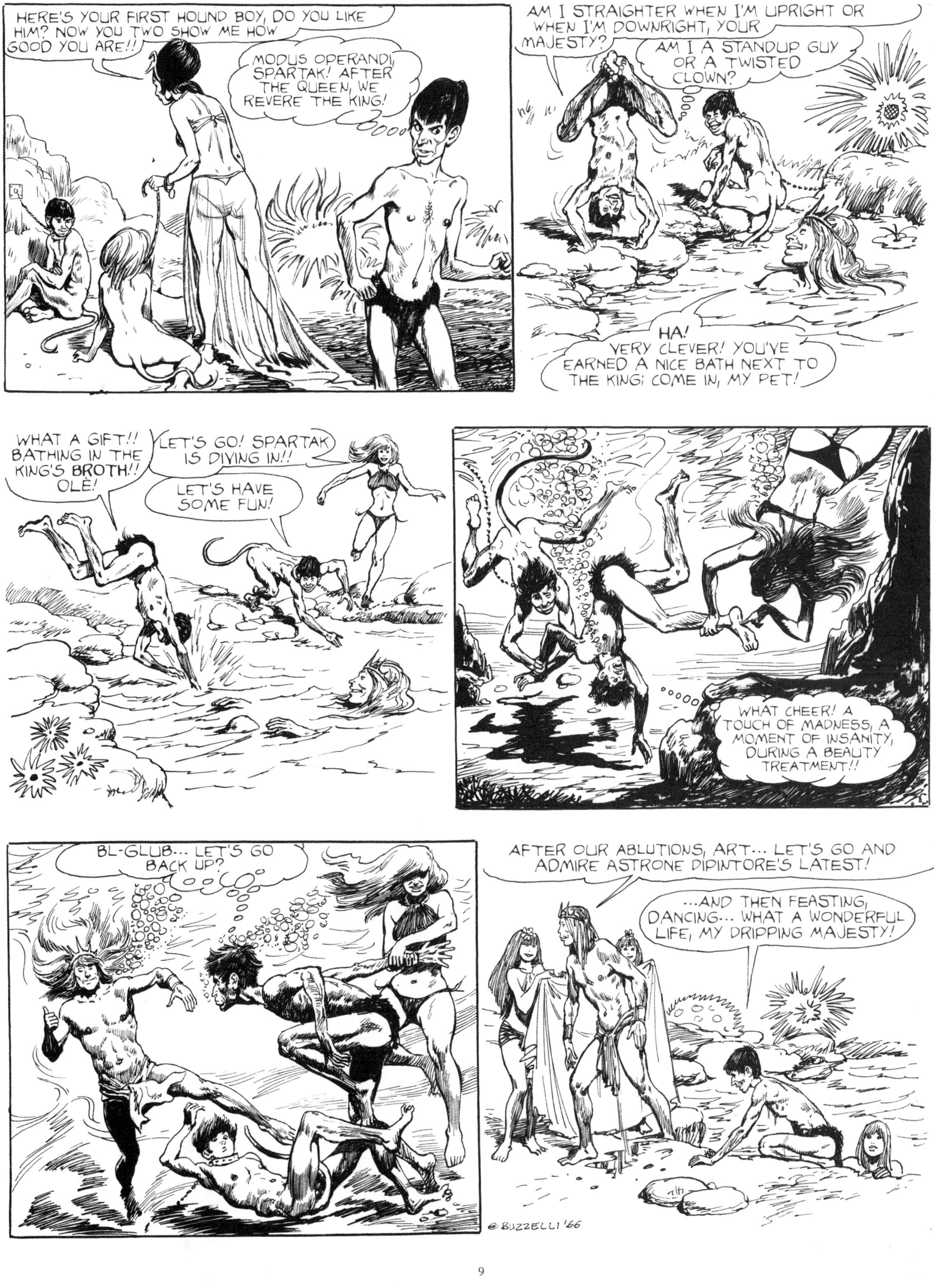
HERE'S YOUR FIRST HOUND BOY, DO YOU LIKE HIM? NOW YOU TWO SHOW ME HOW GOOD YOU ARE!!
MODUS OPERANDI, SPARTAK! AFTER THE QUEEN, WE REVERE THE KING!
AM I STRAIGHTER WHEN I'M UPRIGHT OR WHEN I'M DOWNRIGHT, YOUR MAJESTY?
AM I A STANDUP GUY OR A TWISTED CLOWN?
HA! VERY CLEVER! YOU'VE EARNED A NICE BATH NEXT TO THE KING; COME IN, MY PET!
WHAT A GIFT!! BATHING IN THE KING'S BROTH!! OLÈ!
LET'S GO! SPARTAK IS DIVING IN!!
LET'S HAVE SOME FUN!
WHAT CHEER! A TOUCH OF MADNESS, A MOMENT OF INSANITY, DURING A BEAUTY TREATMENT!!
BL-GLUB... LET'S GO BACK UP?
AFTER OUR ABLUTIONS, ART... LET'S GO AND ADMIRE ASTRONE DIPINTORE'S LATEST!
...AND THEN FEASTING, DANCING... WHAT A WONDERFUL LIFE, MY DRIPPING MAJESTY!
©BUZZELLI '66

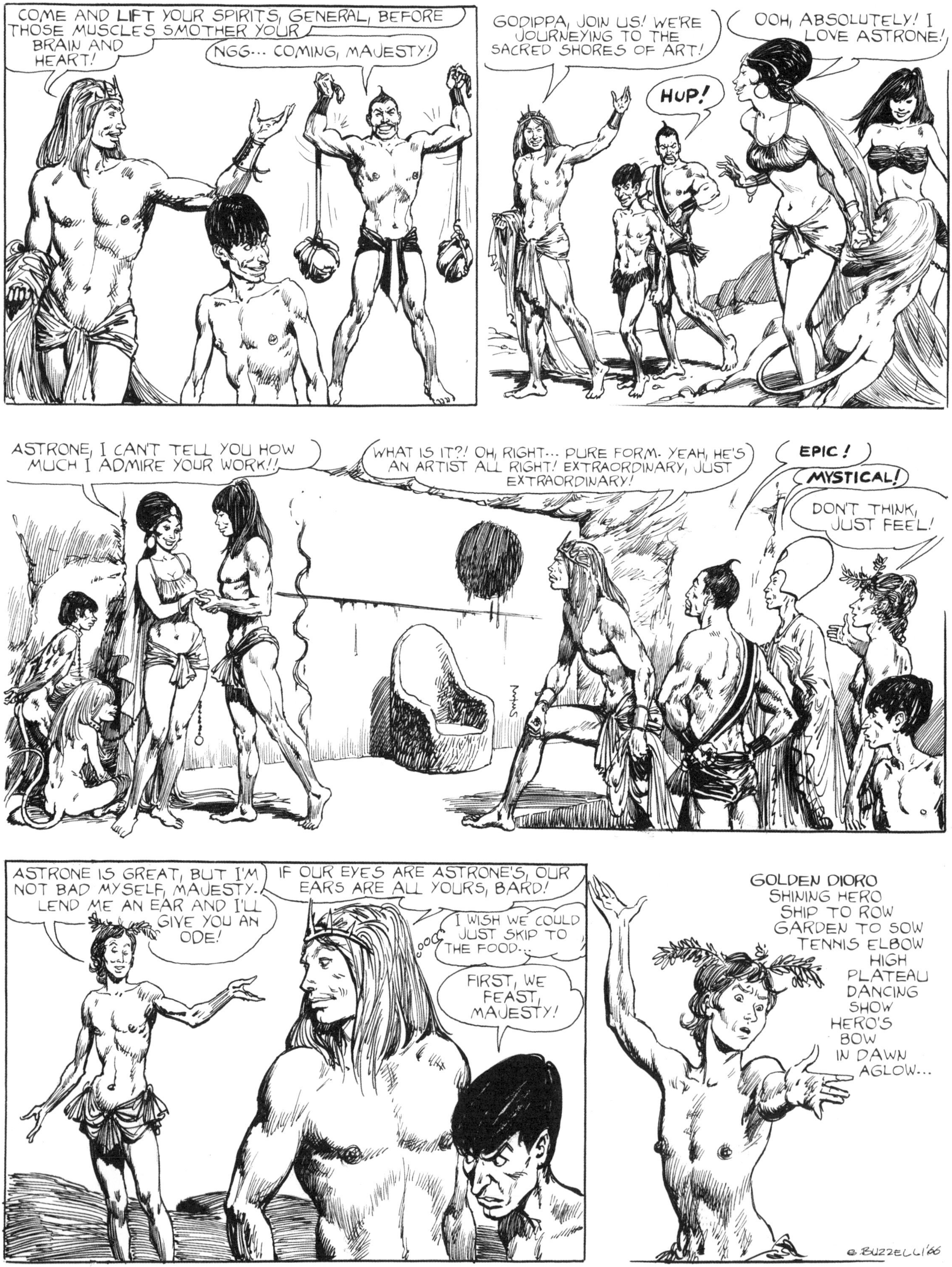
COME AND LIFT YOUR SPIRITS, GENERAL, BEFORE THOSE MUSCLES SMOTHER YOUR BRAIN AND HEART!
NGG... COMING, MAJESTY!
GODIPPA, JOIN US! WE'RE JOURNEYING TO THE SACRED SHORES OF ART!
HUP!
OOH, ABSOLUTELY! I LOVE ASTRONE!
ASTRONE, I CAN'T TELL YOU HOW MUCH I ADMIRE YOUR WORK!!
WHAT IS IT?! OH, RIGHT... PURE FORM. YEAH, HE'S AN ARTIST ALL RIGHT! EXTRAORDINARY, JUST EXTRAORDINARY!
EPIC!
MYSTICAL!
DON'T THINK, JUST FEEL!
ASTRONE IS GREAT, BUT I'M NOT BAD MYSELF, MAJESTY. LEND ME AN EAR AND I'LL GIVE YOU AN ODE!
IF OUR EYES ARE ASTRONE'S, OUR EARS ARE ALL YOURS, BARD!
I WISH WE COULD JUST SKIP TO THE FOOD...
FIRST, WE FEAST, MAJESTY!
GOLDEN DIORO
SHINING HERO
SHIP TO ROW
GARDEN TO SOW
TENNIS ELBOW
HIGH
PLATEAU
DANCING
SHOW
HERO'S
BOW
IN DAWN
AGLOW...
© BUZZELLI '66

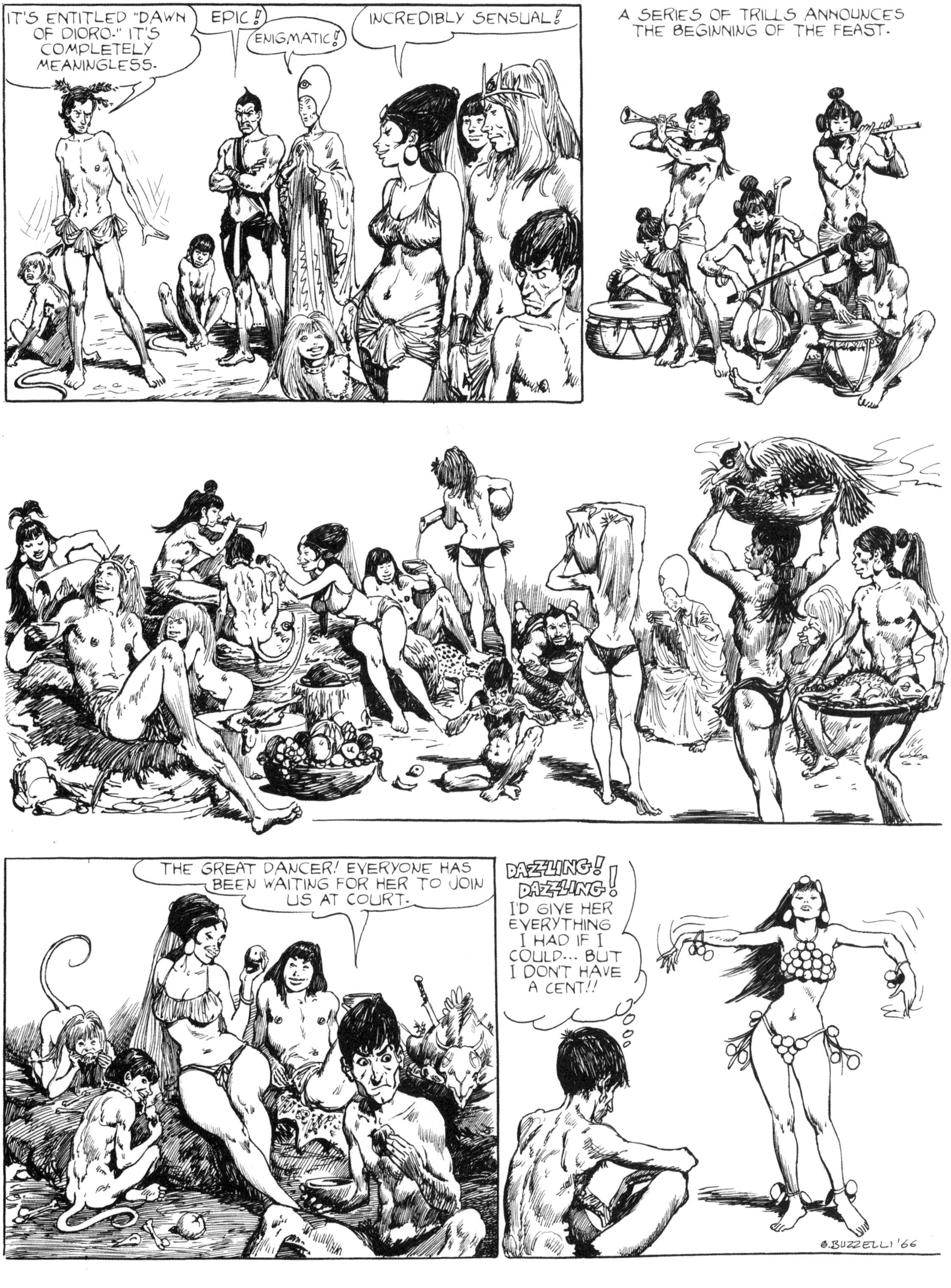
IT'S ENTITLED "DAWN OF DIORO-" IT'S COMPLETELY MEANINGLESS.
EPIC!
ENIGMATIC!
INCREDIBLY SENSUAL!
A SERIES OF TRILLS ANNOUNCES THE BEGINNING OF THE FEAST.
THE GREAT DANCER! EVERYONE HAS BEEN WAITING FOR HER TO JOIN US AT COURT.
DAZZLING! DAZZLING!
I'D GIVE HER EVERYTHING I HAD IF I COULD... BUT I DON'T HAVE A CENT!!
G. BUZZELLI '66

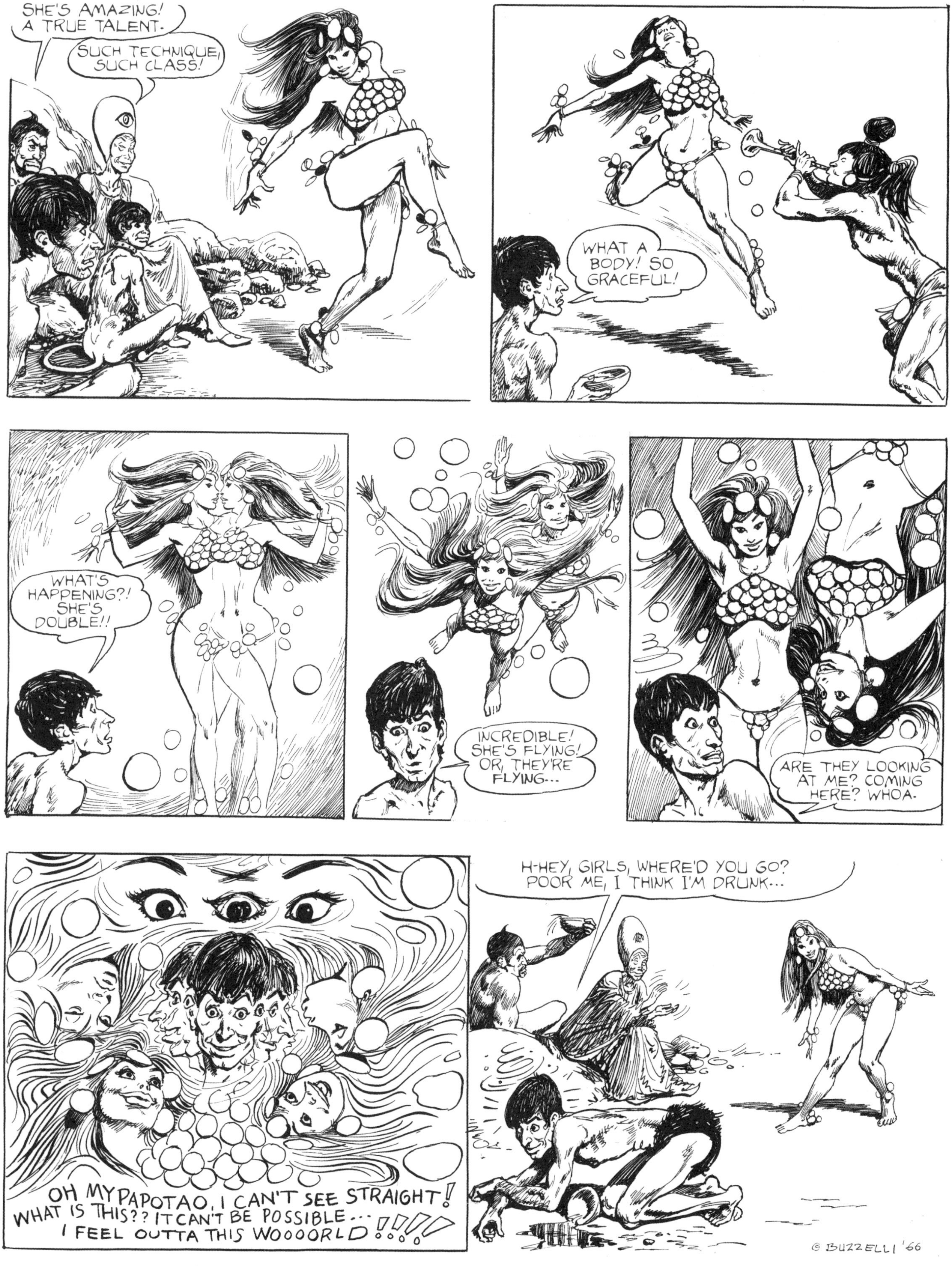
SHE'S AMAZING! A TRUE TALENT.
SUCH TECHNIQUE, SUCH CLASS!
WHAT A BODY! SO GRACEFUL!
WHAT'S HAPPENING?! SHE'S DOUBLE!!
INCREDIBLE! SHE'S FLYING! OR, THEY'RE FLYING...
ARE THEY LOOKING AT ME? COMING HERE? WHOA.
OH MY PAPOTAO, I CAN'T SEE STRAIGHT! WHAT IS THIS?? IT CAN'T BE POSSIBLE... I FEEL OUTTA THIS WOOOORLD!!!!!
H-HEY, GIRLS, WHERE'D YOU GO? POOR ME, I THINK I'M DRUNK...
© BUZZELLI '66

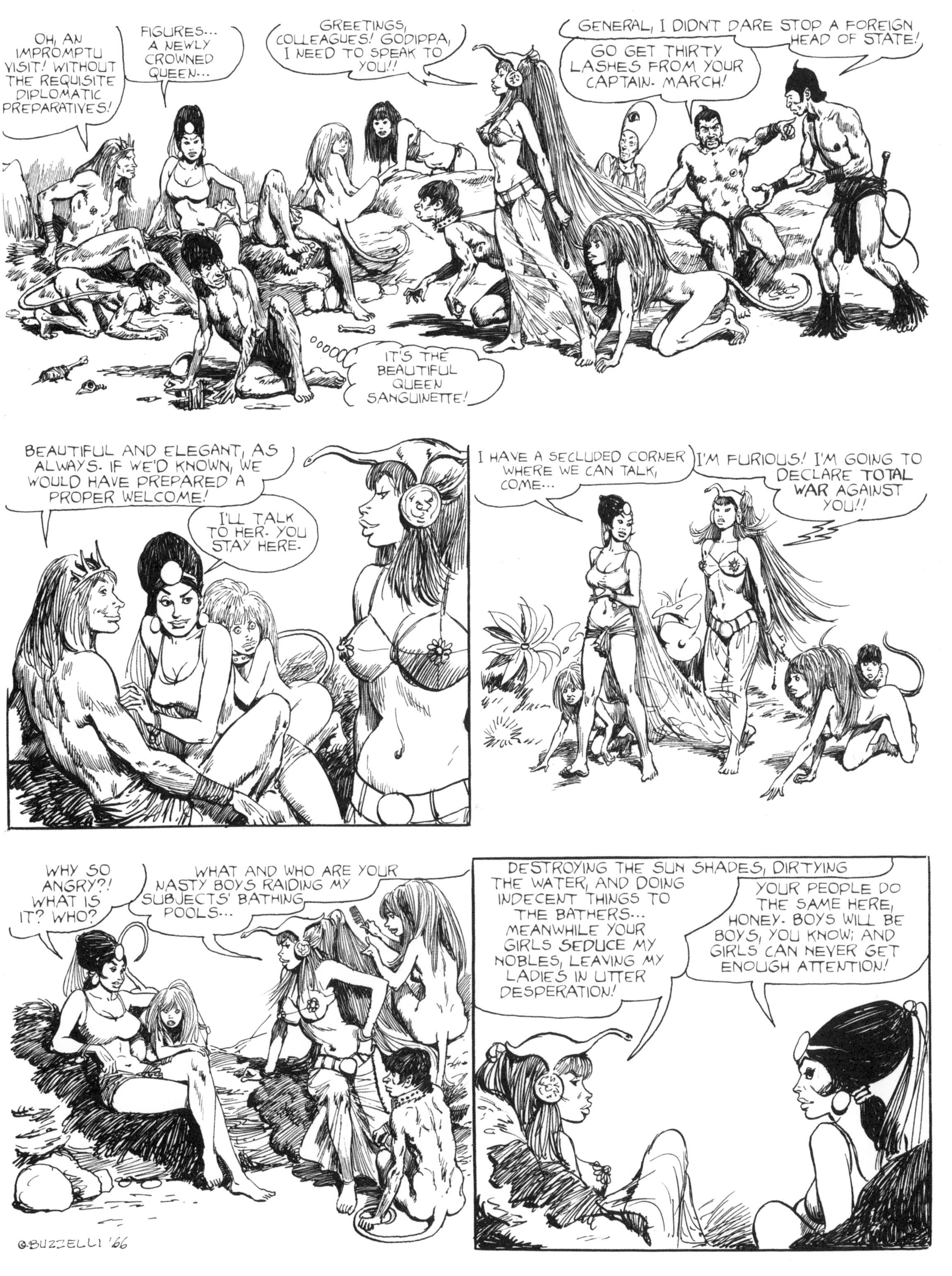
OH, AN IMPROMPTU VISIT! WITHOUT THE REQUISITE DIPLOMATIC PREPARATIVES!
FIGURES... A NEWLY CROWNED QUEEN...
GREETINGS, COLLEAGUES! GODIPPA, I NEED TO SPEAK TO YOU!!
GENERAL, I DIDN'T DARE STOP A FOREIGN HEAD OF STATE!
GO GET THIRTY LASHES FROM YOUR CAPTAIN. MARCH!
IT'S THE BEAUTIFUL QUEEN SANGUINETTE!
BEAUTIFUL AND ELEGANT, AS ALWAYS. IF WE'D KNOWN, WE WOULD HAVE PREPARED A PROPER WELCOME!
I'LL TALK TO HER. YOU STAY HERE.
I HAVE A SECLUDED CORNER WHERE WE CAN TALK, COME...
I'M FURIOUS! I'M GOING TO DECLARE TOTAL WAR AGAINST YOU!!
WHY SO ANGRY?! WHAT IS IT? WHO?
WHAT AND WHO ARE YOUR NASTY BOYS RAIDING MY SUBJECTS' BATHING POOLS...
DESTROYING THE SUN SHADES, DIRTYING THE WATER, AND DOING INDECENT THINGS TO THE BATHERS... MEANWHILE YOUR GIRLS SEDUCE MY NOBLES, LEAVING MY LADIES IN UTTER DESPERATION!
YOUR PEOPLE DO THE SAME HERE, HONEY. BOYS WILL BE BOYS, YOU KNOW; AND GIRLS CAN NEVER GET ENOUGH ATTENTION!
©BUZZELLI '66

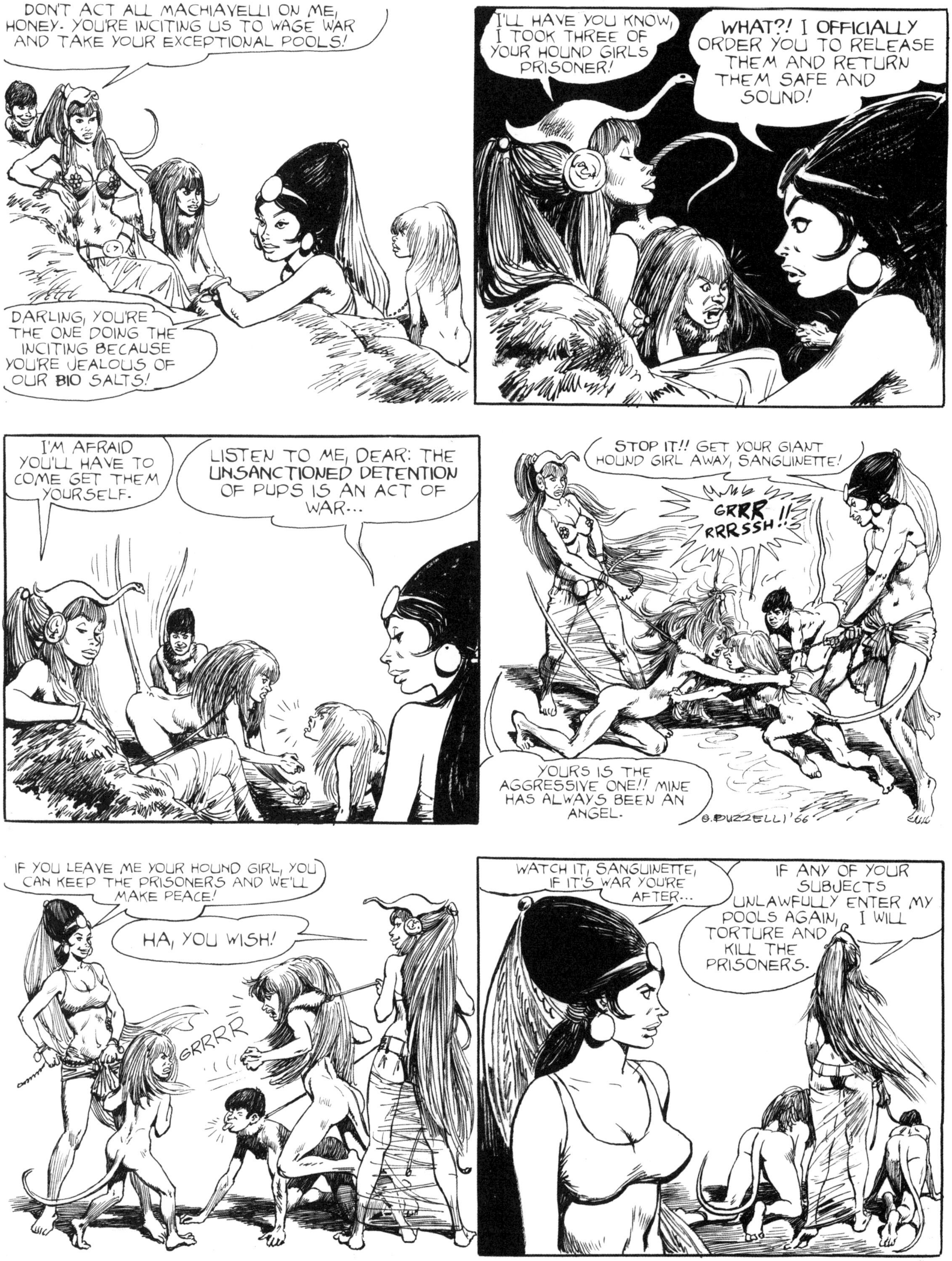

DON'T ACT ALL MACHIAVELLI ON ME, HONEY- YOU'RE INCITING US TO WAGE WAR AND TAKE YOUR EXCEPTIONAL POOLS!
DARLING, YOU'RE THE ONE DOING THE INCITING BECAUSE YOU'RE JEALOUS OF OUR BIO SALTS!
I'LL HAVE YOU KNOW, I TOOK THREE OF YOUR HOUND GIRLS PRISONER!
WHAT?! I OFFICIALLY ORDER YOU TO RELEASE THEM AND RETURN THEM SAFE AND SOUND!
I'M AFRAID YOU'LL HAVE TO COME GET THEM YOURSELF.
LISTEN TO ME, DEAR: THE UNSANCTIONED DETENTION OF PUPS IS AN ACT OF WAR...
STOP IT!! GET YOUR GIANT HOUND GIRL AWAY, SANGUINETTE!
GRRR RRRSSH!!
YOURS IS THE AGGRESSIVE ONE!! MINE HAS ALWAYS BEEN AN ANGEL.
G. PUZZELLI '66
IF YOU LEAVE ME YOUR HOUND GIRL, YOU CAN KEEP THE PRISONERS AND WE'LL MAKE PEACE!
HA, YOU WISH!
GRRRR
WATCH IT, SANGUINETTE, IF IT'S WAR YOU'RE AFTER...
IF ANY OF YOUR SUBJECTS UNLAWFULLY ENTER MY POOLS AGAIN, I WILL TORTURE AND KILL THE PRISONERS.

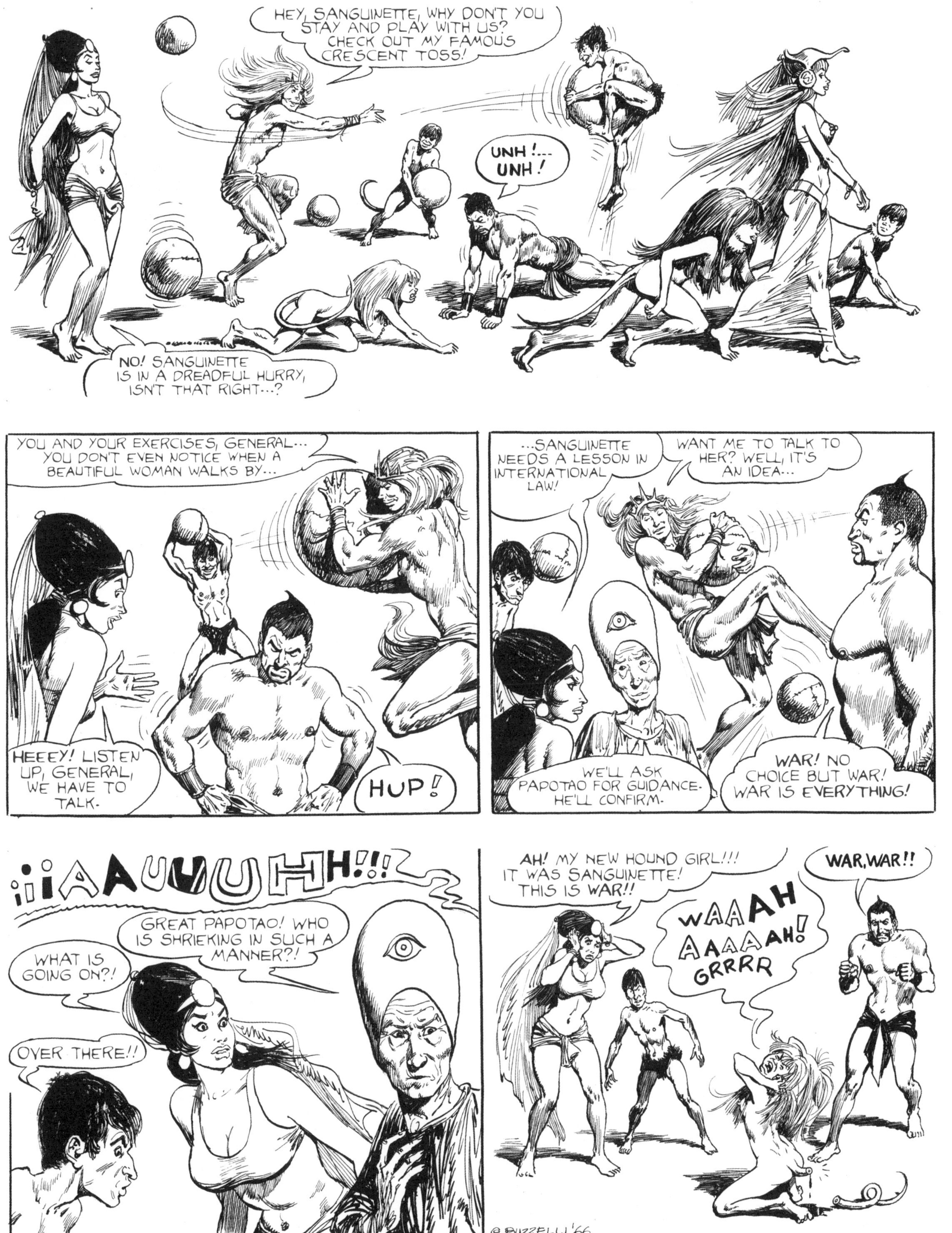

HEY, SANGUINETTE, WHY DON'T YOU STAY AND PLAY WITH US? CHECK OUT MY FAMOUS CRESCENT TOSS!
UNH!... UNH!
NO! SANGUINETTE IS IN A DREADFUL HURRY, ISN'T THAT RIGHT...?
YOU AND YOUR EXERCISES, GENERAL... YOU DON'T EVEN NOTICE WHEN A BEAUTIFUL WOMAN WALKS BY...
HEEEY! LISTEN UP, GENERAL, WE HAVE TO TALK.
HUP!
...SANGUINETTE NEEDS A LESSON IN INTERNATIONAL LAW!
WANT ME TO TALK TO HER? WELL, IT'S AN IDEA...
WE'LL ASK PAPOTAO FOR GUIDANCE. HE'LL CONFIRM.
WAR! NO CHOICE BUT WAR! WAR IS EVERYTHING!
¡¡IAAUUUHHH!!!
WHAT IS GOING ON?!
GREAT PAPOTAO! WHO IS SHRIEKING IN SUCH A MANNER?!
OVER THERE!!
AH! MY NEW HOUND GIRL!!! IT WAS SANGUINETTE! THIS IS WAR!!
WAAAH AAAAAH! GRRRR
WAR, WAR!!
G. BUZZELLI '66

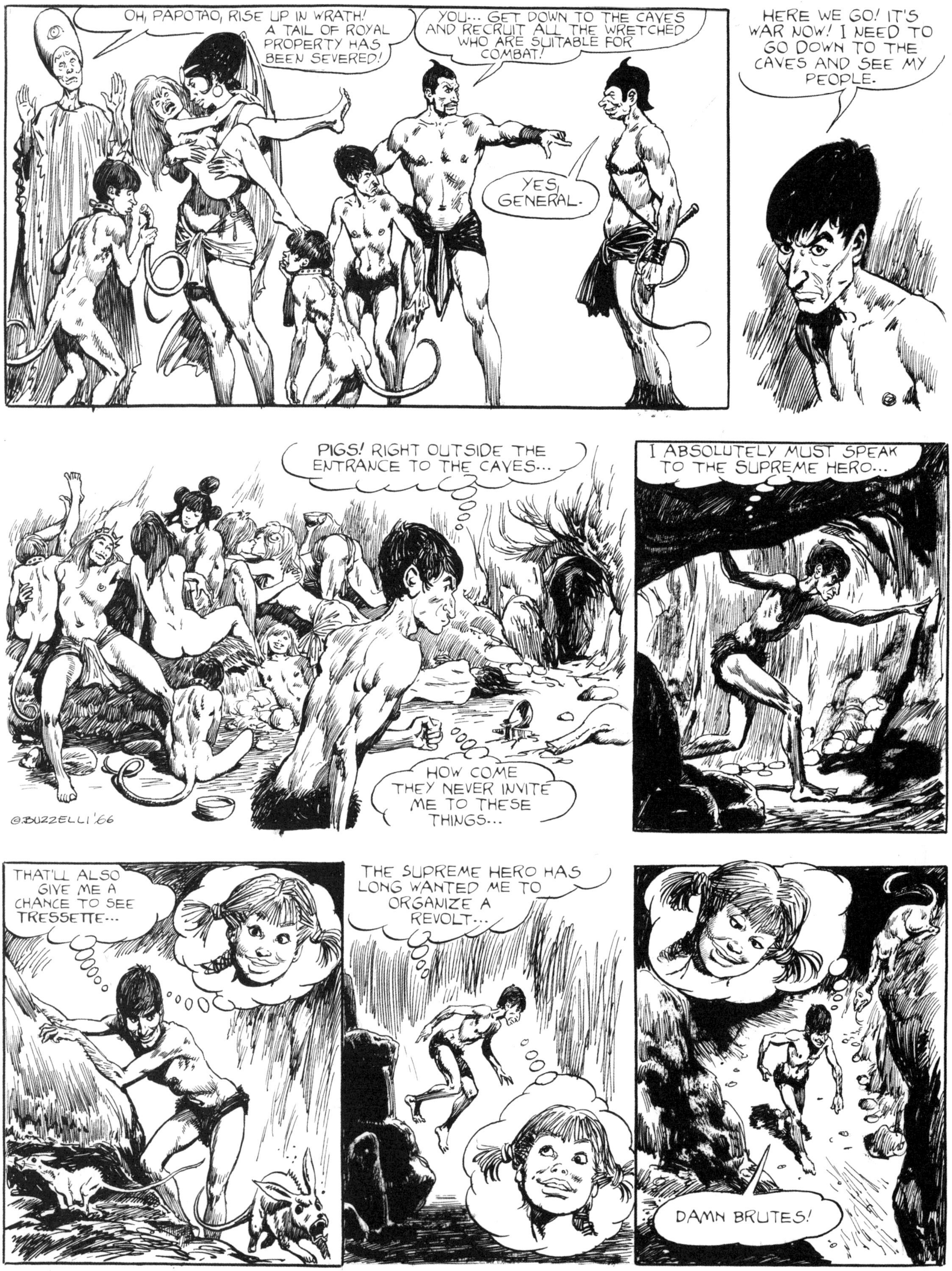
OH, PAPOTAO, RISE UP IN WRATH! A TAIL OF ROYAL PROPERTY HAS BEEN SEVERED!
YOU... GET DOWN TO THE CAVES AND RECRUIT ALL THE WRETCHED WHO ARE SUITABLE FOR COMBAT!
YES, GENERAL.
HERE WE GO! IT'S WAR NOW! I NEED TO GO DOWN TO THE CAVES AND SEE MY PEOPLE.
PIGS! RIGHT OUTSIDE THE ENTRANCE TO THE CAVES...
HOW COME THEY NEVER INVITE ME TO THESE THINGS...
©BUZZELLI '66
I ABSOLUTELY MUST SPEAK TO THE SUPREME HERO...
THAT'LL ALSO GIVE ME A CHANCE TO SEE TRESSETTE...
THE SUPREME HERO HAS LONG WANTED ME TO ORGANIZE A REVOLT...
DAMN BRUTES!

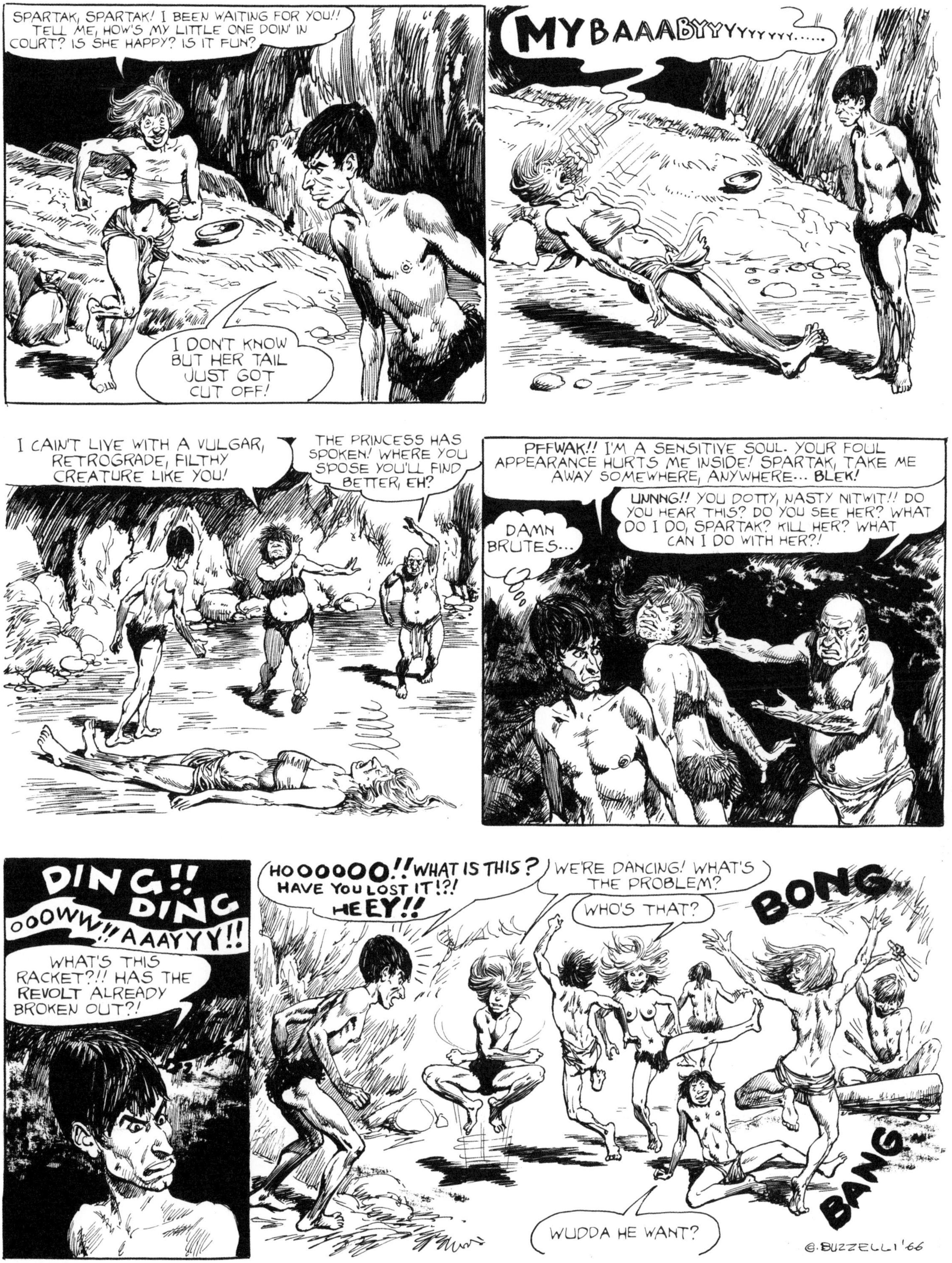
SPARTAK, SPARTAK! I BEEN WAITING FOR YOU!! TELL ME, HOW'S MY LITTLE ONE DOIN' IN COURT? IS SHE HAPPY? IS IT FUN?
I DON'T KNOW BUT HER TAIL JUST GOT CUT OFF!
MYBAAABYYYYYYYY......
I CAIN'T LIVE WITH A VULGAR, RETROGRADE, FILTHY CREATURE LIKE YOU!
THE PRINCESS HAS SPOKEN! WHERE YOU S'POSE YOU'LL FIND BETTER, EH?
PFFWAK!! I'M A SENSITIVE SOUL. YOUR FOUL APPEARANCE HURTS ME INSIDE! SPARTAK, TAKE ME AWAY SOMEWHERE, ANYWHERE... BLEK!
DAMN BRUTES...
UNNNG!! YOU DOTTY, NASTY NITWIT!! DO YOU HEAR THIS? DO YOU SEE HER? WHAT DO I DO, SPARTAK? KILL HER? WHAT CAN I DO WITH HER?!
DING!! DING
OOOWW!! AAAYYY!!
WHAT'S THIS RACKET?!! HAS THE REVOLT ALREADY BROKEN OUT?!
HOOOOOO!! WHAT IS THIS? HAVE YOU LOST IT!?! HEEY!!
WE'RE DANCING! WHAT'S THE PROBLEM?
WHO'S THAT?
BONG
BANG
WUDDA HE WANT?
©. BUZZELLI '66

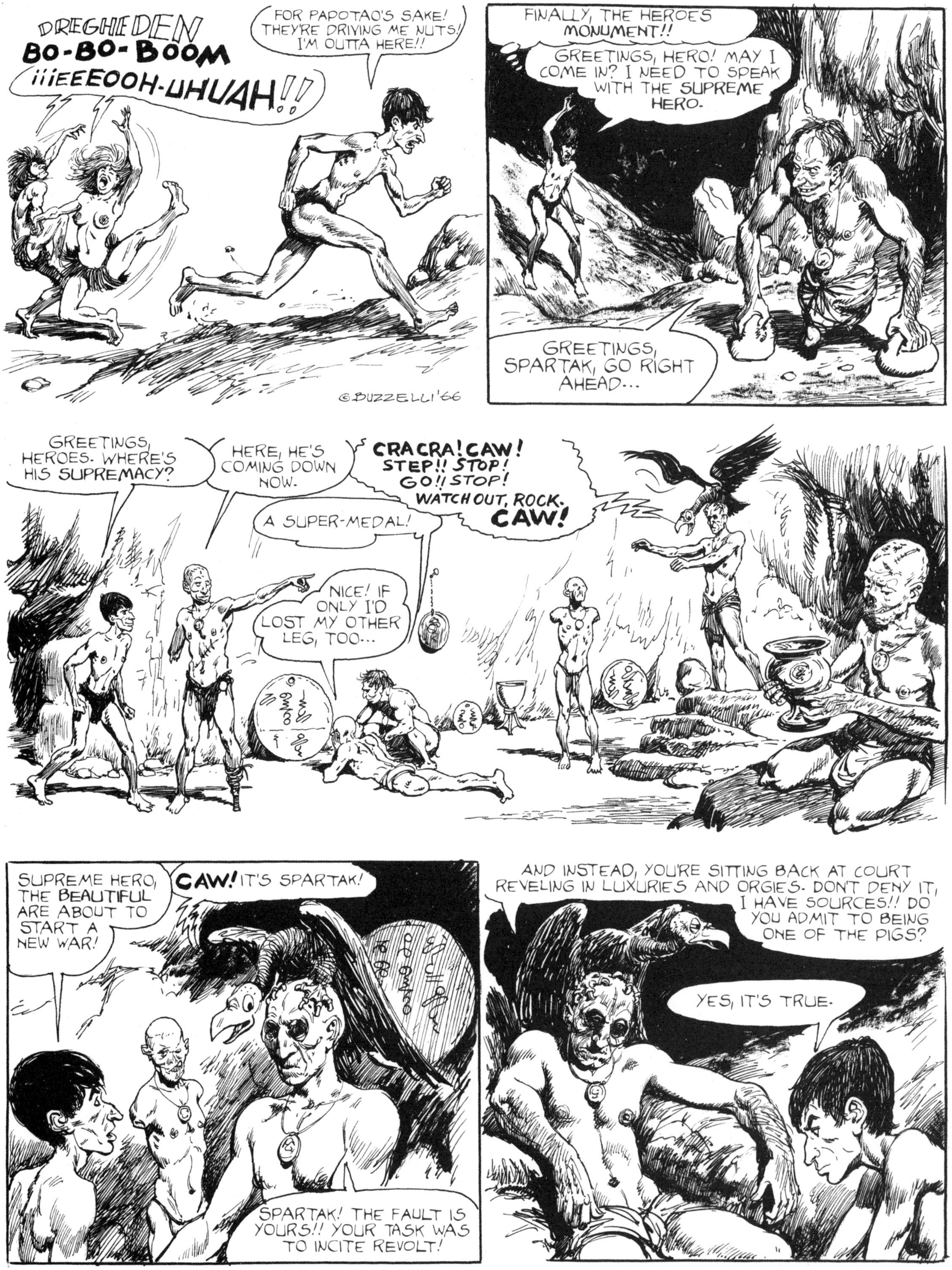
DREGHEDEN
BO-BO-BOOM
¡¡¡EEEOOH-UHUAH!!
FOR PAPOTAO'S SAKE! THEY'RE DRIVING ME NUTS! I'M OUTTA HERE!!
©BUZZELLI'66
FINALLY, THE HEROES MONUMENT!!
GREETINGS, HERO! MAY I COME IN? I NEED TO SPEAK WITH THE SUPREME HERO.
GREETINGS, SPARTAK, GO RIGHT AHEAD...
GREETINGS, HEROES. WHERE'S HIS SUPREMACY?
HERE, HE'S COMING DOWN NOW.
CRACRA! CAW! STEP!! STOP! GO!! STOP! WATCH OUT, ROCK. CAW!
A SUPER-MEDAL!
NICE! IF ONLY I'D LOST MY OTHER LEG, TOO...
SUPREME HERO, THE BEAUTIFUL ARE ABOUT TO START A NEW WAR!
CAW! IT'S SPARTAK!
SPARTAK! THE FAULT IS YOURS!! YOUR TASK WAS TO INCITE REVOLT!
AND INSTEAD, YOU'RE SITTING BACK AT COURT REVELING IN LUXURIES AND ORGIES. DON'T DENY IT, I HAVE SOURCES!! DO YOU ADMIT TO BEING ONE OF THE PIGS?
YES, IT'S TRUE.

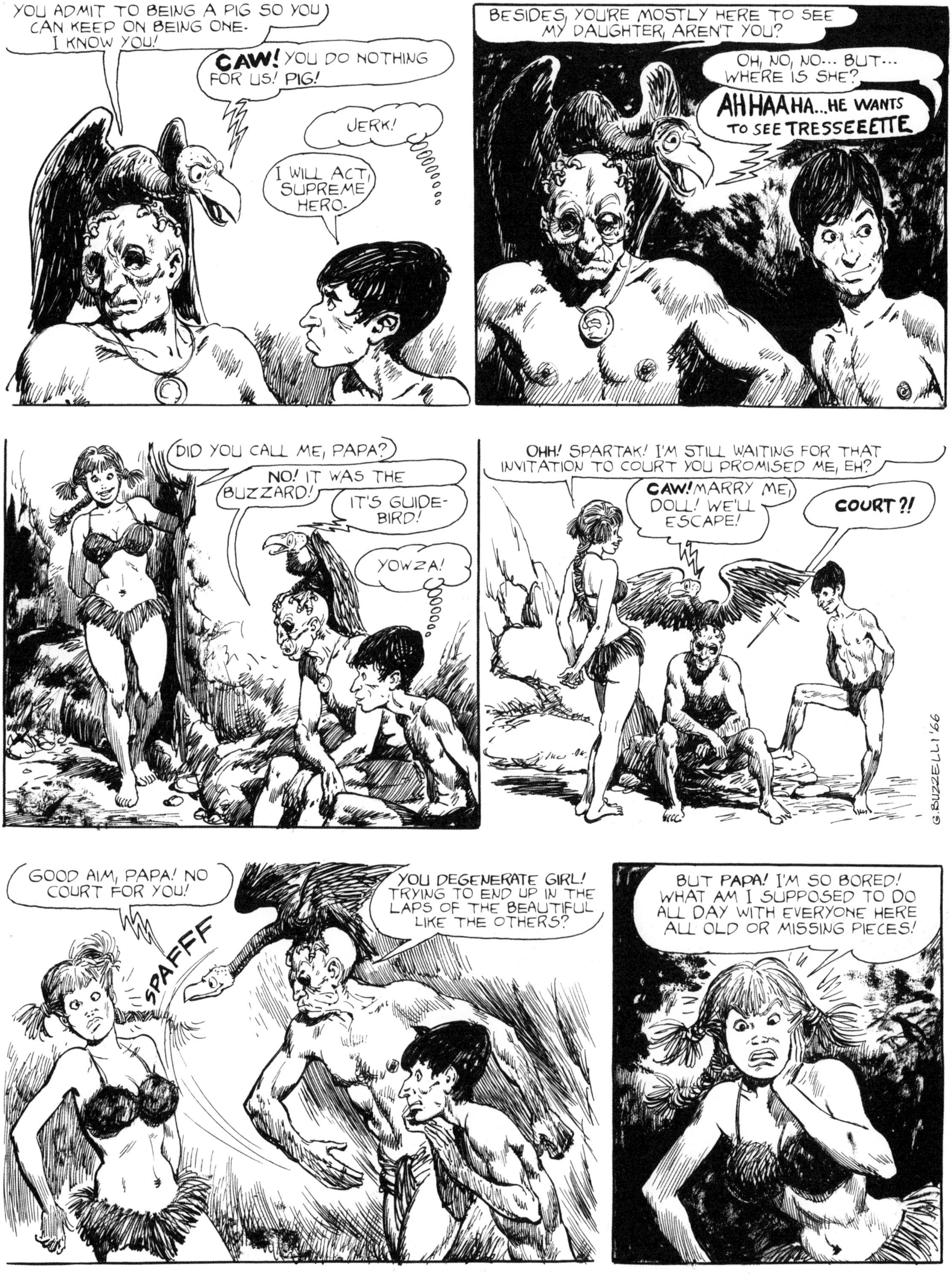
YOU ADMIT TO BEING A PIG SO YOU CAN KEEP ON BEING ONE- I KNOW YOU!
CAW! YOU DO NOTHING FOR US! PIG!
JERK!
I WILL ACT, SUPREME HERO.
BESIDES, YOU'RE MOSTLY HERE TO SEE MY DAUGHTER, AREN'T YOU?
OH, NO, NO... BUT... WHERE IS SHE?
AHHAAHA...HE WANTS TO SEE TRESSEEETTE
DID YOU CALL ME, PAPA?
NO! IT WAS THE BUZZARD!
IT'S GUIDE-BIRD!
YOWZA!
OHH! SPARTAK! I'M STILL WAITING FOR THAT INVITATION TO COURT YOU PROMISED ME, EH?
CAW! MARRY ME, DOLL! WE'LL ESCAPE!
COURT?!
G.BUZZELLI '66
GOOD AIM, PAPA! NO COURT FOR YOU!
SPAFFF
YOU DEGENERATE GIRL! TRYING TO END UP IN THE LAPS OF THE BEAUTIFUL LIKE THE OTHERS?
BUT PAPA! I'M SO BORED! WHAT AM I SUPPOSED TO DO ALL DAY WITH EVERYONE HERE ALL OLD OR MISSING PIECES!

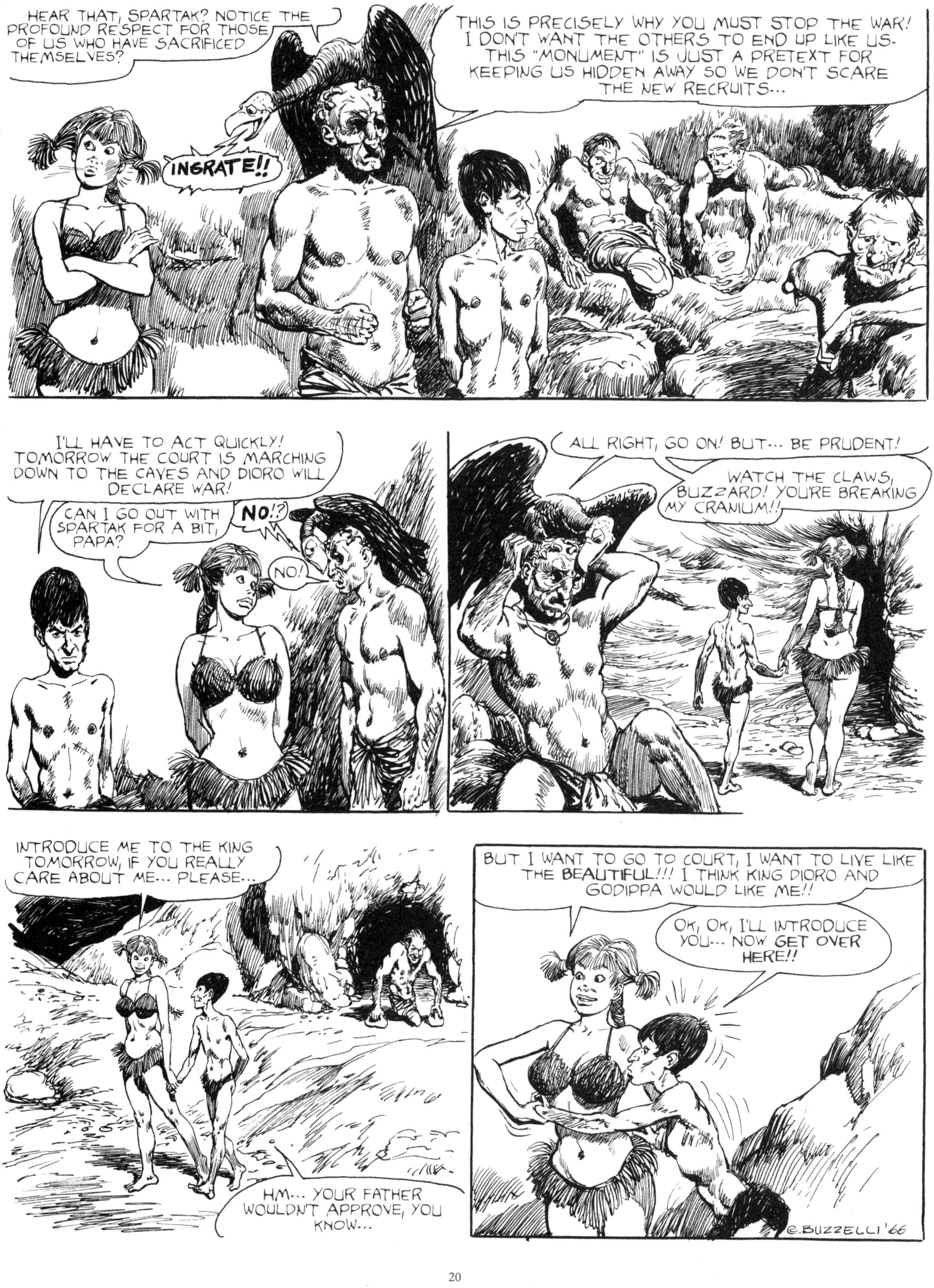
HEAR THAT, SPARTAK? NOTICE THE PROFOUND RESPECT FOR THOSE OF US WHO HAVE SACRIFICED THEMSELVES?
INGRATE!!
THIS IS PRECISELY WHY YOU MUST STOP THE WAR! I DON'T WANT THE OTHERS TO END UP LIKE US. THIS "MONUMENT" IS JUST A PRETEXT FOR KEEPING US HIDDEN AWAY SO WE DON'T SCARE THE NEW RECRUITS...
I'LL HAVE TO ACT QUICKLY! TOMORROW THE COURT IS MARCHING DOWN TO THE CAVES AND DIORO WILL DECLARE WAR!
CAN I GO OUT WITH SPARTAK FOR A BIT, PAPA?
NO!?
NO!
ALL RIGHT, GO ON! BUT... BE PRUDENT!
WATCH THE CLAWS, BUZZARD! YOU'RE BREAKING MY CRANIUM!!
INTRODUCE ME TO THE KING TOMORROW, IF YOU REALLY CARE ABOUT ME... PLEASE...
HM... YOUR FATHER WOULDN'T APPROVE, YOU KNOW...
BUT I WANT TO GO TO COURT, I WANT TO LIVE LIKE THE BEAUTIFUL!!! I THINK KING DIORO AND GODIPPA WOULD LIKE ME!!
OK, OK, I'LL INTRODUCE YOU... NOW GET OVER HERE!!
©.BUZZELLI '66

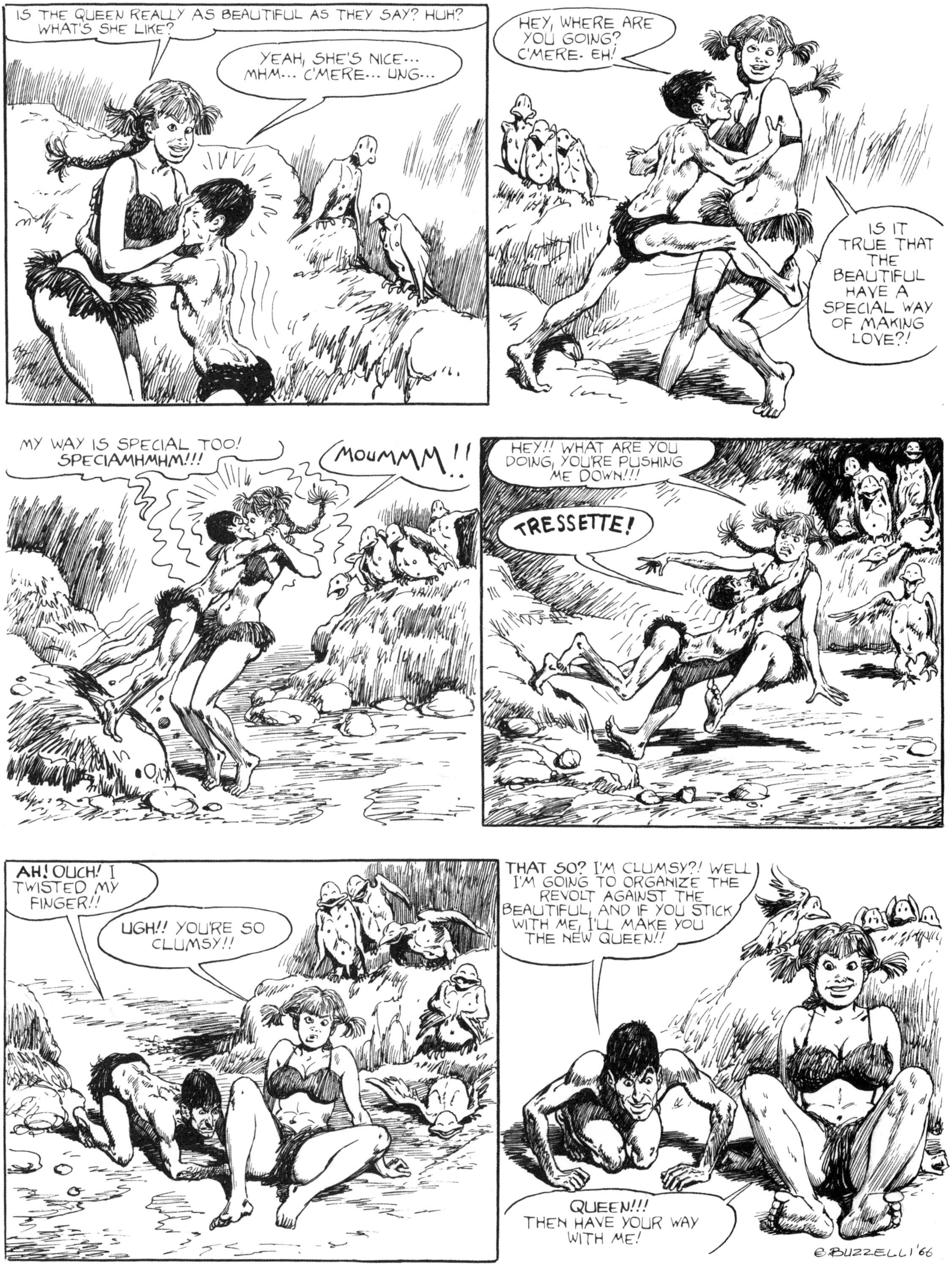
IS THE QUEEN REALLY AS BEAUTIFUL AS THEY SAY? HUH? WHAT'S SHE LIKE?
YEAH, SHE'S NICE... MHM... C'MERE... UNG...
HEY, WHERE ARE YOU GOING? C'MERE. EH!
IS IT TRUE THAT THE BEAUTIFUL HAVE A SPECIAL WAY OF MAKING LOVE?!
MY WAY IS SPECIAL TOO! SPECIAMHMHM!!!
MOUMMM!!
HEY!! WHAT ARE YOU DOING, YOU'RE PUSHING ME DOWN!!!
TRESSETTE!
AH! OUCH! I TWISTED MY FINGER!!
UGH!! YOU'RE SO CLUMSY!!
THAT SO? I'M CLUMSY?! WELL I'M GOING TO ORGANIZE THE REVOLT AGAINST THE BEAUTIFUL, AND IF YOU STICK WITH ME, I'LL MAKE YOU THE NEW QUEEN!!
QUEEN!!! THEN HAVE YOUR WAY WITH ME!
G. BUZZELLI '66

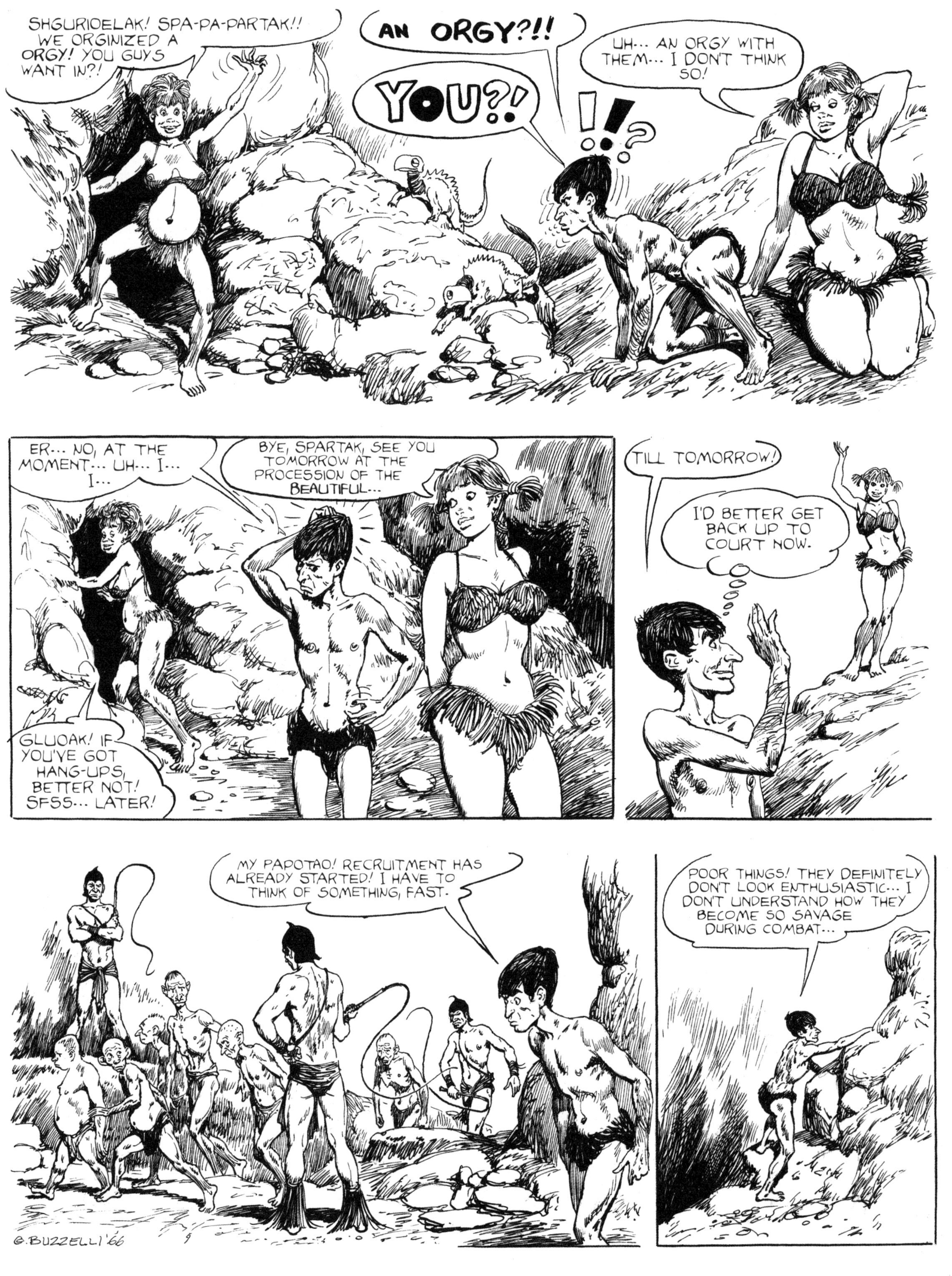
SHGURIOELAK! SPA-PA-PARTAK!! WE ORGINIZED A ORGY! YOU GUYS WANT IN?!
AN ORGY?!!
YOU?!
!!?
UH... AN ORGY WITH THEM... I DON'T THINK SO!
ER... NO, AT THE MOMENT... UH... I... I...
BYE, SPARTAK, SEE YOU TOMORROW AT THE PROCESSION OF THE BEAUTIFUL...
GLUOAK! IF YOU'VE GOT HANG-UPS, BETTER NOT! SFSS... LATER!
TILL TOMORROW!
I'D BETTER GET BACK UP TO COURT NOW.
MY PAPOTAO! RECRUITMENT HAS ALREADY STARTED! I HAVE TO THINK OF SOMETHING, FAST.
POOR THINGS! THEY DEFINITELY DON'T LOOK ENTHUSIASTIC... I DON'T UNDERSTAND HOW THEY BECOME SO SAVAGE DURING COMBAT...
G. BUZZELLI '66

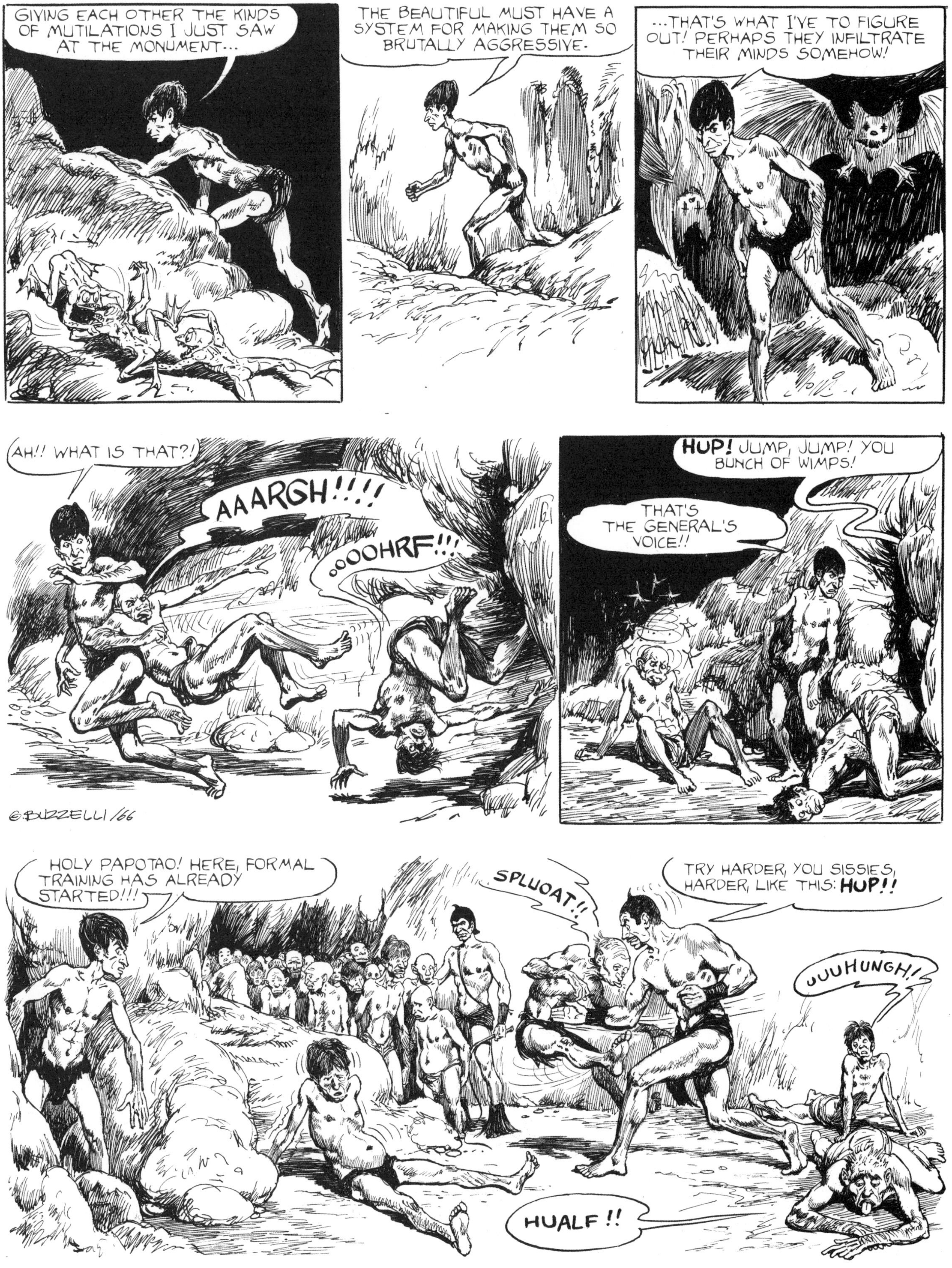

GIVING EACH OTHER THE KINDS OF MUTILATIONS I JUST SAW AT THE MONUMENT...
THE BEAUTIFUL MUST HAVE A SYSTEM FOR MAKING THEM SO BRUTALLY AGGRESSIVE.
...THAT'S WHAT I'VE TO FIGURE OUT! PERHAPS THEY INFILTRATE THEIR MINDS SOMEHOW!
AH!! WHAT IS THAT?!
AAARGH!!!!!
OOOOHRF!!!
©BUZZELLI /66
HUP! JUMP, JUMP! YOU BUNCH OF WIMPS!
THAT'S THE GENERAL'S VOICE!!
HOLY PAPOTAO! HERE, FORMAL TRAINING HAS ALREADY STARTED!!!
SPLUOAT!!
TRY HARDER, YOU SISSIES, HARDER, LIKE THIS: HUP!!
UUUHUNGH!!
HUALF!!

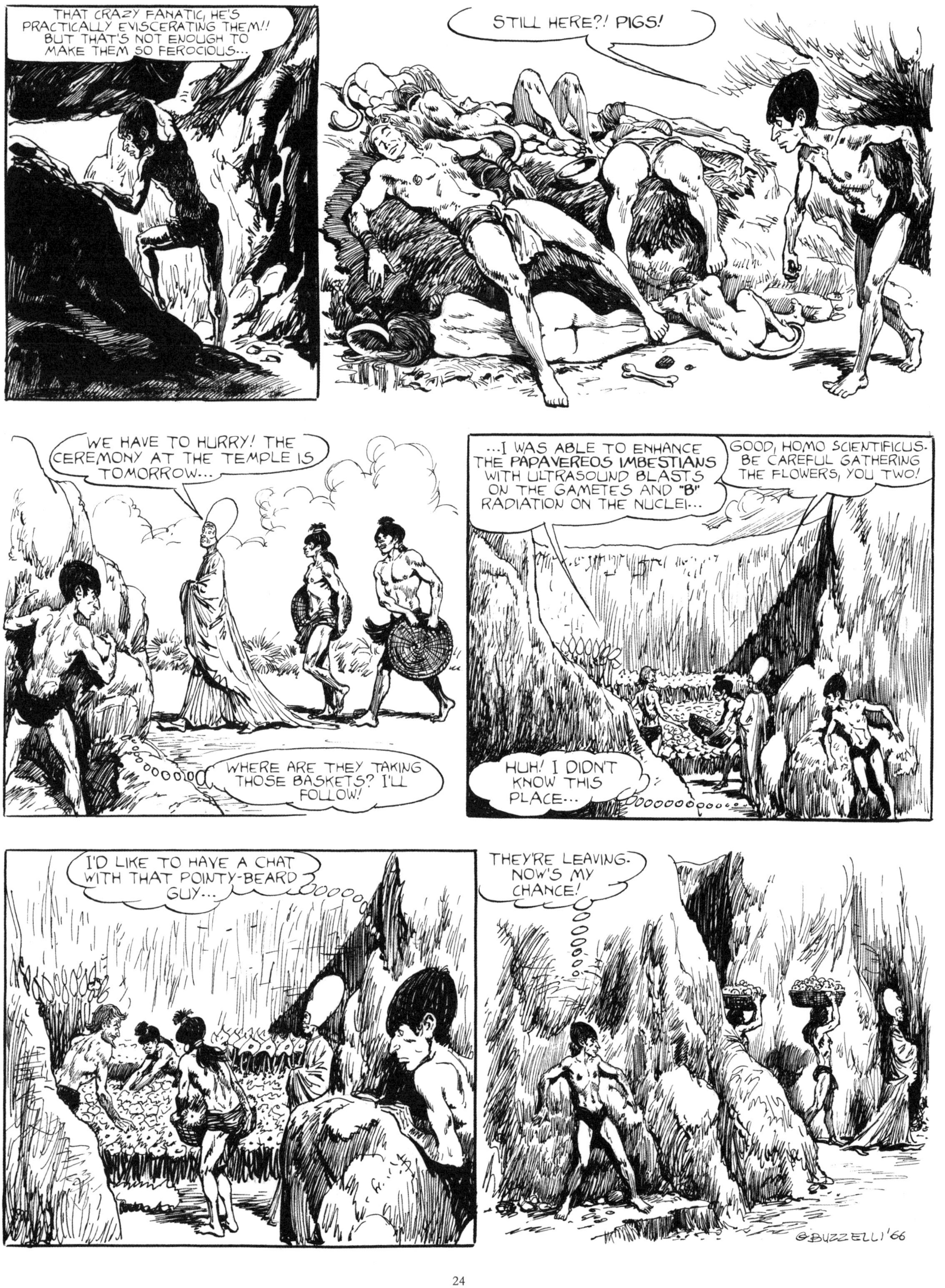
THAT CRAZY FANATIC, HE'S PRACTICALLY EVISCERATING THEM!! BUT THAT'S NOT ENOUGH TO MAKE THEM SO FEROCIOUS...
STILL HERE?! PIGS!
WE HAVE TO HURRY! THE CEREMONY AT THE TEMPLE IS TOMORROW...
WHERE ARE THEY TAKING THOSE BASKETS? I'LL FOLLOW!
...I WAS ABLE TO ENHANCE THE PAPAVEREOS IMBESTIANS WITH ULTRASOUND BLASTS ON THE GAMETES AND "B" RADIATION ON THE NUCLEI...
GOOD, HOMO SCIENTIFICUS. BE CAREFUL GATHERING THE FLOWERS, YOU TWO!
HUH! I DIDN'T KNOW THIS PLACE...
I'D LIKE TO HAVE A CHAT WITH THAT POINTY-BEARD GUY...
THEY'RE LEAVING. NOW'S MY CHANCE!
©BUZZELLI '66

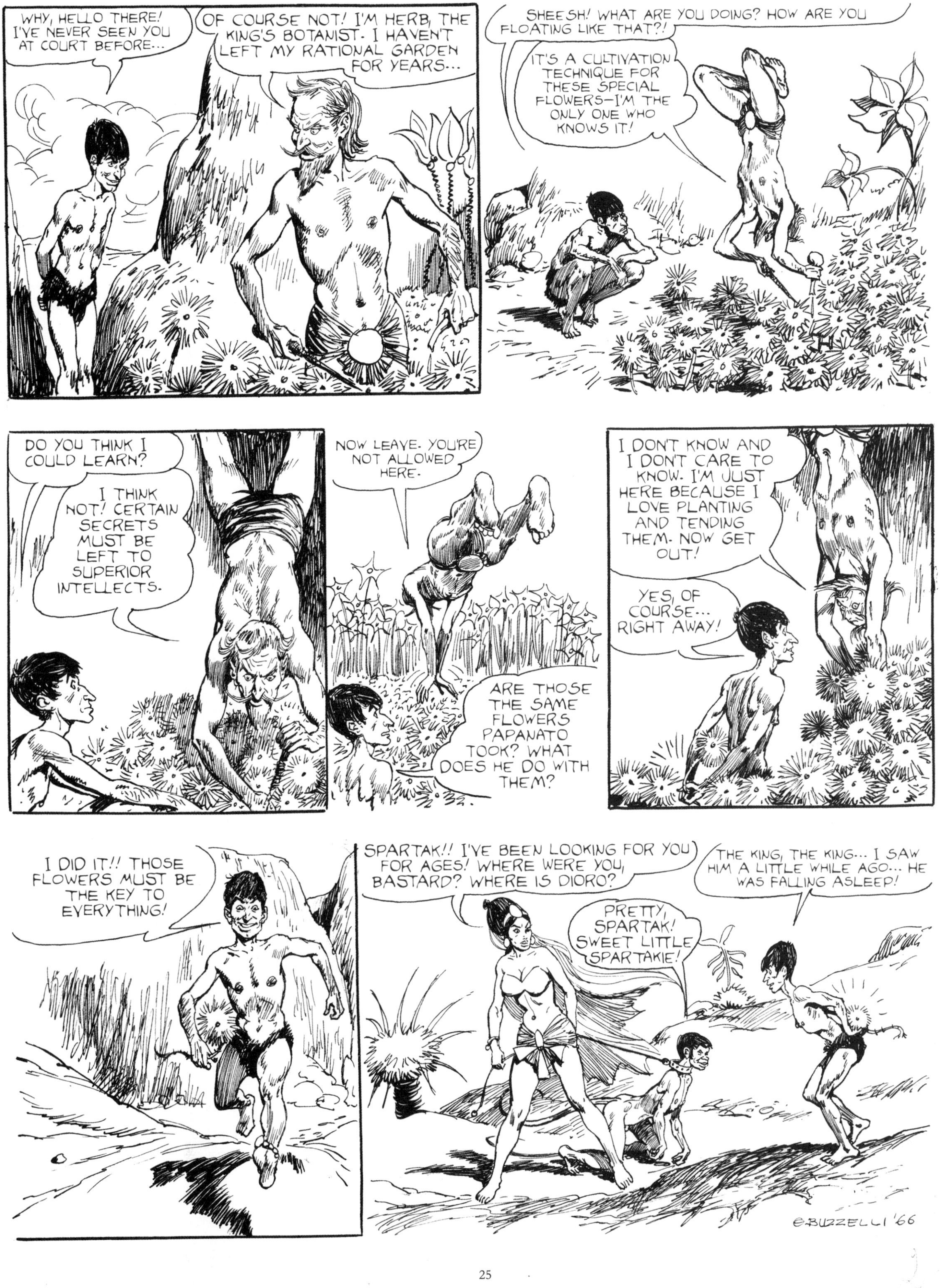
WHY, HELLO THERE! I'VE NEVER SEEN YOU AT COURT BEFORE...
OF COURSE NOT! I'M HERB, THE KING'S BOTANIST. I HAVEN'T LEFT MY RATIONAL GARDEN FOR YEARS...
SHEESH! WHAT ARE YOU DOING? HOW ARE YOU FLOATING LIKE THAT?!
IT'S A CULTIVATION TECHNIQUE FOR THESE SPECIAL FLOWERS—I'M THE ONLY ONE WHO KNOWS IT!
DO YOU THINK I COULD LEARN?
I THINK NOT! CERTAIN SECRETS MUST BE LEFT TO SUPERIOR INTELLECTS.
NOW LEAVE. YOU'RE NOT ALLOWED HERE.
ARE THOSE THE SAME FLOWERS PAPANATO TOOK? WHAT DOES HE DO WITH THEM?
I DON'T KNOW AND I DON'T CARE TO KNOW. I'M JUST HERE BECAUSE I LOVE PLANTING AND TENDING THEM. NOW GET OUT!
YES, OF COURSE... RIGHT AWAY!
I DID IT!! THOSE FLOWERS MUST BE THE KEY TO EVERYTHING!
SPARTAK!! I'VE BEEN LOOKING FOR YOU FOR AGES! WHERE WERE YOU, BASTARD? WHERE IS DIORO?
PRETTY, SPARTAK! SWEET LITTLE SPARTAKIE!
THE KING, THE KING... I SAW HIM A LITTLE WHILE AGO... HE WAS FALLING ASLEEP!
G. BUZZELLI '66

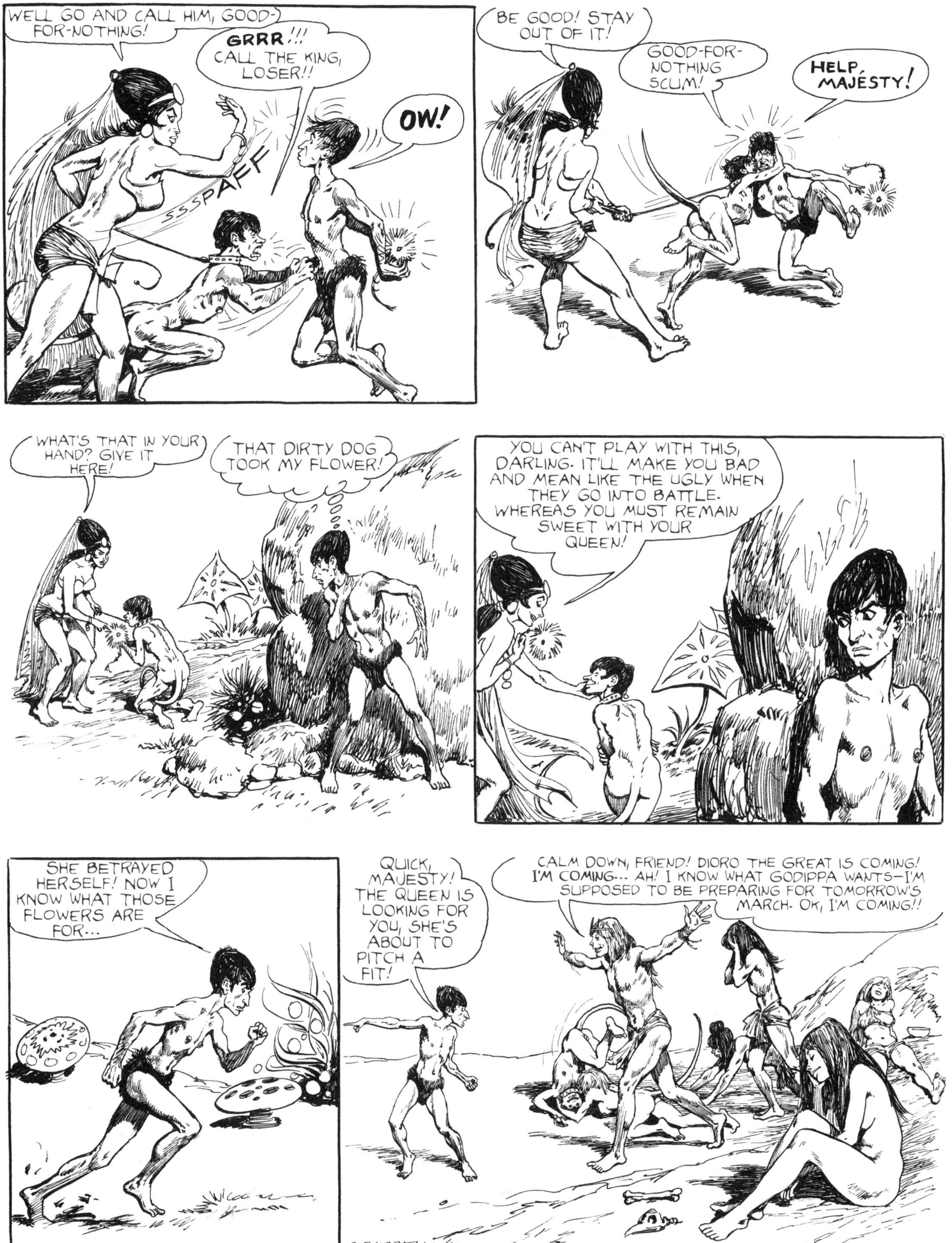
WELL GO AND CALL HIM, GOOD-FOR-NOTHING!
GRRR!!! CALL THE KING, LOSER!!
SSSPAFF
OW!
BE GOOD! STAY OUT OF IT!
GOOD-FOR-NOTHING SCUM!
HELP, MAJESTY!
WHAT'S THAT IN YOUR HAND? GIVE IT HERE!
THAT DIRTY DOG TOOK MY FLOWER!
YOU CAN'T PLAY WITH THIS, DARLING. IT'LL MAKE YOU BAD AND MEAN LIKE THE UGLY WHEN THEY GO INTO BATTLE. WHEREAS YOU MUST REMAIN SWEET WITH YOUR QUEEN!
SHE BETRAYED HERSELF! NOW I KNOW WHAT THOSE FLOWERS ARE FOR...
QUICK, MAJESTY! THE QUEEN IS LOOKING FOR YOU, SHE'S ABOUT TO PITCH A FIT!
CALM DOWN, FRIEND! DIORO THE GREAT IS COMING! I'M COMING... AH! I KNOW WHAT GODIPPA WANTS—I'M SUPPOSED TO BE PREPARING FOR TOMORROW'S MARCH. OK, I'M COMING!!
©BUZZELLI/66

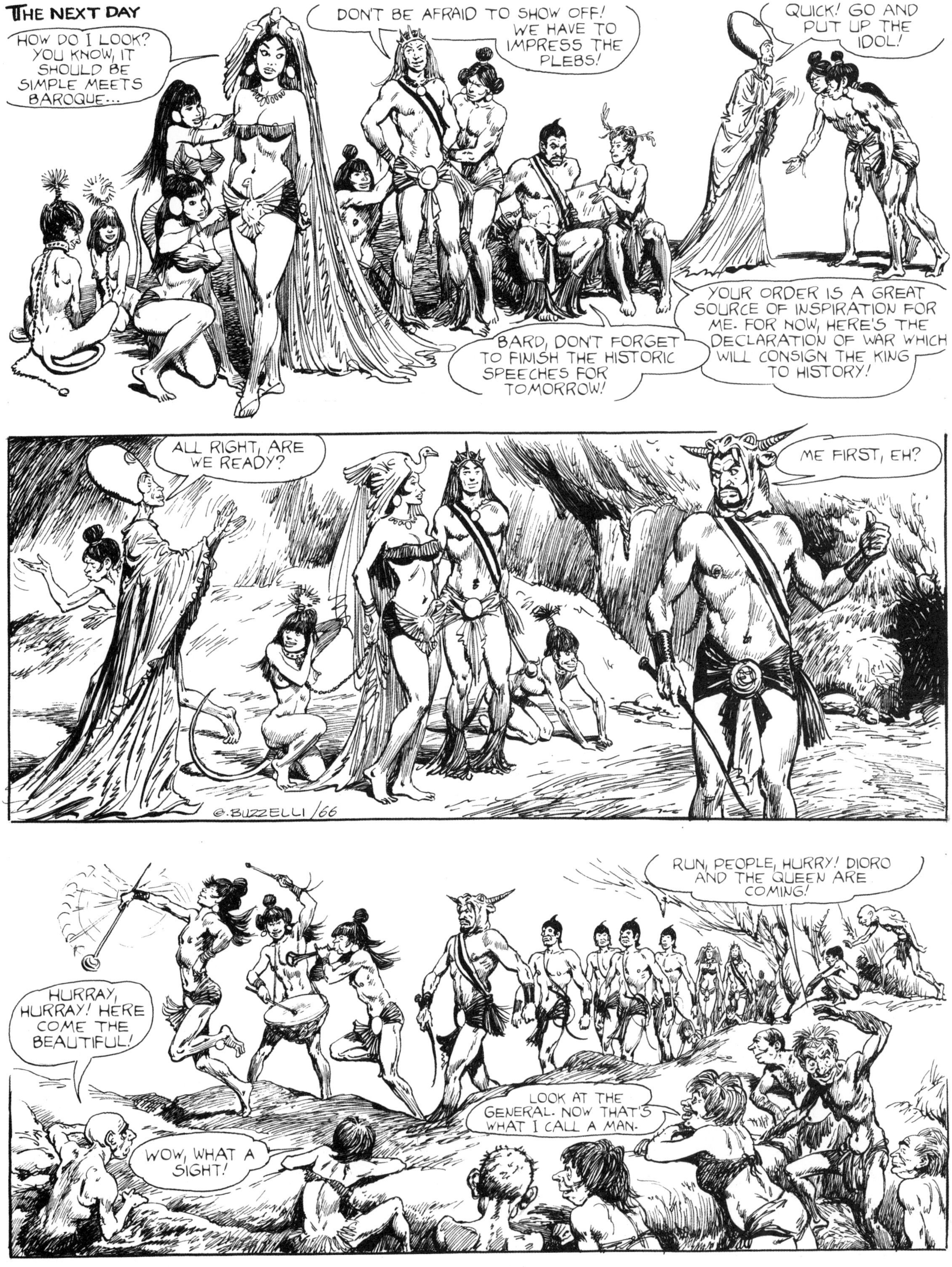
THE NEXT DAY
HOW DO I LOOK? YOU KNOW, IT SHOULD BE SIMPLE MEETS BAROQUE...
DON'T BE AFRAID TO SHOW OFF! WE HAVE TO IMPRESS THE PLEBS!
BARD, DON'T FORGET TO FINISH THE HISTORIC SPEECHES FOR TOMORROW!
YOUR ORDER IS A GREAT SOURCE OF INSPIRATION FOR ME. FOR NOW, HERE'S THE DECLARATION OF WAR WHICH WILL CONSIGN THE KING TO HISTORY!
QUICK! GO AND PUT UP THE IDOL!
ALL RIGHT, ARE WE READY?
ME FIRST, EH?
G. BUZZELLI /66
HURRAY, HURRAY! HERE COME THE BEAUTIFUL!
RUN, PEOPLE, HURRY! DIORO AND THE QUEEN ARE COMING!
LOOK AT THE GENERAL. NOW THAT'S WHAT I CALL A MAN.
WOW, WHAT A SIGHT!

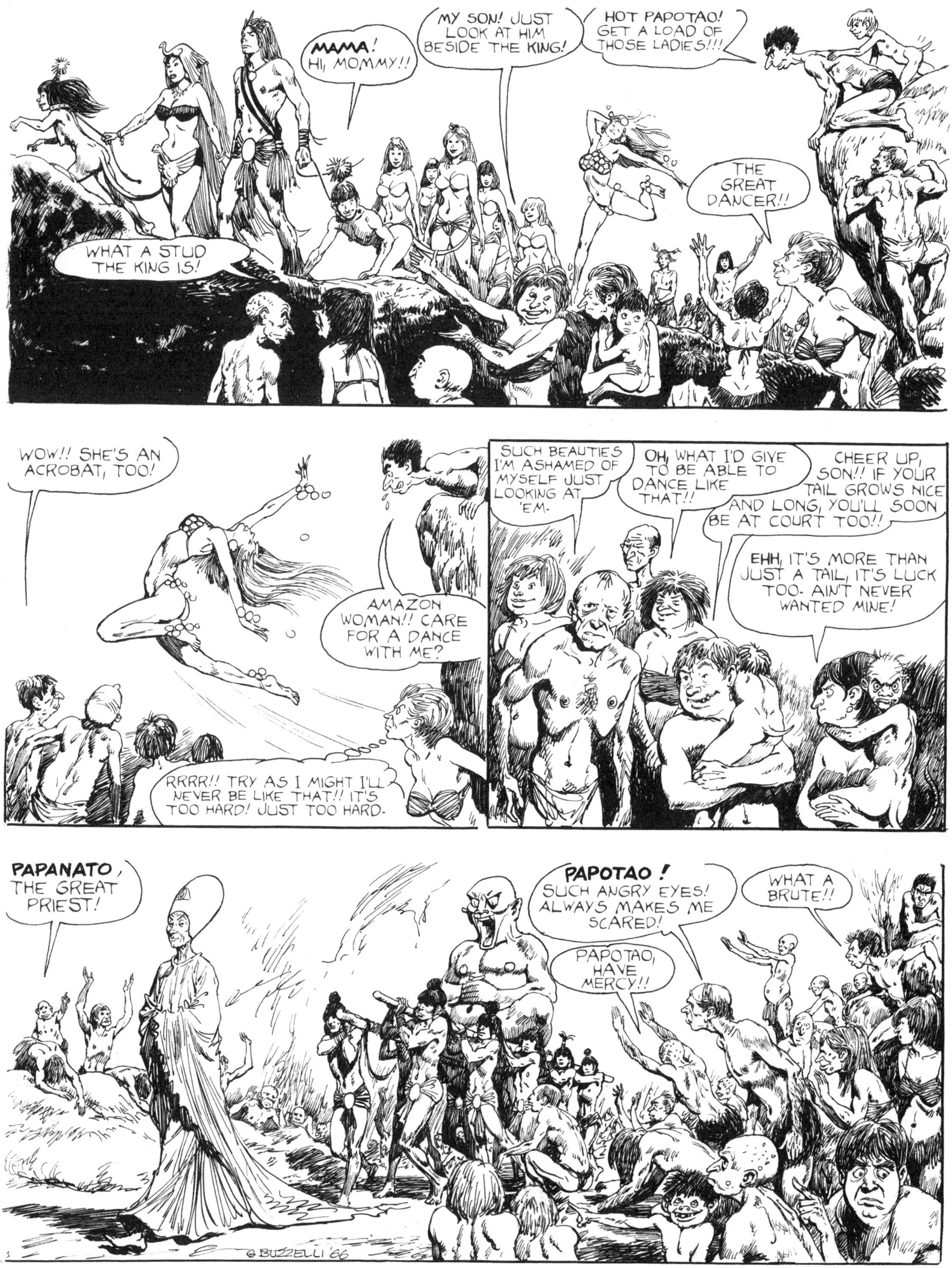
MAMA! HI, MOMMY!!
MY SON! JUST LOOK AT HIM BESIDE THE KING!
HOT PAPOTAO! GET A LOAD OF THOSE LADIES!!!
WHAT A STUD THE KING IS!
THE GREAT DANCER!!
WOW!! SHE'S AN ACROBAT, TOO!
AMAZON WOMAN!! CARE FOR A DANCE WITH ME?
RRRR!! TRY AS I MIGHT I'LL NEVER BE LIKE THAT!! IT'S TOO HARD! JUST TOO HARD.
SUCH BEAUTIES I'M ASHAMED OF MYSELF JUST LOOKING AT 'EM.
OH, WHAT I'D GIVE TO BE ABLE TO DANCE LIKE THAT!!
CHEER UP, SON!! IF YOUR TAIL GROWS NICE AND LONG, YOU'LL SOON BE AT COURT TOO!!
EHH, IT'S MORE THAN JUST A TAIL, IT'S LUCK TOO- AIN'T NEVER WANTED MINE!
PAPANATO, THE GREAT PRIEST!
PAPOTAO! SUCH ANGRY EYES! ALWAYS MAKES ME SCARED!
PAPOTAO, HAVE MERCY!!
WHAT A BRUTE!!
1
© BUZZELLI '66

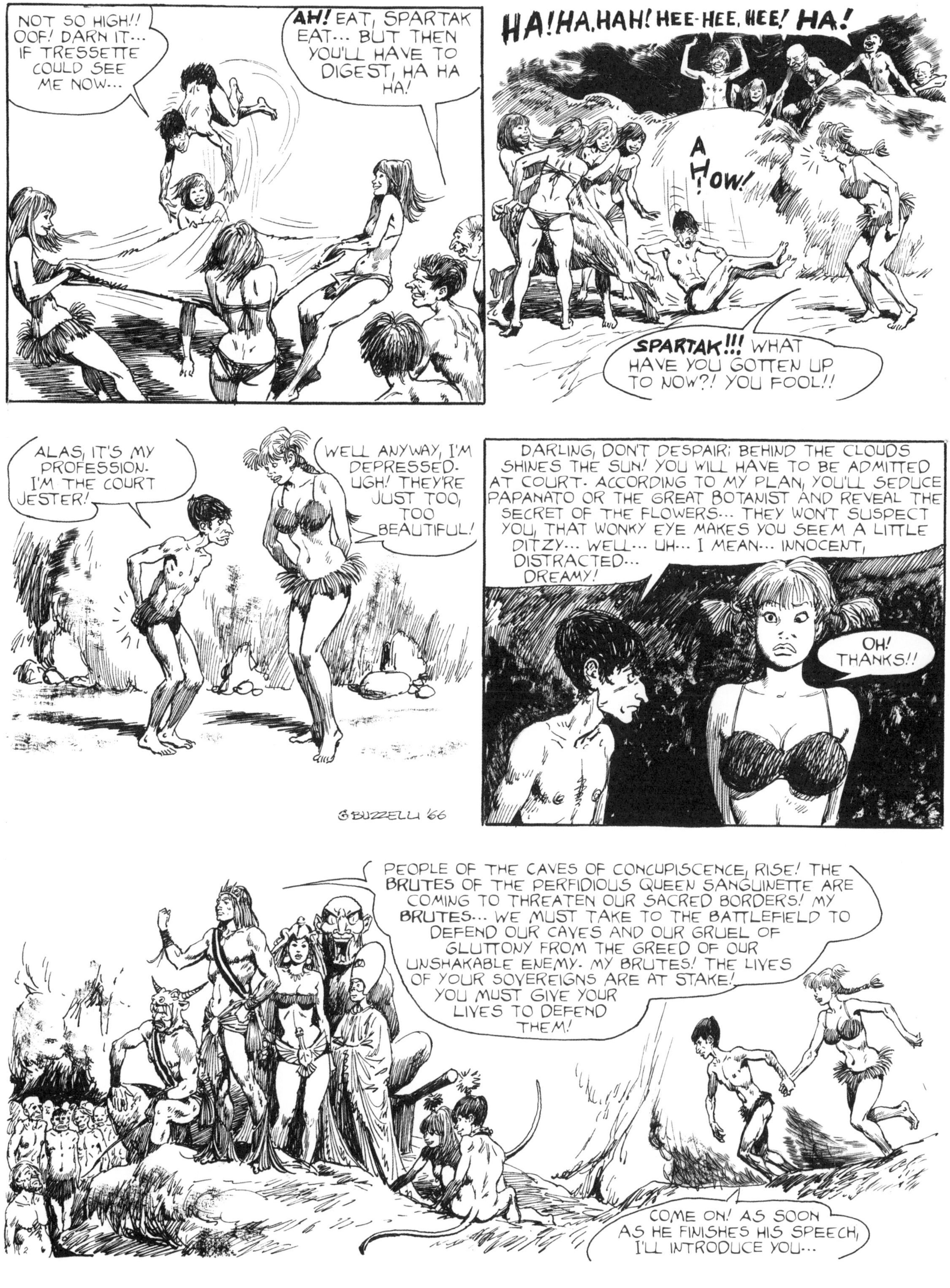
NOT SO HIGH!! OOF! DARN IT... IF TRESSETTE COULD SEE ME NOW...
AH! EAT, SPARTAK EAT... BUT THEN YOU'LL HAVE TO DIGEST, HA HA HA!
HA! HA, HAH! HEE-HEE, HEE! HA!
A H! OW!
SPARTAK!!! WHAT HAVE YOU GOTTEN UP TO NOW?! YOU FOOL!!
ALAS, IT'S MY PROFESSION- I'M THE COURT JESTER!
WELL ANYWAY, I'M DEPRESSED- UGH! THEY'RE JUST TOO, TOO BEAUTIFUL!
© BUZZELLI '66
DARLING, DON'T DESPAIR; BEHIND THE CLOUDS SHINES THE SUN! YOU WILL HAVE TO BE ADMITTED AT COURT. ACCORDING TO MY PLAN, YOU'LL SEDUCE PAPANATO OR THE GREAT BOTANIST AND REVEAL THE SECRET OF THE FLOWERS... THEY WON'T SUSPECT YOU, THAT WONKY EYE MAKES YOU SEEM A LITTLE DITZY... WELL... UH... I MEAN... INNOCENT, DISTRACTED... DREAMY!
OH! THANKS!!
PEOPLE OF THE CAVES OF CONCUPISCENCE, RISE! THE BRUTES OF THE PERFIDIOUS QUEEN SANGUINETTE ARE COMING TO THREATEN OUR SACRED BORDERS! MY BRUTES... WE MUST TAKE TO THE BATTLEFIELD TO DEFEND OUR CAVES AND OUR GRUEL OF GLUTTONY FROM THE GREED OF OUR UNSHAKABLE ENEMY. MY BRUTES! THE LIVES OF YOUR SOVEREIGNS ARE AT STAKE! YOU MUST GIVE YOUR LIVES TO DEFEND THEM!
COME ON! AS SOON AS HE FINISHES HIS SPEECH, I'LL INTRODUCE YOU...

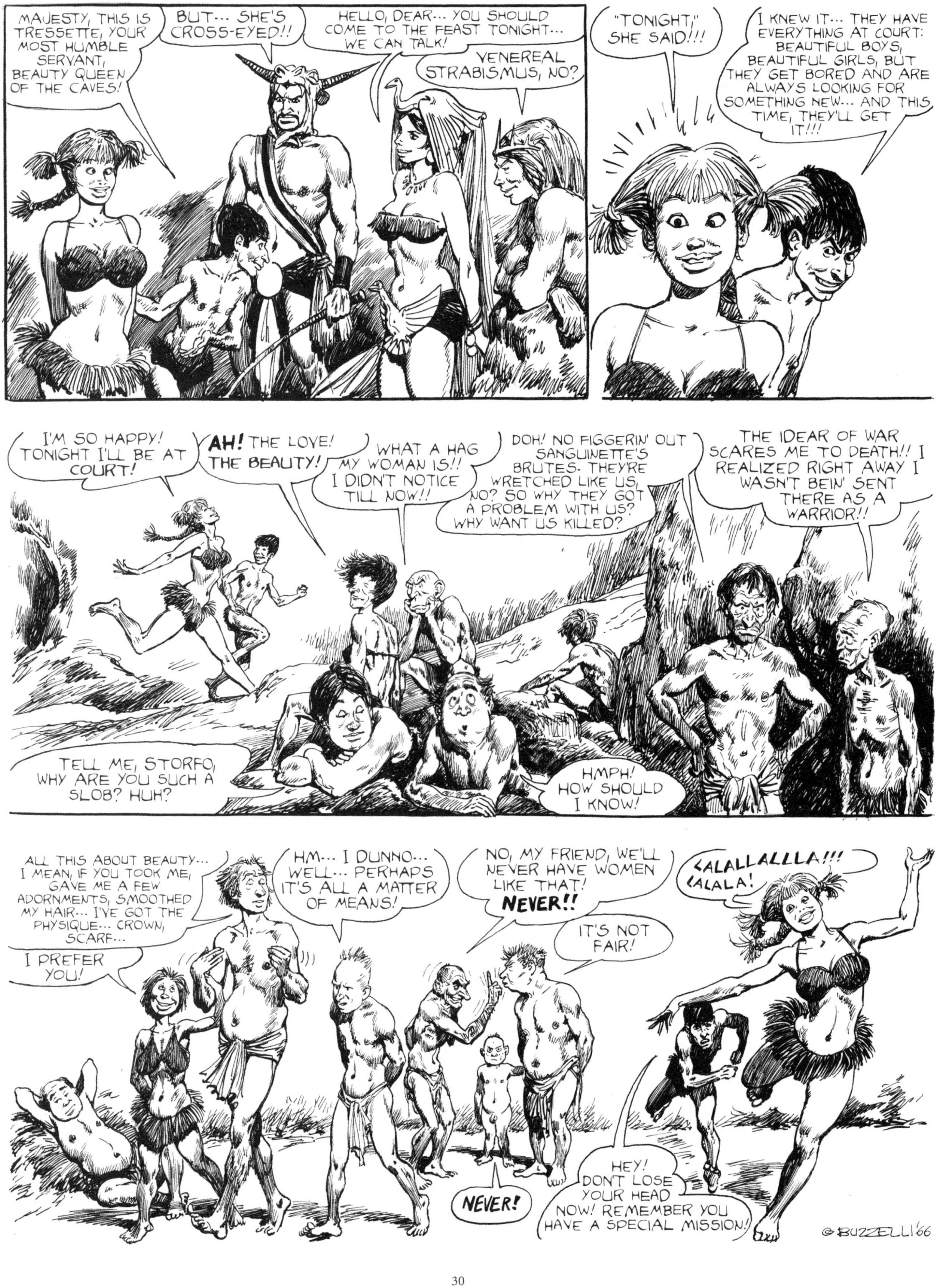
MAJESTY, THIS IS TRESSETTE, YOUR MOST HUMBLE SERVANT, BEAUTY QUEEN OF THE CAVES!
BUT... SHE'S CROSS-EYED!!
HELLO, DEAR... YOU SHOULD COME TO THE FEAST TONIGHT... WE CAN TALK!
VENEREAL STRABISMUS, NO?
"TONIGHT," SHE SAID!!!
I KNEW IT... THEY HAVE EVERYTHING AT COURT: BEAUTIFUL BOYS, BEAUTIFUL GIRLS, BUT THEY GET BORED AND ARE ALWAYS LOOKING FOR SOMETHING NEW... AND THIS TIME, THEY'LL GET IT!!!
I'M SO HAPPY! TONIGHT I'LL BE AT COURT!
AH! THE LOVE! THE BEAUTY!
WHAT A HAG MY WOMAN IS!! I DIDN'T NOTICE TILL NOW!!
DOH! NO FIGGERIN' OUT SANGUINETTE'S BRUTES. THEY'RE WRETCHED LIKE US, NO? SO WHY THEY GOT A PROBLEM WITH US? WHY WANT US KILLED?
THE IDEAR OF WAR SCARES ME TO DEATH!! I REALIZED RIGHT AWAY I WASN'T BEIN' SENT THERE AS A WARRIOR!!
TELL ME, STORFO, WHY ARE YOU SUCH A SLOB? HUH?
HMPH! HOW SHOULD I KNOW!
ALL THIS ABOUT BEAUTY... I MEAN, IF YOU TOOK ME, GAVE ME A FEW ADORNMENTS, SMOOTHED MY HAIR... I'VE GOT THE PHYSIQUE... CROWN, SCARF...
I PREFER YOU!
HM... I DUNNO... WELL... PERHAPS IT'S ALL A MATTER OF MEANS!
NO, MY FRIEND, WE'LL NEVER HAVE WOMEN LIKE THAT! NEVER!!
IT'S NOT FAIR!
LALALLALLLA!!! LALALA!
NEVER!
HEY! DON'T LOSE YOUR HEAD NOW! REMEMBER YOU HAVE A SPECIAL MISSION!
© BUZZELLI '66

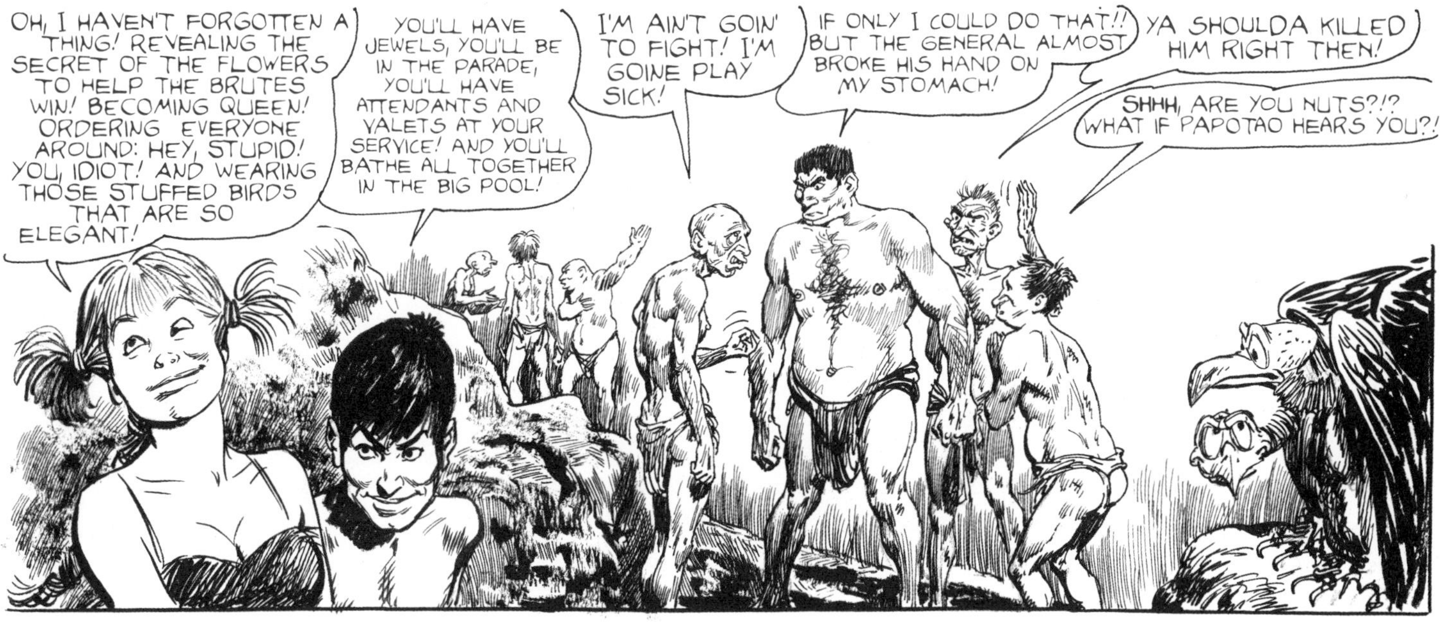
OH, I HAVEN'T FORGOTTEN A THING! REVEALING THE SECRET OF THE FLOWERS TO HELP THE BRUTES WIN! BECOMING QUEEN! ORDERING EVERYONE AROUND: HEY, STUPID! YOU, IDIOT! AND WEARING THOSE STUFFED BIRDS THAT ARE SO ELEGANT!
YOU'LL HAVE JEWELS, YOU'LL BE IN THE PARADE, YOU'LL HAVE ATTENDANTS AND VALETS AT YOUR SERVICE! AND YOU'LL BATHE ALL TOGETHER IN THE BIG POOL!
I'M AIN'T GOIN' TO FIGHT! I'M GOINE PLAY SICK!
IF ONLY I COULD DO THAT!! BUT THE GENERAL ALMOST BROKE HIS HAND ON MY STOMACH!
YA SHOULDA KILLED HIM RIGHT THEN!
SHHH, ARE YOU NUTS?!? WHAT IF PAPOTAO HEARS YOU?!

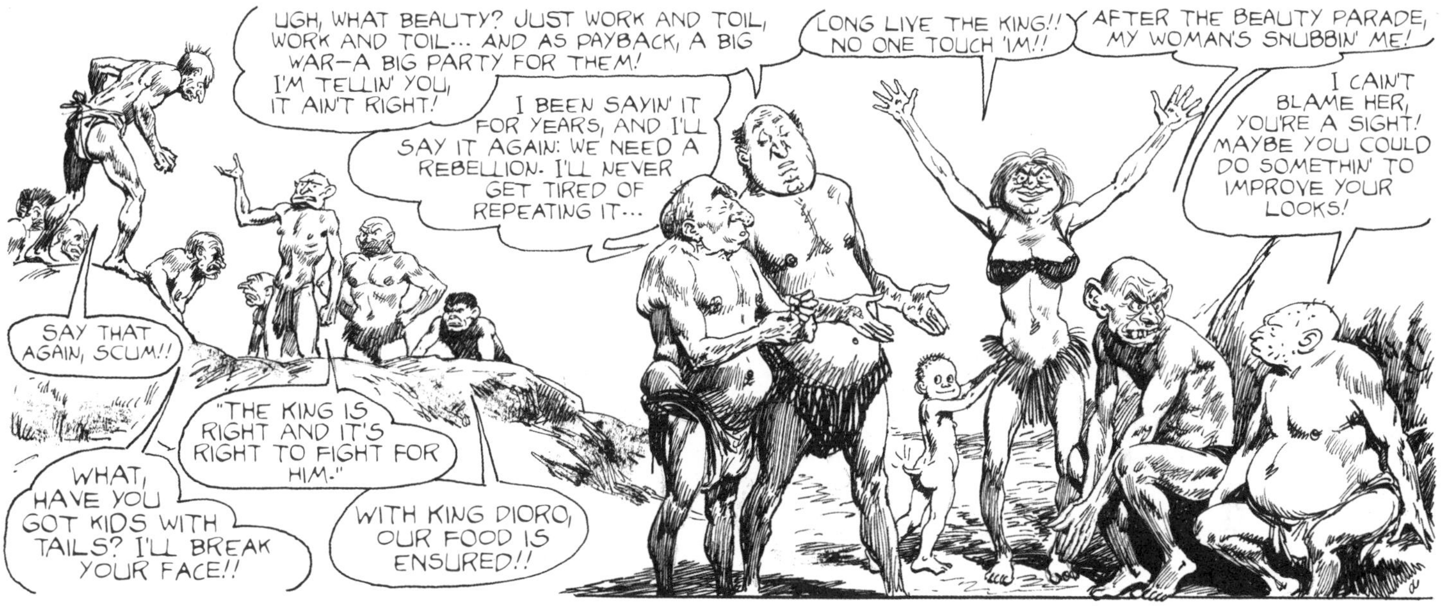
UGH, WHAT BEAUTY? JUST WORK AND TOIL, WORK AND TOIL... AND AS PAYBACK, A BIG WAR—A BIG PARTY FOR THEM! I'M TELLIN' YOU, IT AIN'T RIGHT!
I BEEN SAYIN' IT FOR YEARS, AND I'LL SAY IT AGAIN: WE NEED A REBELLION. I'LL NEVER GET TIRED OF REPEATING IT...
LONG LIVE THE KING!! NO ONE TOUCH 'IM!!
AFTER THE BEAUTY PARADE, MY WOMAN'S SNUBBIN' ME!
I CAIN'T BLAME HER, YOU'RE A SIGHT! MAYBE YOU COULD DO SOMETHIN' TO IMPROVE YOUR LOOKS!
SAY THAT AGAIN, SCUM!!
"THE KING IS RIGHT AND IT'S RIGHT TO FIGHT FOR HIM."
WHAT, HAVE YOU GOT KIDS WITH TAILS? I'LL BREAK YOUR FACE!!
WITH KING DIORO, OUR FOOD IS ENSURED!!

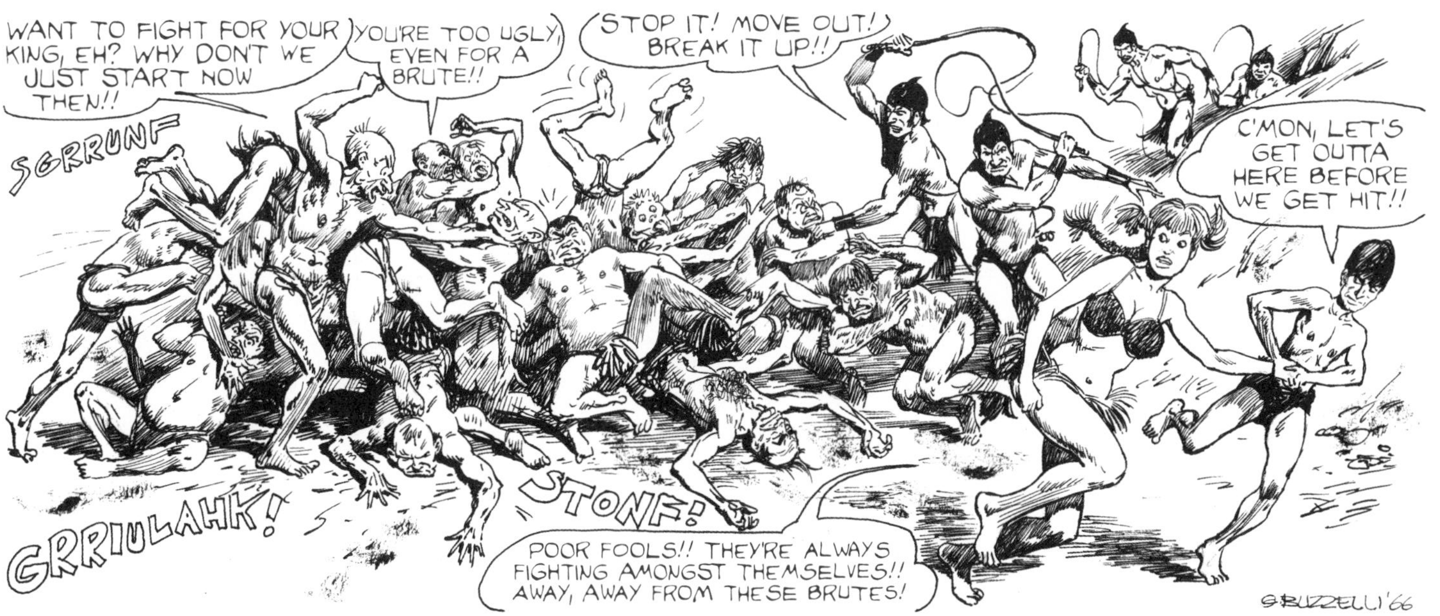
WANT TO FIGHT FOR YOUR KING, EH? WHY DON'T WE JUST START NOW THEN!!
YOU'RE TOO UGLY, EVEN FOR A BRUTE!!
STOP IT! MOVE OUT! BREAK IT UP!!
C'MON, LET'S GET OUTTA HERE BEFORE WE GET HIT!!
SGRRUNF
GRRIULAHK!
STONF!
POOR FOOLS!! THEY'RE ALWAYS FIGHTING AMONGST THEMSELVES!! AWAY, AWAY FROM THESE BRUTES!
G. BUZZELLI '66

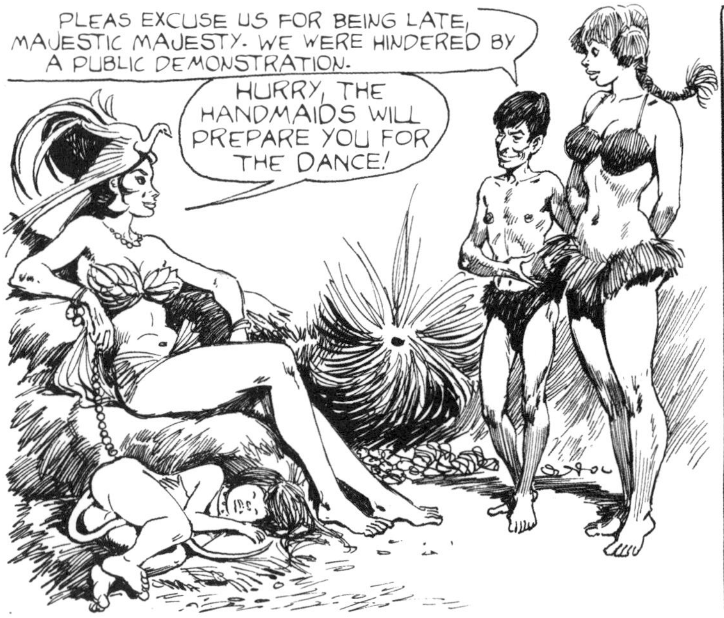
PLEAS EXCUSE US FOR BEING LATE, MAJESTIC MAJESTY. WE WERE HINDERED BY A PUBLIC DEMONSTRATION.
HURRY, THE HANDMAIDS WILL PREPARE YOU FOR THE DANCE!

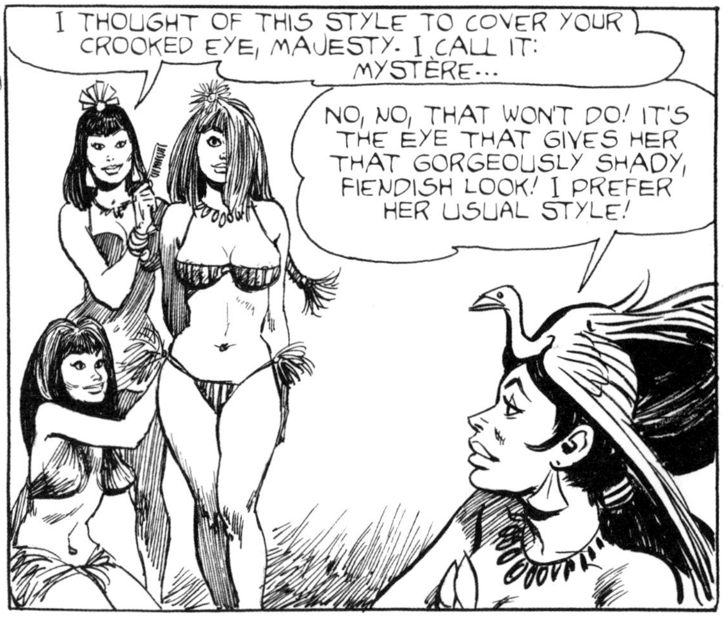
I THOUGHT OF THIS STYLE TO COVER YOUR CROOKED EYE, MAJESTY. I CALL IT: MYSTÈRE...
NO, NO, THAT WON'T DO! IT'S THE EYE THAT GIVES HER THAT GORGEOUSLY SHADY, FIENDISH LOOK! I PREFER HER USUAL STYLE!

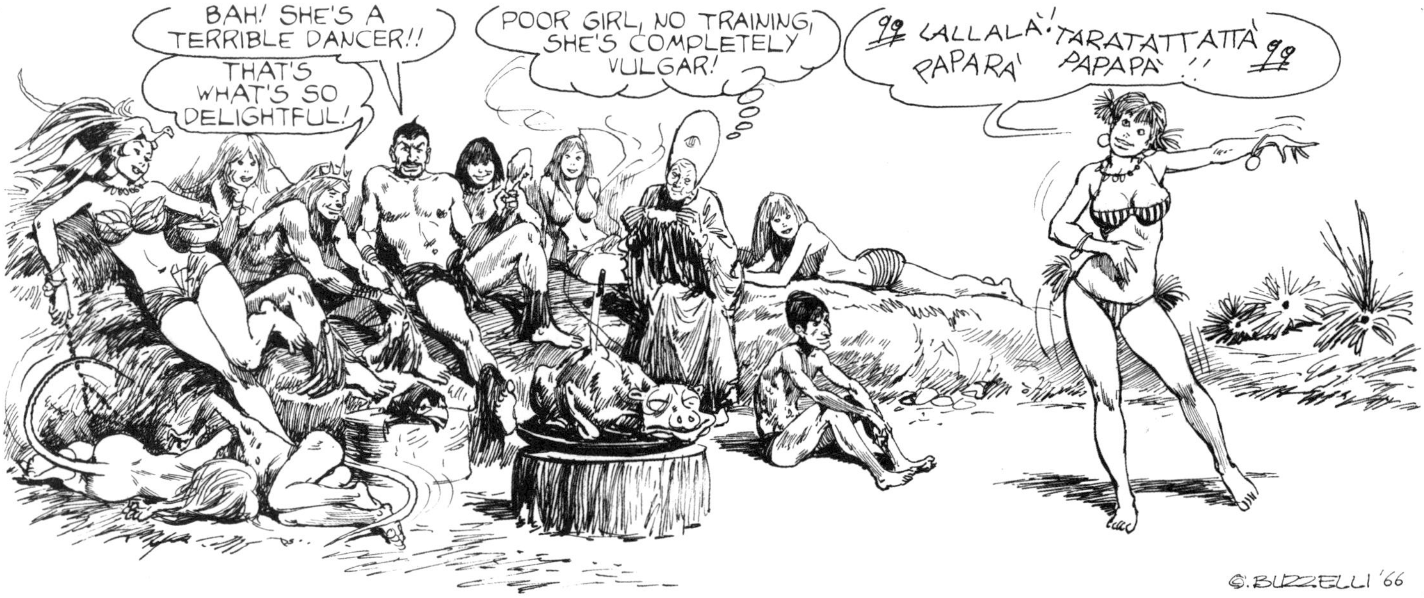
BAH! SHE'S A TERRIBLE DANCER!!
THAT'S WHAT'S SO DELIGHTFUL!
POOR GIRL, NO TRAINING, SHE'S COMPLETELY VULGAR!
LALLALÀ! TARATATTATTÀ PAPARÀ PAPAPÀ!!
©. BUZZELLI '66

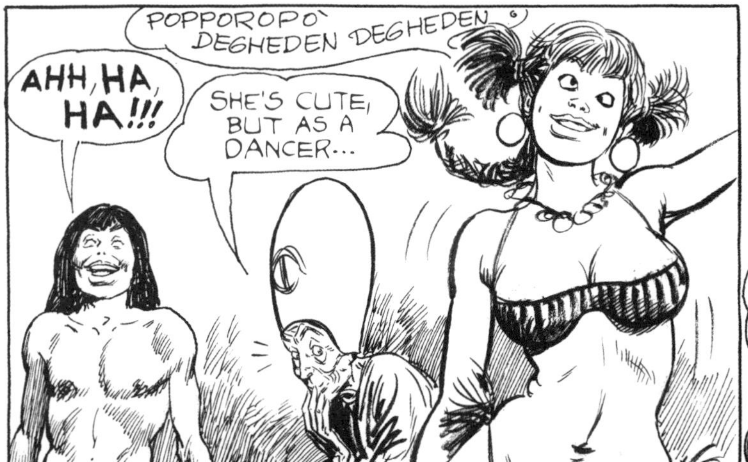
POPPOROPÒ DEGHEDEN DEGHEDEN
AHH, HA, HA!!!
SHE'S CUTE, BUT AS A DANCER...

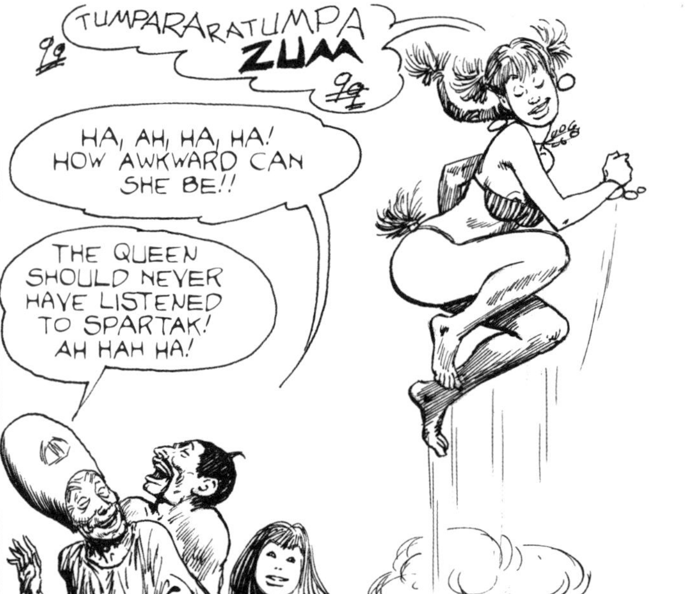
TUMPARARATUMPA ZUM
HA, AH, HA, HA! HOW AWKWARD CAN SHE BE!!
THE QUEEN SHOULD NEVER HAVE LISTENED TO SPARTAK! AH HAH HA!

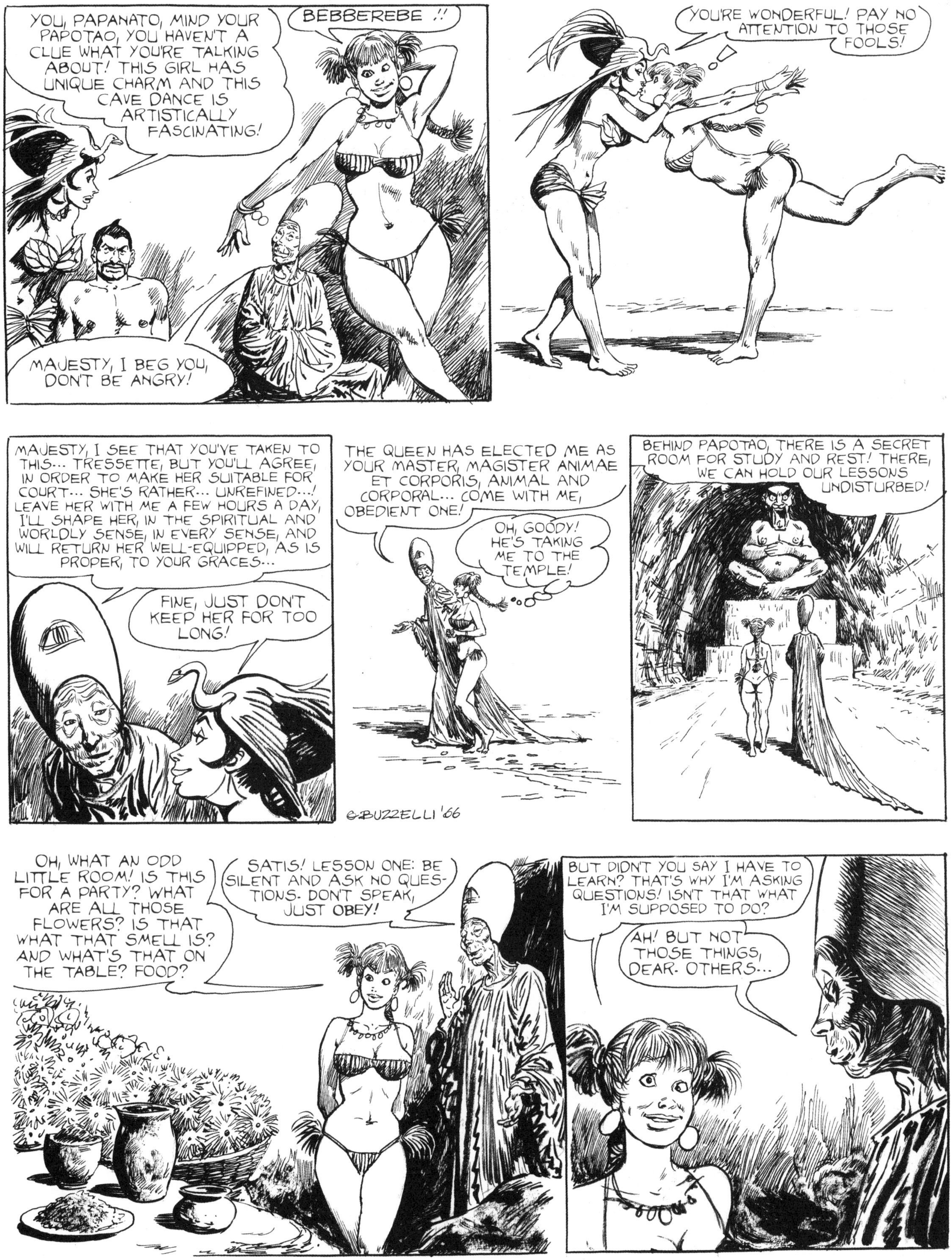

YOU, PAPANATO, MIND YOUR PAPOTAO, YOU HAVEN'T A CLUE WHAT YOU'RE TALKING ABOUT! THIS GIRL HAS UNIQUE CHARM AND THIS CAVE DANCE IS ARTISTICALLY FASCINATING!
BEBBEREBE !!
MAJESTY, I BEG YOU, DON'T BE ANGRY!
YOU'RE WONDERFUL! PAY NO ATTENTION TO THOSE FOOLS!
!
MAJESTY, I SEE THAT YOU'VE TAKEN TO THIS... TRESSETTE, BUT YOU'LL AGREE, IN ORDER TO MAKE HER SUITABLE FOR COURT... SHE'S RATHER... UNREFINED...! LEAVE HER WITH ME A FEW HOURS A DAY, I'LL SHAPE HER, IN THE SPIRITUAL AND WORLDLY SENSE, IN EVERY SENSE, AND WILL RETURN HER WELL-EQUIPPED, AS IS PROPER, TO YOUR GRACES...
FINE, JUST DON'T KEEP HER FOR TOO LONG!
THE QUEEN HAS ELECTED ME AS YOUR MASTER, MAGISTER ANIMAE ET CORPORIS, ANIMAL AND CORPORAL... COME WITH ME, OBEDIENT ONE!
OH, GOODY! HE'S TAKING ME TO THE TEMPLE!
G. BUZZELLI '66
BEHIND PAPOTAO, THERE IS A SECRET ROOM FOR STUDY AND REST! THERE, WE CAN HOLD OUR LESSONS UNDISTURBED!
OH, WHAT AN ODD LITTLE ROOM! IS THIS FOR A PARTY? WHAT ARE ALL THOSE FLOWERS? IS THAT WHAT THAT SMELL IS? AND WHAT'S THAT ON THE TABLE? FOOD?
SATIS! LESSON ONE: BE SILENT AND ASK NO QUESTIONS. DON'T SPEAK, JUST OBEY!
BUT DIDN'T YOU SAY I HAVE TO LEARN? THAT'S WHY I'M ASKING QUESTIONS! ISN'T THAT WHAT I'M SUPPOSED TO DO?
AH! BUT NOT THOSE THINGS, DEAR. OTHERS...

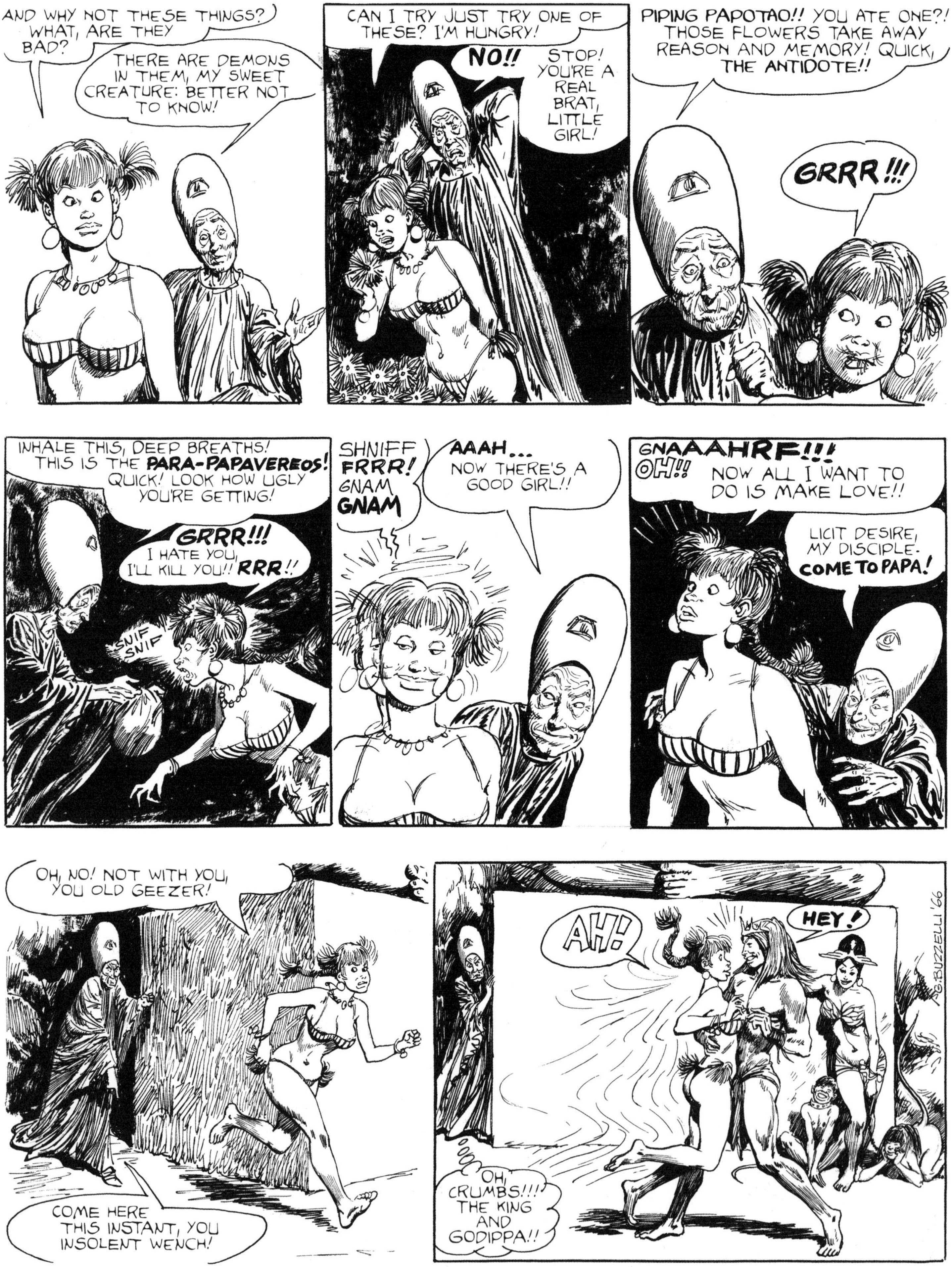
AND WHY NOT THESE THINGS? WHAT, ARE THEY BAD?
THERE ARE DEMONS IN THEM, MY SWEET CREATURE: BETTER NOT TO KNOW!
CAN I TRY JUST TRY ONE OF THESE? I'M HUNGRY!
NO!!
STOP! YOU'RE A REAL BRAT, LITTLE GIRL!
PIPING PAPOTAO!! YOU ATE ONE?! THOSE FLOWERS TAKE AWAY REASON AND MEMORY! QUICK, THE ANTIDOTE!!
GRRR!!!
INHALE THIS, DEEP BREATHS! THIS IS THE PARA-PAPAVEREOS! QUICK! LOOK HOW UGLY YOU'RE GETTING!
GRRR!!! I HATE YOU, I'LL KILL YOU!! RRR!!
SNIF SNIF
SHNIFF FRRR! GNAM GNAM
AAAH... NOW THERE'S A GOOD GIRL!!
GNAAAHRF!!! OH!! NOW ALL I WANT TO DO IS MAKE LOVE!!
LICIT DESIRE, MY DISCIPLE. COME TO PAPA!
OH, NO! NOT WITH YOU, YOU OLD GEEZER!
COME HERE THIS INSTANT, YOU INSOLENT WENCH!
AH!
HEY!
OH, CRUMBS!!! THE KING AND GODIPPA!!
G. BUZZELLI '66

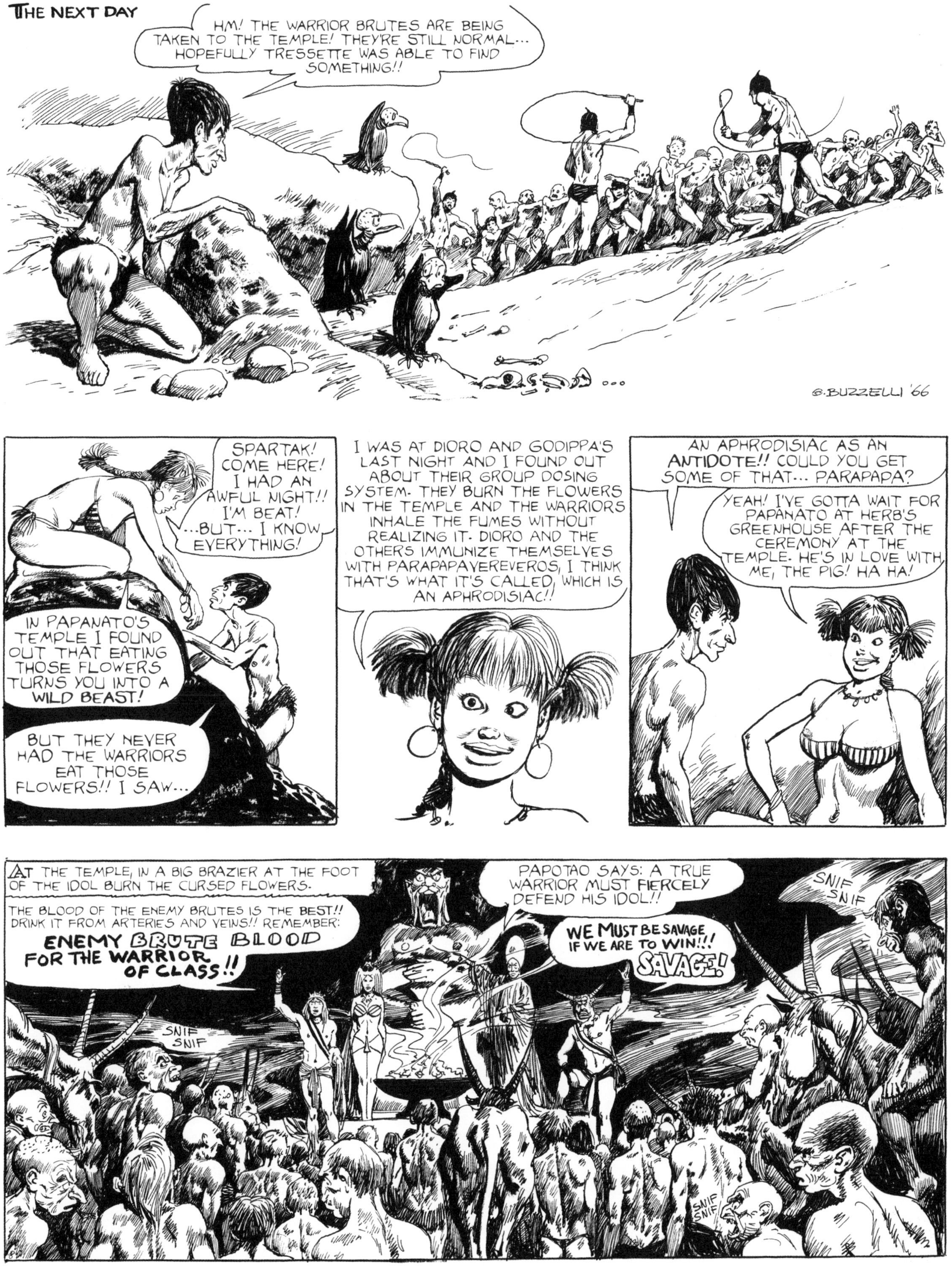
THE NEXT DAY
HM! THE WARRIOR BRUTES ARE BEING TAKEN TO THE TEMPLE! THEY'RE STILL NORMAL... HOPEFULLY TRESSETTE WAS ABLE TO FIND SOMETHING!!
G. BUZZELLI '66
SPARTAK! COME HERE! I HAD AN AWFUL NIGHT!! I'M BEAT! ...BUT... I KNOW EVERYTHING!
IN PAPANATO'S TEMPLE I FOUND OUT THAT EATING THOSE FLOWERS TURNS YOU INTO A WILD BEAST!
BUT THEY NEVER HAD THE WARRIORS EAT THOSE FLOWERS!! I SAW...
I WAS AT DIORO AND GODIPPA'S LAST NIGHT AND I FOUND OUT ABOUT THEIR GROUP DOSING SYSTEM. THEY BURN THE FLOWERS IN THE TEMPLE AND THE WARRIORS INHALE THE FUMES WITHOUT REALIZING IT. DIORO AND THE OTHERS IMMUNIZE THEMSELVES WITH PARAPAPAVEREVEROS, I THINK THAT'S WHAT IT'S CALLED, WHICH IS AN APHRODISIAC!!
AN APHRODISIAC AS AN ANTIDOTE!! COULD YOU GET SOME OF THAT... PARAPAPA?
YEAH! I'VE GOTTA WAIT FOR PAPANATO AT HERB'S GREENHOUSE AFTER THE CEREMONY AT THE TEMPLE. HE'S IN LOVE WITH ME, THE PIG! HA HA!
AT THE TEMPLE, IN A BIG BRAZIER AT THE FOOT OF THE IDOL BURN THE CURSED FLOWERS.
THE BLOOD OF THE ENEMY BRUTES IS THE BEST!! DRINK IT FROM ARTERIES AND VEINS!! REMEMBER:
ENEMY BRUTE BLOOD FOR THE WARRIOR OF CLASS!!
PAPOTAO SAYS: A TRUE WARRIOR MUST FIERCELY DEFEND HIS IDOL!!
WE MUST BE SAVAGE IF WE ARE TO WIN!!!
SAVAGE!
SNIF SNIF
SNIF SNIF
SNIF SNIF

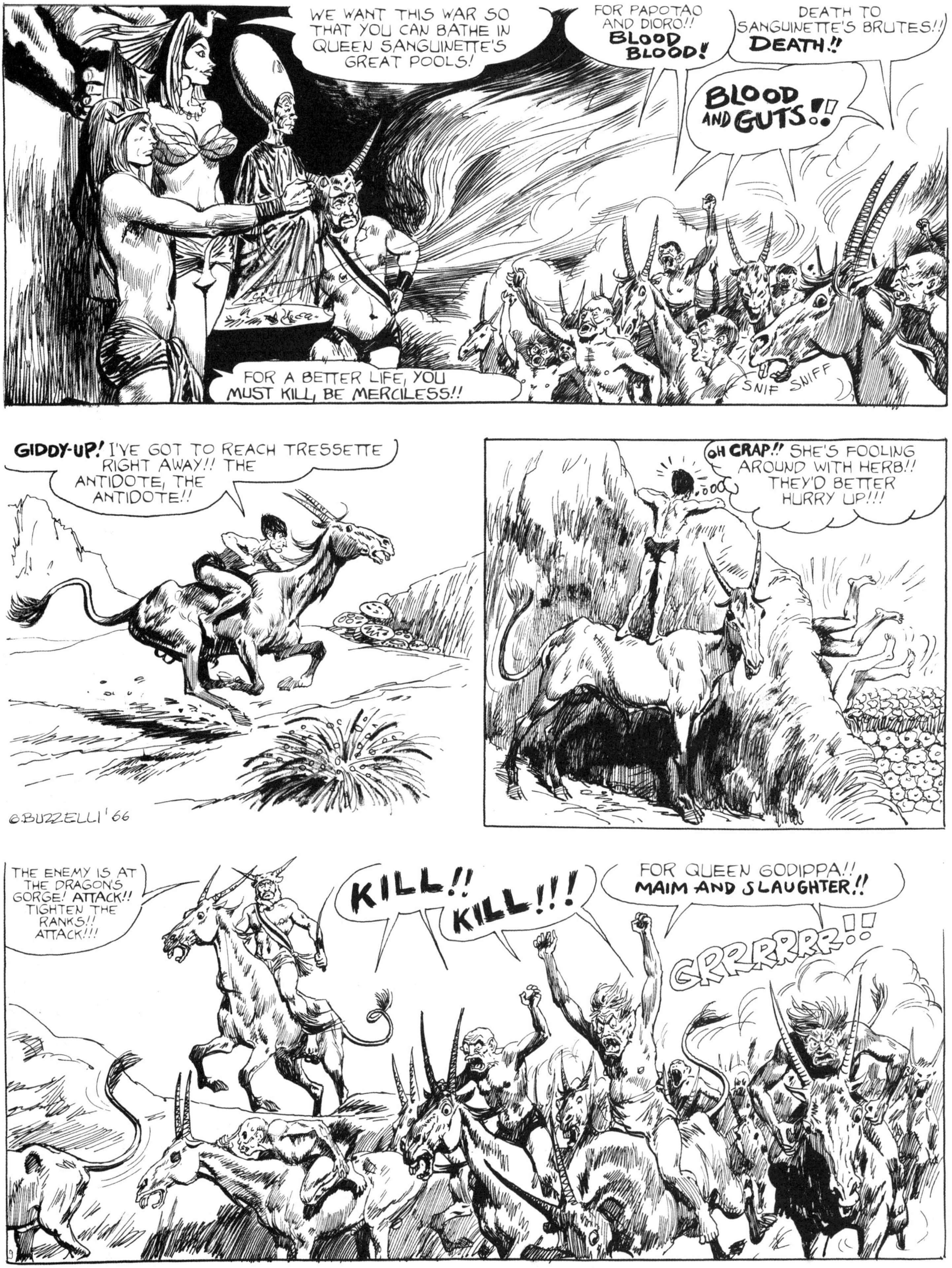

WE WANT THIS WAR SO THAT YOU CAN BATHE IN QUEEN SANGUINETTE'S GREAT POOLS!
FOR PAPOTAO AND DIORO!! BLOOD BLOOD!
DEATH TO SANGUINETTE'S BRUTES!! DEATH!!
BLOOD AND GUTS!!
FOR A BETTER LIFE, YOU MUST KILL, BE MERCILESS!!
SNIF SNIFF
GIDDY-UP! I'VE GOT TO REACH TRESSETTE RIGHT AWAY!! THE ANTIDOTE, THE ANTIDOTE!!
©BUZZELLI '66
OH CRAP!! SHE'S FOOLING AROUND WITH HERB!! THEY'D BETTER HURRY UP!!!
THE ENEMY IS AT THE DRAGON'S GORGE! ATTACK!! TIGHTEN THE RANKS!! ATTACK!!!
KILL!! KILL!!!
FOR QUEEN GODIPPA!! MAIM AND SLAUGHTER!!
GRRRRRR!!

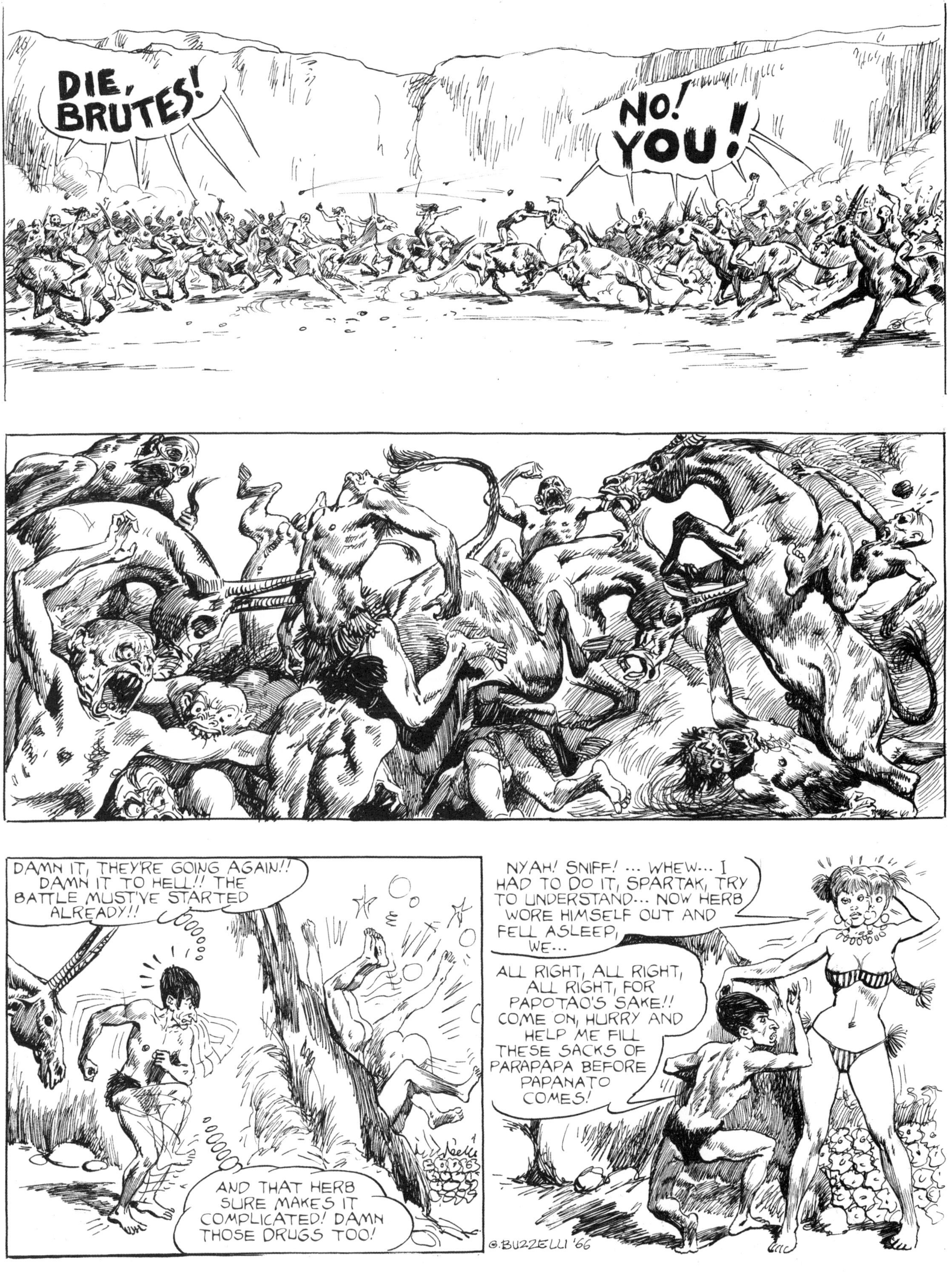
DIE, BRUTES!
NO! YOU!
DAMN IT, THEY'RE GOING AGAIN!! DAMN IT TO HELL!! THE BATTLE MUST'VE STARTED ALREADY!!
AND THAT HERB SURE MAKES IT COMPLICATED! DAMN THOSE DRUGS TOO!
NYAH! SNIFF! ... WHEW... I HAD TO DO IT, SPARTAK, TRY TO UNDERSTAND... NOW HERB WORE HIMSELF OUT AND FELL ASLEEP, WE...
ALL RIGHT, ALL RIGHT, ALL RIGHT, FOR PAPOTAO'S SAKE!! COME ON, HURRY AND HELP ME FILL THESE SACKS OF PARAPAPA BEFORE PAPANATO COMES!
©.BUZZELLI '66

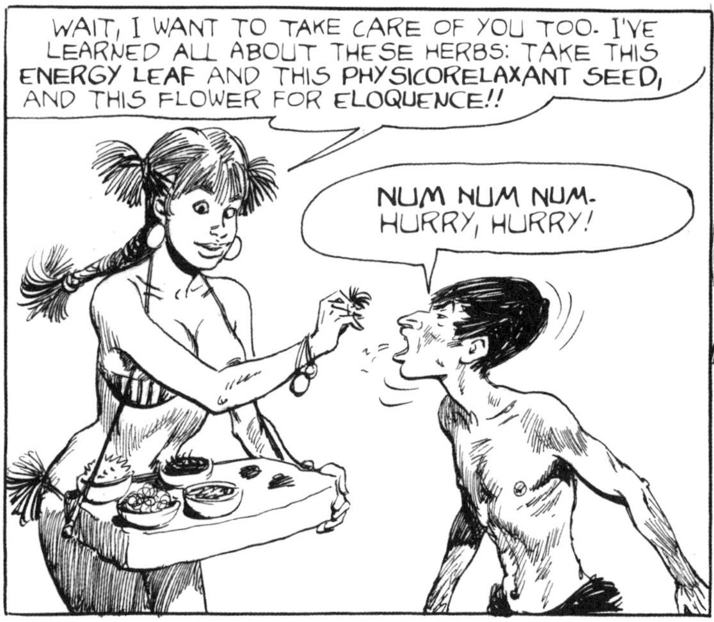
WAIT, I WANT TO TAKE CARE OF YOU TOO. I'VE LEARNED ALL ABOUT THESE HERBS: TAKE THIS ENERGY LEAF AND THIS PHYSICORELAXANT SEED, AND THIS FLOWER FOR ELOQUENCE!!
NUM NUM NUM. HURRY, HURRY!

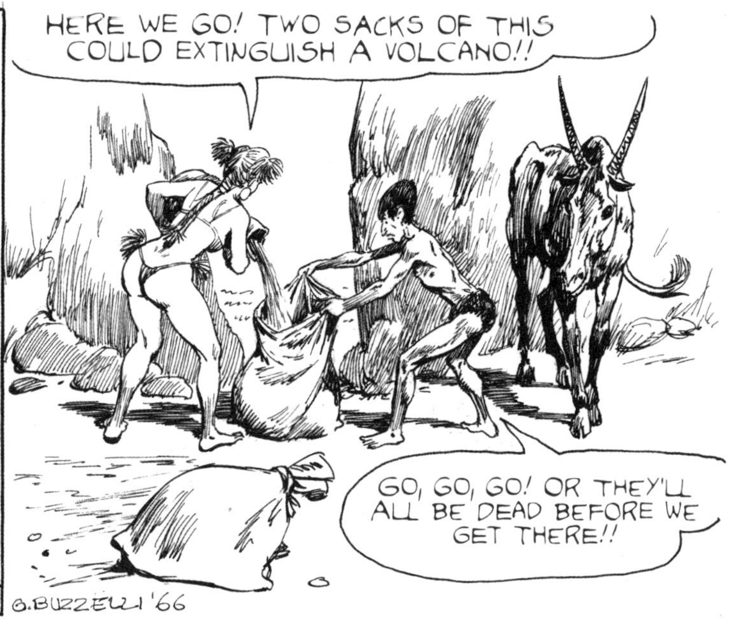
HERE WE GO! TWO SACKS OF THIS COULD EXTINGUISH A VOLCANO!!
GO, GO, GO! OR THEY'LL ALL BE DEAD BEFORE WE GET THERE!!
G. BUZZELLI '66

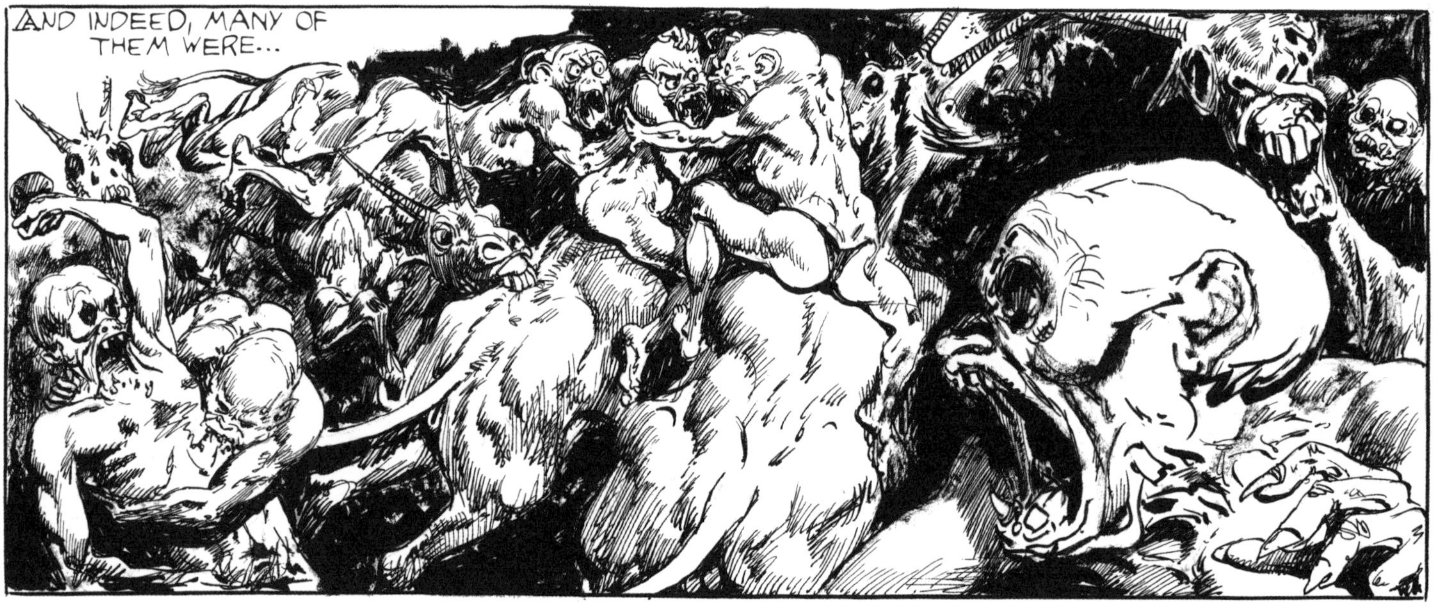
AND INDEED, MANY OF THEM WERE...

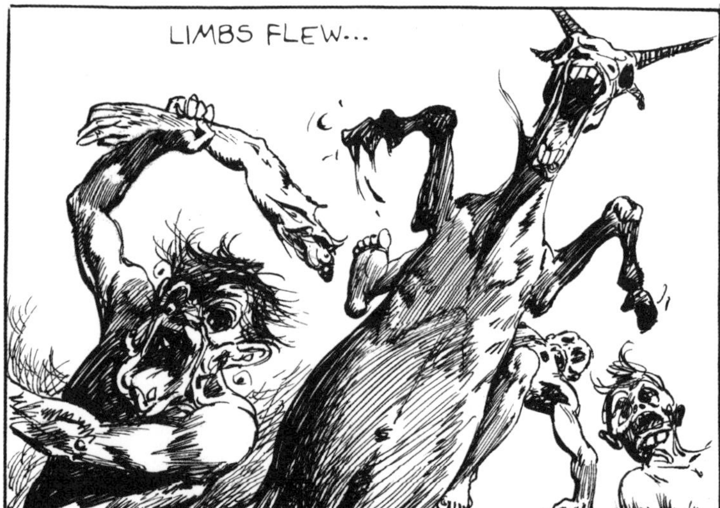
LIMBS FLEW...
11

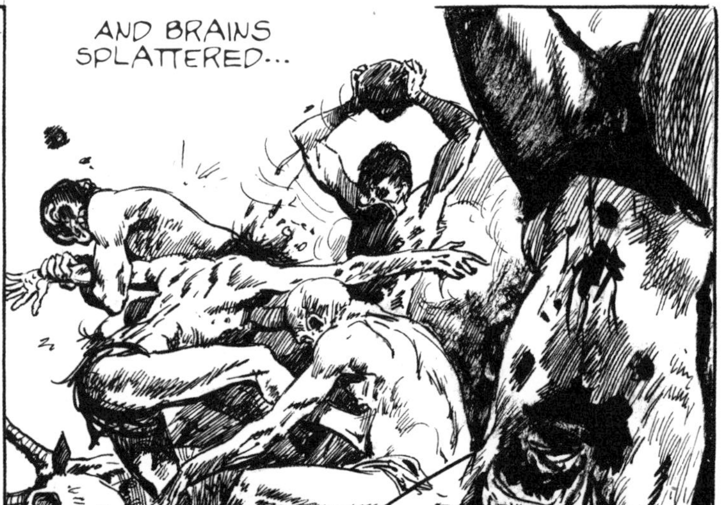
AND BRAINS SPLATTERED...

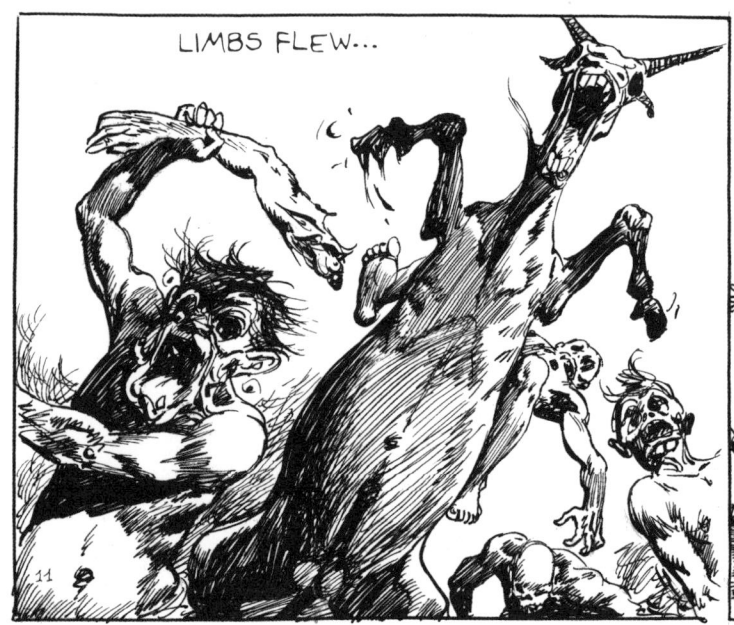

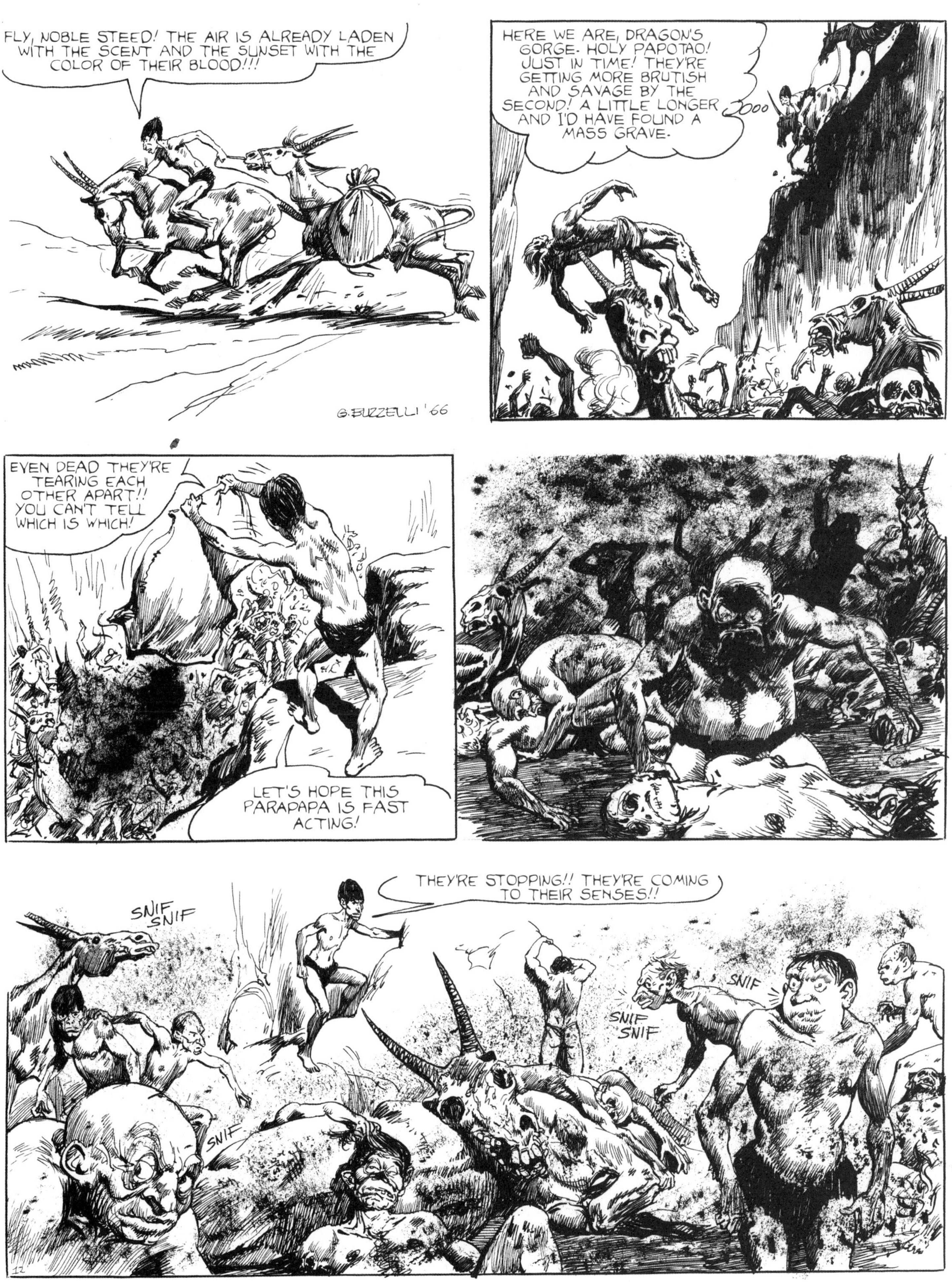
FLY, NOBLE STEED! THE AIR IS ALREADY LADEN WITH THE SCENT AND THE SUNSET WITH THE COLOR OF THEIR BLOOD!!!
G. BUZZELLI '66
HERE WE ARE, DRAGON'S GORGE- HOLY PAPOTAO! JUST IN TIME! THEY'RE GETTING MORE BRUTISH AND SAVAGE BY THE SECOND! A LITTLE LONGER AND I'D HAVE FOUND A MASS GRAVE-
EVEN DEAD THEY'RE TEARING EACH OTHER APART!! YOU CAN'T TELL WHICH IS WHICH!
LET'S HOPE THIS PARAPAPA IS FAST ACTING!
THEY'RE STOPPING!! THEY'RE COMING TO THEIR SENSES!!
SNIF SNIF
SNIF
SNIF SNIF
SNIF
12

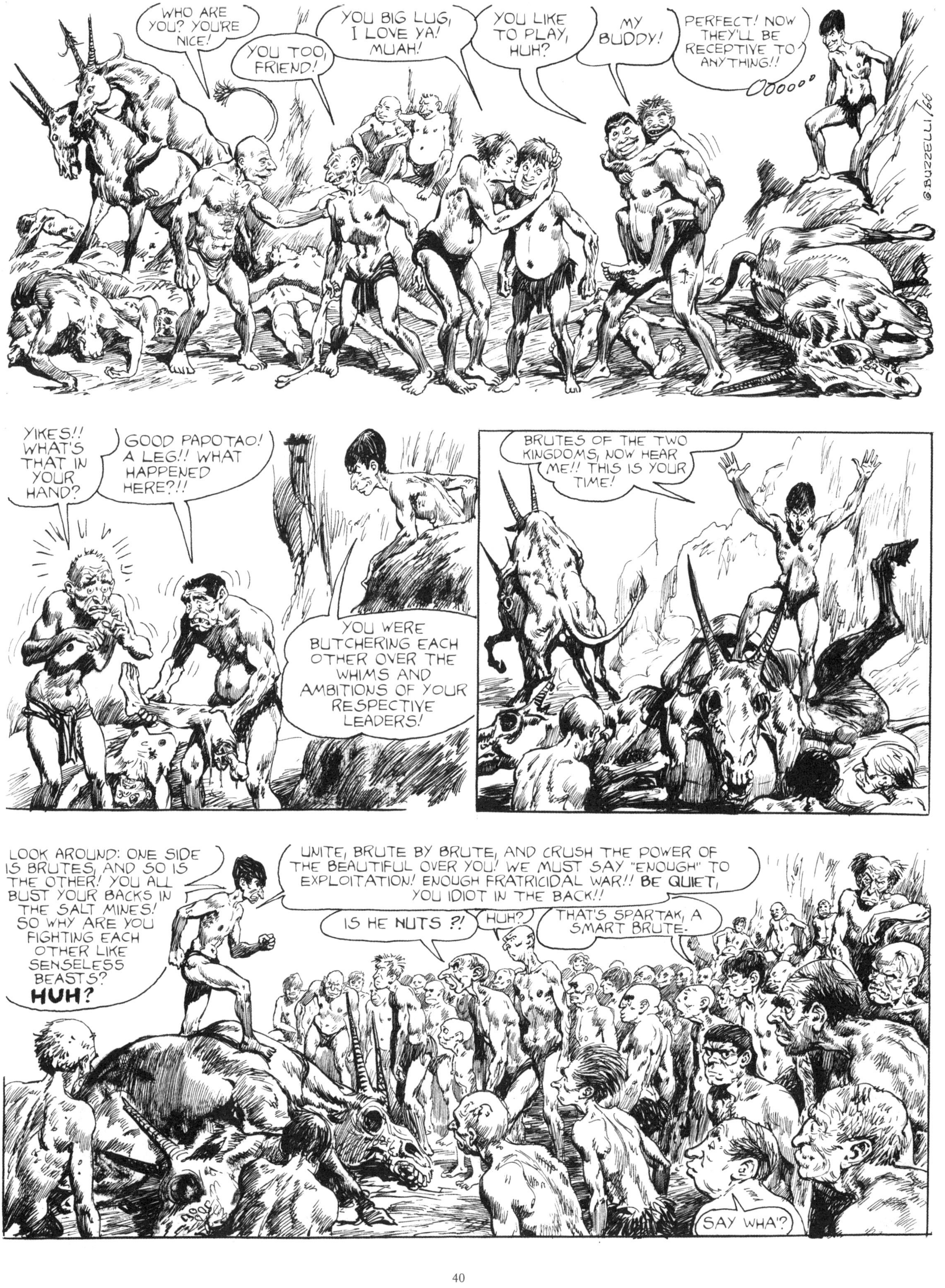
WHO ARE YOU? YOU'RE NICE!
YOU TOO, FRIEND!
YOU BIG LUG, I LOVE YA! MUAH!
YOU LIKE TO PLAY, HUH?
MY BUDDY!
PERFECT! NOW THEY'LL BE RECEPTIVE TO ANYTHING!! OOOOOO
©BUZZELLI/66
YIKES!! WHAT'S THAT IN YOUR HAND?
GOOD PAPOTAO! A LEG!! WHAT HAPPENED HERE?!!
YOU WERE BUTCHERING EACH OTHER OVER THE WHIMS AND AMBITIONS OF YOUR RESPECTIVE LEADERS!
BRUTES OF THE TWO KINGDOMS, NOW HEAR ME!! THIS IS YOUR TIME!
LOOK AROUND: ONE SIDE IS BRUTES, AND SO IS THE OTHER! YOU ALL BUST YOUR BACKS IN THE SALT MINES! SO WHY ARE YOU FIGHTING EACH OTHER LIKE SENSELESS BEASTS? HUH?
UNITE, BRUTE BY BRUTE, AND CRUSH THE POWER OF THE BEAUTIFUL OVER YOU! WE MUST SAY "ENOUGH" TO EXPLOITATION! ENOUGH FRATRICIDAL WAR!! BE QUIET, YOU IDIOT IN THE BACK!!
IS HE NUTS ?!
HUH?
THAT'S SPARTAK, A SMART BRUTE.
SAY WHA'?

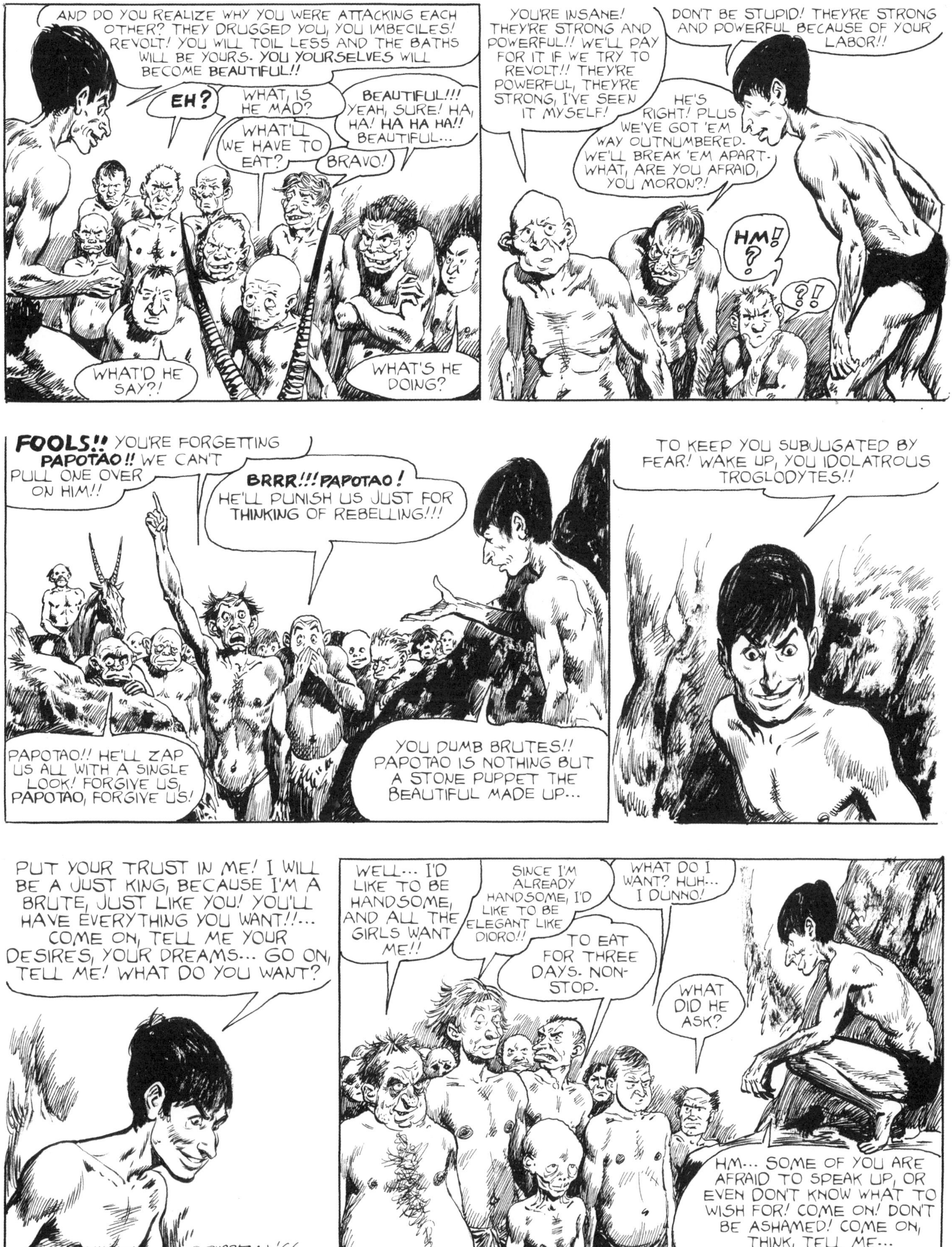
AND DO YOU REALIZE WHY YOU WERE ATTACKING EACH OTHER? THEY DRUGGED YOU, YOU IMBECILES! REVOLT! YOU WILL TOIL LESS AND THE BATHS WILL BE YOURS. YOU YOURSELVES WILL BECOME BEAUTIFUL!!
EH?
WHAT, IS HE MAD?
WHAT'LL WE HAVE TO EAT?
BEAUTIFUL!!! YEAH, SURE! HA, HA! HA HA HA!! BEAUTIFUL...
BRAVO!
WHAT'D HE SAY?!
WHAT'S HE DOING?
YOU'RE INSANE! THEY'RE STRONG AND POWERFUL!! WE'LL PAY FOR IT IF WE TRY TO REVOLT!! THEY'RE POWERFUL, THEY'RE STRONG, I'VE SEEN IT MYSELF!
DON'T BE STUPID! THEY'RE STRONG AND POWERFUL BECAUSE OF YOUR LABOR!!
HE'S RIGHT! PLUS WE'VE GOT 'EM WAY OUTNUMBERED. WE'LL BREAK 'EM APART. WHAT, ARE YOU AFRAID, YOU MORON?!
HM!! ?
?!
FOOLS!! YOU'RE FORGETTING PAPOTAO!! WE CAN'T PULL ONE OVER ON HIM!!
BRRR!!! PAPOTAO! HE'LL PUNISH US JUST FOR THINKING OF REBELLING!!!
PAPOTAO!! HE'LL ZAP US ALL WITH A SINGLE LOOK! FORGIVE US, PAPOTAO, FORGIVE US!
YOU DUMB BRUTES!! PAPOTAO IS NOTHING BUT A STONE PUPPET THE BEAUTIFUL MADE UP...
TO KEEP YOU SUBJUGATED BY FEAR! WAKE UP, YOU IDOLATROUS TROGLODYTES!!
PUT YOUR TRUST IN ME! I WILL BE A JUST KING, BECAUSE I'M A BRUTE, JUST LIKE YOU! YOU'LL HAVE EVERYTHING YOU WANT!!... COME ON, TELL ME YOUR DESIRES, YOUR DREAMS... GO ON, TELL ME! WHAT DO YOU WANT?
G. BUZZELLI '66
WELL... I'D LIKE TO BE HANDSOME, AND ALL THE GIRLS WANT ME!!
SINCE I'M ALREADY HANDSOME, I'D LIKE TO BE ELEGANT LIKE DIORO!!
TO EAT FOR THREE DAYS. NON-STOP.
WHAT DO I WANT? HUH... I DUNNO!
WHAT DID HE ASK?
HM... SOME OF YOU ARE AFRAID TO SPEAK UP, OR EVEN DON'T KNOW WHAT TO WISH FOR! COME ON! DON'T BE ASHAMED! COME ON, THINK, TELL ME...

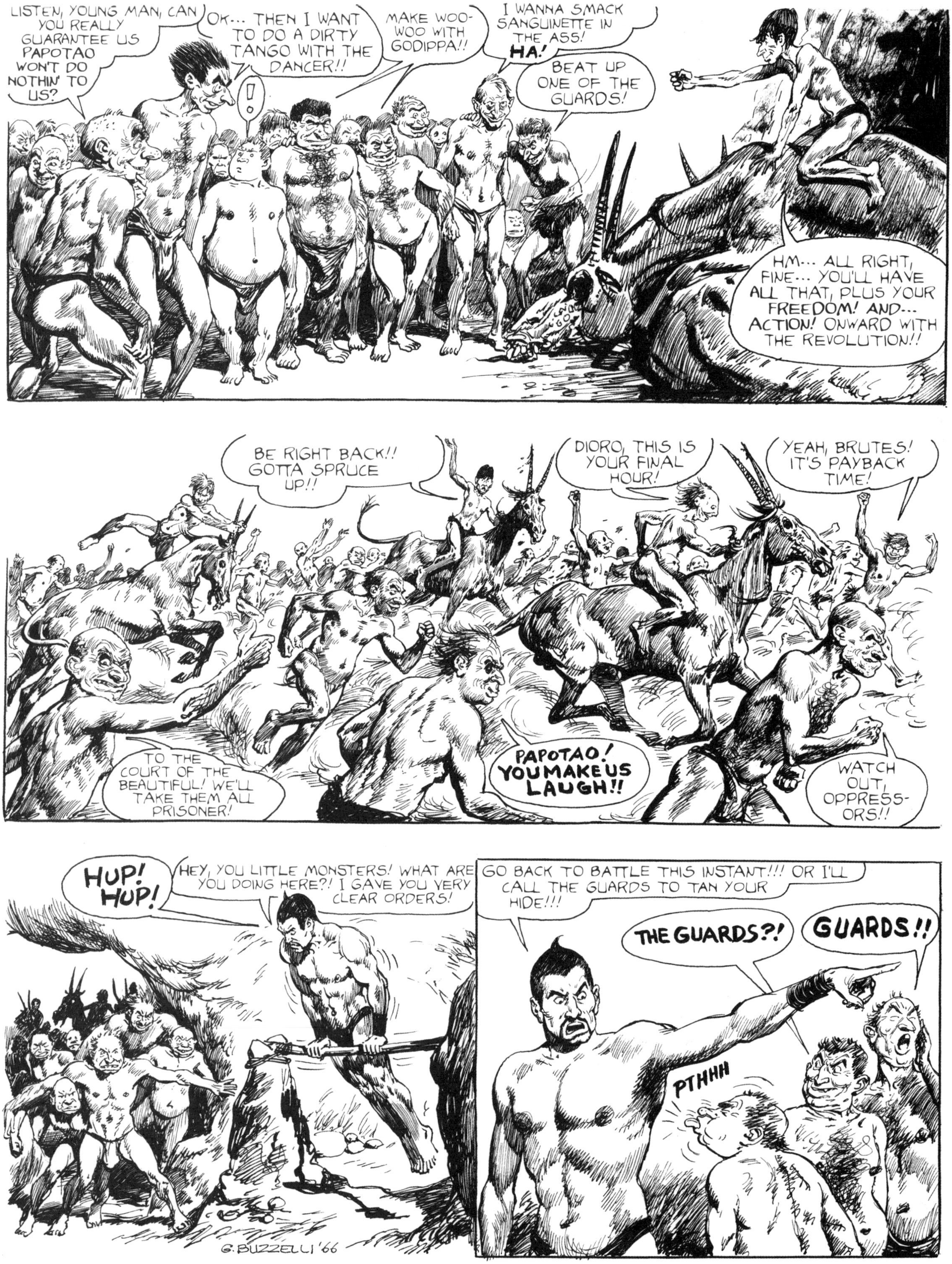
LISTEN, YOUNG MAN, CAN YOU REALLY GUARANTEE US PAPOTAO WON'T DO NOTHIN' TO US?
OK... THEN I WANT TO DO A DIRTY TANGO WITH THE DANCER!!
!
MAKE WOO-WOO WITH GODIPPA!!
I WANNA SMACK SANGUINETTE IN THE ASS! HA!
BEAT UP ONE OF THE GUARDS!
HM... ALL RIGHT, FINE... YOU'LL HAVE ALL THAT, PLUS YOUR FREEDOM! AND... ACTION! ONWARD WITH THE REVOLUTION!!
BE RIGHT BACK!! GOTTA SPRUCE UP!!
DIORO, THIS IS YOUR FINAL HOUR!
YEAH, BRUTES! IT'S PAYBACK TIME!
TO THE COURT OF THE BEAUTIFUL! WE'LL TAKE THEM ALL PRISONER!
PAPOTAO! YOU MAKE US LAUGH!!
WATCH OUT, OPPRESS-ORS!!
HUP! HUP!
HEY, YOU LITTLE MONSTERS! WHAT ARE YOU DOING HERE?! I GAVE YOU VERY CLEAR ORDERS!
G. BUZZELLI '66
GO BACK TO BATTLE THIS INSTANT!!! OR I'LL CALL THE GUARDS TO TAN YOUR HIDE!!!
THE GUARDS?!
GUARDS!!
PTHHH

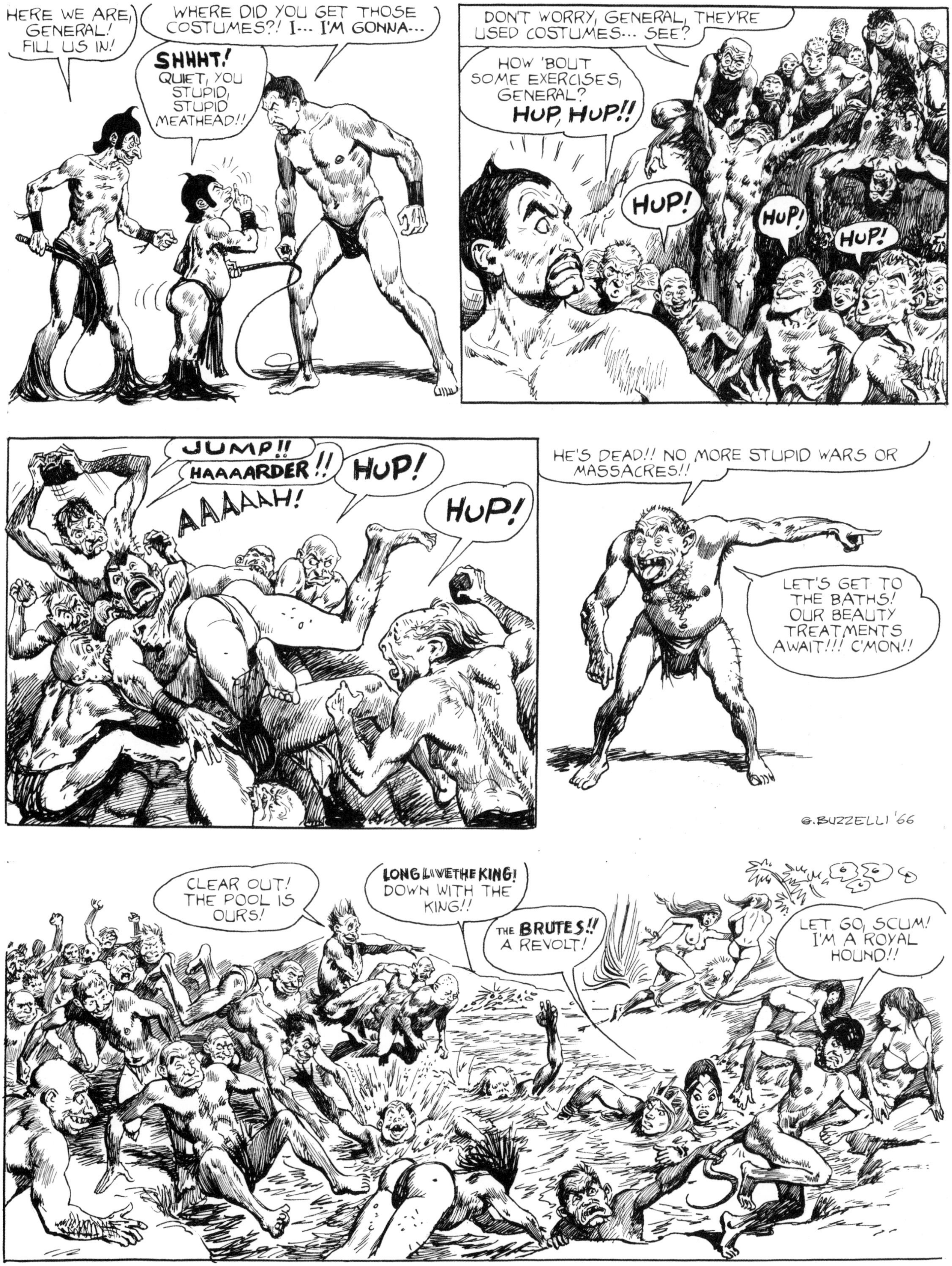
HERE WE ARE, GENERAL! FILL US IN!
WHERE DID YOU GET THOSE COSTUMES?! I... I'M GONNA...
SHHHT! QUIET, YOU STUPID, STUPID MEATHEAD!!
DON'T WORRY, GENERAL, THEY'RE USED COSTUMES... SEE?
HOW 'BOUT SOME EXERCISES, GENERAL? HUP, HUP!!
HUP!
HUP!
HUP!
JUMP!!
HAAAARDER!!
AAAAAH!
HUP!
HUP!
HE'S DEAD!! NO MORE STUPID WARS OR MASSACRES!!
LET'S GET TO THE BATHS! OUR BEAUTY TREATMENTS AWAIT!!! C'MON!!
G. BUZZELLI '66
CLEAR OUT! THE POOL IS OURS!
LONG LIVE THE KING! DOWN WITH THE KING!!
THE BRUTES!! A REVOLT!
LET GO, SCUM! I'M A ROYAL HOUND!!

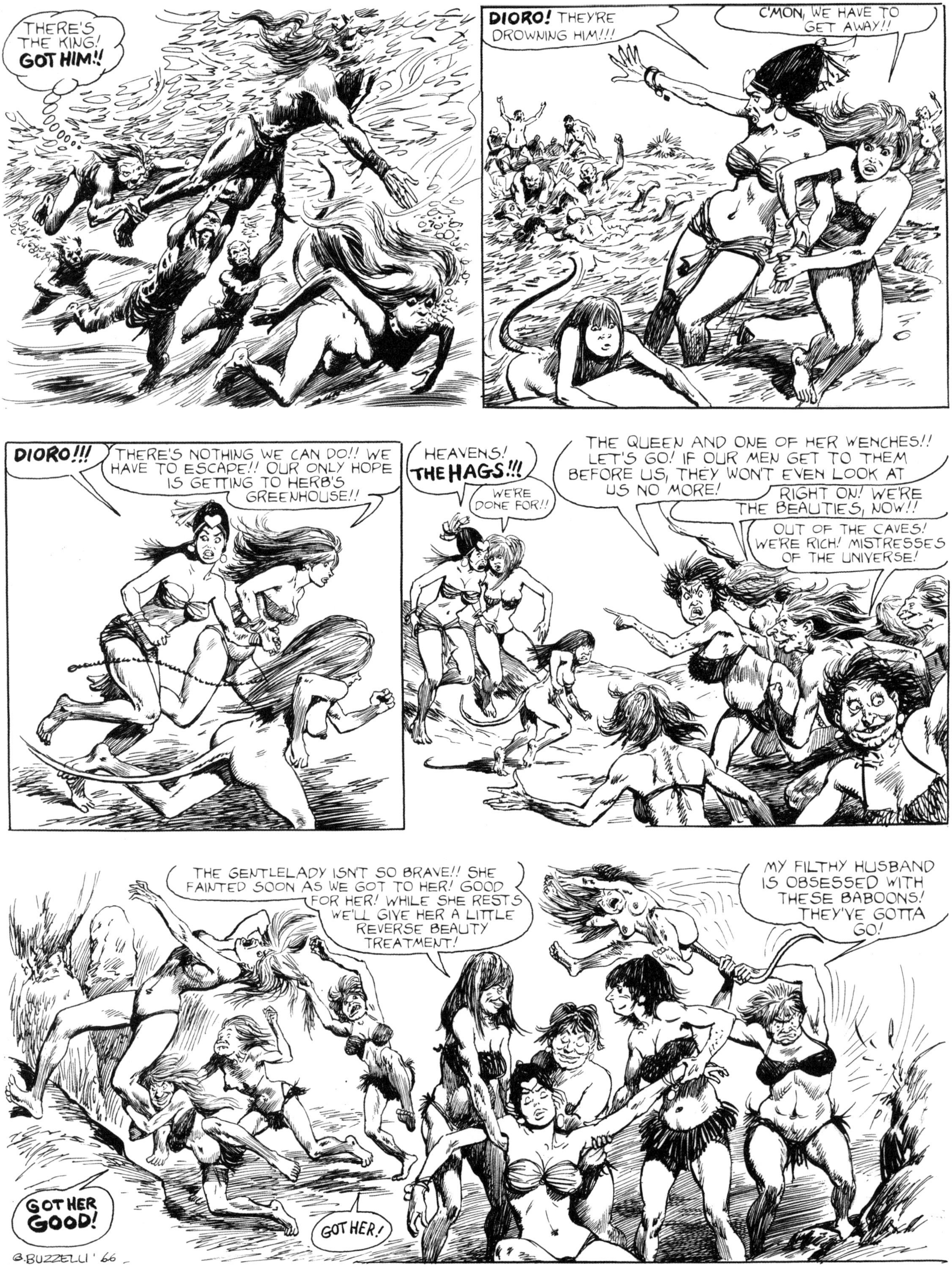
THERE'S THE KING! GOT HIM!!
DIORO! THEY'RE DROWNING HIM!!!
C'MON, WE HAVE TO GET AWAY!!
DIORO!!!
THERE'S NOTHING WE CAN DO!! WE HAVE TO ESCAPE!! OUR ONLY HOPE IS GETTING TO HERB'S GREENHOUSE!!
HEAVENS! THE HAGS!!!
WE'RE DONE FOR!!
THE QUEEN AND ONE OF HER WENCHES!! LET'S GO! IF OUR MEN GET TO THEM BEFORE US, THEY WON'T EVEN LOOK AT US NO MORE!
RIGHT ON! WE'RE THE BEAUTIES, NOW!!
OUT OF THE CAVES! WE'RE RICH! MISTRESSES OF THE UNIVERSE!
THE GENTLELADY ISN'T SO BRAVE!! SHE FAINTED SOON AS WE GOT TO HER! GOOD FOR HER! WHILE SHE RESTS WE'LL GIVE HER A LITTLE REVERSE BEAUTY TREATMENT!
MY FILTHY HUSBAND IS OBSESSED WITH THESE BABOONS! THEY'VE GOTTA GO!
GOT HER GOOD!
GOT HER!
G. BUZZELLI '66

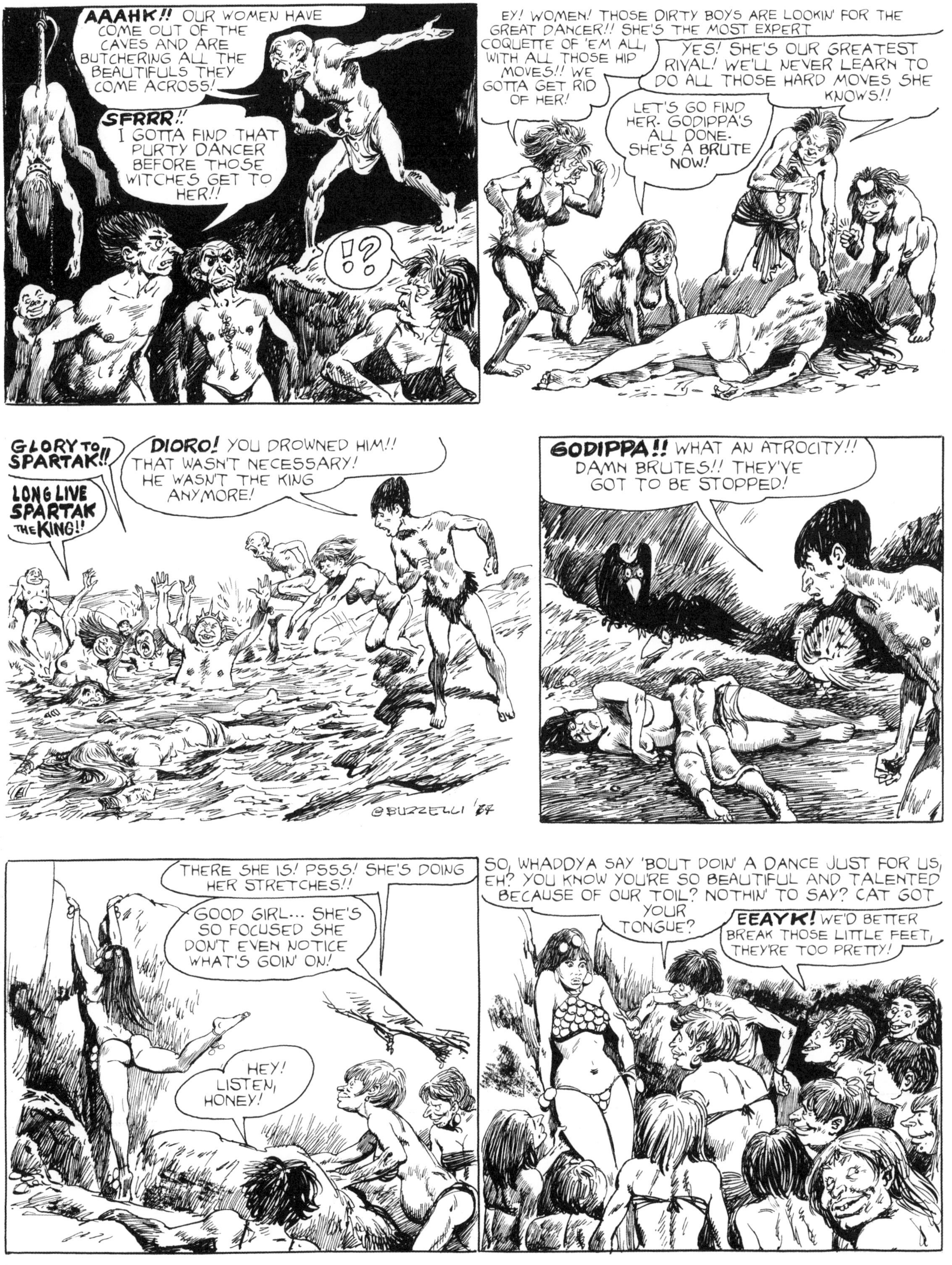
AAAHK!! OUR WOMEN HAVE COME OUT OF THE CAVES AND ARE BUTCHERING ALL THE BEAUTIFULS THEY COME ACROSS!
SFRRR!! I GOTTA FIND THAT PURTY DANCER BEFORE THOSE WITCHES GET TO HER!!
!?
EY! WOMEN! THOSE DIRTY BOYS ARE LOOKIN' FOR THE GREAT DANCER!! SHE'S THE MOST EXPERT COQUETTE OF 'EM ALL, WITH ALL THOSE HIP MOVES!! WE GOTTA GET RID OF HER!
YES! SHE'S OUR GREATEST RIVAL! WE'LL NEVER LEARN TO DO ALL THOSE HARD MOVES SHE KNOWS!!
LET'S GO FIND HER- GODIPPA'S ALL DONE- SHE'S A BRUTE NOW!
GLORY TO SPARTAK!!
LONG LIVE SPARTAK THE KING!!
DIORO! YOU DROWNED HIM!! THAT WASN'T NECESSARY! HE WASN'T THE KING ANYMORE!
©BUZZELLI '87
GODIPPA!! WHAT AN ATROCITY!! DAMN BRUTES!! THEY'VE GOT TO BE STOPPED!
THERE SHE IS! PSSS! SHE'S DOING HER STRETCHES!!
GOOD GIRL... SHE'S SO FOCUSED SHE DON'T EVEN NOTICE WHAT'S GOIN' ON!
HEY! LISTEN, HONEY!
SO, WHADDYA SAY 'BOUT DOIN' A DANCE JUST FOR US, EH? YOU KNOW YOU'RE SO BEAUTIFUL AND TALENTED BECAUSE OF OUR TOIL? NOTHIN' TO SAY? CAT GOT YOUR TONGUE?
EEAYK! WE'D BETTER BREAK THOSE LITTLE FEET, THEY'RE TOO PRETTY!

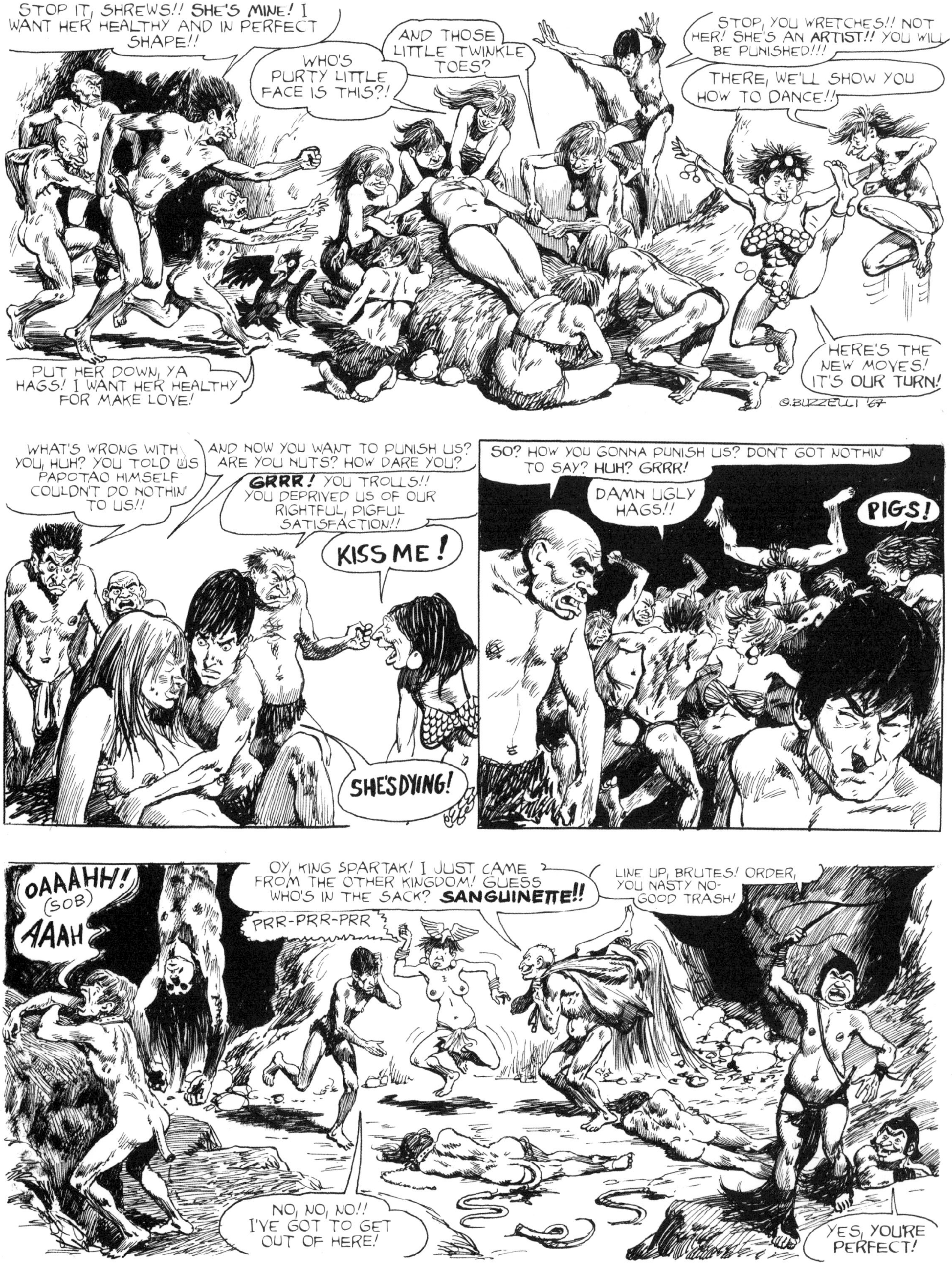

STOP IT, SHREWS!! SHE'S MINE! I WANT HER HEALTHY AND IN PERFECT SHAPE!!
WHO'S PURTY LITTLE FACE IS THIS?!
AND THOSE LITTLE TWINKLE TOES?
STOP, YOU WRETCHES!! NOT HER! SHE'S AN ARTIST!! YOU WILL BE PUNISHED!!!
THERE, WE'LL SHOW YOU HOW TO DANCE!!
PUT HER DOWN, YA HAGS! I WANT HER HEALTHY FOR MAKE LOVE!
HERE'S THE NEW MOVES! IT'S OUR TURN!
G.BUZZELLI '67
WHAT'S WRONG WITH YOU, HUH? YOU TOLD US PAPOTAO HIMSELF COULDN'T DO NOTHIN' TO US!!
AND NOW YOU WANT TO PUNISH US? ARE YOU NUTS? HOW DARE YOU?
GRRR! YOU TROLLS!! YOU DEPRIVED US OF OUR RIGHTFUL, PIGFUL SATISFACTION!!
KISS ME!
SHE'S DYING!
SO? HOW YOU GONNA PUNISH US? DON'T GOT NOTHIN' TO SAY? HUH? GRRR!
DAMN UGLY HAGS!!
PIGS!
OAAAHH! (SOB) AAAH
OY, KING SPARTAK! I JUST CAME FROM THE OTHER KINGDOM! GUESS WHO'S IN THE SACK? SANGUINETTE!!
LINE UP, BRUTES! ORDER, YOU NASTY NO-GOOD TRASH!
PRR-PRR-PRR
NO, NO, NO!! I'VE GOT TO GET OUT OF HERE!
YES, YOU'RE PERFECT!

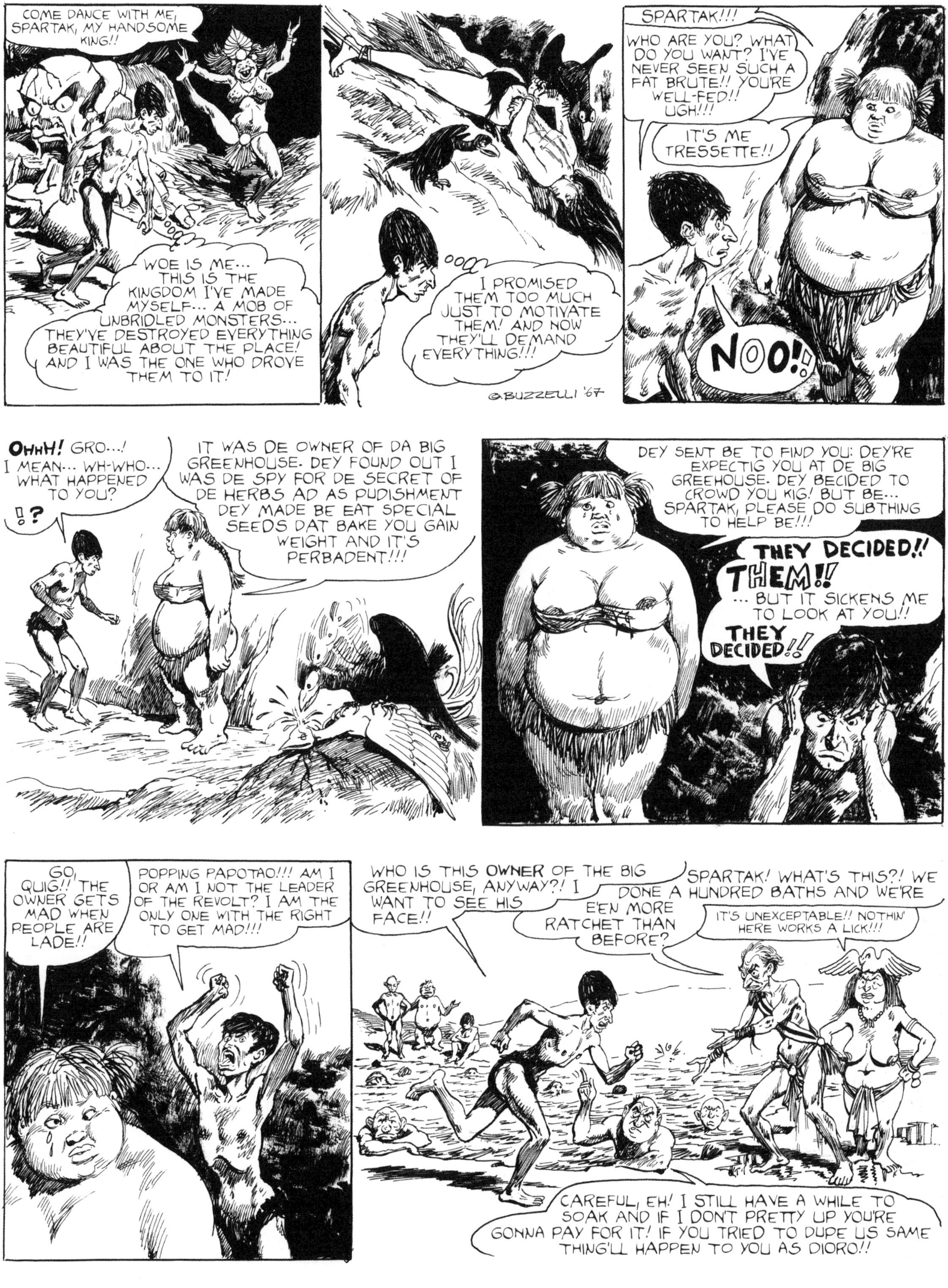
COME DANCE WITH ME, SPARTAK, MY HANDSOME KING!!
WOE IS ME... THIS IS THE KINGDOM I'VE MADE MYSELF... A MOB OF UNBRIDLED MONSTERS... THEY'VE DESTROYED EVERYTHING BEAUTIFUL ABOUT THE PLACE! AND I WAS THE ONE WHO DROVE THEM TO IT!
I PROMISED THEM TOO MUCH JUST TO MOTIVATE THEM! AND NOW THEY'LL DEMAND EVERYTHING!!!
G. BUZZELLI '67
SPARTAK!!!
WHO ARE YOU? WHAT DO YOU WANT? I'VE NEVER SEEN SUCH A FAT BRUTE!! YOU'RE WELL-FED!! UGH!!!
IT'S ME TRESSETTE!!
NOO!!
OHHH! GRO...! I MEAN... WH-WHO... WHAT HAPPENED TO YOU?
!?
IT WAS DE OWNER OF DA BIG GREENHOUSE. DEY FOUND OUT I WAS DE SPY FOR DE SECRET OF DE HERBS AD AS PUDISHMENT DEY MADE BE EAT SPECIAL SEEDS DAT BAKE YOU GAIN WEIGHT AND IT'S PERBADENT!!!
DEY SENT BE TO FIND YOU: DEY'RE EXPECTIG YOU AT DE BIG GREEHOUSE. DEY BECIDED TO CROWD YOU KIG! BUT BE... SPARTAK, PLEASE DO SUBTHING TO HELP BE!!!
THEY DECIDED!! THEM!! ... BUT IT SICKENS ME TO LOOK AT YOU!! THEY DECIDED!!
GO, QUIG!! THE OWNER GETS MAD WHEN PEOPLE ARE LADE!!
POPPING PAPOTAO!!! AM I OR AM I NOT THE LEADER OF THE REVOLT? I AM THE ONLY ONE WITH THE RIGHT TO GET MAD!!!
WHO IS THIS OWNER OF THE BIG GREENHOUSE, ANYWAY?! I WANT TO SEE HIS FACE!!
SPARTAK! WHAT'S THIS?! WE DONE A HUNDRED BATHS AND WE'RE E'EN MORE RATCHET THAN BEFORE?
IT'S UNEXCEPTABLE!! NOTHIN' HERE WORKS A LICK!!!
CAREFUL, EH! I STILL HAVE A WHILE TO SOAK AND IF I DON'T PRETTY UP YOU'RE GONNA PAY FOR IT! IF YOU TRIED TO DUPE US SAME THING'LL HAPPEN TO YOU AS DIORO!!

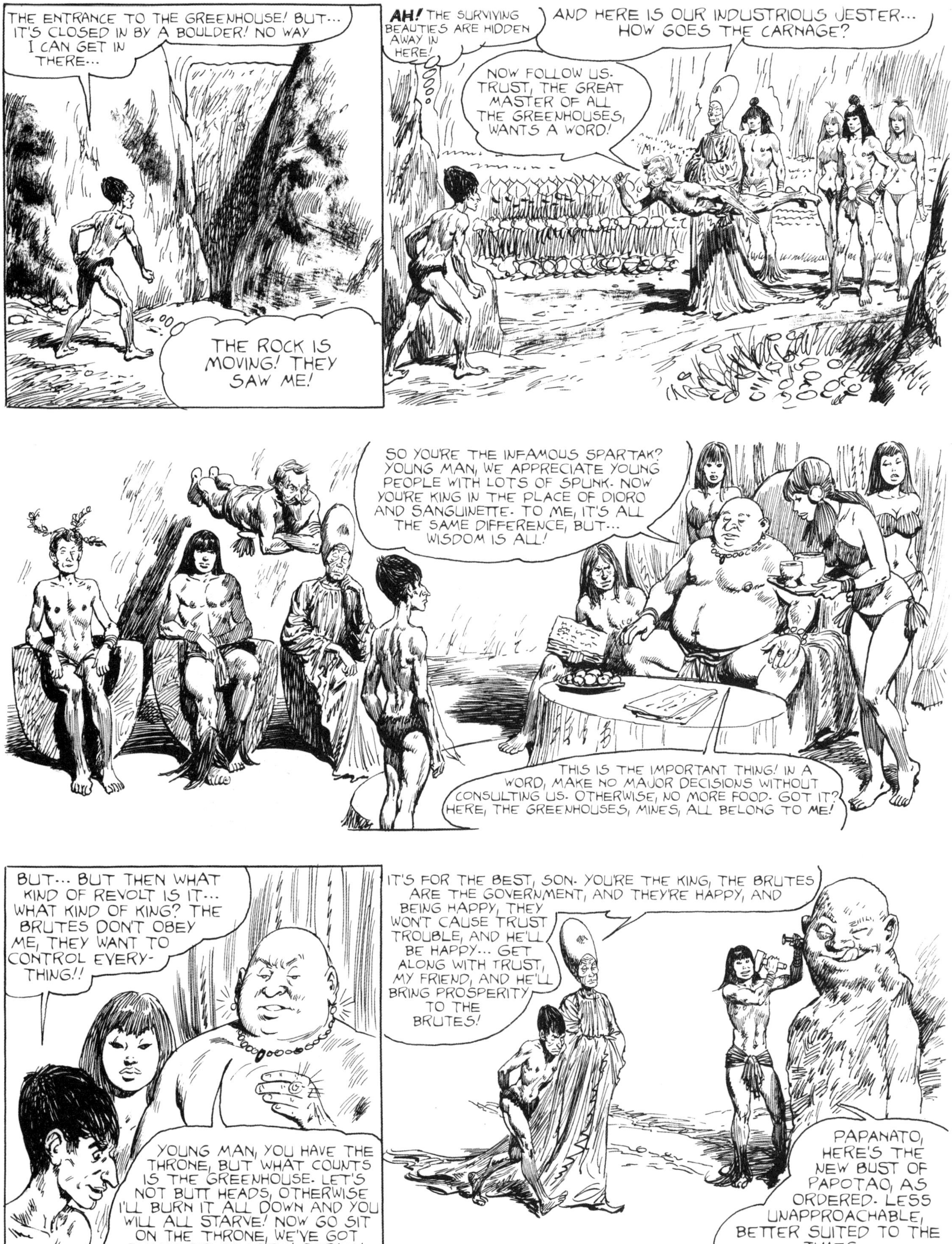
THE ENTRANCE TO THE GREENHOUSE! BUT... IT'S CLOSED IN BY A BOULDER! NO WAY I CAN GET IN THERE...
THE ROCK IS MOVING! THEY SAW ME!
AH! THE SURVIVING BEAUTIES ARE HIDDEN AWAY IN HERE!
AND HERE IS OUR INDUSTRIOUS JESTER... HOW GOES THE CARNAGE?
NOW FOLLOW US. TRUST, THE GREAT MASTER OF ALL THE GREENHOUSES, WANTS A WORD!
SO YOU'RE THE INFAMOUS SPARTAK? YOUNG MAN, WE APPRECIATE YOUNG PEOPLE WITH LOTS OF SPUNK. NOW YOU'RE KING IN THE PLACE OF DIORO AND SANGUINETTE. TO ME, IT'S ALL THE SAME DIFFERENCE, BUT... WISDOM IS ALL!
THIS IS THE IMPORTANT THING! IN A WORD, MAKE NO MAJOR DECISIONS WITHOUT CONSULTING US. OTHERWISE, NO MORE FOOD. GOT IT? HERE, THE GREENHOUSES, MINES, ALL BELONG TO ME!
BUT... BUT THEN WHAT KIND OF REVOLT IS IT... WHAT KIND OF KING? THE BRUTES DON'T OBEY ME, THEY WANT TO CONTROL EVERYTHING!!
YOUNG MAN, YOU HAVE THE THRONE, BUT WHAT COUNTS IS THE GREENHOUSE. LET'S NOT BUTT HEADS, OTHERWISE I'LL BURN IT ALL DOWN AND YOU WILL ALL STARVE! NOW GO SIT ON THE THRONE, WE'VE GOT THINGS TO DO HERE! SCRAM!
IT'S FOR THE BEST, SON. YOU'RE THE KING, THE BRUTES ARE THE GOVERNMENT, AND THEY'RE HAPPY, AND BEING HAPPY, THEY WON'T CAUSE TRUST TROUBLE, AND HE'LL BE HAPPY... GET ALONG WITH TRUST, MY FRIEND, AND HE'LL BRING PROSPERITY TO THE BRUTES!
PAPANATO, HERE'S THE NEW BUST OF PAPOTAO, AS ORDERED. LESS UNAPPROACHABLE, BETTER SUITED TO THE TIMES...
G. BUZZELLI '67

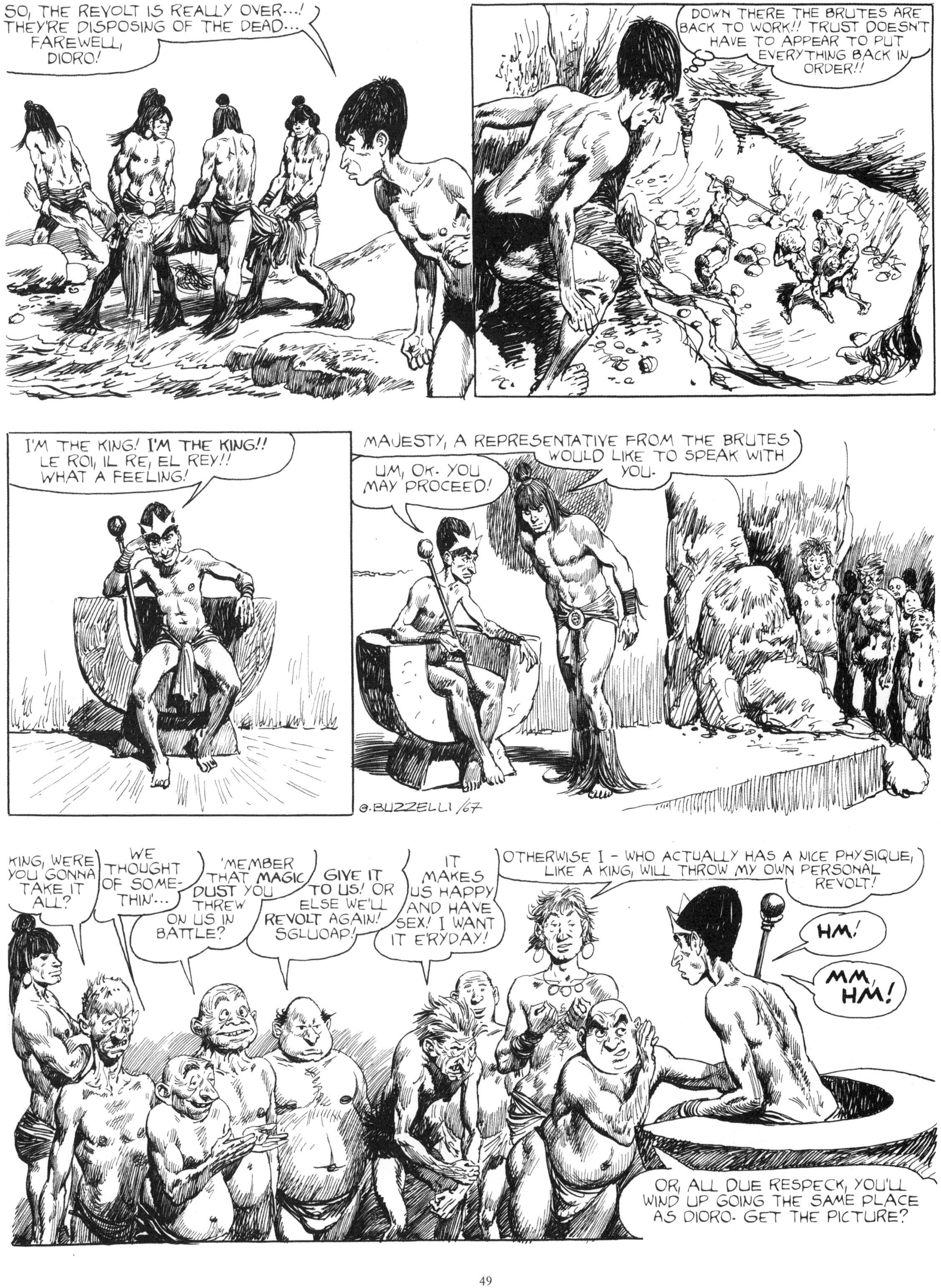

SO, THE REVOLT IS REALLY OVER...! THEY'RE DISPOSING OF THE DEAD... FAREWELL, DIORO!
DOWN THERE THE BRUTES ARE BACK TO WORK!! TRUST DOESN'T HAVE TO APPEAR TO PUT EVERYTHING BACK IN ORDER!!
I'M THE KING! I'M THE KING!! LE ROI, IL RE, EL REY!! WHAT A FEELING!
MAJESTY, A REPRESENTATIVE FROM THE BRUTES WOULD LIKE TO SPEAK WITH YOU.
UM, OK. YOU MAY PROCEED!
G. BUZZELLI /67
KING, WERE YOU GONNA TAKE IT ALL?
WE THOUGHT OF SOME-THIN'...
'MEMBER THAT MAGIC DUST YOU THREW ON US IN BATTLE?
GIVE IT TO US! OR ELSE WE'LL REVOLT AGAIN! SGLUOAP!
IT MAKES US HAPPY AND HAVE SEX! I WANT IT E'RYDAY!
OTHERWISE I - WHO ACTUALLY HAS A NICE PHYSIQUE, LIKE A KING, WILL THROW MY OWN PERSONAL REVOLT!
HM!
MM, HM!
OR, ALL DUE RESPECK, YOU'LL WIND UP GOING THE SAME PLACE AS DIORO- GET THE PICTURE?

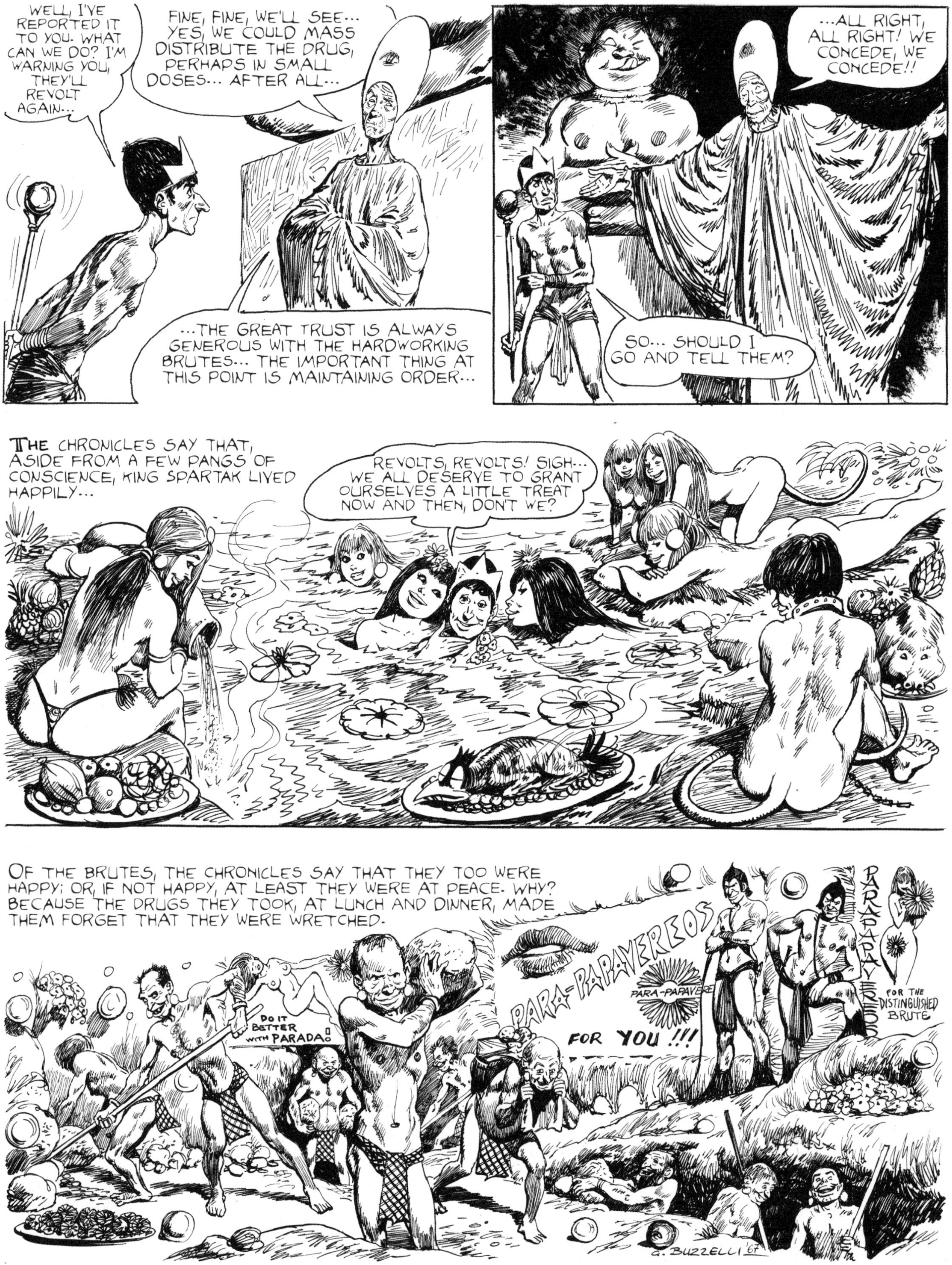
WELL, I'VE REPORTED IT TO YOU. WHAT CAN WE DO? I'M WARNING YOU, THEY'LL REVOLT AGAIN...
FINE, FINE, WE'LL SEE... YES, WE COULD MASS DISTRIBUTE THE DRUG, PERHAPS IN SMALL DOSES... AFTER ALL...
...THE GREAT TRUST IS ALWAYS GENEROUS WITH THE HARDWORKING BRUTES... THE IMPORTANT THING AT THIS POINT IS MAINTAINING ORDER...
...ALL RIGHT, ALL RIGHT! WE CONCEDE, WE CONCEDE!!
SO... SHOULD I GO AND TELL THEM?
THE CHRONICLES SAY THAT, ASIDE FROM A FEW PANGS OF CONSCIENCE, KING SPARTAK LIVED HAPPILY...
REVOLTS, REVOLTS! SIGH... WE ALL DESERVE TO GRANT OURSELVES A LITTLE TREAT NOW AND THEN, DON'T WE?
OF THE BRUTES, THE CHRONICLES SAY THAT THEY TOO WERE HAPPY; OR, IF NOT HAPPY, AT LEAST THEY WERE AT PEACE. WHY? BECAUSE THE DRUGS THEY TOOK, AT LUNCH AND DINNER, MADE THEM FORGET THAT THEY WERE WRETCHED.
DO IT BETTER WITH PARADA!
PARA-PAPAVEREOS
PARA-PAPAVERE
FOR YOU !!!
PARAPAPAVEREOS
FOR THE DISTINGUISHED BRUTE
G. BUZZELLI 67

Resurrection

(1984)

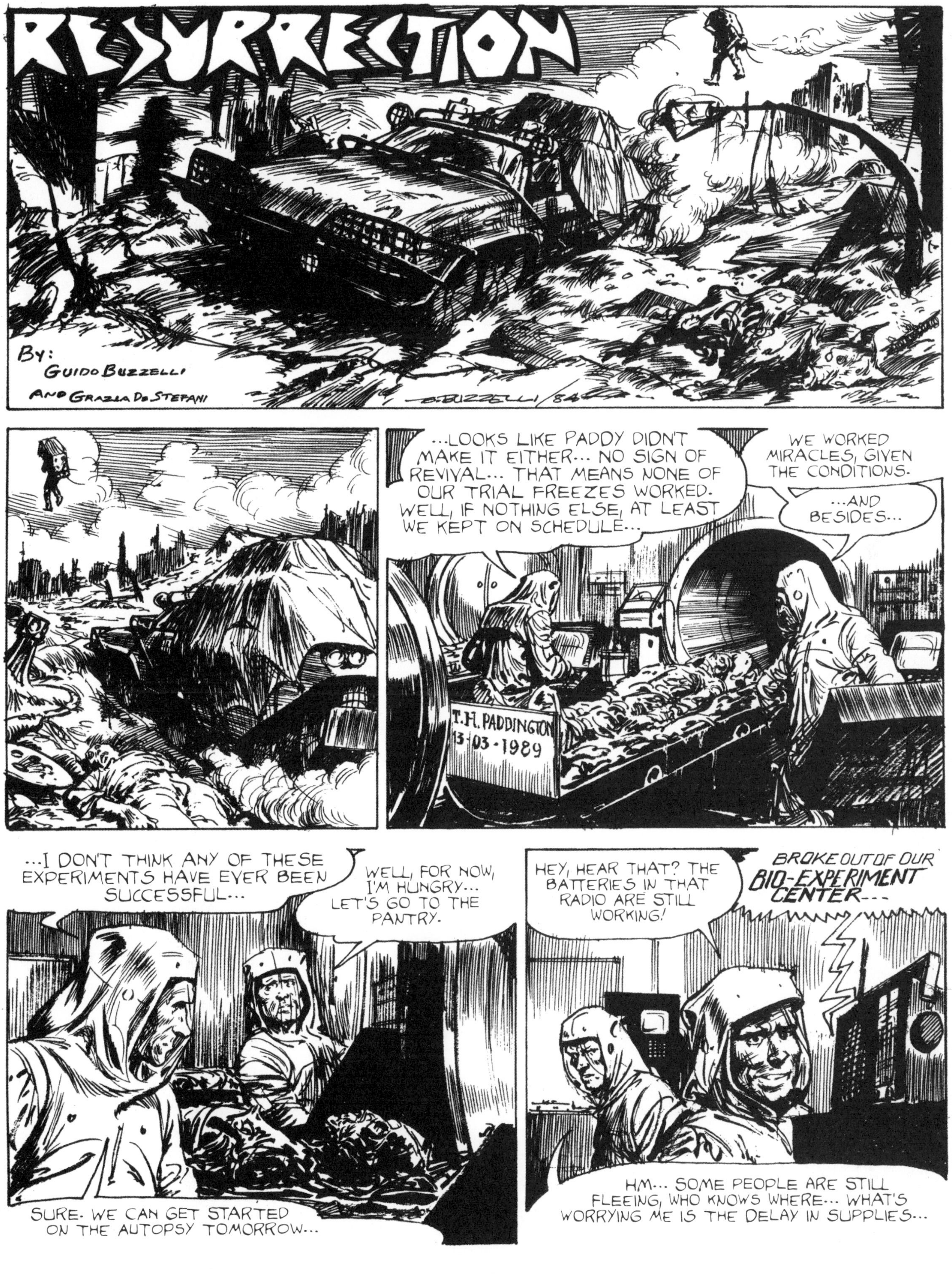
RESURRECTION
BY: GUIDO BUZZELLI AND GRAZIA DE STEFANI
...LOOKS LIKE PADDY DIDN'T MAKE IT EITHER... NO SIGN OF REVIVAL... THAT MEANS NONE OF OUR TRIAL FREEZES WORKED. WELL, IF NOTHING ELSE, AT LEAST WE KEPT ON SCHEDULE...
WE WORKED MIRACLES, GIVEN THE CONDITIONS.
...AND BESIDES...
T.H. PADDINGTON 13-03-1989
...I DON'T THINK ANY OF THESE EXPERIMENTS HAVE EVER BEEN SUCCESSFUL...
WELL, FOR NOW, I'M HUNGRY... LET'S GO TO THE PANTRY.
SURE. WE CAN GET STARTED ON THE AUTOPSY TOMORROW...
HEY, HEAR THAT? THE BATTERIES IN THAT RADIO ARE STILL WORKING!
BROKE OUT OF OUR BIO-EXPERIMENT CENTER---
HM... SOME PEOPLE ARE STILL FLEEING, WHO KNOWS WHERE... WHAT'S WORRYING ME IS THE DELAY IN SUPPLIES...

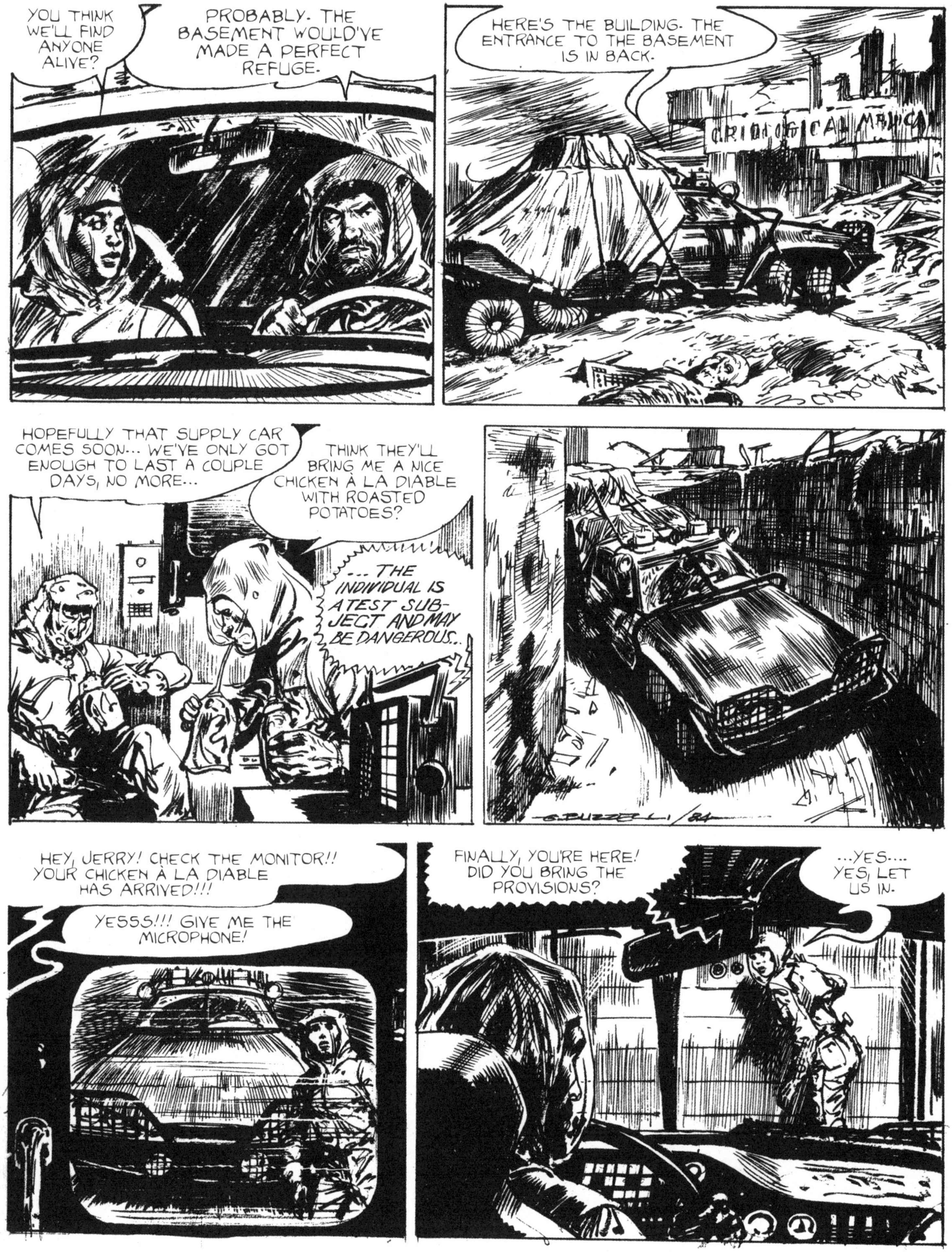
YOU THINK WE'LL FIND ANYONE ALIVE?
PROBABLY. THE BASEMENT WOULD'VE MADE A PERFECT REFUGE.
HERE'S THE BUILDING. THE ENTRANCE TO THE BASEMENT IS IN BACK.
HOPEFULLY THAT SUPPLY CAR COMES SOON... WE'VE ONLY GOT ENOUGH TO LAST A COUPLE DAYS, NO MORE...
THINK THEY'LL BRING ME A NICE CHICKEN À LA DIABLE WITH ROASTED POTATOES?
...THE INDIVIDUAL IS A TEST SUBJECT AND MAY BE DANGEROUS...
G. BUZZELLI /84
HEY, JERRY! CHECK THE MONITOR!! YOUR CHICKEN À LA DIABLE HAS ARRIVED!!!
YESSS!!! GIVE ME THE MICROPHONE!
FINALLY, YOU'RE HERE! DID YOU BRING THE PROVISIONS?
...YES.... YES, LET US IN.

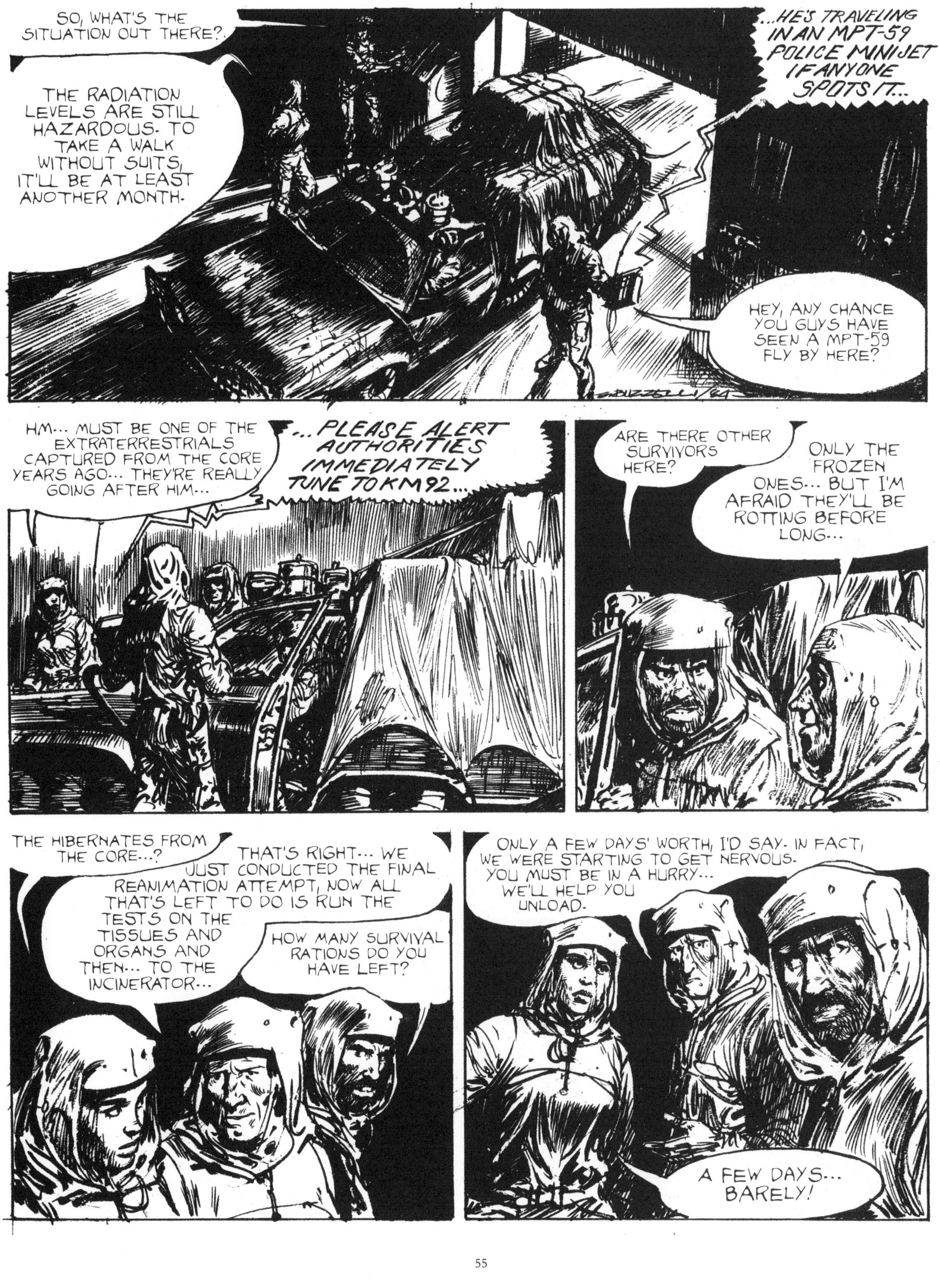

SO, WHAT'S THE SITUATION OUT THERE?
THE RADIATION LEVELS ARE STILL HAZARDOUS. TO TAKE A WALK WITHOUT SUITS, IT'LL BE AT LEAST ANOTHER MONTH.
...HE'S TRAVELING IN AN MPT-59 POLICE MINIJET IF ANYONE SPOTS IT...
HEY, ANY CHANCE YOU GUYS HAVE SEEN A MPT-59 FLY BY HERE?
HM... MUST BE ONE OF THE EXTRATERRESTRIALS CAPTURED FROM THE CORE YEARS AGO... THEY'RE REALLY GOING AFTER HIM...
...PLEASE ALERT AUTHORITIES IMMEDIATELY TUNE TO KM92...
ARE THERE OTHER SURVIVORS HERE?
ONLY THE FROZEN ONES... BUT I'M AFRAID THEY'LL BE ROTTING BEFORE LONG...
THE HIBERNATES FROM THE CORE...?
THAT'S RIGHT... WE JUST CONDUCTED THE FINAL REANIMATION ATTEMPT, NOW ALL THAT'S LEFT TO DO IS RUN THE TESTS ON THE TISSUES AND ORGANS AND THEN... TO THE INCINERATOR...
HOW MANY SURVIVAL RATIONS DO YOU HAVE LEFT?
ONLY A FEW DAYS' WORTH, I'D SAY. IN FACT, WE WERE STARTING TO GET NERVOUS. YOU MUST BE IN A HURRY... WE'LL HELP YOU UNLOAD.
A FEW DAYS... BARELY!

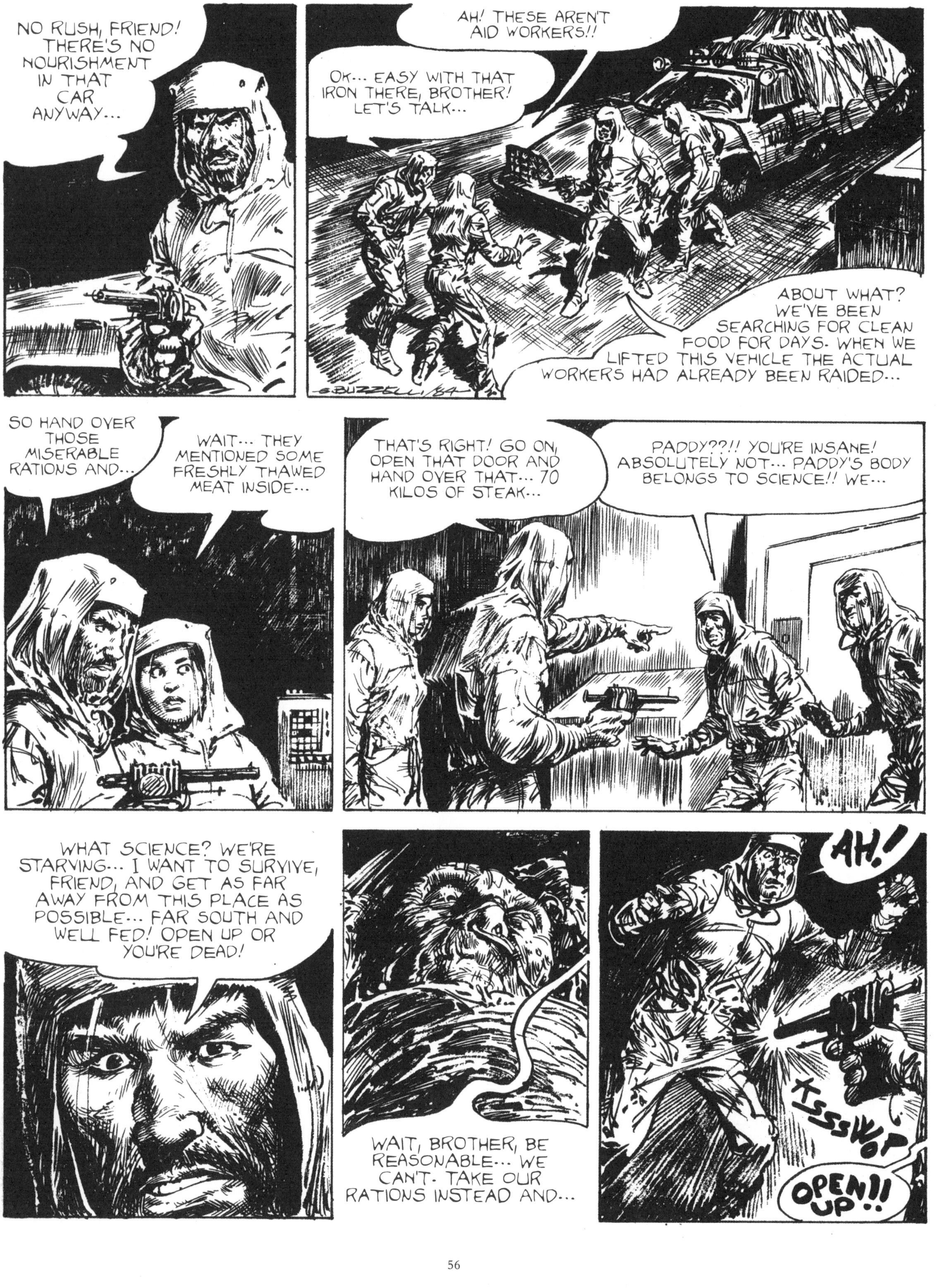
NO RUSH, FRIEND! THERE'S NO NOURISHMENT IN THAT CAR ANYWAY...
AH! THESE AREN'T AID WORKERS!!
OK... EASY WITH THAT IRON THERE, BROTHER! LET'S TALK...
ABOUT WHAT? WE'VE BEEN SEARCHING FOR CLEAN FOOD FOR DAYS. WHEN WE LIFTED THIS VEHICLE THE ACTUAL WORKERS HAD ALREADY BEEN RAIDED...
SO HAND OVER THOSE MISERABLE RATIONS AND...
WAIT... THEY MENTIONED SOME FRESHLY THAWED MEAT INSIDE...
THAT'S RIGHT! GO ON, OPEN THAT DOOR AND HAND OVER THAT... 70 KILOS OF STEAK...
PADDY??!! YOU'RE INSANE! ABSOLUTELY NOT... PADDY'S BODY BELONGS TO SCIENCE!! WE...
WHAT SCIENCE? WE'RE STARVING... I WANT TO SURVIVE, FRIEND, AND GET AS FAR AWAY FROM THIS PLACE AS POSSIBLE... FAR SOUTH AND WELL FED! OPEN UP OR YOU'RE DEAD!
WAIT, BROTHER, BE REASONABLE... WE CAN'T. TAKE OUR RATIONS INSTEAD AND...
AH!
KSSSWOP
OPEN!! UP!!

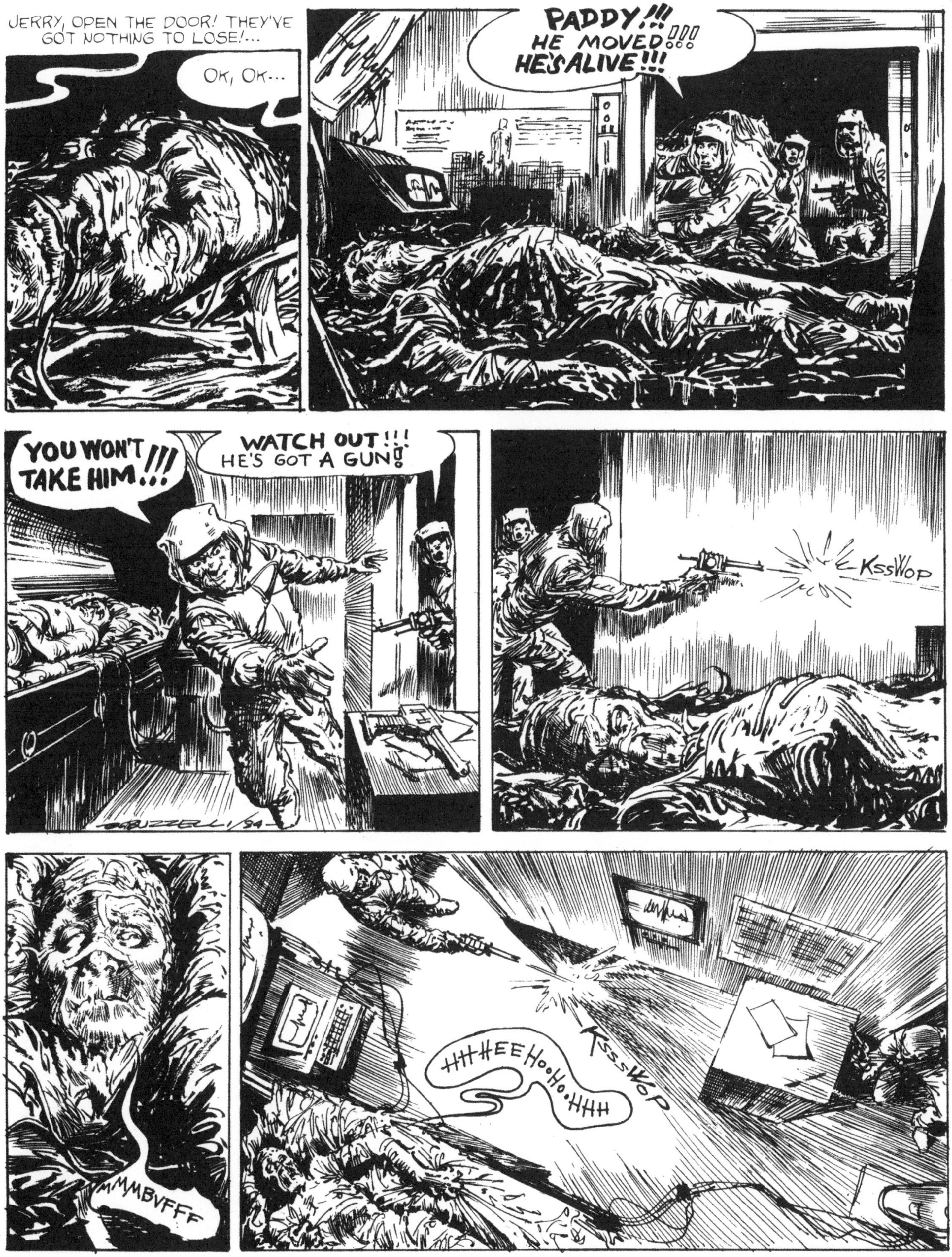

JERRY, OPEN THE DOOR! THEY'VE GOT NOTHING TO LOSE!...
OK, OK...
PADDY!!! HE MOVED!!! HE'S ALIVE!!!
YOU WON'T TAKE HIM!!!
WATCH OUT!!! HE'S GOT A GUN!
KSSWOP
MMMBVFFF
HHHEEHoHoHo..HHH
KSSSWOP

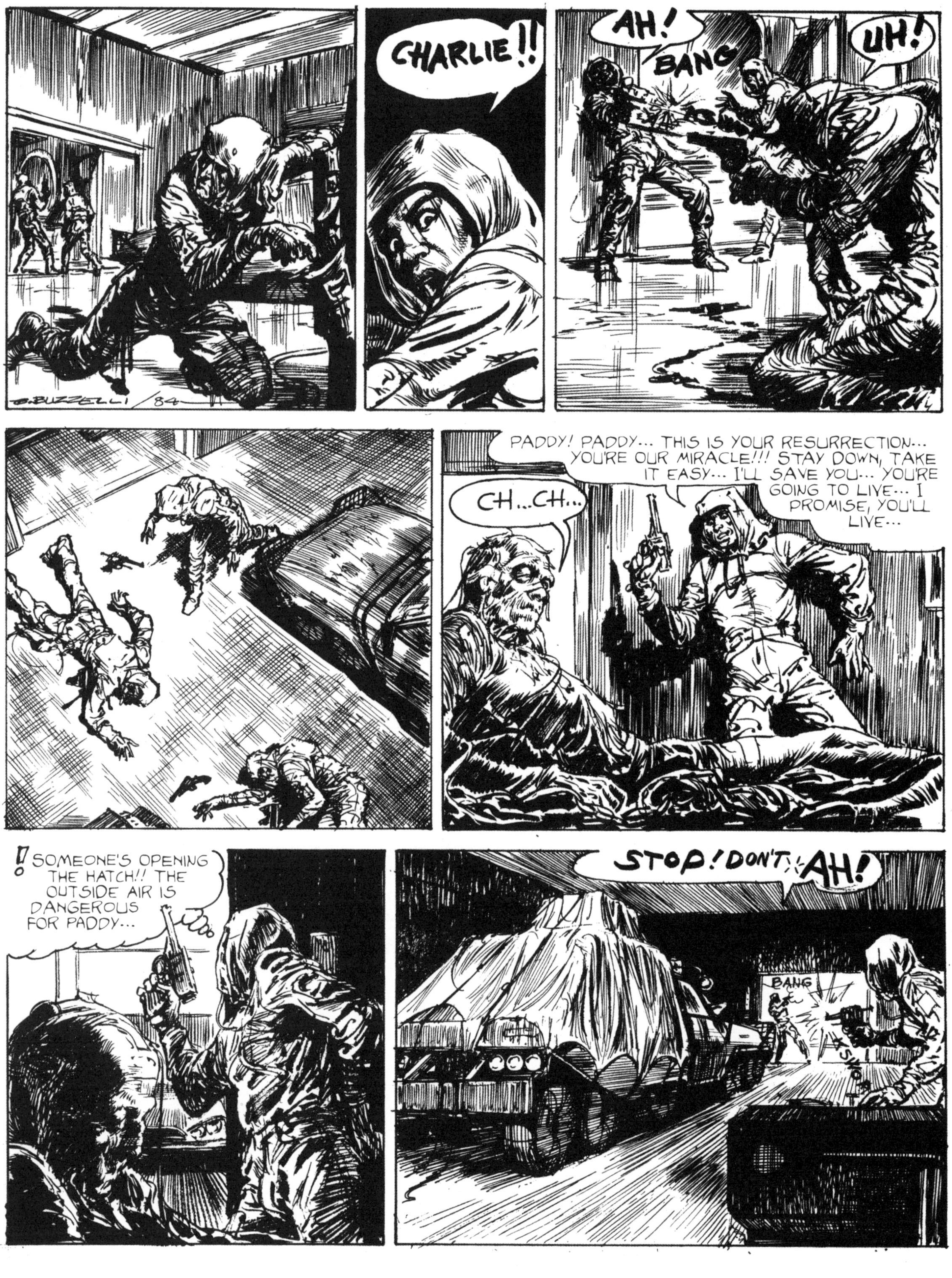

G.BUZZELLI /84
CHARLIE!!
AH!
BANG
UH!
PADDY! PADDY... THIS IS YOUR RESURRECTION... YOU'RE OUR MIRACLE!!! STAY DOWN, TAKE IT EASY... I'LL SAVE YOU... YOU'RE GOING TO LIVE... I PROMISE, YOU'LL LIVE...
CH...CH...
!? SOMEONE'S OPENING THE HATCH!! THE OUTSIDE AIR IS DANGEROUS FOR PADDY...
STOP! DON'T AH!
BANG

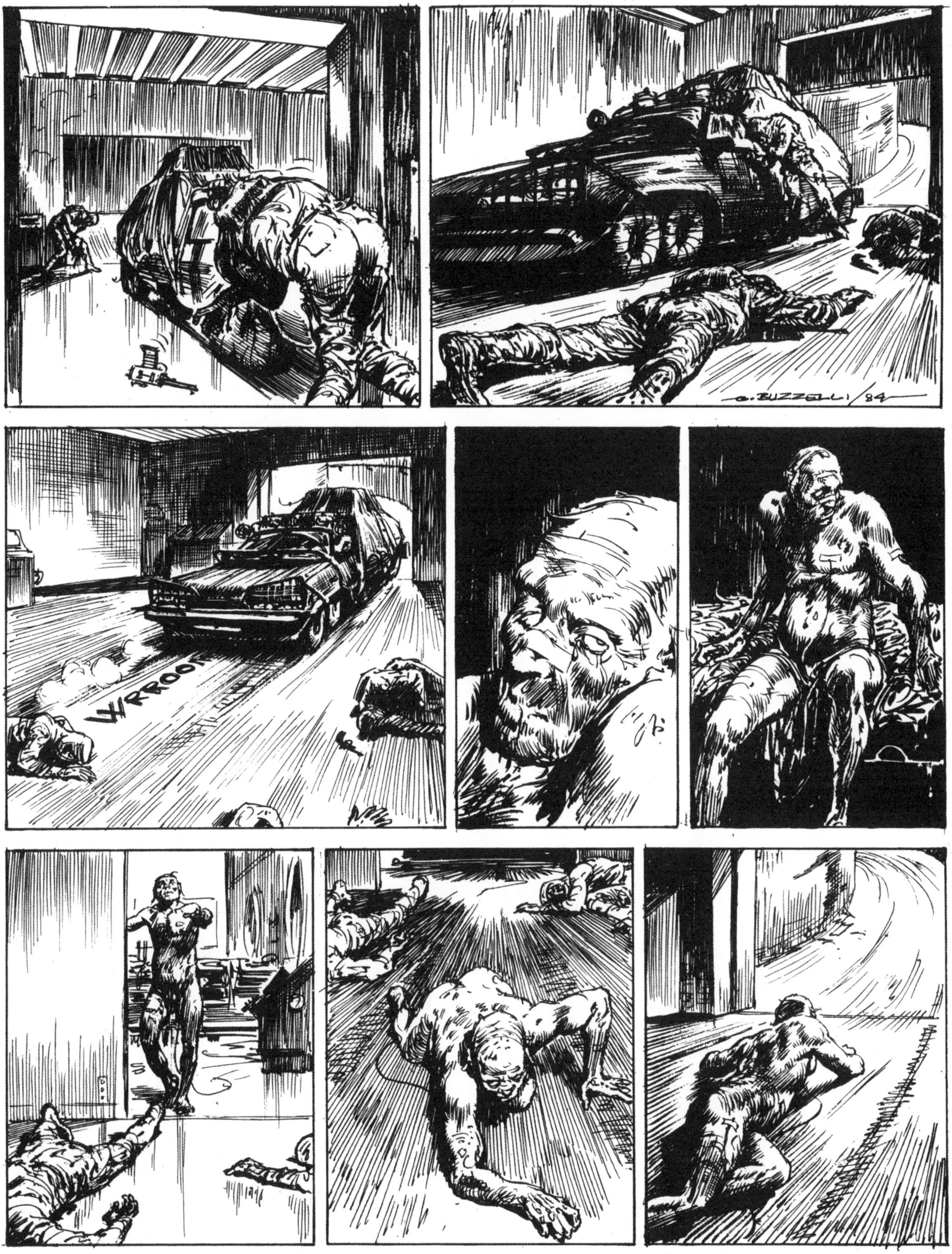
G. BUZZELLI/84
WRROOM

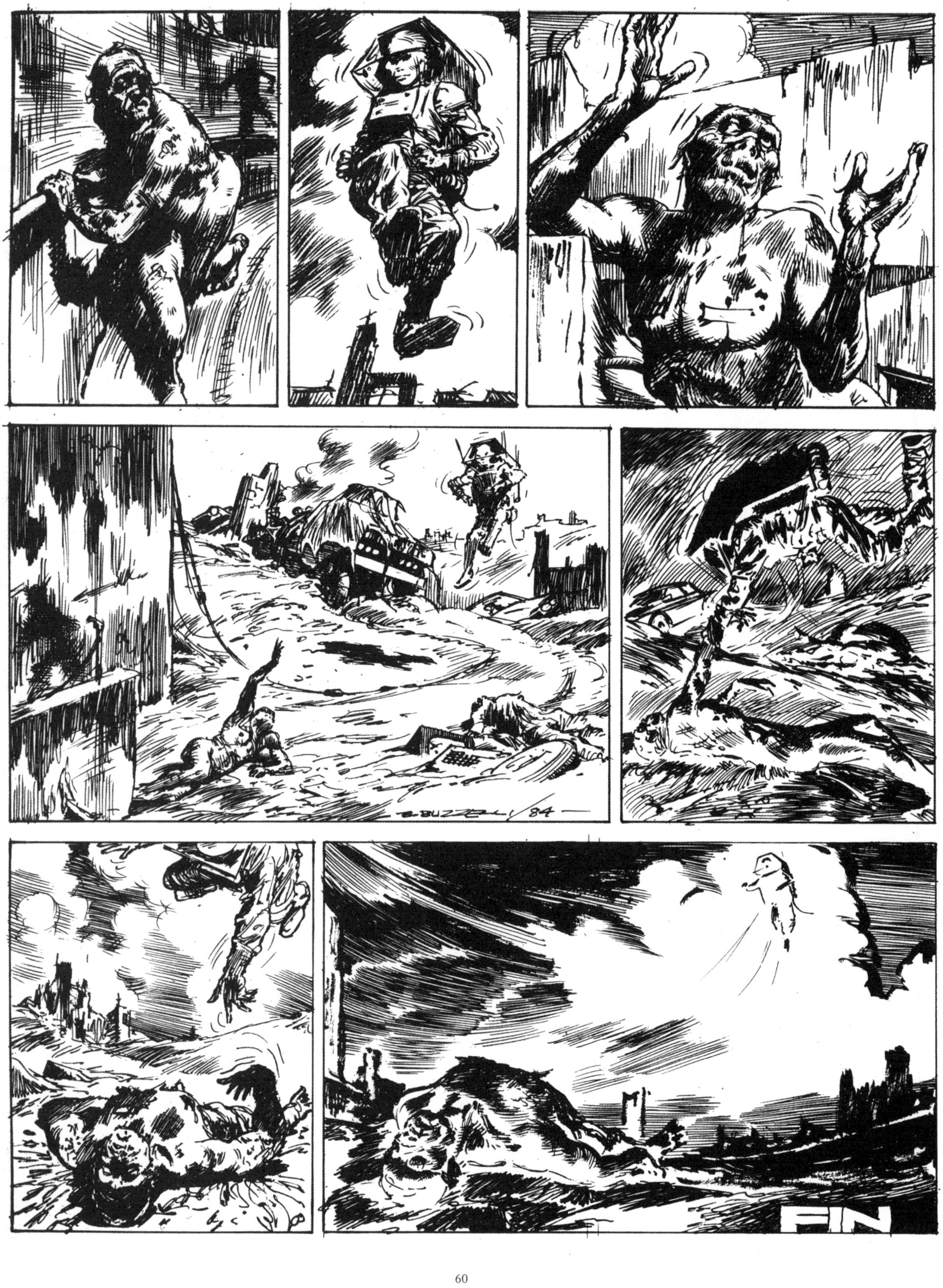
FIN

A Star for Ganymede

(1986)

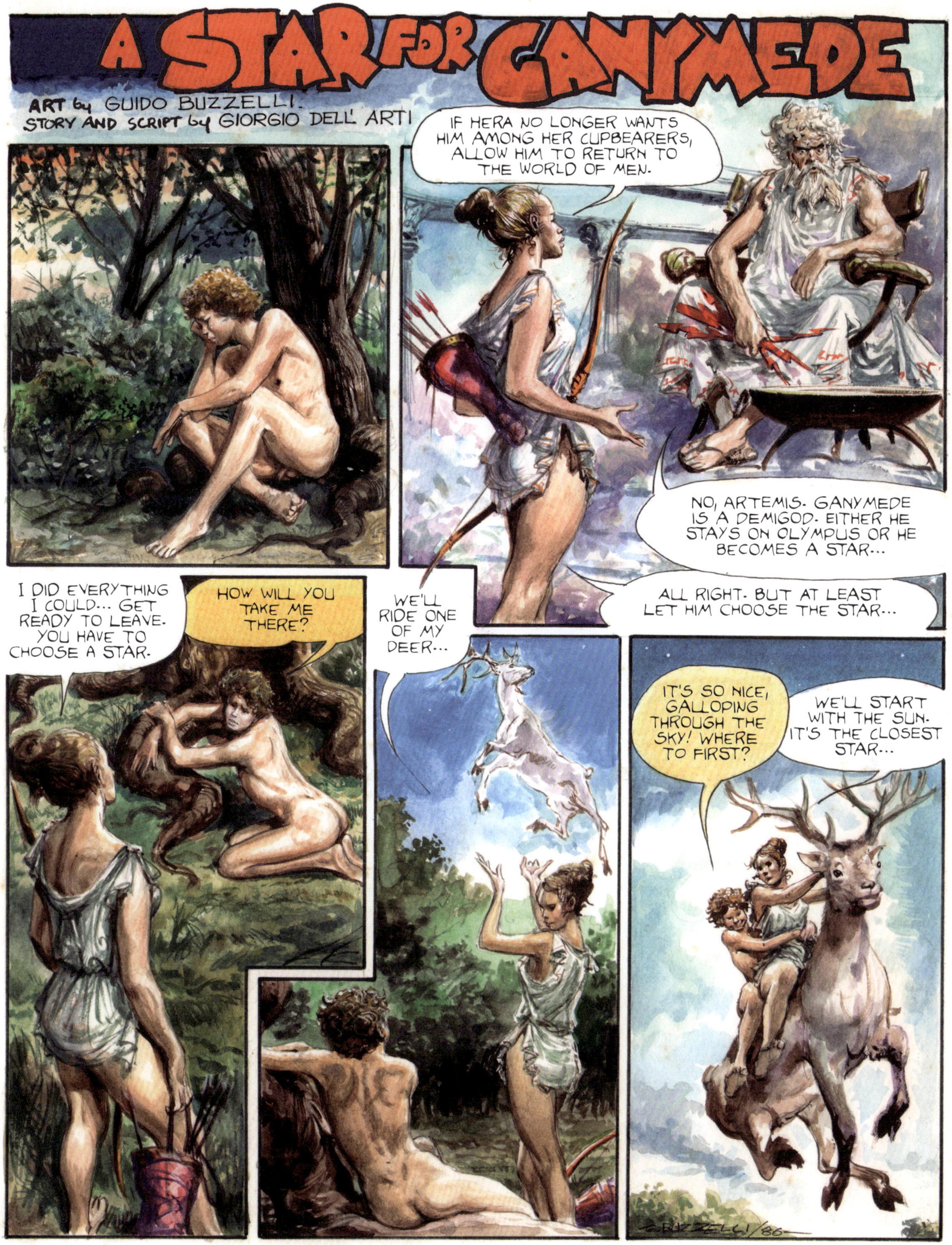
A STAR FOR GANYMEDE
ART by GUIDO BUZZELLI.
STORY AND SCRIPT by GIORGIO DELL' ARTI
IF HERA NO LONGER WANTS HIM AMONG HER CUPBEARERS, ALLOW HIM TO RETURN TO THE WORLD OF MEN.
NO, ARTEMIS. GANYMEDE IS A DEMIGOD. EITHER HE STAYS ON OLYMPUS OR HE BECOMES A STAR...
ALL RIGHT. BUT AT LEAST LET HIM CHOOSE THE STAR...
I DID EVERYTHING I COULD... GET READY TO LEAVE. YOU HAVE TO CHOOSE A STAR.
HOW WILL YOU TAKE ME THERE?
WE'LL RIDE ONE OF MY DEER...
IT'S SO NICE, GALLOPING THROUGH THE SKY! WHERE TO FIRST?
WE'LL START WITH THE SUN. IT'S THE CLOSEST STAR...

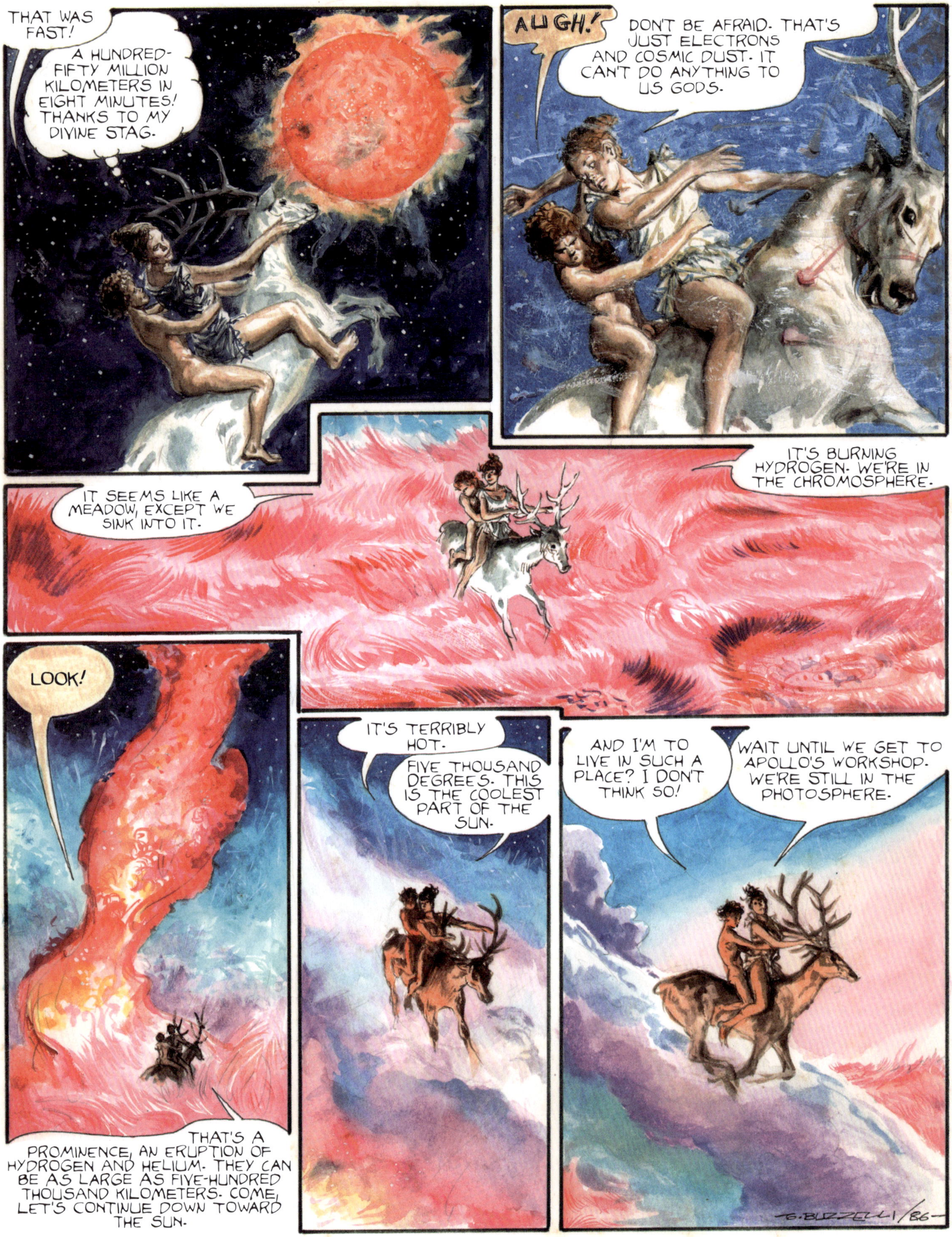

THAT WAS FAST!
A HUNDRED-FIFTY MILLION KILOMETERS IN EIGHT MINUTES! THANKS TO MY DIVINE STAG.
AUGH!
DON'T BE AFRAID. THAT'S JUST ELECTRONS AND COSMIC DUST. IT CAN'T DO ANYTHING TO US GODS.
IT SEEMS LIKE A MEADOW, EXCEPT WE SINK INTO IT.
IT'S BURNING HYDROGEN. WE'RE IN THE CHROMOSPHERE.
LOOK!
THAT'S A PROMINENCE, AN ERUPTION OF HYDROGEN AND HELIUM. THEY CAN BE AS LARGE AS FIVE-HUNDRED THOUSAND KILOMETERS. COME, LET'S CONTINUE DOWN TOWARD THE SUN.
IT'S TERRIBLY HOT.
FIVE THOUSAND DEGREES. THIS IS THE COOLEST PART OF THE SUN.
AND I'M TO LIVE IN SUCH A PLACE? I DON'T THINK SO!
WAIT UNTIL WE GET TO APOLLO'S WORKSHOP. WE'RE STILL IN THE PHOTOSPHERE.
G. BUZZELLI/86

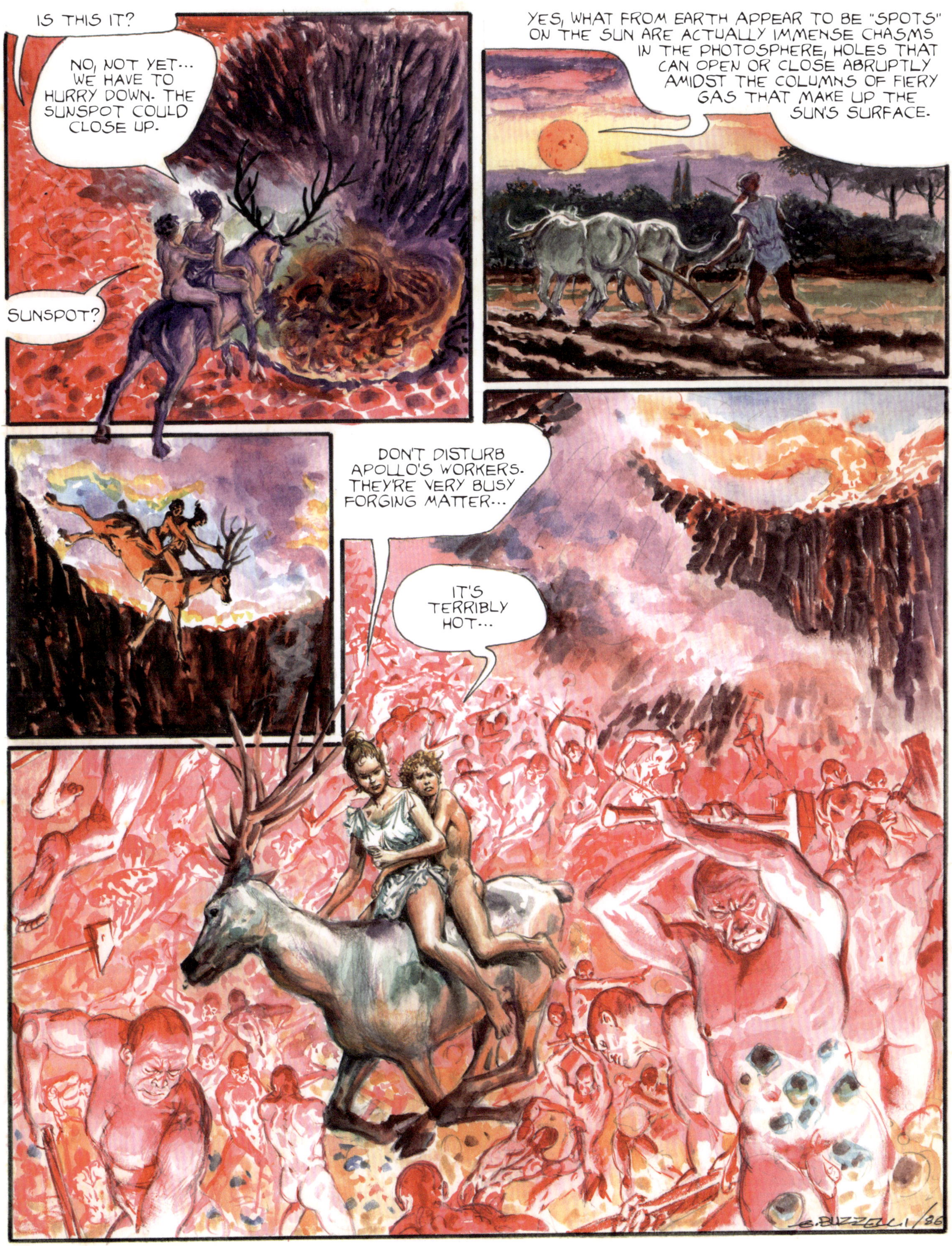
IS THIS IT?
NO, NOT YET... WE HAVE TO HURRY DOWN. THE SUNSPOT COULD CLOSE UP.
SUNSPOT?
YES, WHAT FROM EARTH APPEAR TO BE "SPOTS" ON THE SUN ARE ACTUALLY IMMENSE CHASMS IN THE PHOTOSPHERE, HOLES THAT CAN OPEN OR CLOSE ABRUPTLY AMIDST THE COLUMNS OF FIERY GAS THAT MAKE UP THE SUN'S SURFACE.
DON'T DISTURB APOLLO'S WORKERS. THEY'RE VERY BUSY FORGING MATTER...
IT'S TERRIBLY HOT...
G. BUZZELLI /86

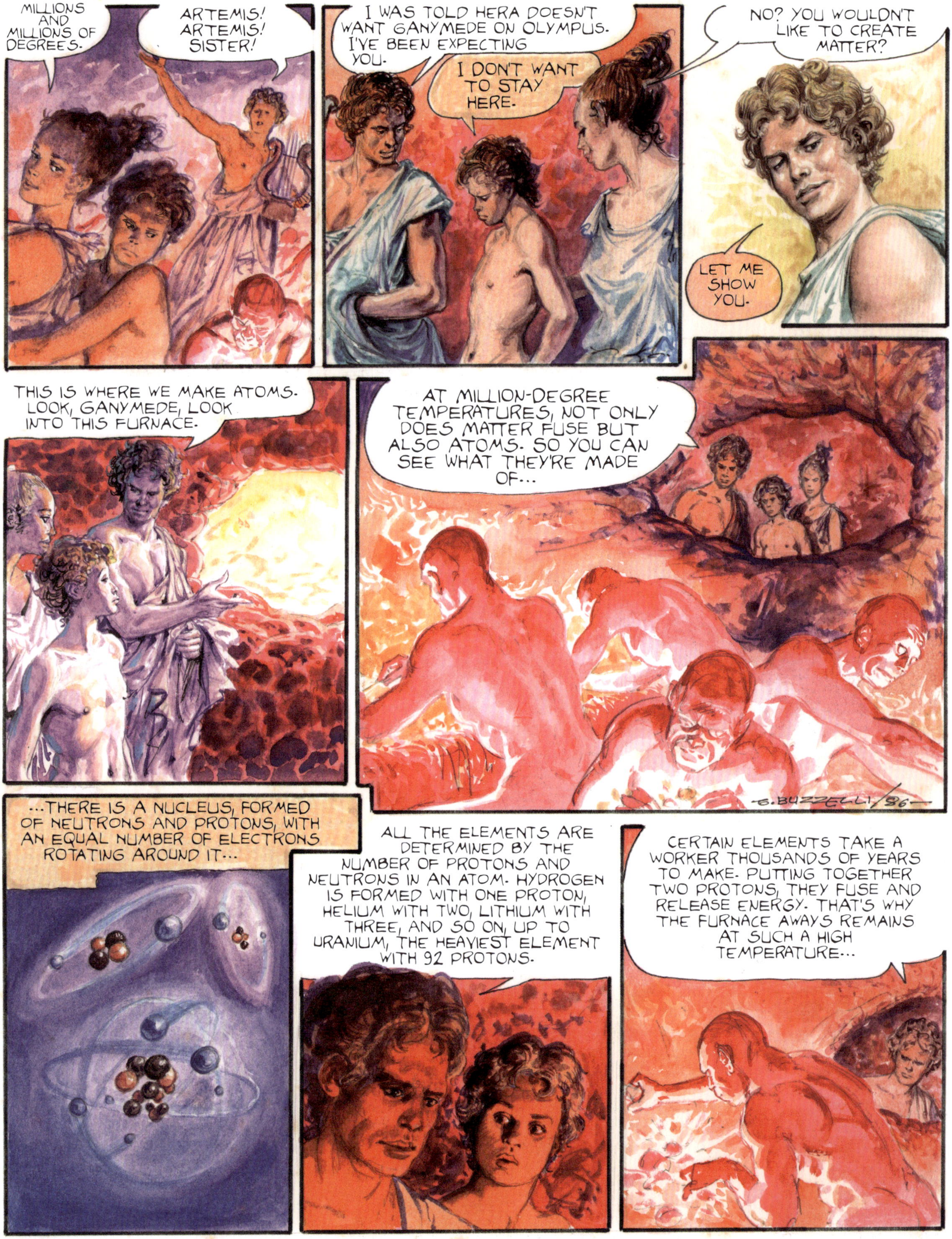
MILLIONS AND MILLIONS OF DEGREES.
ARTEMIS! ARTEMIS! SISTER!
I WAS TOLD HERA DOESN'T WANT GANYMEDE ON OLYMPUS. I'VE BEEN EXPECTING YOU.
I DON'T WANT TO STAY HERE.
NO? YOU WOULDN'T LIKE TO CREATE MATTER?
LET ME SHOW YOU.
THIS IS WHERE WE MAKE ATOMS. LOOK, GANYMEDE, LOOK INTO THIS FURNACE.
AT MILLION-DEGREE TEMPERATURES, NOT ONLY DOES MATTER FUSE BUT ALSO ATOMS. SO YOU CAN SEE WHAT THEY'RE MADE OF...
G. BUZZELLI /86
...THERE IS A NUCLEUS, FORMED OF NEUTRONS AND PROTONS, WITH AN EQUAL NUMBER OF ELECTRONS ROTATING AROUND IT...
ALL THE ELEMENTS ARE DETERMINED BY THE NUMBER OF PROTONS AND NEUTRONS IN AN ATOM. HYDROGEN IS FORMED WITH ONE PROTON, HELIUM WITH TWO, LITHIUM WITH THREE, AND SO ON, UP TO URANIUM, THE HEAVIEST ELEMENT WITH 92 PROTONS.
CERTAIN ELEMENTS TAKE A WORKER THOUSANDS OF YEARS TO MAKE. PUTTING TOGETHER TWO PROTONS, THEY FUSE AND RELEASE ENERGY. THAT'S WHY THE FURNACE AWAYS REMAINS AT SUCH A HIGH TEMPERATURE...

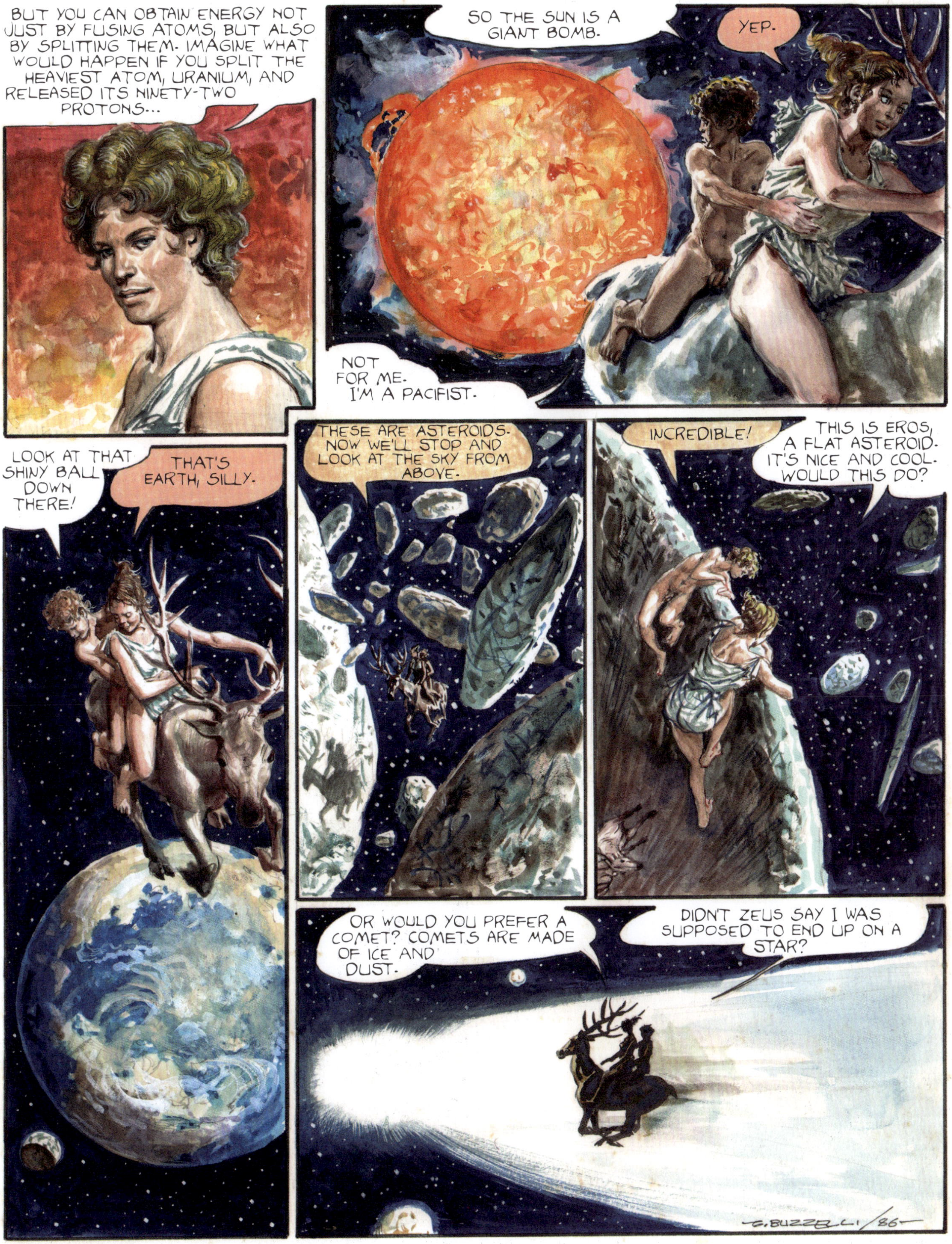

BUT YOU CAN OBTAIN ENERGY NOT JUST BY FUSING ATOMS, BUT ALSO BY SPLITTING THEM. IMAGINE WHAT WOULD HAPPEN IF YOU SPLIT THE HEAVIEST ATOM, URANIUM, AND RELEASED ITS NINETY-TWO PROTONS...
SO THE SUN IS A GIANT BOMB.
YEP.
NOT FOR ME. I'M A PACIFIST.
LOOK AT THAT SHINY BALL DOWN THERE!
THAT'S EARTH, SILLY.
THESE ARE ASTEROIDS. NOW WE'LL STOP AND LOOK AT THE SKY FROM ABOVE.
INCREDIBLE!
THIS IS EROS, A FLAT ASTEROID. IT'S NICE AND COOL. WOULD THIS DO?
OR WOULD YOU PREFER A COMET? COMETS ARE MADE OF ICE AND DUST.
DIDN'T ZEUS SAY I WAS SUPPOSED TO END UP ON A STAR?
G. BUZZELLI/86

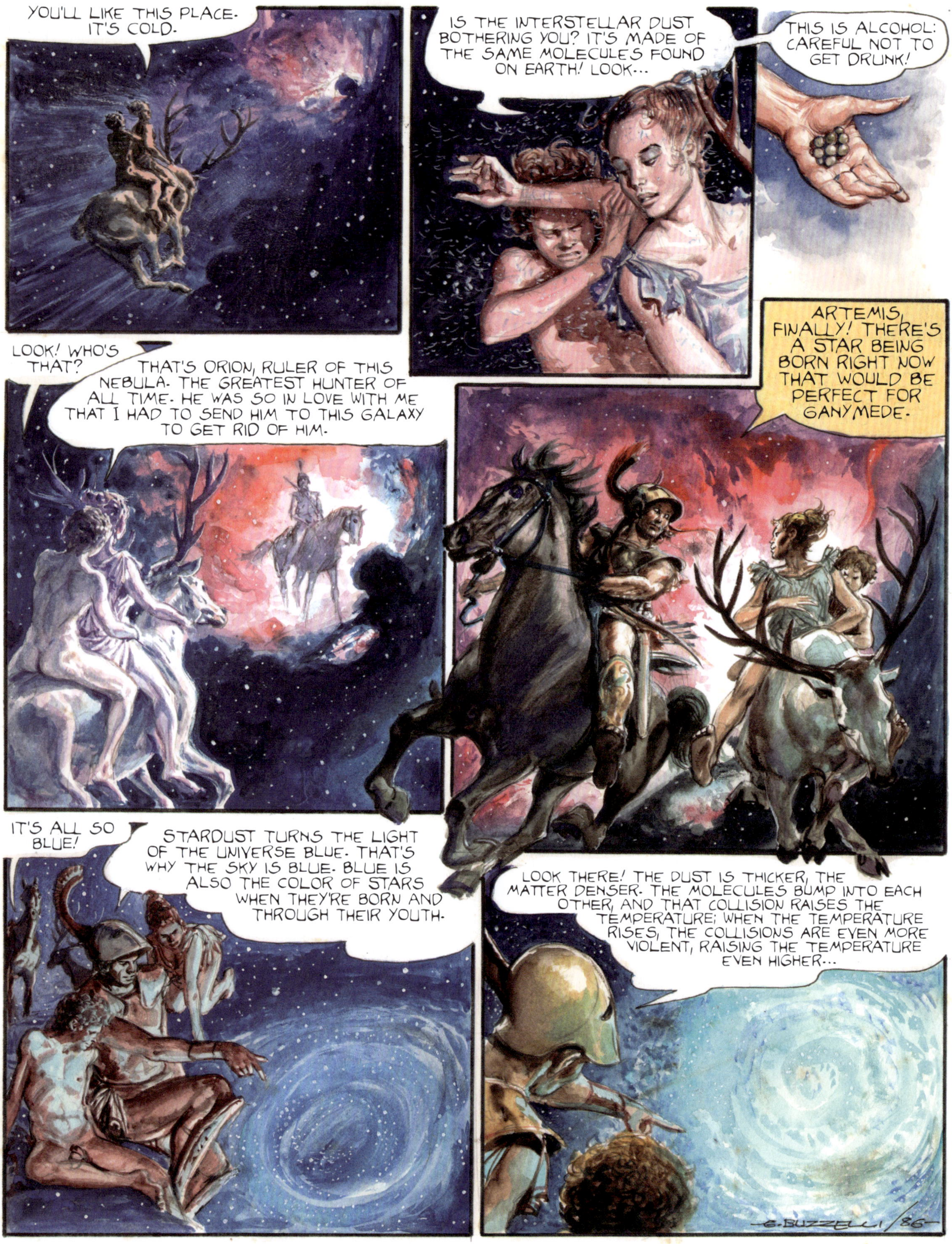
YOU'LL LIKE THIS PLACE. IT'S COLD.
IS THE INTERSTELLAR DUST BOTHERING YOU? IT'S MADE OF THE SAME MOLECULES FOUND ON EARTH! LOOK...
THIS IS ALCOHOL: CAREFUL NOT TO GET DRUNK!
LOOK! WHO'S THAT?
THAT'S ORION, RULER OF THIS NEBULA. THE GREATEST HUNTER OF ALL TIME. HE WAS SO IN LOVE WITH ME THAT I HAD TO SEND HIM TO THIS GALAXY TO GET RID OF HIM.
ARTEMIS, FINALLY! THERE'S A STAR BEING BORN RIGHT NOW THAT WOULD BE PERFECT FOR GANYMEDE.
IT'S ALL SO BLUE!
STARDUST TURNS THE LIGHT OF THE UNIVERSE BLUE. THAT'S WHY THE SKY IS BLUE. BLUE IS ALSO THE COLOR OF STARS WHEN THEY'RE BORN AND THROUGH THEIR YOUTH.
LOOK THERE! THE DUST IS THICKER, THE MATTER DENSER. THE MOLECULES BUMP INTO EACH OTHER, AND THAT COLLISION RAISES THE TEMPERATURE; WHEN THE TEMPERATURE RISES, THE COLLISIONS ARE EVEN MORE VIOLENT, RAISING THE TEMPERATURE EVEN HIGHER...
G. BUZZELLI /86

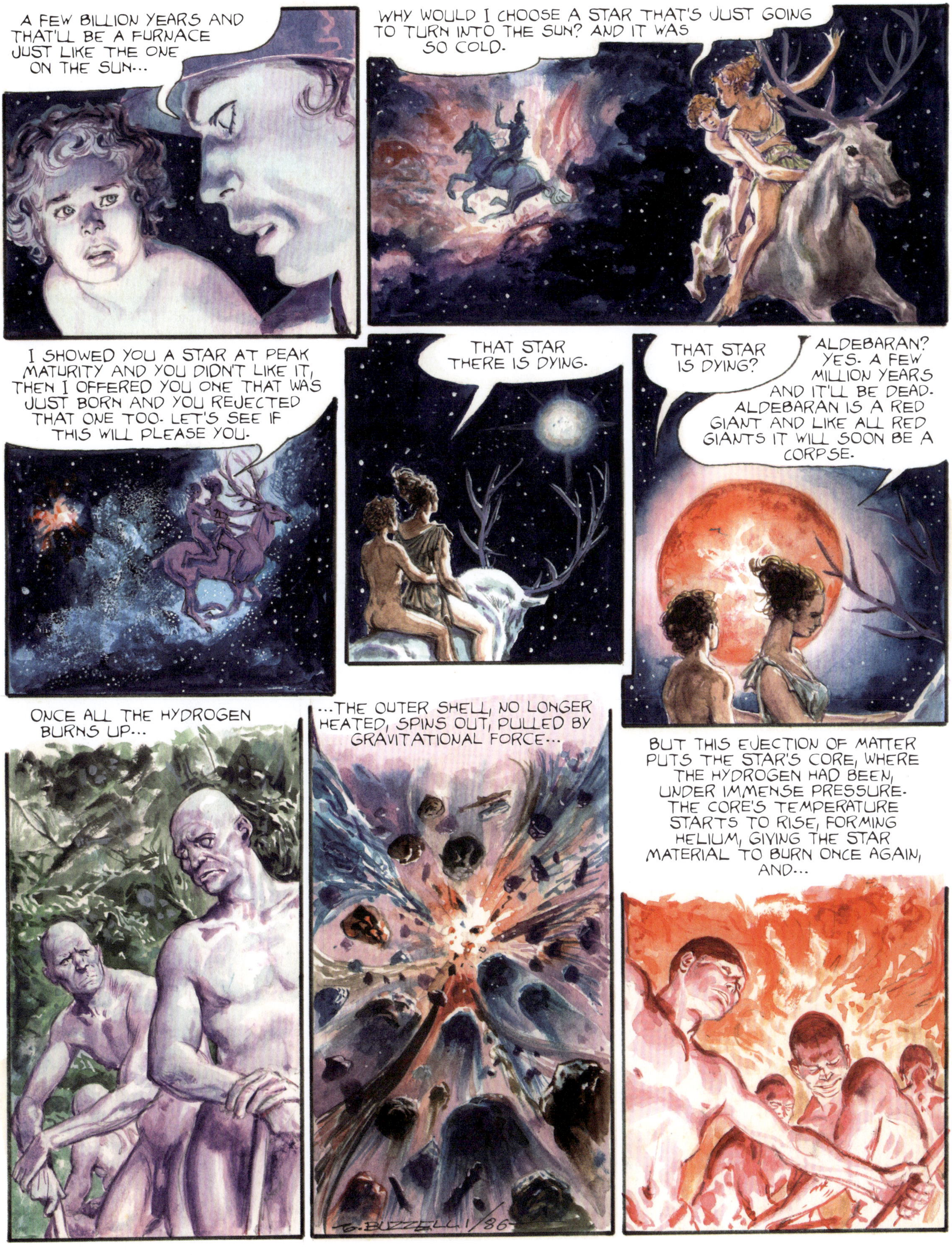
A FEW BILLION YEARS AND THAT'LL BE A FURNACE JUST LIKE THE ONE ON THE SUN...
WHY WOULD I CHOOSE A STAR THAT'S JUST GOING TO TURN INTO THE SUN? AND IT WAS SO COLD.
I SHOWED YOU A STAR AT PEAK MATURITY AND YOU DIDN'T LIKE IT, THEN I OFFERED YOU ONE THAT WAS JUST BORN AND YOU REJECTED THAT ONE TOO. LET'S SEE IF THIS WILL PLEASE YOU.
THAT STAR THERE IS DYING.
THAT STAR IS DYING?
ALDEBARAN? YES. A FEW MILLION YEARS AND IT'LL BE DEAD. ALDEBARAN IS A RED GIANT AND LIKE ALL RED GIANTS IT WILL SOON BE A CORPSE.
ONCE ALL THE HYDROGEN BURNS UP...
...THE OUTER SHELL, NO LONGER HEATED, SPINS OUT, PULLED BY GRAVITATIONAL FORCE...
G. BUZZELLI /86
BUT THIS EJECTION OF MATTER PUTS THE STAR'S CORE, WHERE THE HYDROGEN HAD BEEN, UNDER IMMENSE PRESSURE. THE CORE'S TEMPERATURE STARTS TO RISE, FORMING HELIUM, GIVING THE STAR MATERIAL TO BURN ONCE AGAIN, AND...

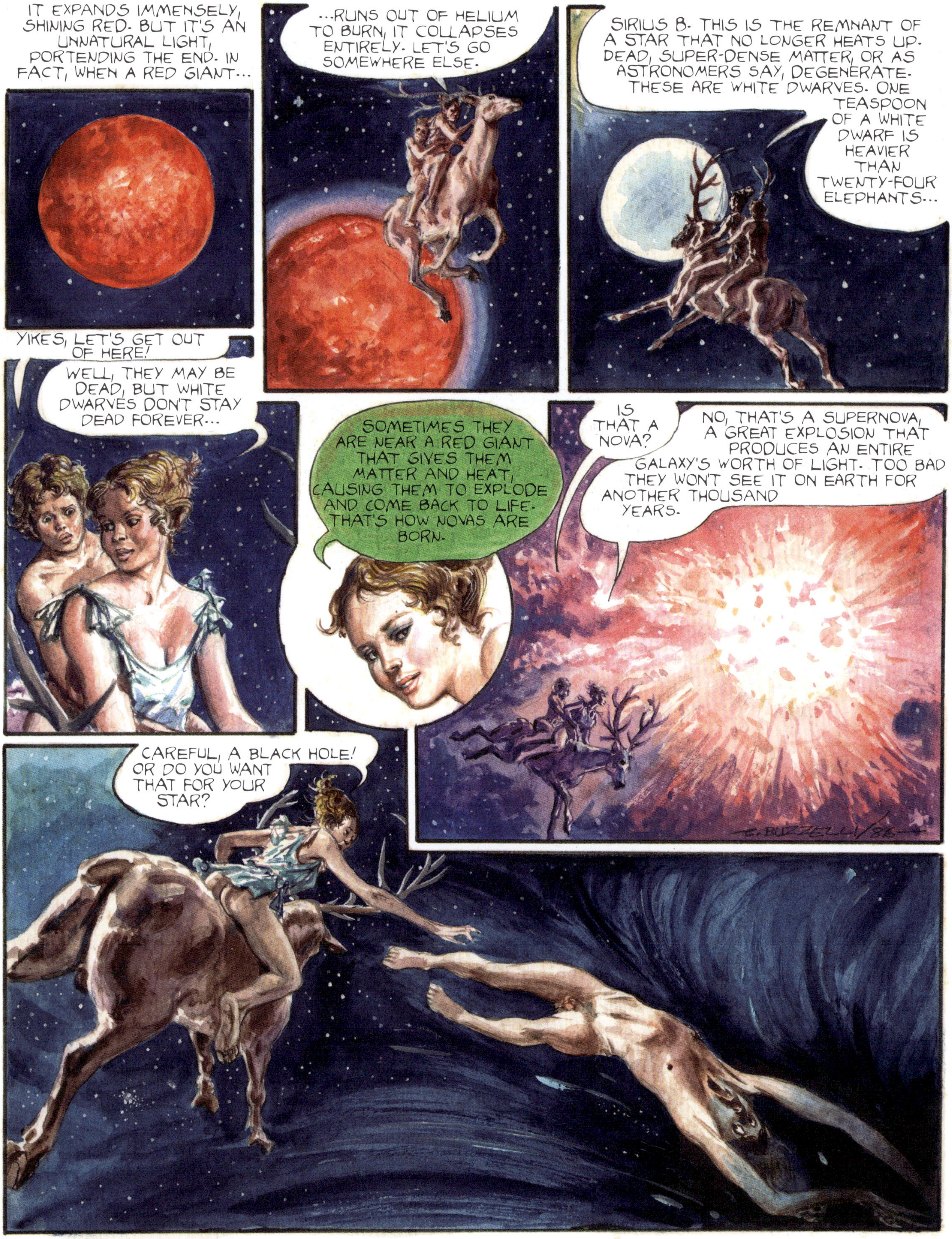
IT EXPANDS IMMENSELY, SHINING RED. BUT IT'S AN UNNATURAL LIGHT, PORTENDING THE END. IN FACT, WHEN A RED GIANT...
...RUNS OUT OF HELIUM TO BURN, IT COLLAPSES ENTIRELY. LET'S GO SOMEWHERE ELSE.
SIRIUS B. THIS IS THE REMNANT OF A STAR THAT NO LONGER HEATS UP. DEAD, SUPER-DENSE MATTER, OR AS ASTRONOMERS SAY, DEGENERATE. THESE ARE WHITE DWARVES. ONE TEASPOON OF A WHITE DWARF IS HEAVIER THAN TWENTY-FOUR ELEPHANTS...
YIKES, LET'S GET OUT OF HERE!
WELL, THEY MAY BE DEAD, BUT WHITE DWARVES DON'T STAY DEAD FOREVER...
SOMETIMES THEY ARE NEAR A RED GIANT THAT GIVES THEM MATTER AND HEAT, CAUSING THEM TO EXPLODE AND COME BACK TO LIFE. THAT'S HOW NOVAS ARE BORN.
IS THAT A NOVA?
NO, THAT'S A SUPERNOVA, A GREAT EXPLOSION THAT PRODUCES AN ENTIRE GALAXY'S WORTH OF LIGHT. TOO BAD THEY WON'T SEE IT ON EARTH FOR ANOTHER THOUSAND YEARS.
C. BUZZELLI/86
CAREFUL, A BLACK HOLE! OR DO YOU WANT THAT FOR YOUR STAR?

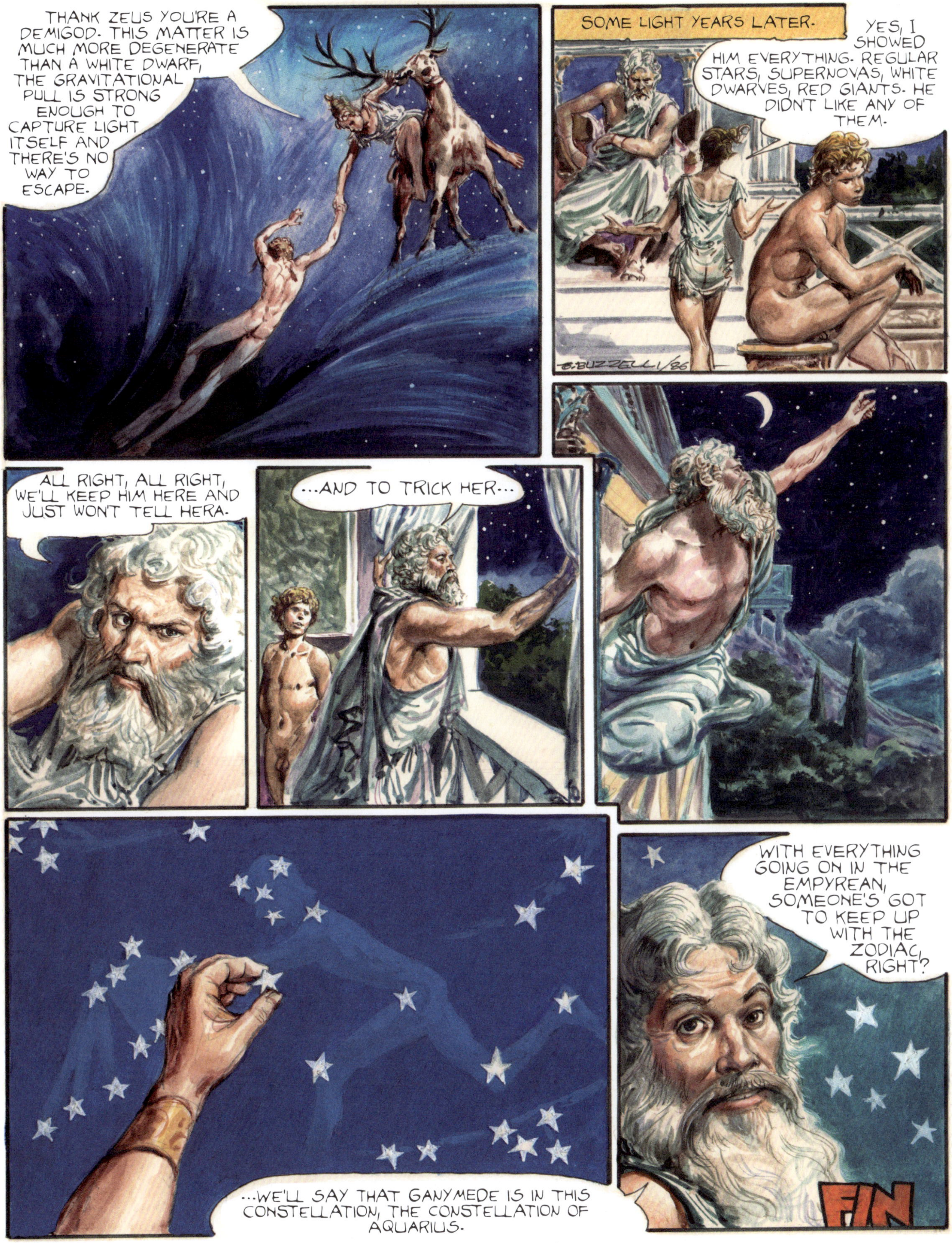
THANK ZEUS YOU'RE A DEMIGOD. THIS MATTER IS MUCH MORE DEGENERATE THAN A WHITE DWARF, THE GRAVITATIONAL PULL IS STRONG ENOUGH TO CAPTURE LIGHT ITSELF AND THERE'S NO WAY TO ESCAPE.
SOME LIGHT YEARS LATER.
YES, I SHOWED HIM EVERYTHING. REGULAR STARS, SUPERNOVAS, WHITE DWARVES, RED GIANTS. HE DIDN'T LIKE ANY OF THEM.
G. BUZZELLI/86
ALL RIGHT, ALL RIGHT, WE'LL KEEP HIM HERE AND JUST WON'T TELL HERA.
...AND TO TRICK HER...
...WE'LL SAY THAT GANYMEDE IS IN THIS CONSTELLATION, THE CONSTELLATION OF AQUARIUS.
WITH EVERYTHING GOING ON IN THE EMPYREAN, SOMEONE'S GOT TO KEEP UP WITH THE ZODIAC, RIGHT?
FIN

Zasafir

(1980)

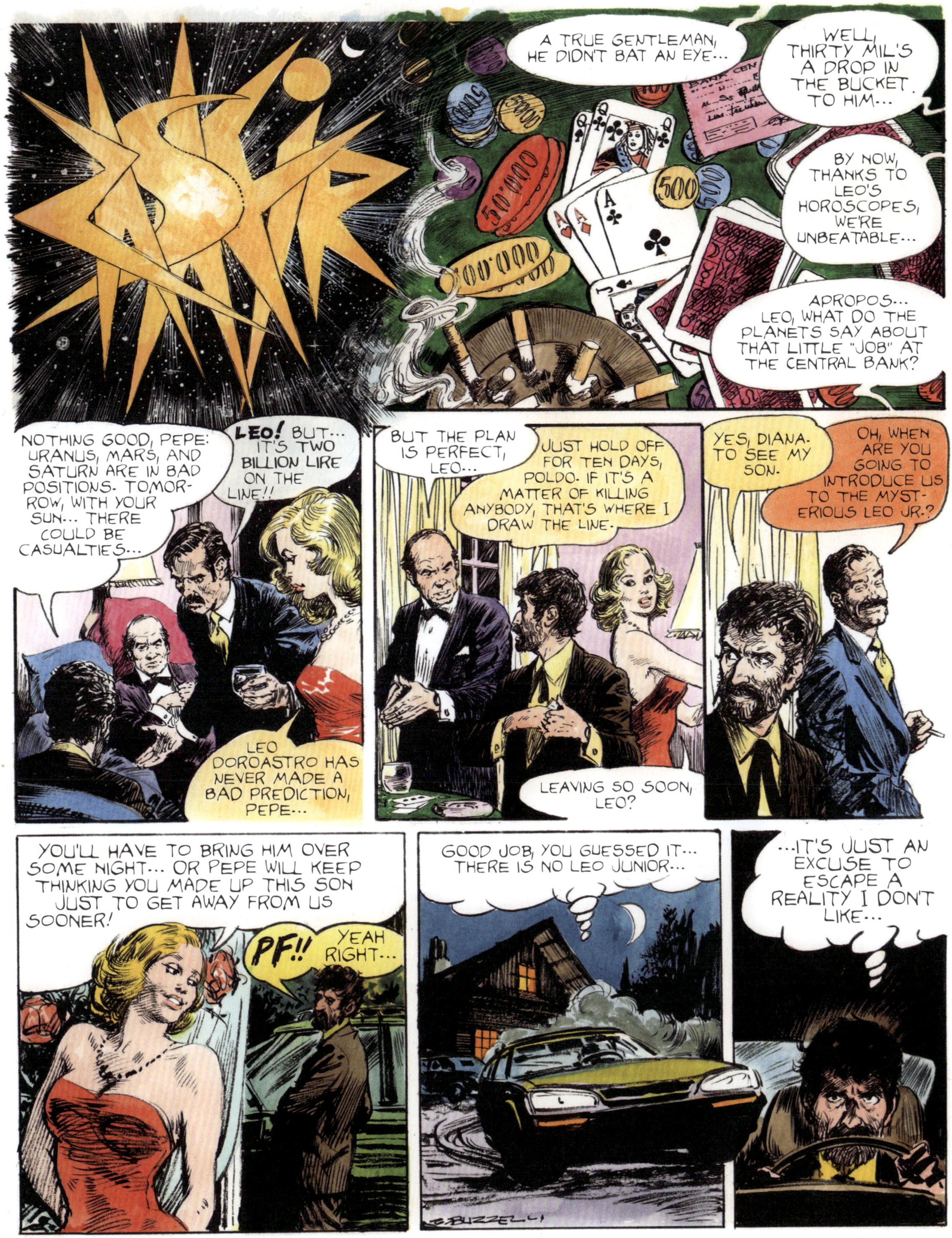
A TRUE GENTLEMAN, HE DIDN'T BAT AN EYE...
WELL, THIRTY MIL'S A DROP IN THE BUCKET. TO HIM...
BY NOW, THANKS TO LEO'S HOROSCOPES, WE'RE UNBEATABLE...
APROPOS... LEO, WHAT DO THE PLANETS SAY ABOUT THAT LITTLE "JOB" AT THE CENTRAL BANK?
NOTHING GOOD, PEPE: URANUS, MARS, AND SATURN ARE IN BAD POSITIONS. TOMORROW, WITH YOUR SUN... THERE COULD BE CASUALTIES...
LEO! BUT... IT'S TWO BILLION LIRE ON THE LINE!!
LEO DOROASTRO HAS NEVER MADE A BAD PREDICTION, PEPE...
BUT THE PLAN IS PERFECT, LEO...
JUST HOLD OFF FOR TEN DAYS, POLDO. IF IT'S A MATTER OF KILLING ANYBODY, THAT'S WHERE I DRAW THE LINE.
LEAVING SO SOON, LEO?
YES, DIANA. TO SEE MY SON.
OH, WHEN ARE YOU GOING TO INTRODUCE US TO THE MYSTERIOUS LEO JR.?
YOU'LL HAVE TO BRING HIM OVER SOME NIGHT... OR PEPE WILL KEEP THINKING YOU MADE UP THIS SON JUST TO GET AWAY FROM US SOONER!
PF!!
YEAH RIGHT...
GOOD JOB, YOU GUESSED IT... THERE IS NO LEO JUNIOR...
...IT'S JUST AN EXCUSE TO ESCAPE A REALITY I DON'T LIKE...

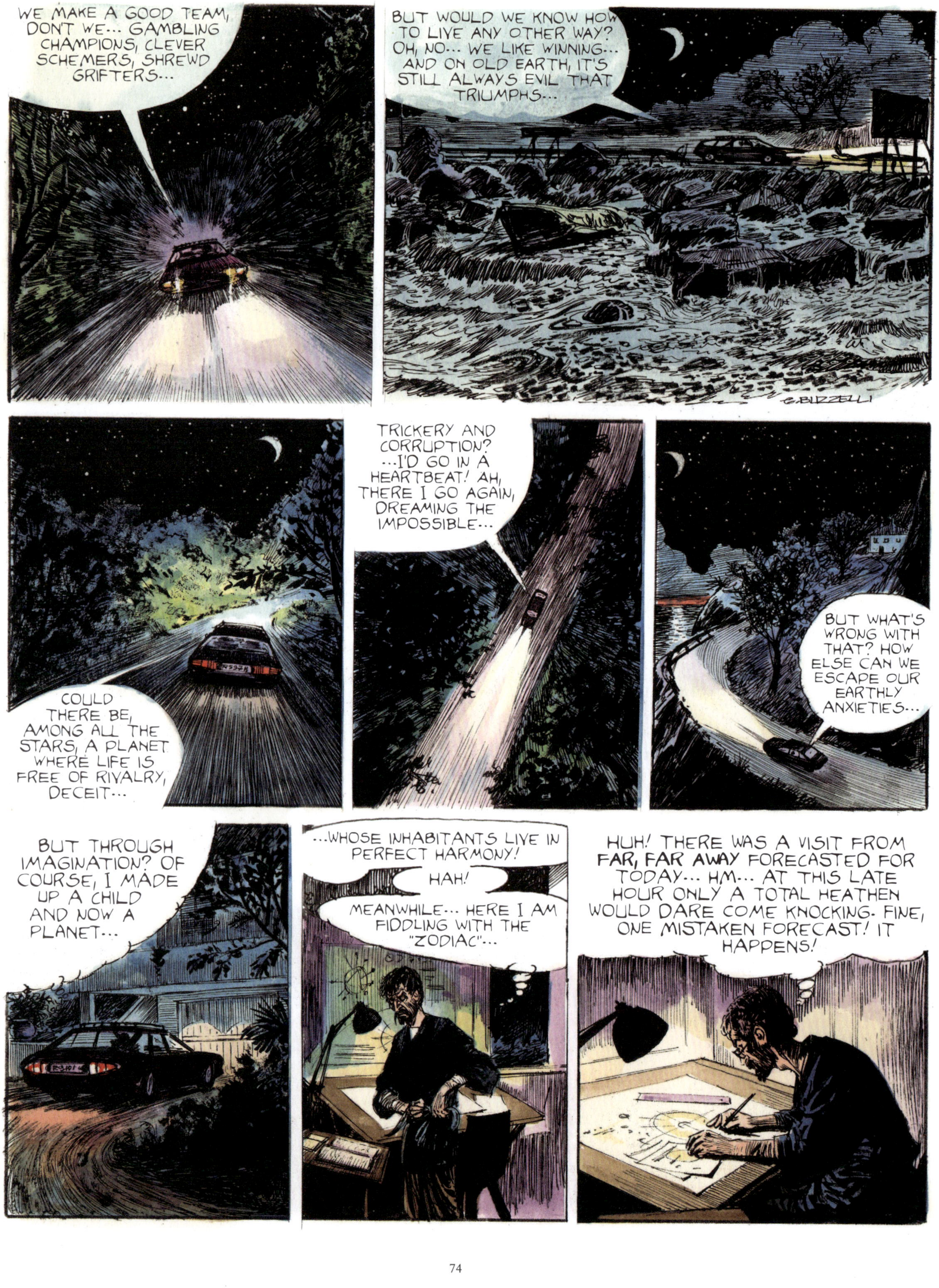

WE MAKE A GOOD TEAM, DON'T WE... GAMBLING CHAMPIONS, CLEVER SCHEMERS, SHREWD GRIFTERS...
BUT WOULD WE KNOW HOW TO LIVE ANY OTHER WAY? OH, NO... WE LIKE WINNING... AND ON OLD EARTH, IT'S STILL ALWAYS EVIL THAT TRIUMPHS...
G. BUZZELLI
COULD THERE BE, AMONG ALL THE STARS, A PLANET WHERE LIFE IS FREE OF RIVALRY, DECEIT...
TRICKERY AND CORRUPTION? ...I'D GO IN A HEARTBEAT! AH, THERE I GO AGAIN, DREAMING THE IMPOSSIBLE...
BUT WHAT'S WRONG WITH THAT? HOW ELSE CAN WE ESCAPE OUR EARTHLY ANXIETIES...
BUT THROUGH IMAGINATION? OF COURSE, I MADE UP A CHILD AND NOW A PLANET...
...WHOSE INHABITANTS LIVE IN PERFECT HARMONY!
HAH!
MEANWHILE... HERE I AM FIDDLING WITH THE "ZODIAC"...
HUH! THERE WAS A VISIT FROM FAR, FAR AWAY FORECASTED FOR TODAY... HM... AT THIS LATE HOUR ONLY A TOTAL HEATHEN WOULD DARE COME KNOCKING. FINE, ONE MISTAKEN FORECAST! IT HAPPENS!

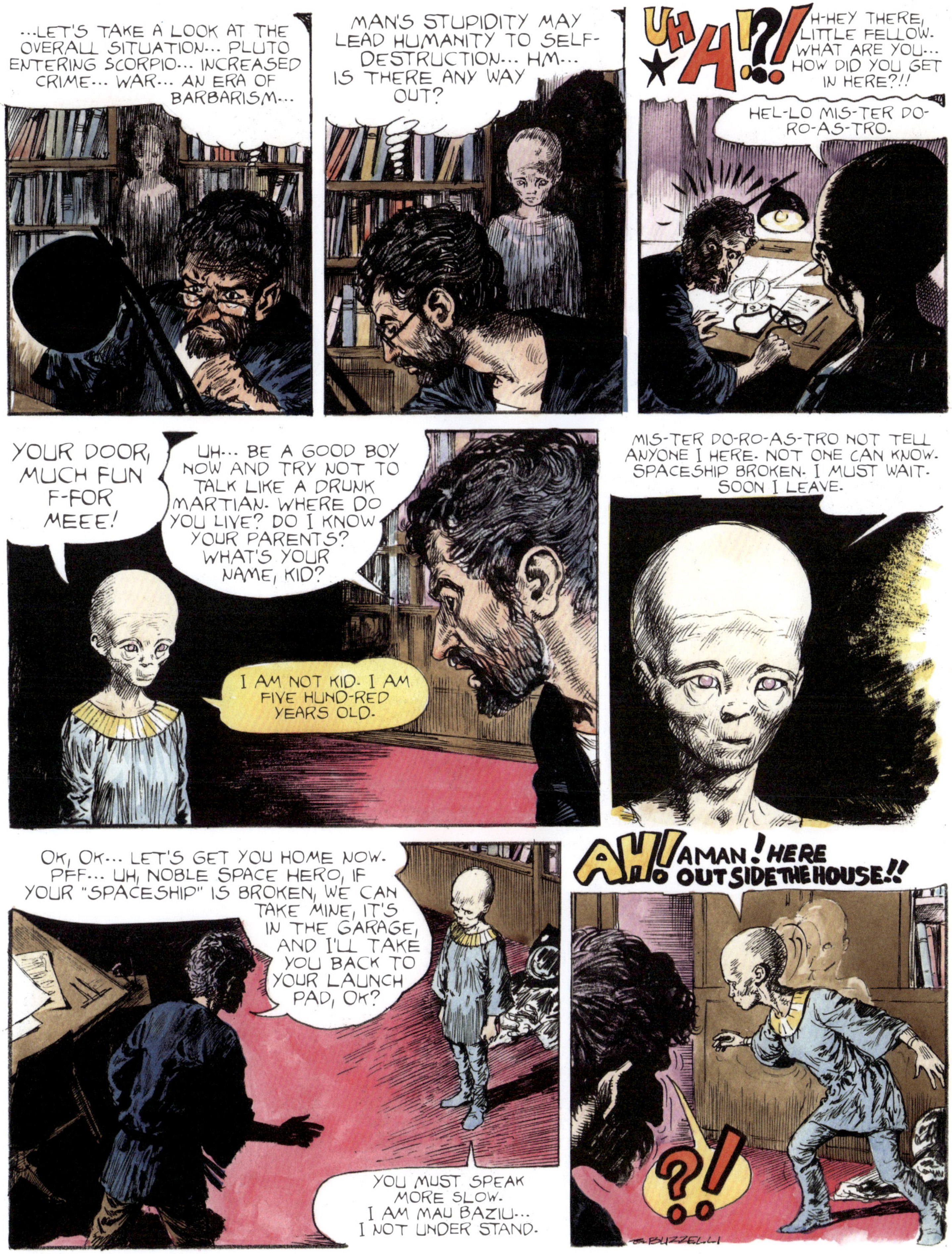
...LET'S TAKE A LOOK AT THE OVERALL SITUATION... PLUTO ENTERING SCORPIO... INCREASED CRIME... WAR... AN ERA OF BARBARISM...
MAN'S STUPIDITY MAY LEAD HUMANITY TO SELF-DESTRUCTION... HM... IS THERE ANY WAY OUT?
UH A!?!
H-HEY THERE, LITTLE FELLOW. WHAT ARE YOU... HOW DID YOU GET IN HERE?!!
HEL-LO MIS-TER DO-RO-AS-TRO.
YOUR DOOR, MUCH FUN F-FOR MEEE!
UH... BE A GOOD BOY NOW AND TRY NOT TO TALK LIKE A DRUNK MARTIAN. WHERE DO YOU LIVE? DO I KNOW YOUR PARENTS? WHAT'S YOUR NAME, KID?
I AM NOT KID. I AM FIVE HUND-RED YEARS OLD.
MIS-TER DO-RO-AS-TRO NOT TELL ANYONE I HERE. NOT ONE CAN KNOW. SPACESHIP BROKEN. I MUST WAIT. SOON I LEAVE.
OK, OK... LET'S GET YOU HOME NOW. PFF... UH, NOBLE SPACE HERO, IF YOUR "SPACESHIP" IS BROKEN, WE CAN TAKE MINE, IT'S IN THE GARAGE, AND I'LL TAKE YOU BACK TO YOUR LAUNCH PAD, OK?
YOU MUST SPEAK MORE SLOW. I AM MAU BAZIU... I NOT UNDER STAND.
AH! A MAN! HERE OUT SIDE THE HOUSE!!
?!
BUZZELLI

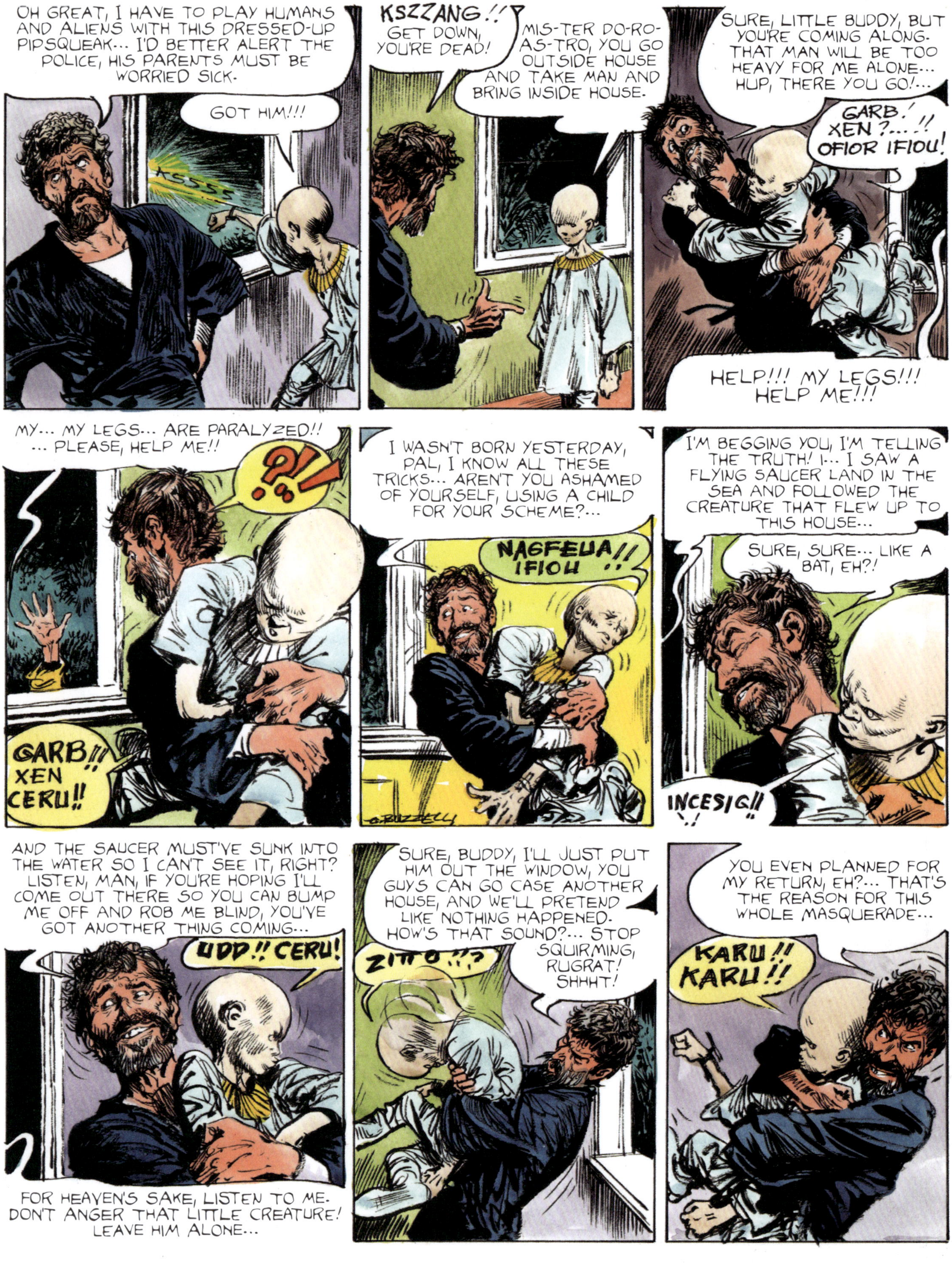
OH GREAT, I HAVE TO PLAY HUMANS AND ALIENS WITH THIS DRESSED-UP PIPSQUEAK... I'D BETTER ALERT THE POLICE, HIS PARENTS MUST BE WORRIED SICK.
GOT HIM!!!
KSZZANG!!
GET DOWN, YOU'RE DEAD!
MIS-TER DO-RO-AS-TRO, YOU GO OUTSIDE HOUSE AND TAKE MAN AND BRING INSIDE HOUSE.
SURE, LITTLE BUDDY, BUT YOU'RE COMING ALONG. THAT MAN WILL BE TOO HEAVY FOR ME ALONE... HUP, THERE YOU GO!...
GARB.! XEN?...!! OFIOR IFIOU!
HELP!!! MY LEGS!!! HELP ME!!!
MY... MY LEGS... ARE PARALYZED!! ... PLEASE, HELP ME!!
?!
GARB!! XEN CERU!!
I WASN'T BORN YESTERDAY, PAL, I KNOW ALL THESE TRICKS... AREN'T YOU ASHAMED OF YOURSELF, USING A CHILD FOR YOUR SCHEME?...
NAGFEUA!! IFIOU!!
I'M BEGGING YOU, I'M TELLING THE TRUTH! I... I SAW A FLYING SAUCER LAND IN THE SEA AND FOLLOWED THE CREATURE THAT FLEW UP TO THIS HOUSE...
SURE, SURE... LIKE A BAT, EH?!
INCESIG!!
AND THE SAUCER MUST'VE SUNK INTO THE WATER SO I CAN'T SEE IT, RIGHT? LISTEN, MAN, IF YOU'RE HOPING I'LL COME OUT THERE SO YOU CAN BUMP ME OFF AND ROB ME BLIND, YOU'VE GOT ANOTHER THING COMING...
UDD!! CERU!
FOR HEAVEN'S SAKE, LISTEN TO ME. DON'T ANGER THAT LITTLE CREATURE! LEAVE HIM ALONE...
SURE, BUDDY, I'LL JUST PUT HIM OUT THE WINDOW, YOU GUYS CAN GO CASE ANOTHER HOUSE, AND WE'LL PRETEND LIKE NOTHING HAPPENED. HOW'S THAT SOUND?... STOP SQUIRMING, RUGRAT! SHHHT!
ZITTO!?
YOU EVEN PLANNED FOR MY RETURN, EH?... THAT'S THE REASON FOR THIS WHOLE MASQUERADE...
KARU!! KARU!!

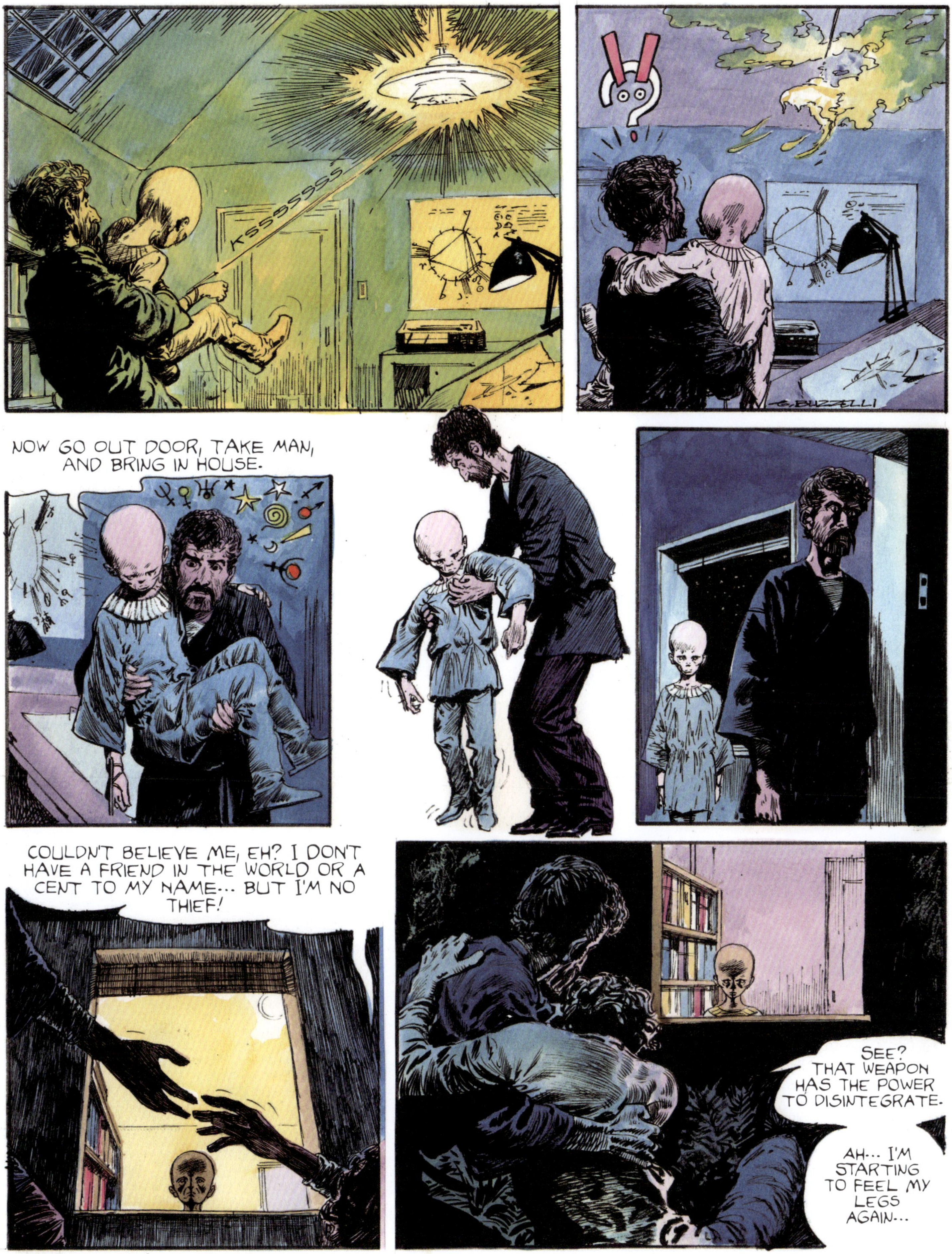
KSSSSSSS
G. BUZZELLI
NOW GO OUT DOOR, TAKE MAN, AND BRING IN HOUSE.
COULDN'T BELIEVE ME, EH? I DON'T HAVE A FRIEND IN THE WORLD OR A CENT TO MY NAME... BUT I'M NO THIEF!
SEE? THAT WEAPON HAS THE POWER TO DISINTEGRATE.
AH... I'M STARTING TO FEEL MY LEGS AGAIN...

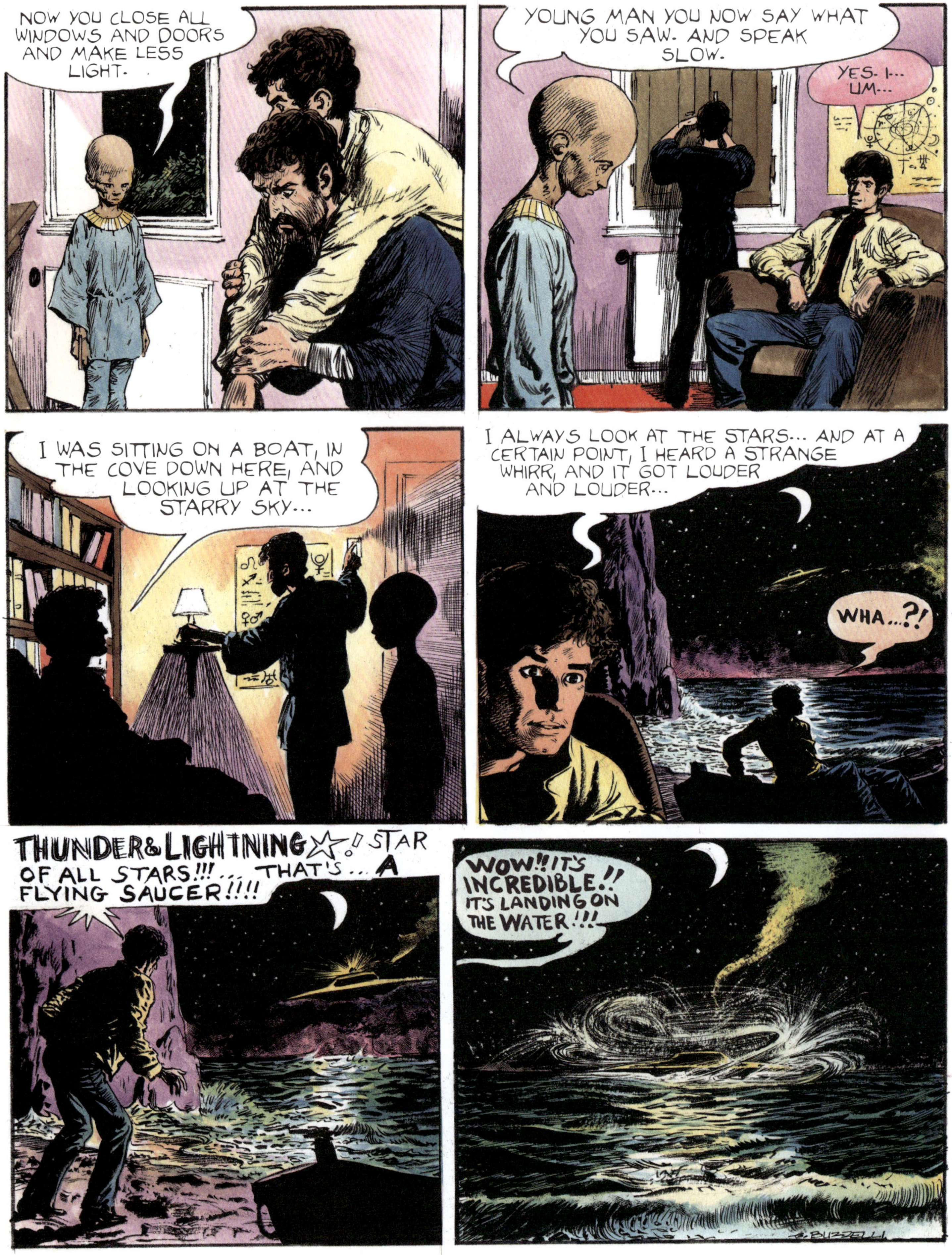
NOW YOU CLOSE ALL WINDOWS AND DOORS AND MAKE LESS LIGHT.
YOUNG MAN YOU NOW SAY WHAT YOU SAW. AND SPEAK SLOW.
YES. I... UM...
I WAS SITTING ON A BOAT, IN THE COVE DOWN HERE, AND LOOKING UP AT THE STARRY SKY...
I ALWAYS LOOK AT THE STARS... AND AT A CERTAIN POINT, I HEARD A STRANGE WHIRR, AND IT GOT LOUDER AND LOUDER...
WHA...?!
THUNDER & LIGHTNING ☆!! STAR OF ALL STARS!!!... THAT'S... A FLYING SAUCER!!!!
WOW!! IT'S INCREDIBLE!! IT'S LANDING ON THE WATER!!!
BUZZELLI

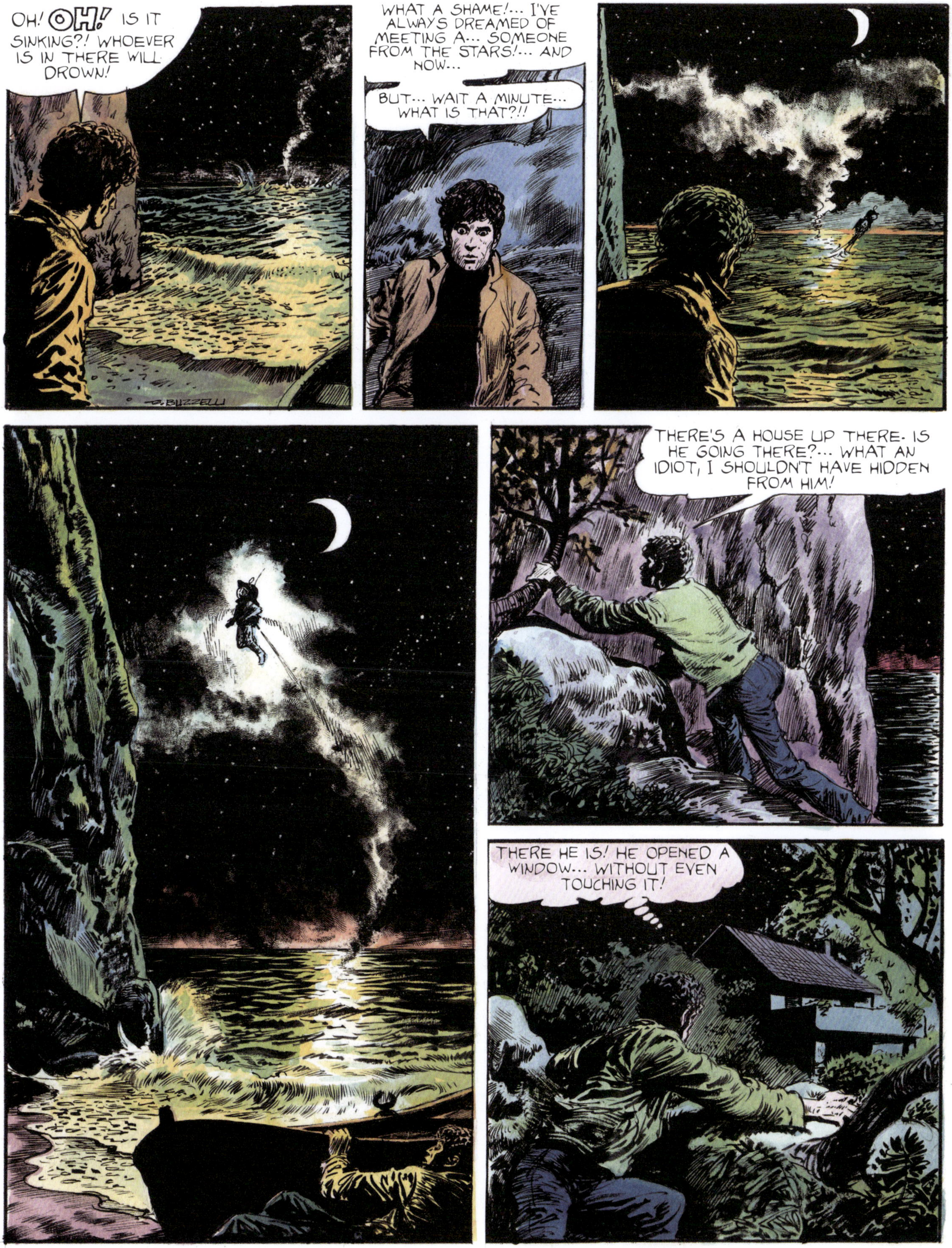
OH! OH! IS IT SINKING?! WHOEVER IS IN THERE WILL DROWN!
G. BUZZELLI
WHAT A SHAME!... I'VE ALWAYS DREAMED OF MEETING A... SOMEONE FROM THE STARS!... AND NOW...
BUT... WAIT A MINUTE... WHAT IS THAT?!!
THERE'S A HOUSE UP THERE. IS HE GOING THERE?... WHAT AN IDIOT, I SHOULDN'T HAVE HIDDEN FROM HIM!
THERE HE IS! HE OPENED A WINDOW... WITHOUT EVEN TOUCHING IT!

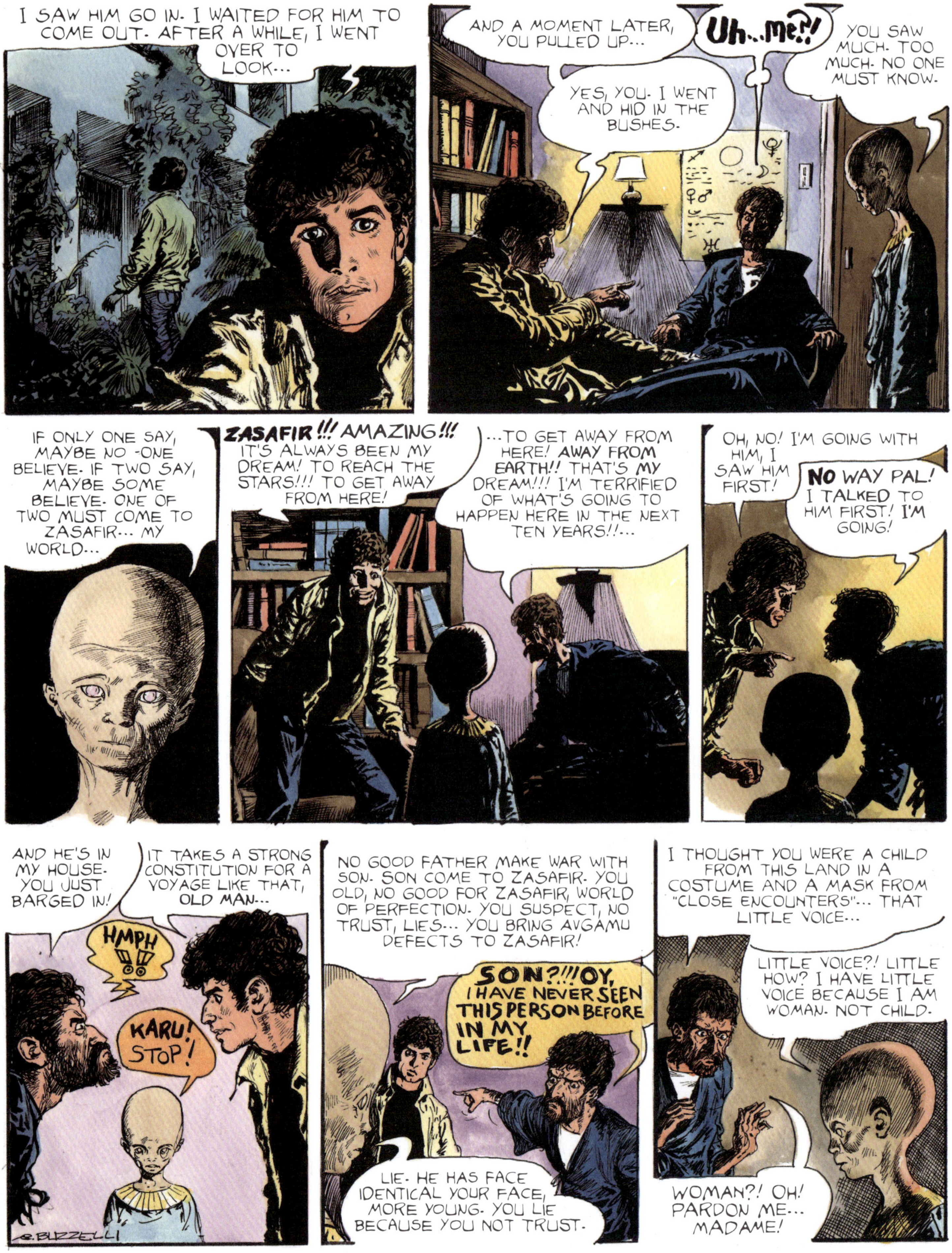

I SAW HIM GO IN. I WAITED FOR HIM TO COME OUT. AFTER A WHILE, I WENT OVER TO LOOK...
AND A MOMENT LATER, YOU PULLED UP...
Uh...me?!
YES, YOU. I WENT AND HID IN THE BUSHES.
YOU SAW MUCH. TOO MUCH. NO ONE MUST KNOW.
IF ONLY ONE SAY, MAYBE NO -ONE BELIEVE. IF TWO SAY, MAYBE SOME BELIEVE. ONE OF TWO MUST COME TO ZASAFIR... MY WORLD...
ZASAFIR!!! AMAZING!!! IT'S ALWAYS BEEN MY DREAM! TO REACH THE STARS!!! TO GET AWAY FROM HERE!
...TO GET AWAY FROM HERE! AWAY FROM EARTH!! THAT'S MY DREAM!!! I'M TERRIFIED OF WHAT'S GOING TO HAPPEN HERE IN THE NEXT TEN YEARS!!...
OH, NO! I'M GOING WITH HIM, I SAW HIM FIRST!
NO WAY PAL! I TALKED TO HIM FIRST! I'M GOING!
AND HE'S IN MY HOUSE. YOU JUST BARGED IN!
IT TAKES A STRONG CONSTITUTION FOR A VOYAGE LIKE THAT, OLD MAN...
HMPH!!
KARU! STOP!
NO GOOD FATHER MAKE WAR WITH SON. SON COME TO ZASAFIR. YOU OLD, NO GOOD FOR ZASAFIR, WORLD OF PERFECTION. YOU SUSPECT, NO TRUST, LIES... YOU BRING AVGAMU DEFECTS TO ZASAFIR!
SON?!!! OY, I HAVE NEVER SEEN THIS PERSON BEFORE IN MY LIFE!!
LIE. HE HAS FACE IDENTICAL YOUR FACE, MORE YOUNG. YOU LIE BECAUSE YOU NOT TRUST.
I THOUGHT YOU WERE A CHILD FROM THIS LAND IN A COSTUME AND A MASK FROM "CLOSE ENCOUNTERS"... THAT LITTLE VOICE...
LITTLE VOICE?! LITTLE HOW? I HAVE LITTLE VOICE BECAUSE I AM WOMAN. NOT CHILD.
WOMAN?! OH! PARDON ME... MADAME!
G. BUZZELLI

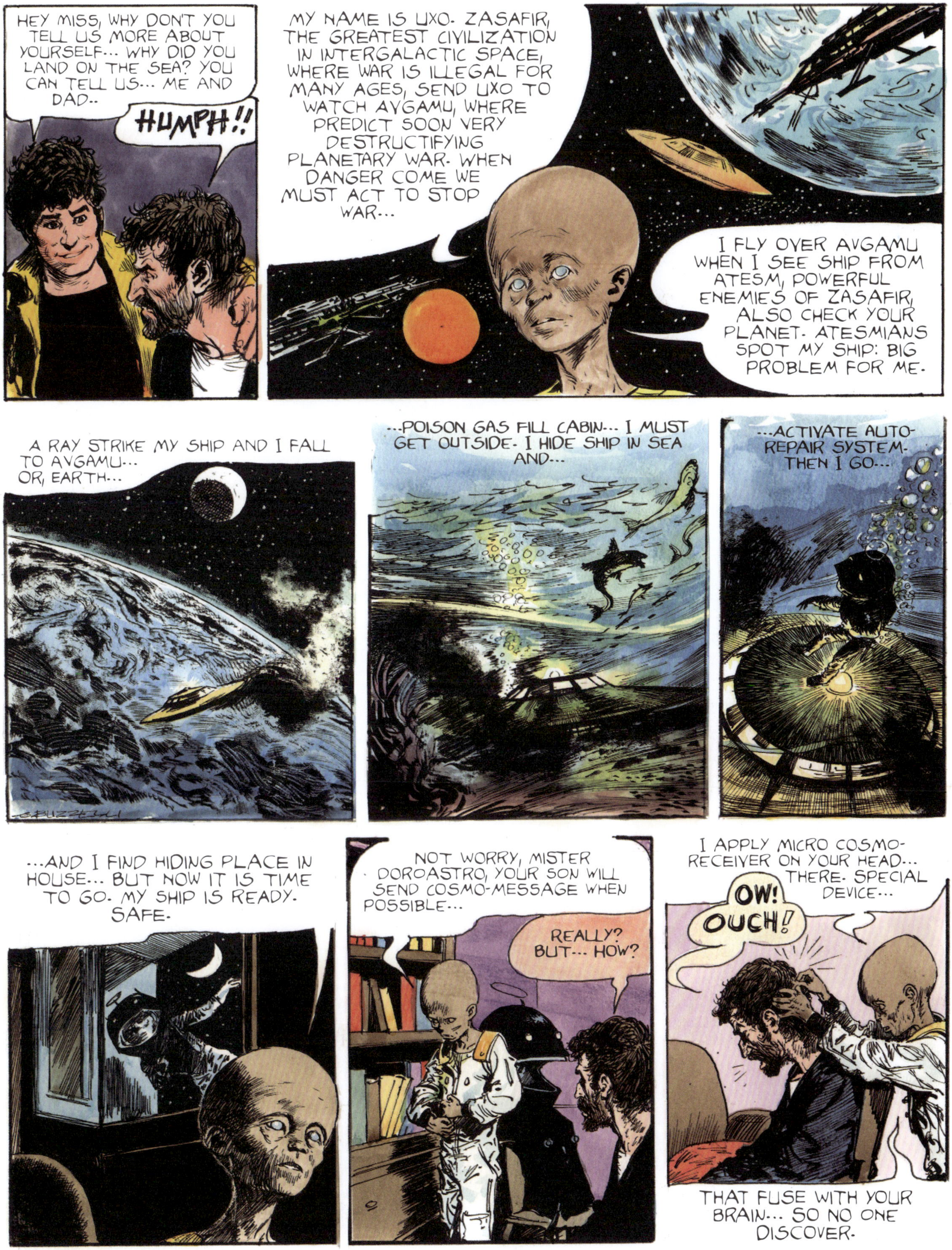
HEY MISS, WHY DON'T YOU TELL US MORE ABOUT YOURSELF... WHY DID YOU LAND ON THE SEA? YOU CAN TELL US... ME AND DAD..
HUMPH!!
MY NAME IS UXO. ZASAFIR, THE GREATEST CIVILIZATION IN INTERGALACTIC SPACE, WHERE WAR IS ILLEGAL FOR MANY AGES, SEND UXO TO WATCH AVGAMU, WHERE PREDICT SOON VERY DESTRUCTIFYING PLANETARY WAR. WHEN DANGER COME WE MUST ACT TO STOP WAR...
I FLY OVER AVGAMU WHEN I SEE SHIP FROM ATESM, POWERFUL ENEMIES OF ZASAFIR, ALSO CHECK YOUR PLANET. ATESMIANS SPOT MY SHIP: BIG PROBLEM FOR ME.
A RAY STRIKE MY SHIP AND I FALL TO AVGAMU... OR, EARTH...
...POISON GAS FILL CABIN... I MUST GET OUTSIDE. I HIDE SHIP IN SEA AND...
...ACTIVATE AUTO-REPAIR SYSTEM. THEN I GO...
...AND I FIND HIDING PLACE IN HOUSE... BUT NOW IT IS TIME TO GO. MY SHIP IS READY. SAFE.
NOT WORRY, MISTER DOROASTRO, YOUR SON WILL SEND COSMO-MESSAGE WHEN POSSIBLE...
REALLY? BUT... HOW?
I APPLY MICRO COSMO-RECEIVER ON YOUR HEAD... THERE. SPECIAL DEVICE...
OW! OUCH!!
THAT FUSE WITH YOUR BRAIN... SO NO ONE DISCOVER.

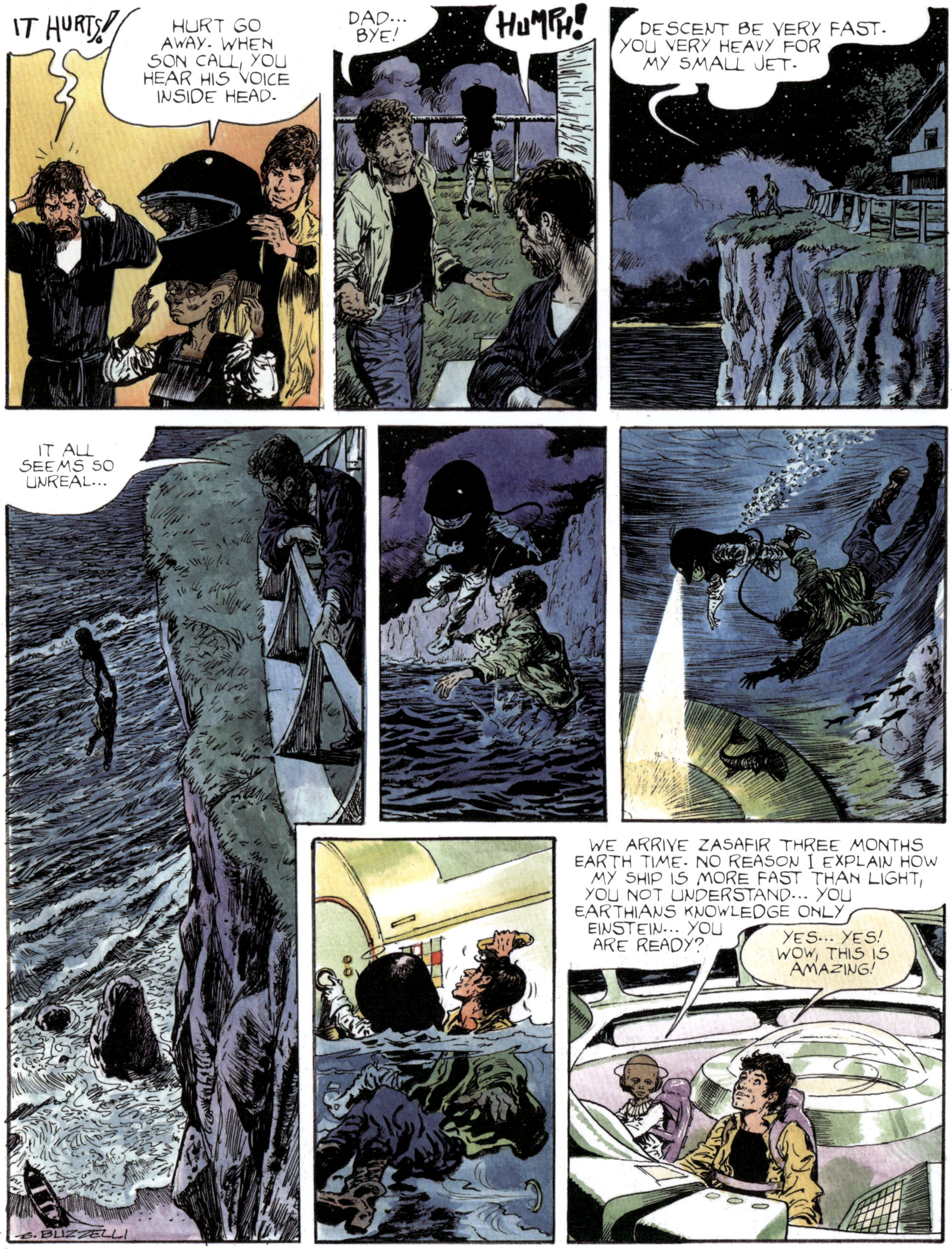
IT HURTS!
HURT GO AWAY. WHEN SON CALL, YOU HEAR HIS VOICE INSIDE HEAD.
DAD... BYE!
HUMPH!
DESCENT BE VERY FAST. YOU VERY HEAVY FOR MY SMALL JET.
IT ALL SEEMS SO UNREAL...
G. BUZZELLI
WE ARRIVE ZASAFIR THREE MONTHS EARTH TIME. NO REASON I EXPLAIN HOW MY SHIP IS MORE FAST THAN LIGHT, YOU NOT UNDERSTAND... YOU EARTHIANS KNOWLEDGE ONLY EINSTEIN... YOU ARE READY?
YES... YES! WOW, THIS IS AMAZING!

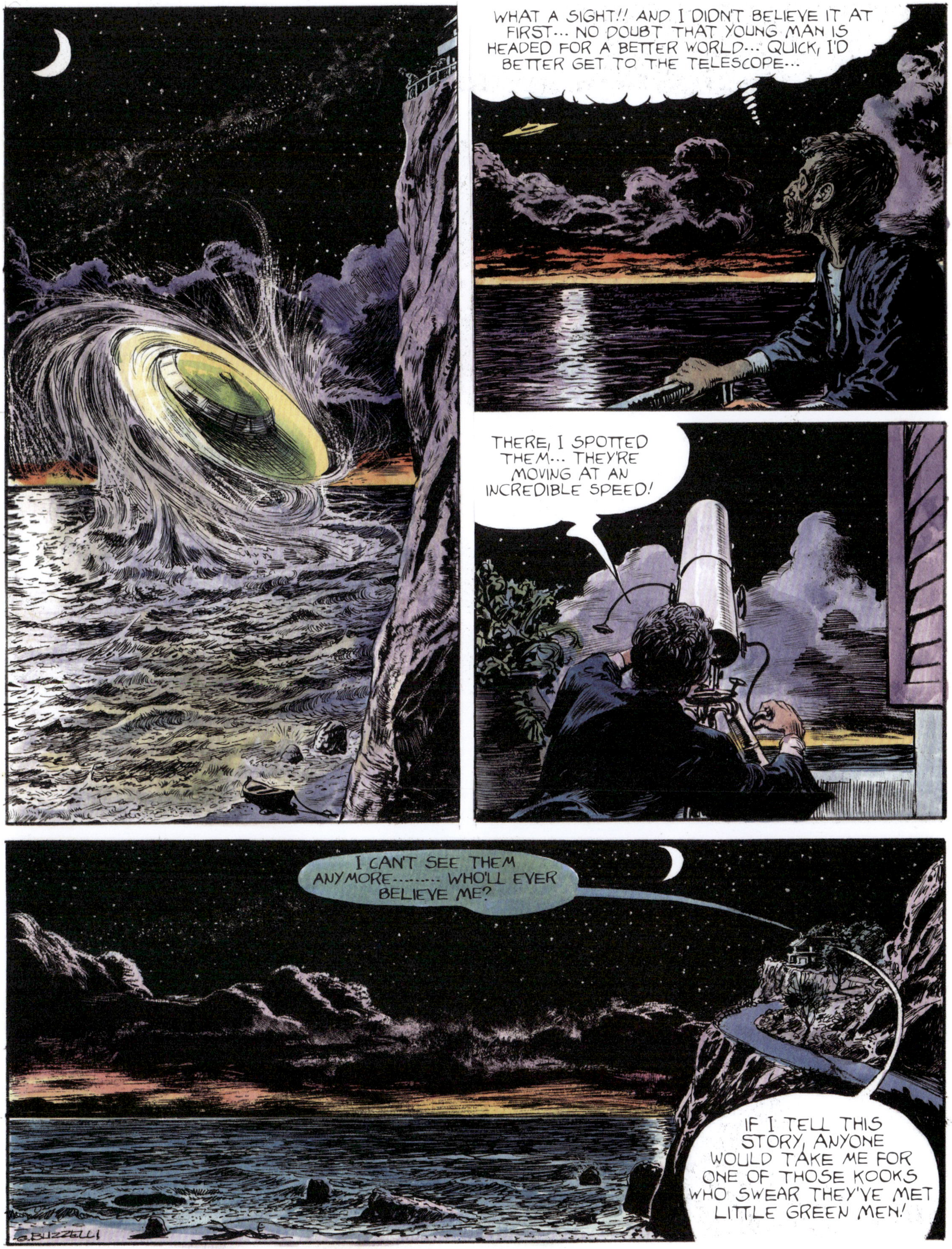
WHAT A SIGHT!! AND I DIDN'T BELIEVE IT AT FIRST... NO DOUBT THAT YOUNG MAN IS HEADED FOR A BETTER WORLD... QUICK, I'D BETTER GET TO THE TELESCOPE...
THERE, I SPOTTED THEM... THEY'RE MOVING AT AN INCREDIBLE SPEED!
I CAN'T SEE THEM ANYMORE......... WHO'LL EVER BELIEVE ME?
IF I TELL THIS STORY, ANYONE WOULD TAKE ME FOR ONE OF THOSE KOOKS WHO SWEAR THEY'VE MET LITTLE GREEN MEN!
G. BUZZELLI

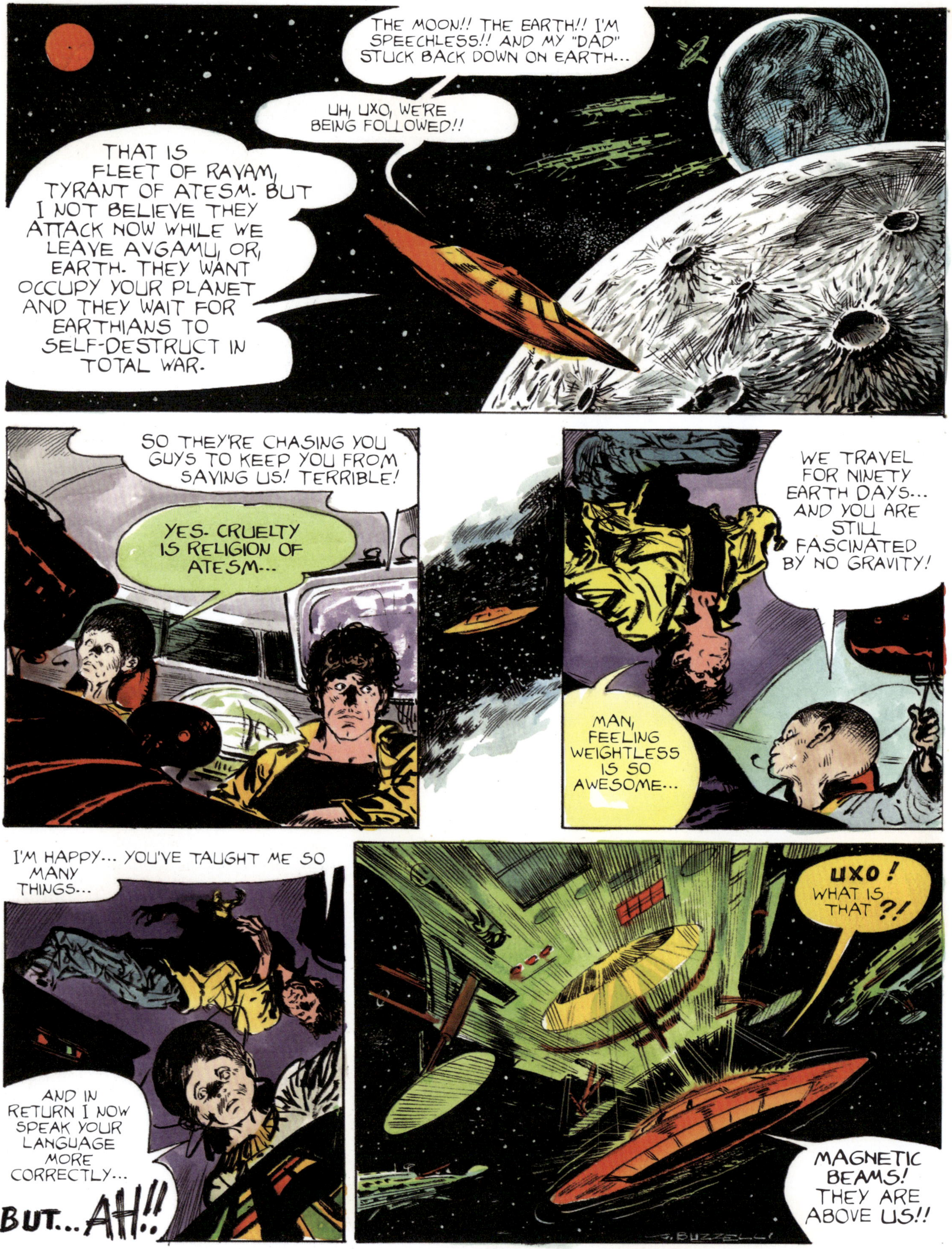
THE MOON!! THE EARTH!! I'M SPEECHLESS!! AND MY "DAD" STUCK BACK DOWN ON EARTH...
UH, UXO, WE'RE BEING FOLLOWED!!
THAT IS FLEET OF RAVAM, TYRANT OF ATESM. BUT I NOT BELIEVE THEY ATTACK NOW WHILE WE LEAVE AVGAMU, OR, EARTH. THEY WANT OCCUPY YOUR PLANET AND THEY WAIT FOR EARTHIANS TO SELF-DESTRUCT IN TOTAL WAR.
SO THEY'RE CHASING YOU GUYS TO KEEP YOU FROM SAVING US! TERRIBLE!
YES. CRUELTY IS RELIGION OF ATESM...
WE TRAVEL FOR NINETY EARTH DAYS... AND YOU ARE STILL FASCINATED BY NO GRAVITY!
MAN, FEELING WEIGHTLESS IS SO AWESOME...
I'M HAPPY... YOU'VE TAUGHT ME SO MANY THINGS...
AND IN RETURN I NOW SPEAK YOUR LANGUAGE MORE CORRECTLY...
BUT... AH!!
UXO! WHAT IS THAT ?!
MAGNETIC BEAMS! THEY ARE ABOVE US!!
G. BUZZELLI

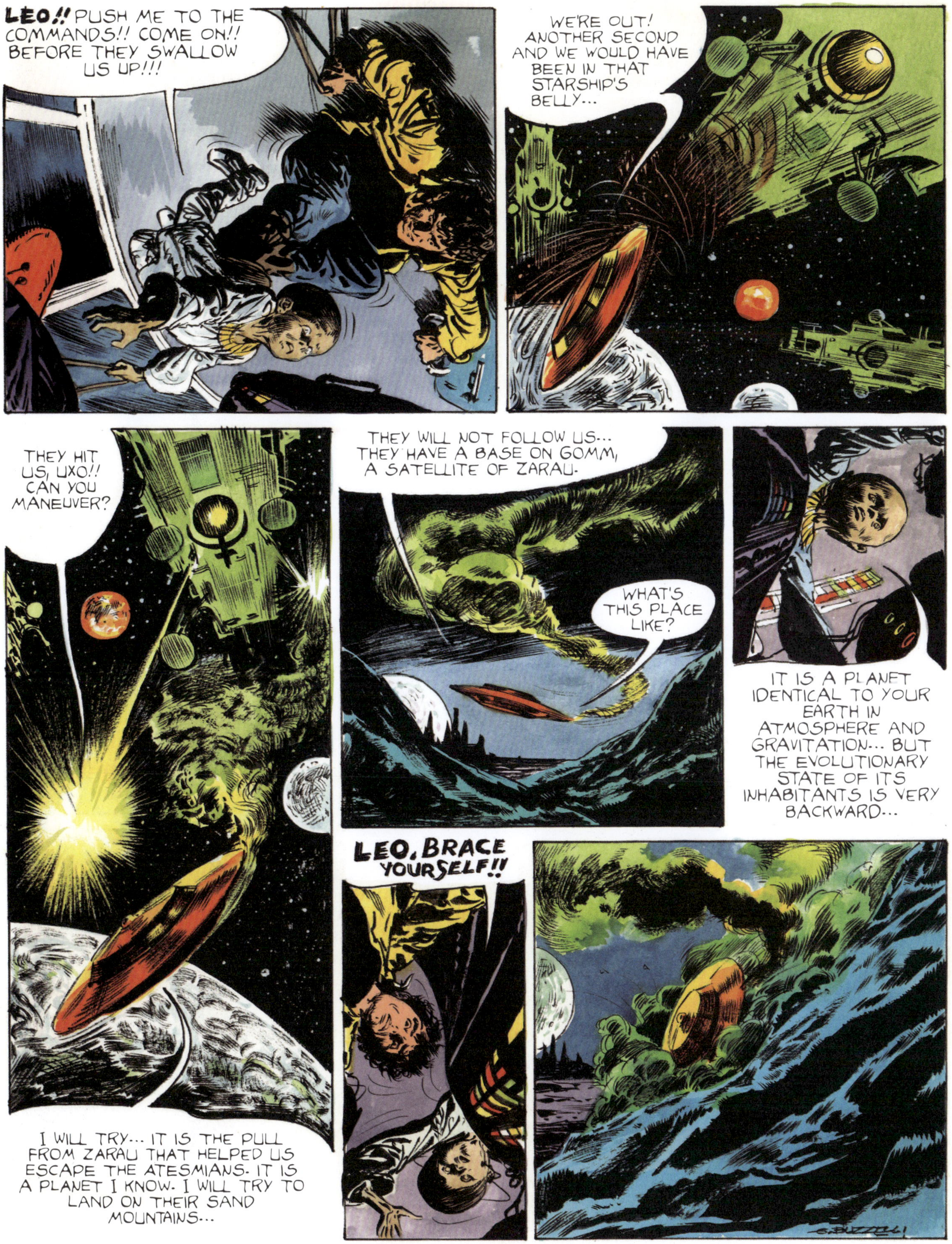
LEO!! PUSH ME TO THE COMMANDS!! COME ON!! BEFORE THEY SWALLOW US UP!!!
WE'RE OUT! ANOTHER SECOND AND WE WOULD HAVE BEEN IN THAT STARSHIP'S BELLY...
THEY HIT US, UXO!! CAN YOU MANEUVER?
I WILL TRY... IT IS THE PULL FROM ZARAU THAT HELPED US ESCAPE THE ATESMIANS. IT IS A PLANET I KNOW. I WILL TRY TO LAND ON THEIR SAND MOUNTAINS...
THEY WILL NOT FOLLOW US... THEY HAVE A BASE ON GOMM, A SATELLITE OF ZARAU.
WHAT'S THIS PLACE LIKE?
IT IS A PLANET IDENTICAL TO YOUR EARTH IN ATMOSPHERE AND GRAVITATION... BUT THE EVOLUTIONARY STATE OF ITS INHABITANTS IS VERY BACKWARD...
LEO, BRACE YOURSELF!!

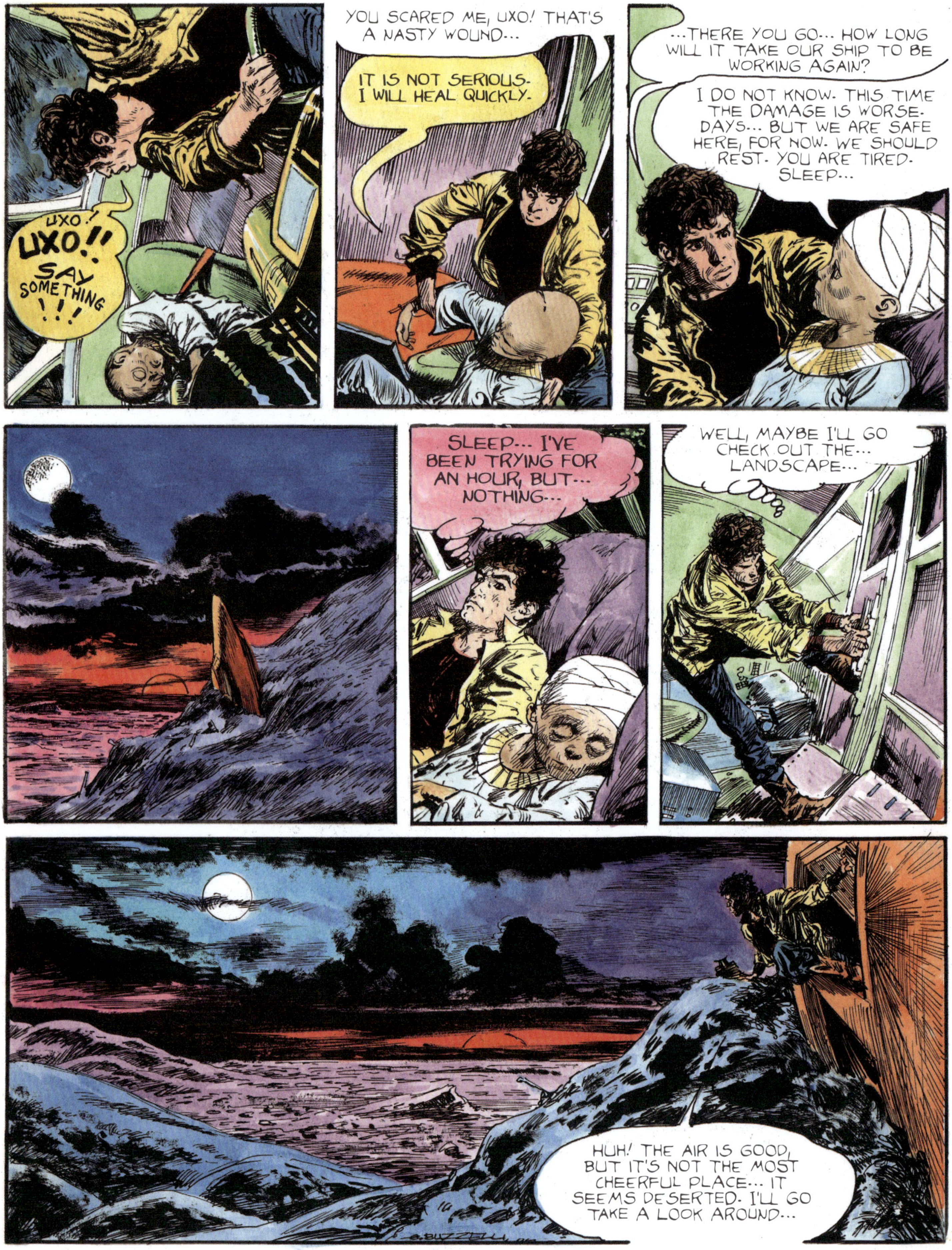
UXO! UXO!! SAY SOMETHING!!!
YOU SCARED ME, UXO! THAT'S A NASTY WOUND...
IT IS NOT SERIOUS. I WILL HEAL QUICKLY.
...THERE YOU GO... HOW LONG WILL IT TAKE OUR SHIP TO BE WORKING AGAIN?
I DO NOT KNOW. THIS TIME THE DAMAGE IS WORSE. DAYS... BUT WE ARE SAFE HERE, FOR NOW. WE SHOULD REST. YOU ARE TIRED. SLEEP...
SLEEP... I'VE BEEN TRYING FOR AN HOUR, BUT... NOTHING...
WELL, MAYBE I'LL GO CHECK OUT THE... LANDSCAPE...
HUH! THE AIR IS GOOD, BUT IT'S NOT THE MOST CHEERFUL PLACE... IT SEEMS DESERTED. I'LL GO TAKE A LOOK AROUND...
S. BUZZELLI

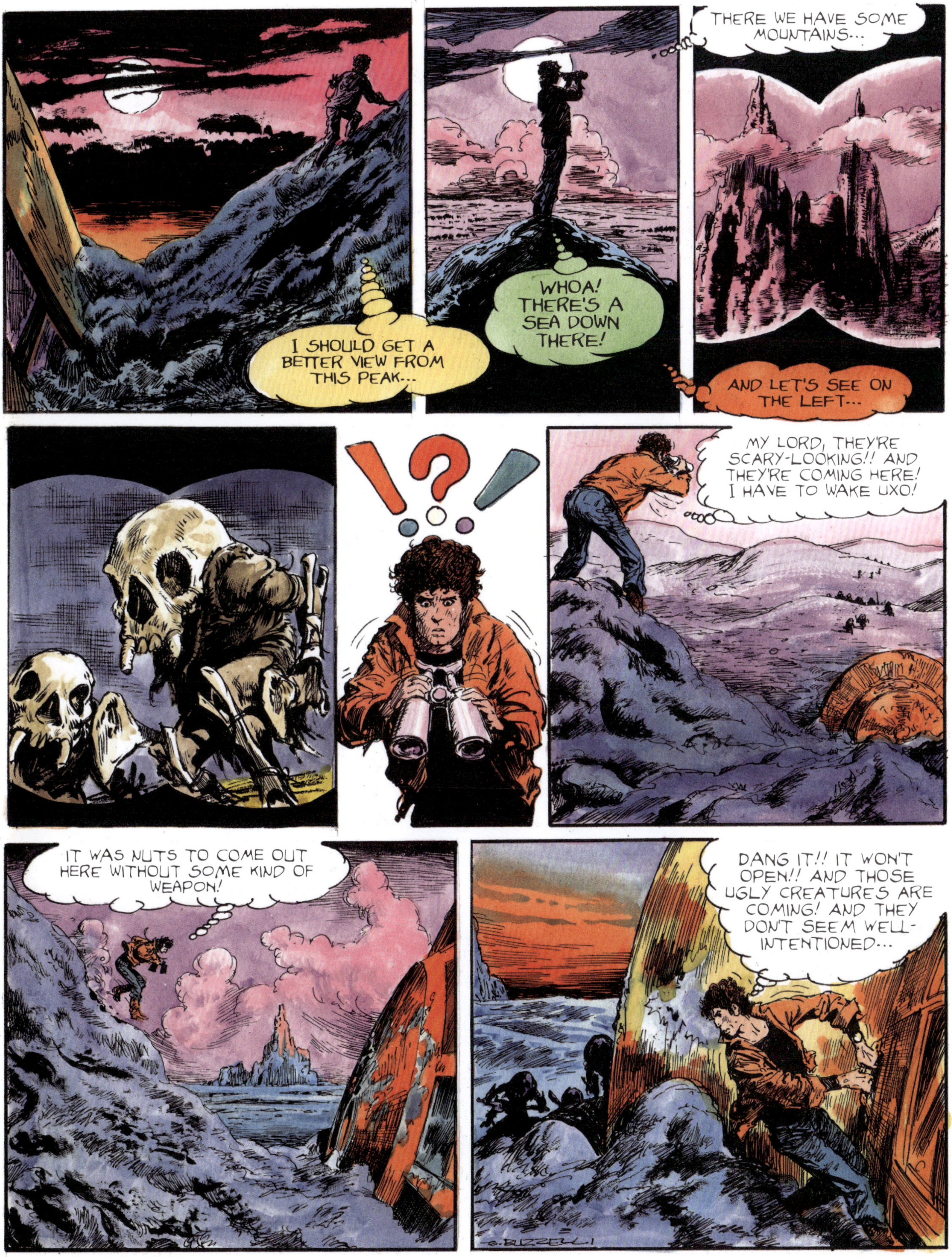
I SHOULD GET A BETTER VIEW FROM THIS PEAK...
WHOA! THERE'S A SEA DOWN THERE!
THERE WE HAVE SOME MOUNTAINS...
AND LET'S SEE ON THE LEFT...
MY LORD, THEY'RE SCARY-LOOKING!! AND THEY'RE COMING HERE! I HAVE TO WAKE UXO!
IT WAS NUTS TO COME OUT HERE WITHOUT SOME KIND OF WEAPON!
DANG IT!! IT WON'T OPEN!! AND THOSE UGLY CREATURES ARE COMING! AND THEY DON'T SEEM WELL-INTENTIONED...

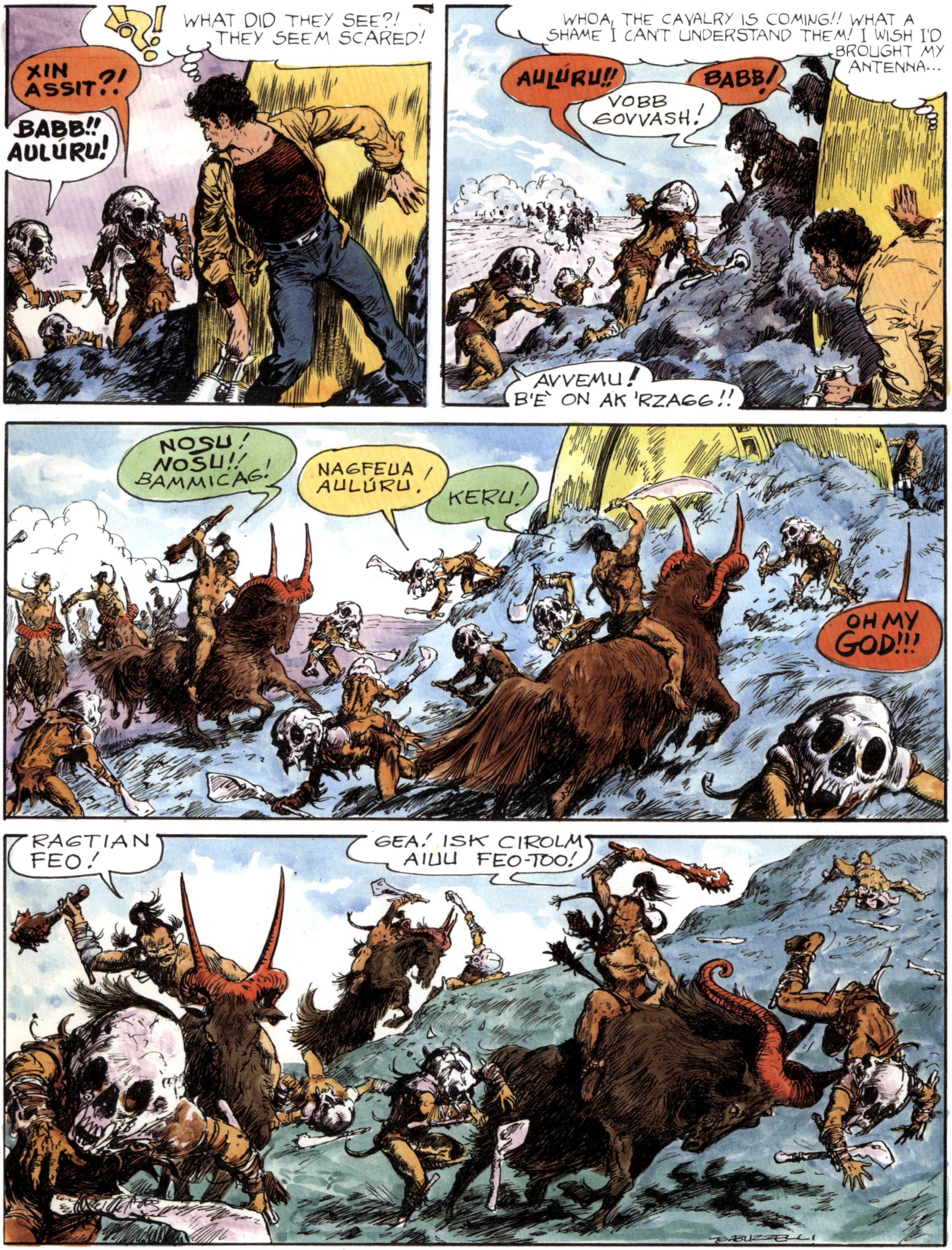
WHAT DID THEY SEE?! THEY SEEM SCARED!
XIN ASSIT?!
BABB!! AULÚRU!
WHOA, THE CAVALRY IS COMING!! WHAT A SHAME I CAN'T UNDERSTAND THEM! I WISH I'D BROUGHT MY ANTENNA...
AULÚRU!!
VOBB GOVVASH!
BABB!
AVVEMU! B'È ON AK'RZAGG!!
NOSU! NOSU!! BAMMICAG!
NAGFEUA AULÚRU!
KERU!
OH MY GOD!!!
RAGTIAN FEO!
GEA! ISK CIROLM AIUU FEO-TOO!

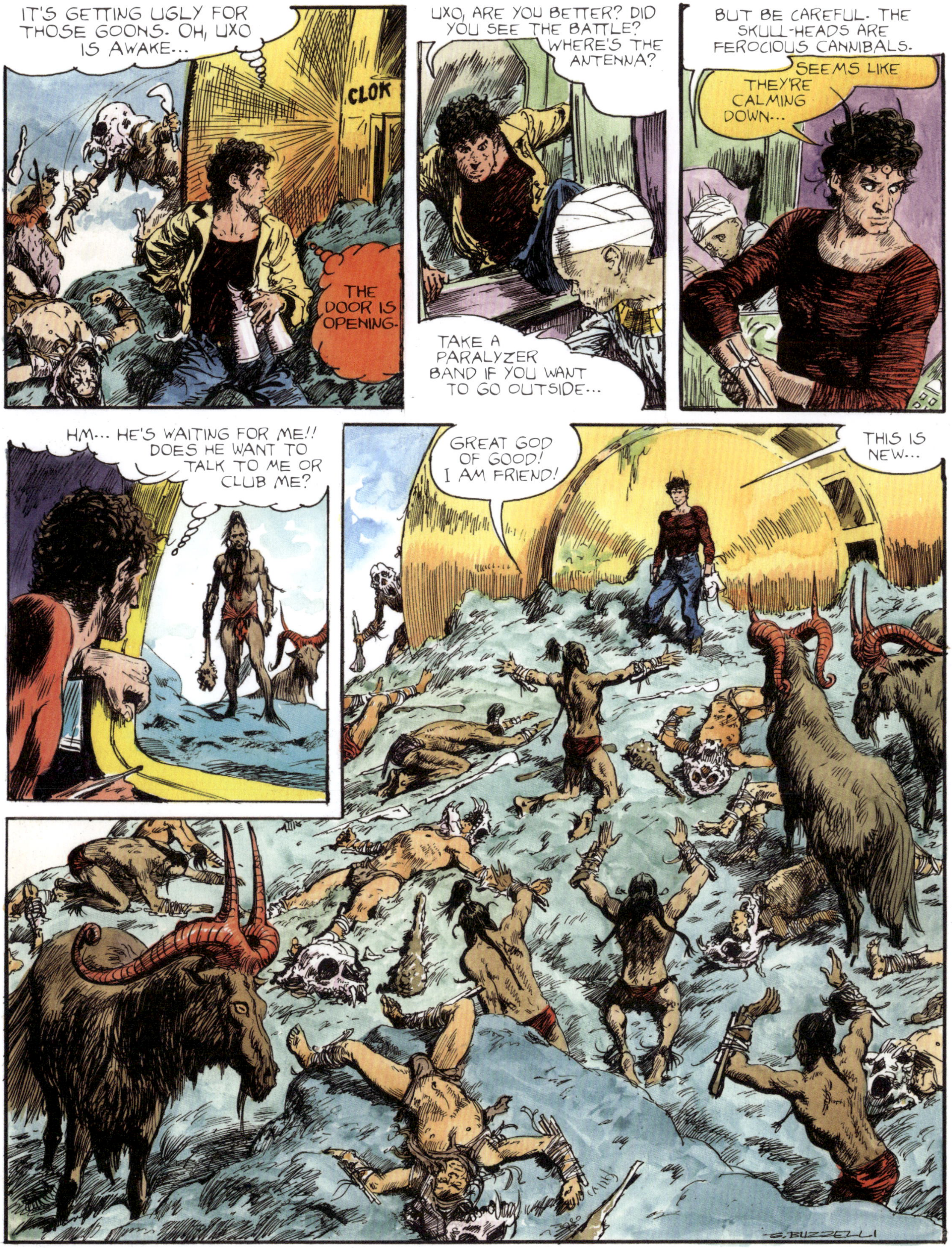
IT'S GETTING UGLY FOR THOSE GOONS. OH, UXO IS AWAKE...
CLOK
THE DOOR IS OPENING.
UXO, ARE YOU BETTER? DID YOU SEE THE BATTLE? WHERE'S THE ANTENNA?
TAKE A PARALYZER BAND IF YOU WANT TO GO OUTSIDE...
BUT BE CAREFUL. THE SKULL-HEADS ARE FEROCIOUS CANNIBALS.
SEEMS LIKE THEY'RE CALMING DOWN...
HM... HE'S WAITING FOR ME!! DOES HE WANT TO TALK TO ME OR CLUB ME?
GREAT GOD OF GOOD! I AM FRIEND!
THIS IS NEW...
G. BUZZELLI

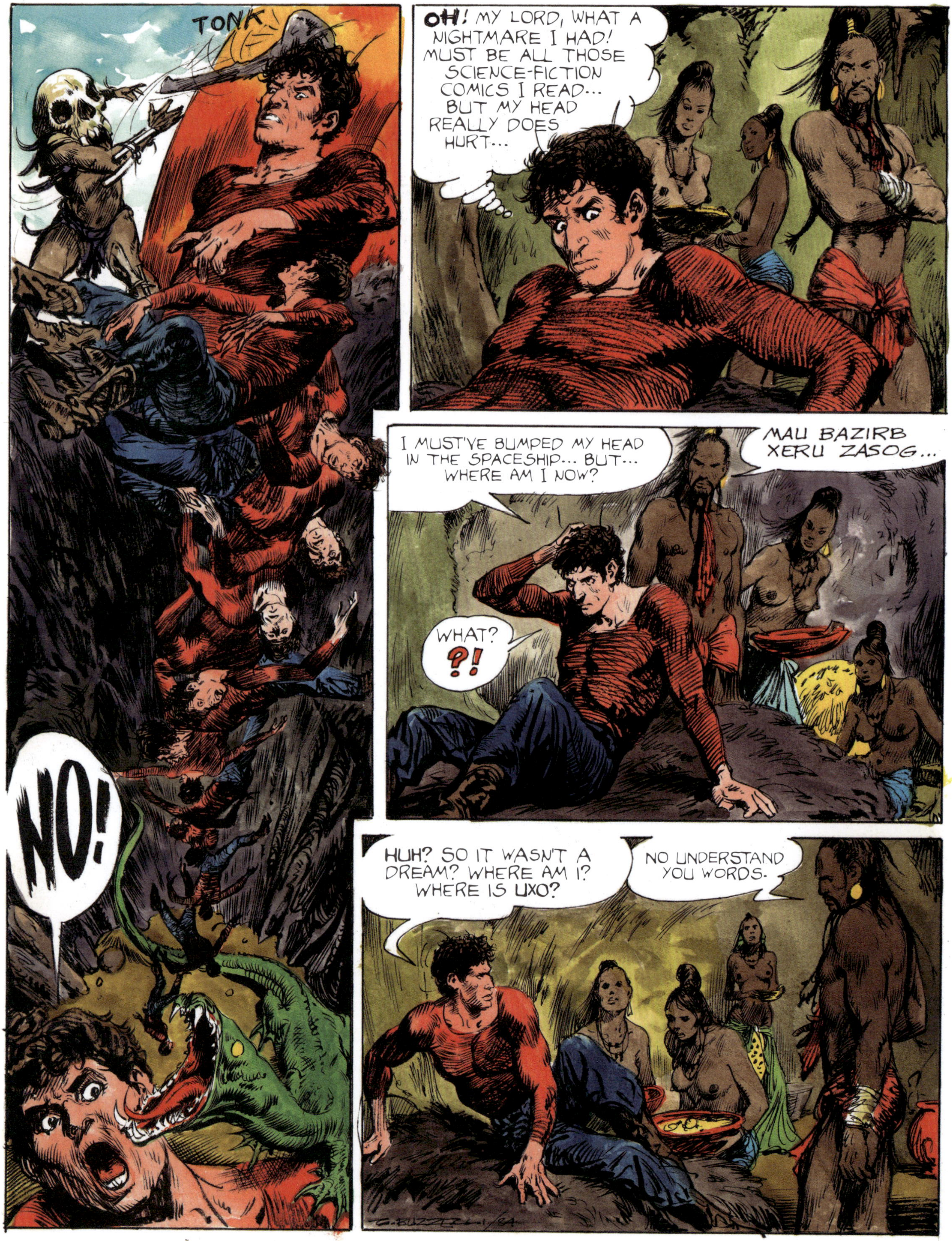
TONK
NO!
OH! MY LORD, WHAT A NIGHTMARE I HAD! MUST BE ALL THOSE SCIENCE-FICTION COMICS I READ... BUT MY HEAD REALLY DOES HURT...
I MUST'VE BUMPED MY HEAD IN THE SPACESHIP... BUT... WHERE AM I NOW?
MAU BAZIRB XERU ZASOG...
WHAT? ?!
HUH? SO IT WASN'T A DREAM? WHERE AM I? WHERE IS UXO?
NO UNDERSTAND YOU WORDS.

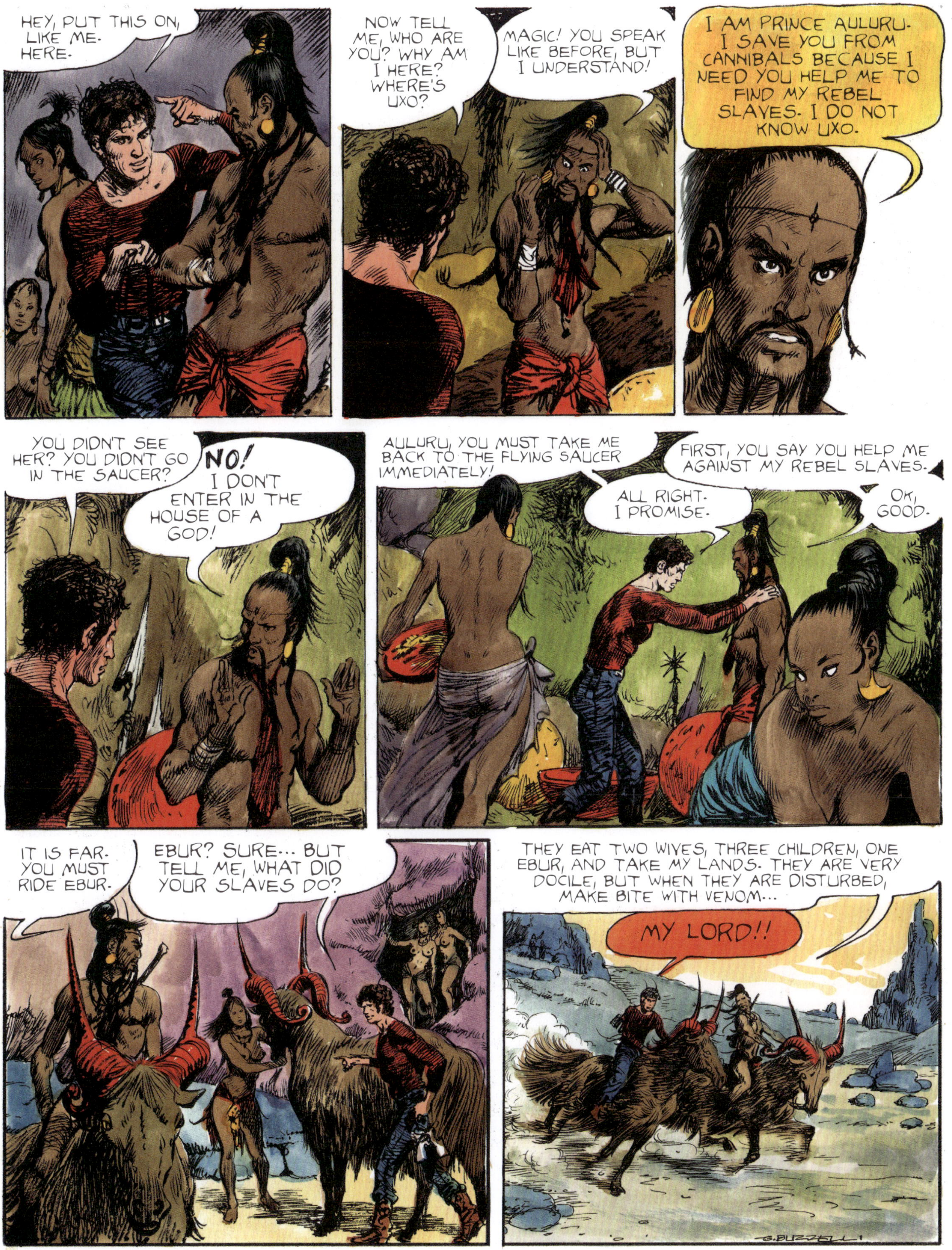
HEY, PUT THIS ON, LIKE ME. HERE.
NOW TELL ME, WHO ARE YOU? WHY AM I HERE? WHERE'S UXO?
MAGIC! YOU SPEAK LIKE BEFORE, BUT I UNDERSTAND!
I AM PRINCE AULURU. I SAVE YOU FROM CANNIBALS BECAUSE I NEED YOU HELP ME TO FIND MY REBEL SLAVES. I DO NOT KNOW UXO.
YOU DIDN'T SEE HER? YOU DIDN'T GO IN THE SAUCER?
NO! I DON'T ENTER IN THE HOUSE OF A GOD!
AULURU, YOU MUST TAKE ME BACK TO THE FLYING SAUCER IMMEDIATELY!
FIRST, YOU SAY YOU HELP ME AGAINST MY REBEL SLAVES.
ALL RIGHT. I PROMISE.
OK, GOOD.
IT IS FAR. YOU MUST RIDE EBUR.
EBUR? SURE... BUT TELL ME, WHAT DID YOUR SLAVES DO?
THEY EAT TWO WIVES, THREE CHILDREN, ONE EBUR, AND TAKE MY LANDS. THEY ARE VERY DOCILE, BUT WHEN THEY ARE DISTURBED, MAKE BITE WITH VENOM...
MY LORD!!
G.BUZZELLI

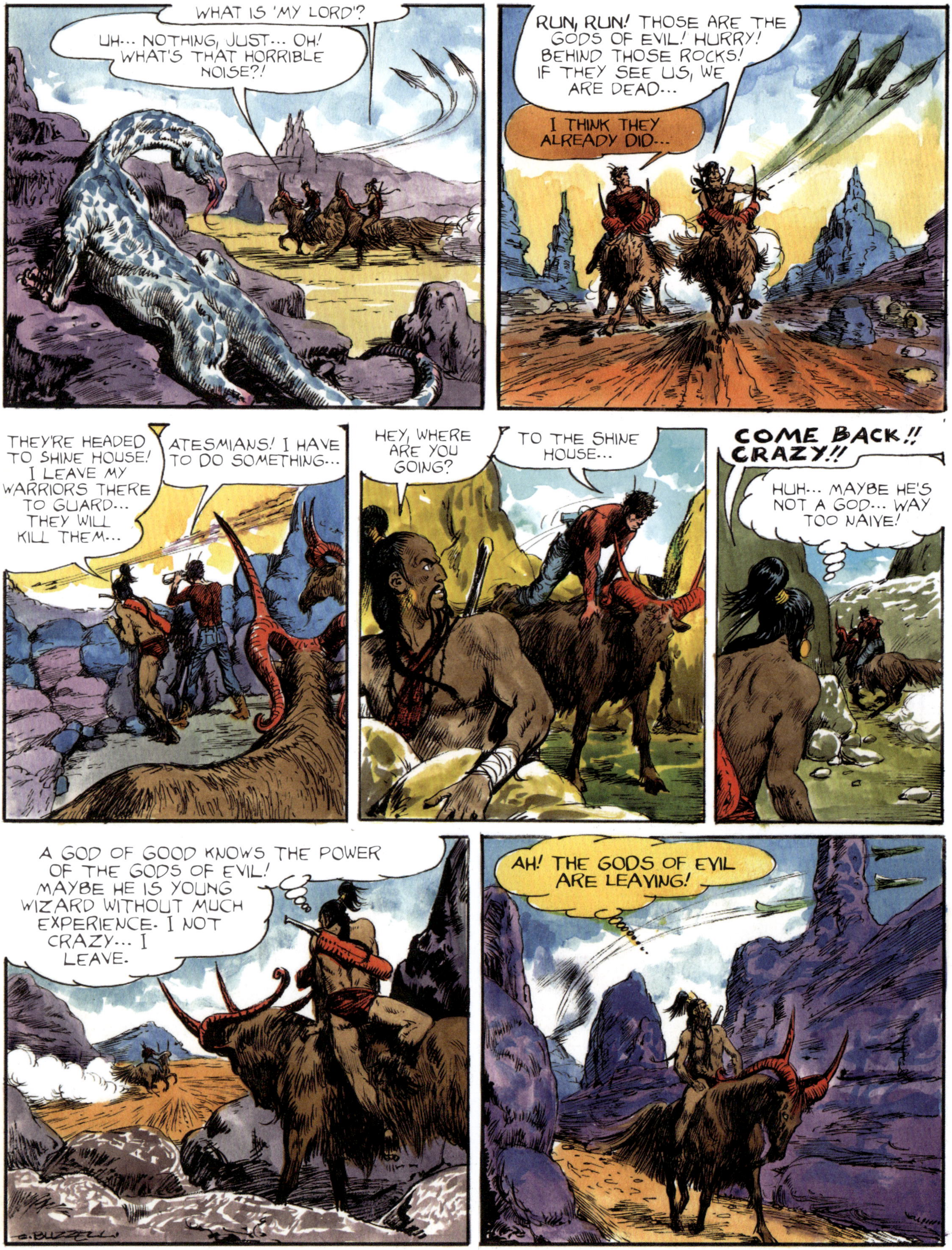

WHAT IS 'MY LORD'?
UH... NOTHING, JUST... OH! WHAT'S THAT HORRIBLE NOISE?!
RUN, RUN! THOSE ARE THE GODS OF EVIL! HURRY! BEHIND THOSE ROCKS! IF THEY SEE US, WE ARE DEAD...
I THINK THEY ALREADY DID...
THEY'RE HEADED TO SHINE HOUSE! I LEAVE MY WARRIORS THERE TO GUARD... THEY WILL KILL THEM...
ATESMIANS! I HAVE TO DO SOMETHING...
HEY, WHERE ARE YOU GOING?
TO THE SHINE HOUSE...
COME BACK!! CRAZY!!
HUH... MAYBE HE'S NOT A GOD... WAY TOO NAIVE!
A GOD OF GOOD KNOWS THE POWER OF THE GODS OF EVIL! MAYBE HE IS YOUNG WIZARD WITHOUT MUCH EXPERIENCE. I NOT CRAZY... I LEAVE.
AH! THE GODS OF EVIL ARE LEAVING!
G. BUZZELLI

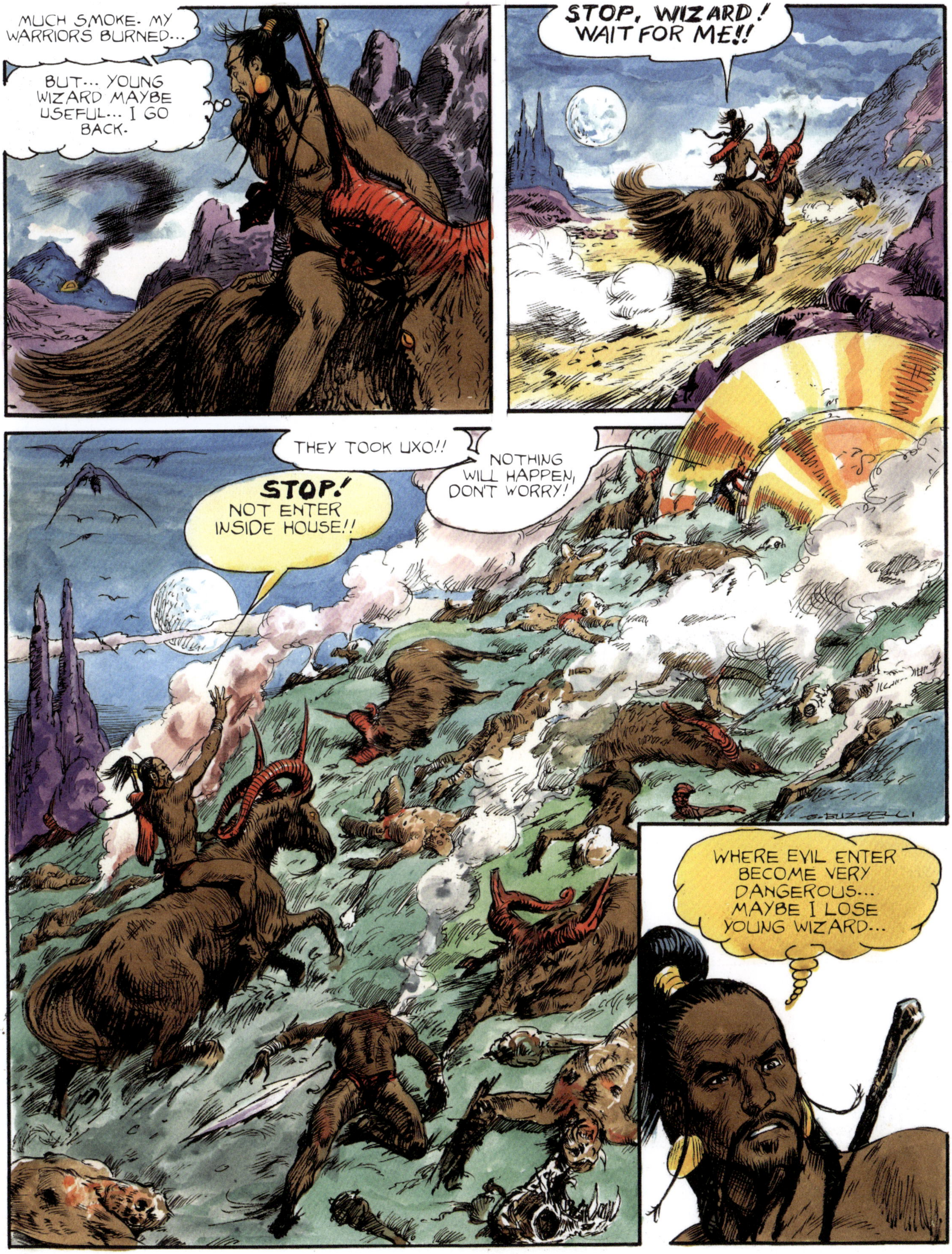
MUCH SMOKE. MY WARRIORS BURNED...
BUT... YOUNG WIZARD MAYBE USEFUL... I GO BACK.
STOP, WIZARD! WAIT FOR ME!!
THEY TOOK UXO!!
NOTHING WILL HAPPEN, DON'T WORRY!
STOP! NOT ENTER INSIDE HOUSE!!
WHERE EVIL ENTER BECOME VERY DANGEROUS... MAYBE I LOSE YOUNG WIZARD...

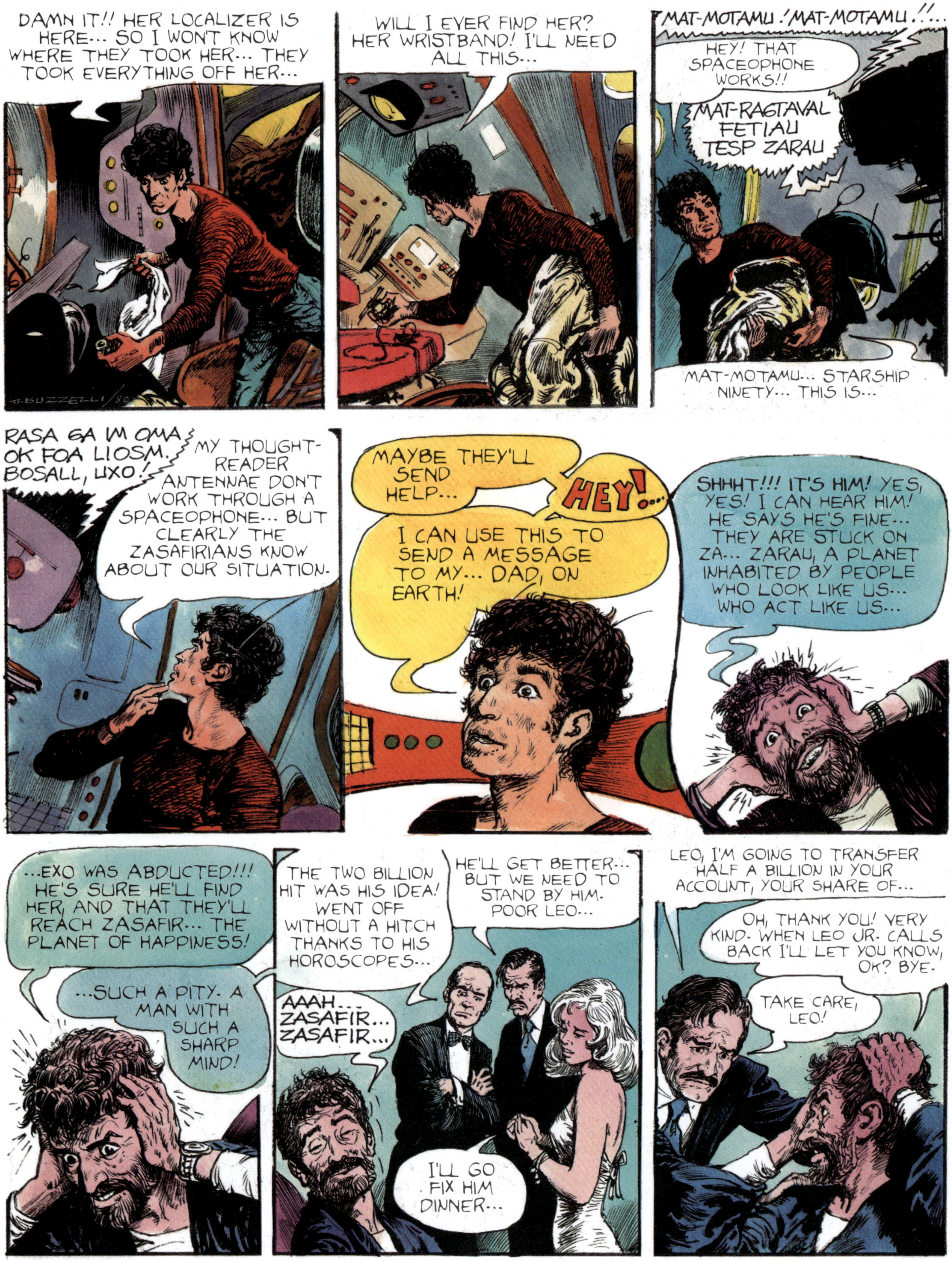

DAMN IT!! HER LOCALIZER IS HERE... SO I WON'T KNOW WHERE THEY TOOK HER... THEY TOOK EVERYTHING OFF HER...
B. BUZZELLI/89
WILL I EVER FIND HER? HER WRISTBAND! I'LL NEED ALL THIS...
MAT-MOTAMU! MAT-MOTAMU!!...
HEY! THAT SPACEOPHONE WORKS!!
MAT-RAGTAVAL FETIAU TESP ZARAU
MAT-MOTAMU... STARSHIP NINETY... THIS IS...
RASA GA IM OMA OK FOA LIOSM. BOSALL, UXO!
MY THOUGHT-READER ANTENNAE DON'T WORK THROUGH A SPACEOPHONE... BUT CLEARLY THE ZASAFIRIANS KNOW ABOUT OUR SITUATION.
MAYBE THEY'LL SEND HELP...
HEY!...
I CAN USE THIS TO SEND A MESSAGE TO MY... DAD, ON EARTH!
SHHHT!!! IT'S HIM! YES, YES! I CAN HEAR HIM! HE SAYS HE'S FINE... THEY ARE STUCK ON ZA... ZARAU, A PLANET INHABITED BY PEOPLE WHO LOOK LIKE US... WHO ACT LIKE US...
...EXO WAS ABDUCTED!!! HE'S SURE HE'LL FIND HER, AND THAT THEY'LL REACH ZASAFIR... THE PLANET OF HAPPINESS!
...SUCH A PITY. A MAN WITH SUCH A SHARP MIND!
THE TWO BILLION HIT WAS HIS IDEA! WENT OFF WITHOUT A HITCH THANKS TO HIS HOROSCOPES...
HE'LL GET BETTER... BUT WE NEED TO STAND BY HIM. POOR LEO...
AAAH... ZASAFIR... ZASAFIR...
I'LL GO FIX HIM DINNER...
LEO, I'M GOING TO TRANSFER HALF A BILLION IN YOUR ACCOUNT, YOUR SHARE OF...
OH, THANK YOU! VERY KIND. WHEN LEO JR. CALLS BACK I'LL LET YOU KNOW, OK? BYE.
TAKE CARE, LEO!

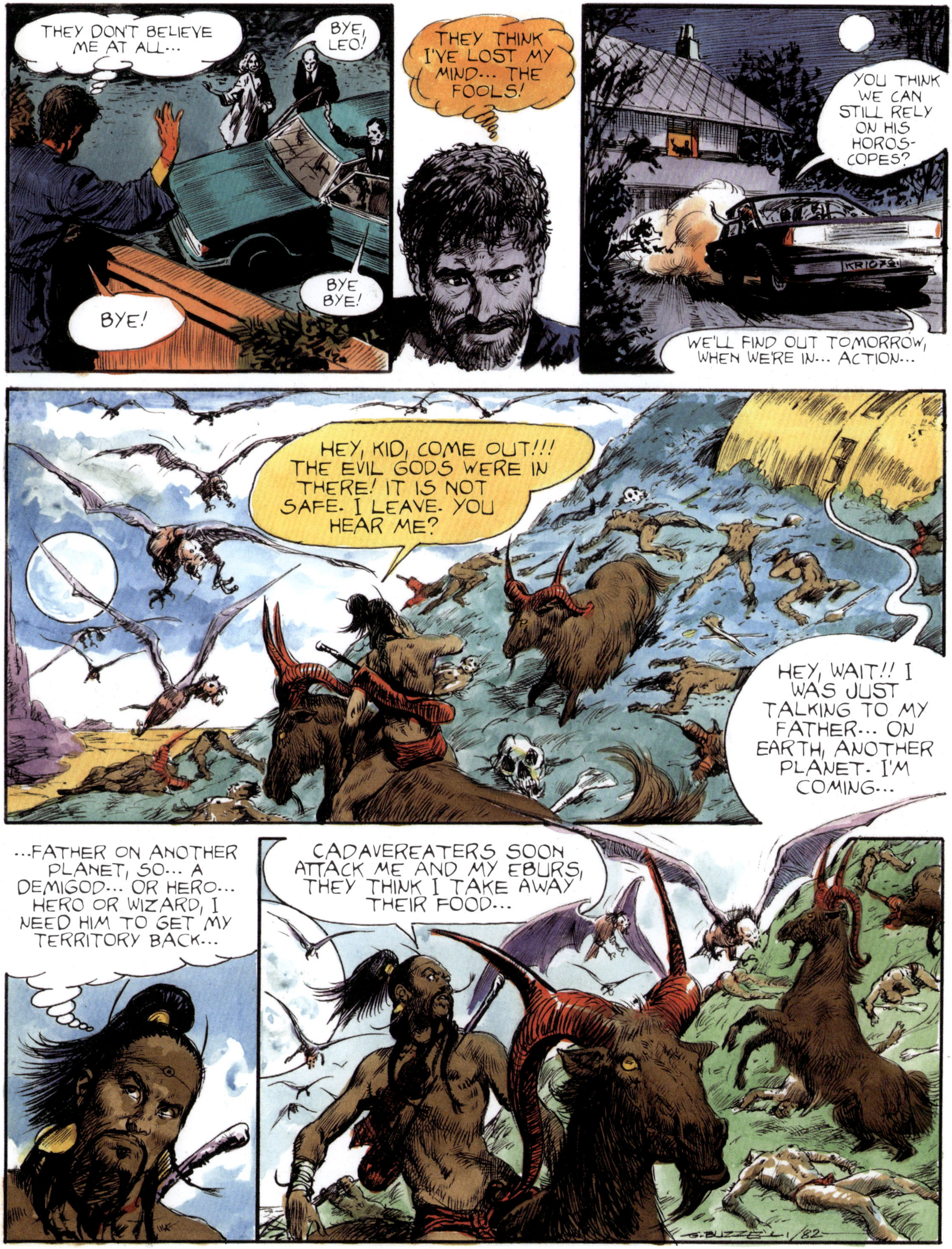
THEY DON'T BELIEVE ME AT ALL...
BYE, LEO!
BYE BYE!
BYE!
THEY THINK I'VE LOST MY MIND... THE FOOLS!
YOU THINK WE CAN STILL RELY ON HIS HOROS-COPES?
WE'LL FIND OUT TOMORROW, WHEN WE'RE IN... ACTION...
HEY, KID, COME OUT!!! THE EVIL GODS WERE IN THERE! IT IS NOT SAFE. I LEAVE. YOU HEAR ME?
HEY, WAIT!! I WAS JUST TALKING TO MY FATHER... ON EARTH, ANOTHER PLANET. I'M COMING...
...FATHER ON ANOTHER PLANET, SO... A DEMIGOD... OR HERO... HERO OR WIZARD, I NEED HIM TO GET MY TERRITORY BACK...
CADAVEREATERS SOON ATTACK ME AND MY EBURS, THEY THINK I TAKE AWAY THEIR FOOD...
G. BUZZELLI /82

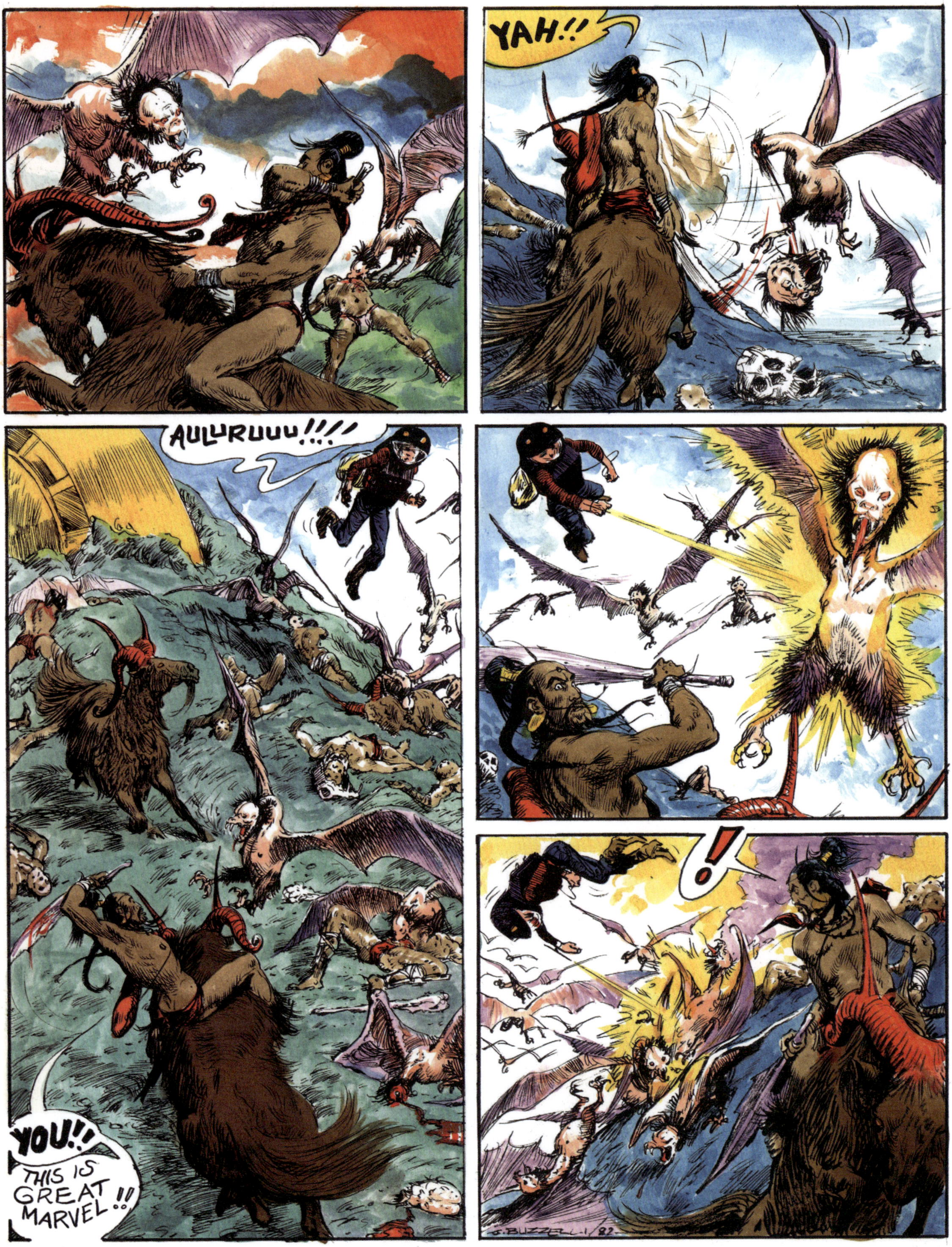

YAH!!
AULURUUU!!!!
!
YOU!!
THIS IS GREAT MARVEL!!

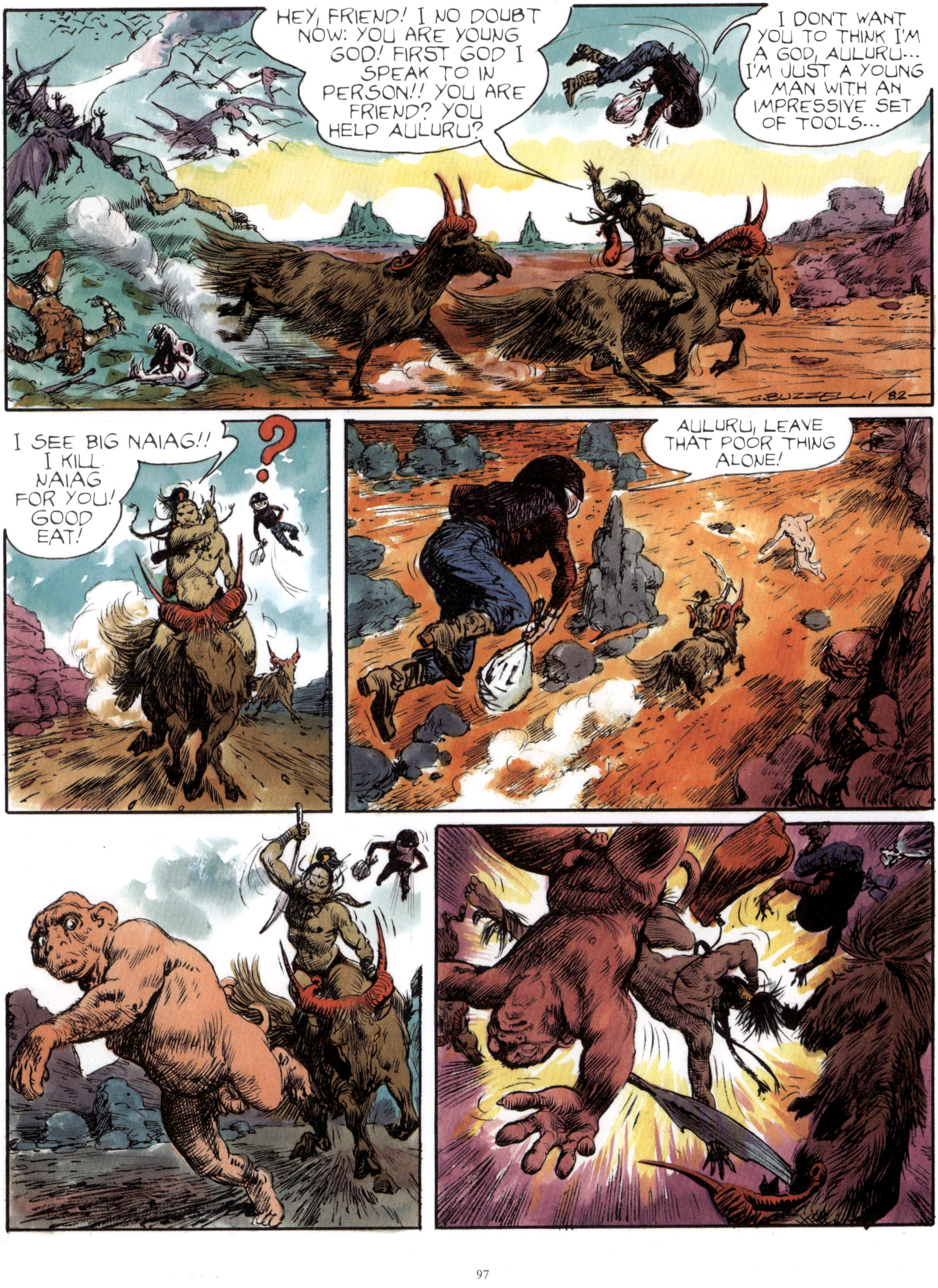
HEY, FRIEND! I NO DOUBT NOW: YOU ARE YOUNG GOD! FIRST GOD I SPEAK TO IN PERSON!! YOU ARE FRIEND? YOU HELP AULURU?
I DON'T WANT YOU TO THINK I'M A GOD, AULURU... I'M JUST A YOUNG MAN WITH AN IMPRESSIVE SET OF TOOLS...
G. BUZZELLI / 82
I SEE BIG NAIAG!! I KILL NAIAG FOR YOU! GOOD EAT!
?
AULURU, LEAVE THAT POOR THING ALONE!

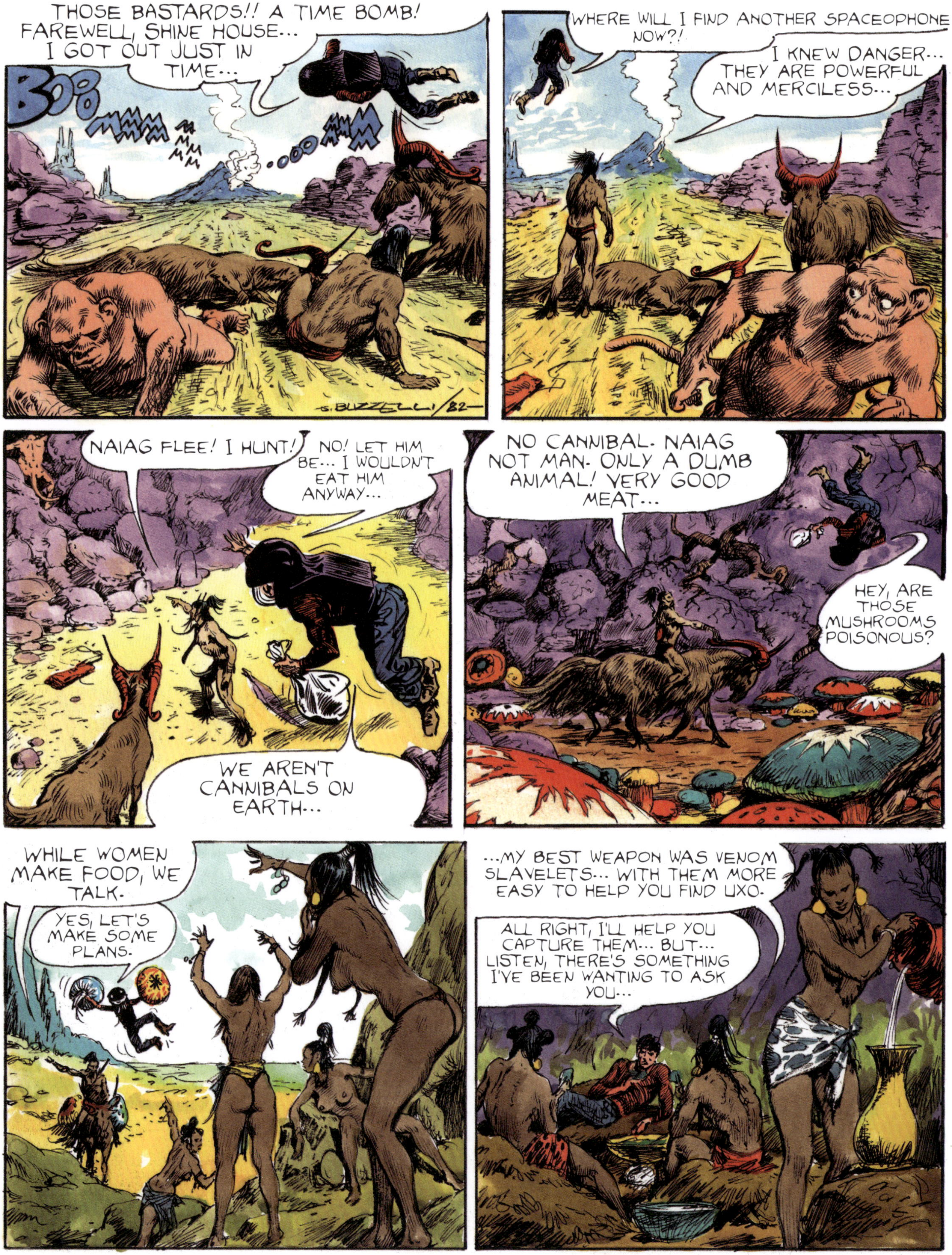
THOSE BASTARDS!! A TIME BOMB! FAREWELL, SHINE HOUSE... I GOT OUT JUST IN TIME...
BOOMMMMMMMMM...OOOMMMM
S. BUZZELLI/82
WHERE WILL I FIND ANOTHER SPACEOPHONE NOW?!
I KNEW DANGER... THEY ARE POWERFUL AND MERCILESS...
NAIAG FLEE! I HUNT!
NO! LET HIM BE... I WOULDN'T EAT HIM ANYWAY...
WE AREN'T CANNIBALS ON EARTH...
NO CANNIBAL. NAIAG NOT MAN. ONLY A DUMB ANIMAL! VERY GOOD MEAT...
HEY, ARE THOSE MUSHROOMS POISONOUS?
WHILE WOMEN MAKE FOOD, WE TALK.
YES, LET'S MAKE SOME PLANS.
...MY BEST WEAPON WAS VENOM SLAVELETS... WITH THEM MORE EASY TO HELP YOU FIND UXO.
ALL RIGHT, I'LL HELP YOU CAPTURE THEM... BUT... LISTEN, THERE'S SOMETHING I'VE BEEN WANTING TO ASK YOU...

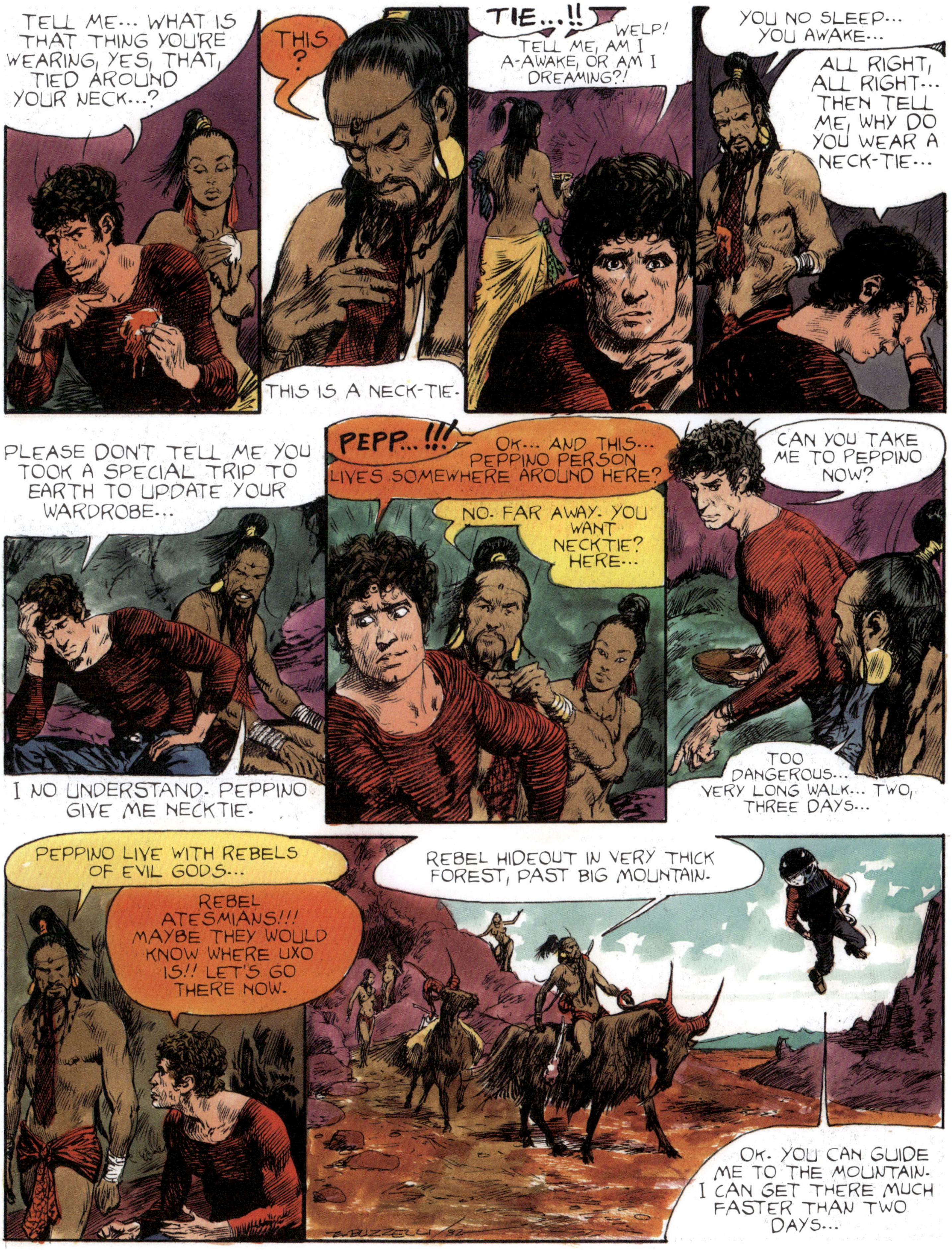
TELL ME... WHAT IS THAT THING YOU'RE WEARING, YES, THAT, TIED AROUND YOUR NECK...?
THIS ?
THIS IS A NECK-TIE.
TIE...!!
WELP! TELL ME, AM I A-AWAKE, OR AM I DREAMING?!
YOU NO SLEEP... YOU AWAKE...
ALL RIGHT, ALL RIGHT... THEN TELL ME, WHY DO YOU WEAR A NECK-TIE...
PLEASE DON'T TELL ME YOU TOOK A SPECIAL TRIP TO EARTH TO UPDATE YOUR WARDROBE...
I NO UNDERSTAND. PEPPINO GIVE ME NECKTIE.
PEPP...!!!
OK... AND THIS... PEPPINO PERSON LIVES SOMEWHERE AROUND HERE?
NO. FAR AWAY. YOU WANT NECKTIE? HERE...
CAN YOU TAKE ME TO PEPPINO NOW?
TOO DANGEROUS... VERY LONG WALK... TWO, THREE DAYS...
PEPPINO LIVE WITH REBELS OF EVIL GODS...
REBEL ATESMIANS!!! MAYBE THEY WOULD KNOW WHERE UXO IS!! LET'S GO THERE NOW.
REBEL HIDEOUT IN VERY THICK FOREST, PAST BIG MOUNTAIN.
OK. YOU CAN GUIDE ME TO THE MOUNTAIN. I CAN GET THERE MUCH FASTER THAN TWO DAYS...
BUZZELLI /92

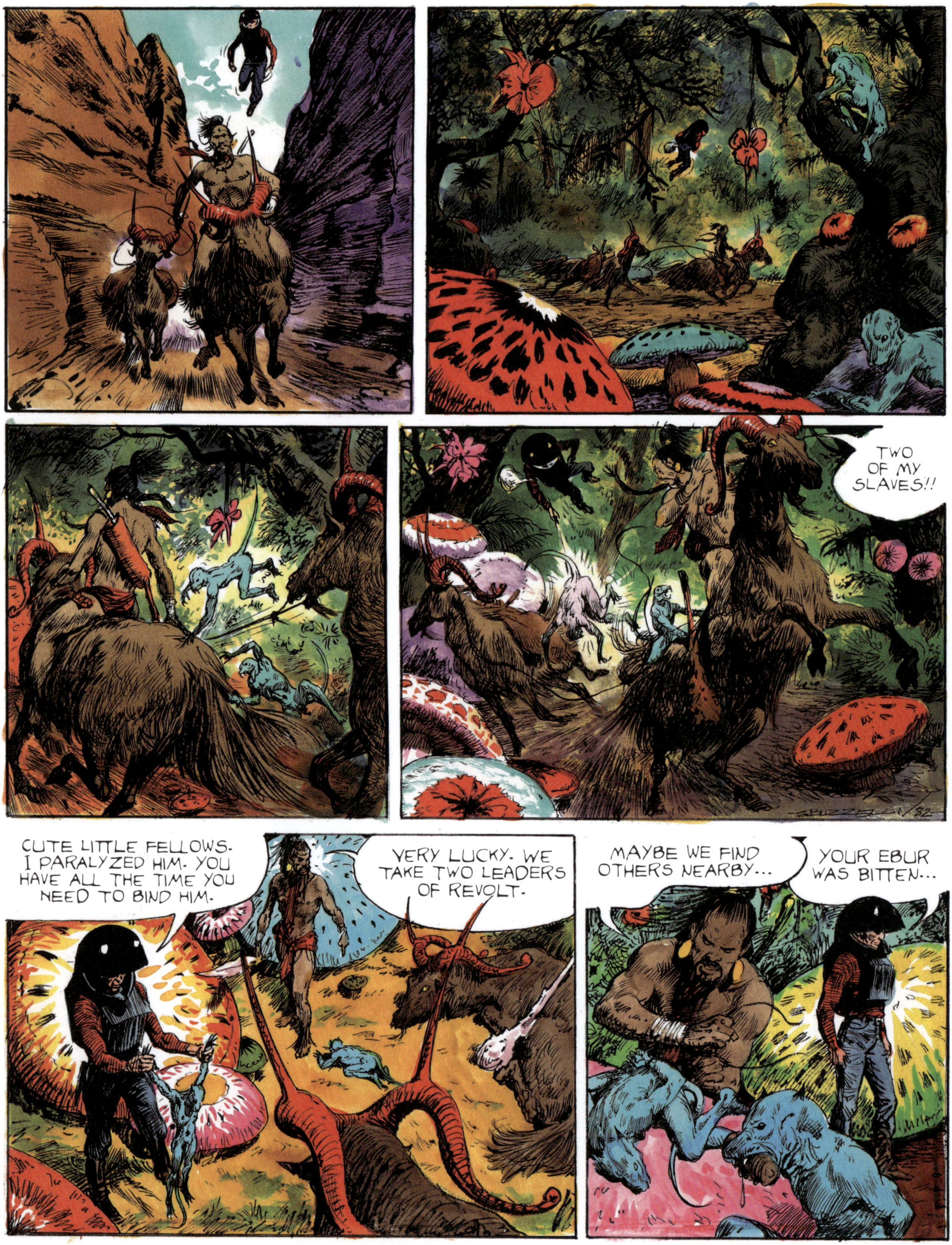
TWO OF MY SLAVES!!
CUTE LITTLE FELLOWS. I PARALYZED HIM. YOU HAVE ALL THE TIME YOU NEED TO BIND HIM.
VERY LUCKY. WE TAKE TWO LEADERS OF REVOLT.
MAYBE WE FIND OTHERS NEARBY...
YOUR EBUR WAS BITTEN...

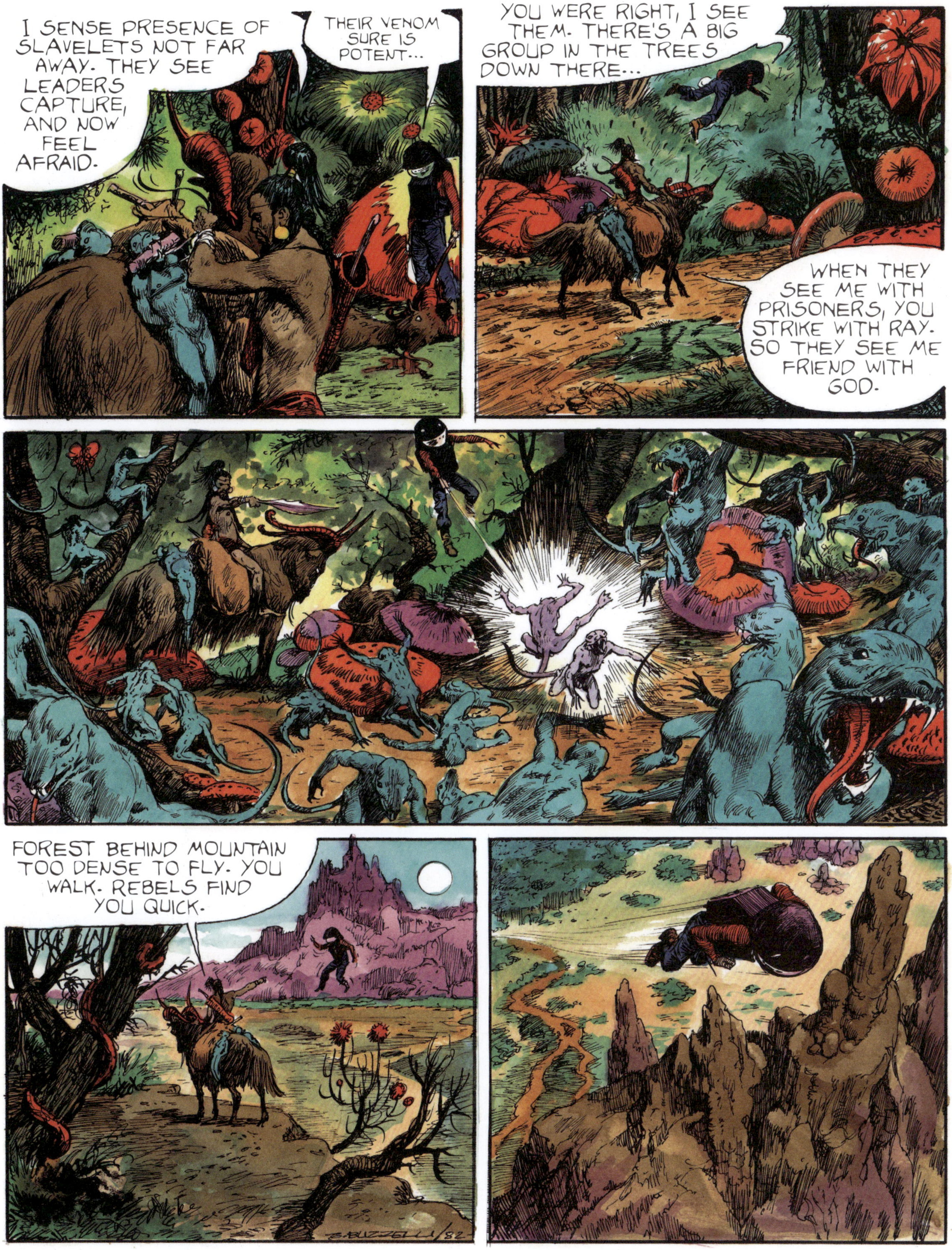
I SENSE PRESENCE OF SLAVELETS NOT FAR AWAY. THEY SEE LEADERS CAPTURE, AND NOW FEEL AFRAID.
THEIR VENOM SURE IS POTENT...
YOU WERE RIGHT, I SEE THEM. THERE'S A BIG GROUP IN THE TREES DOWN THERE...
WHEN THEY SEE ME WITH PRISONERS, YOU STRIKE WITH RAY. SO THEY SEE ME FRIEND WITH GOD.
FOREST BEHIND MOUNTAIN TOO DENSE TO FLY. YOU WALK. REBELS FIND YOU QUICK.
E. BUZZELLI /82

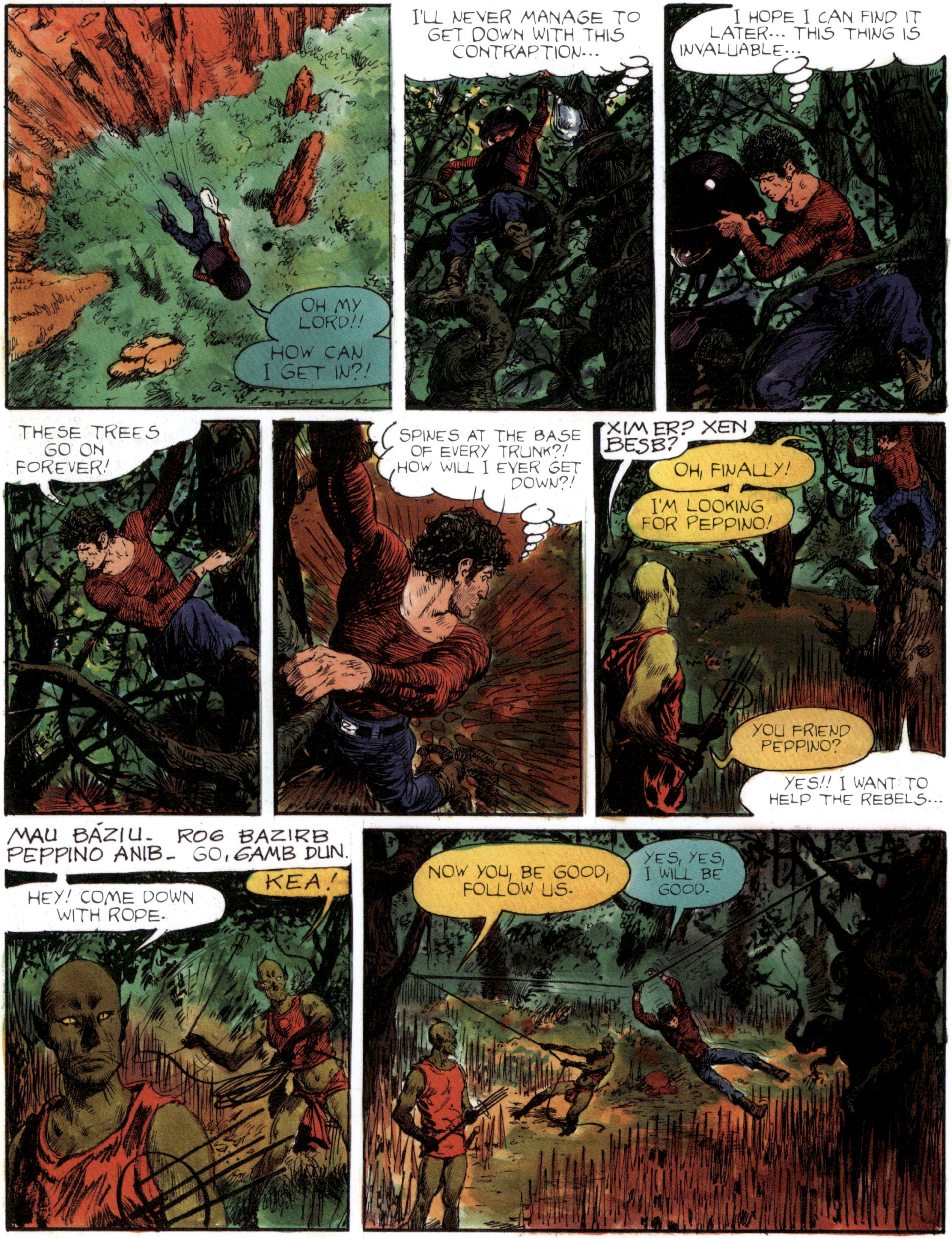
OH MY LORD!!
HOW CAN I GET IN?!
I'LL NEVER MANAGE TO GET DOWN WITH THIS CONTRAPTION...
I HOPE I CAN FIND IT LATER... THIS THING IS INVALUABLE...
THESE TREES GO ON FOREVER!
SPINES AT THE BASE OF EVERY TRUNK?! HOW WILL I EVER GET DOWN?!
XIM ER? XEN BESB?
OH, FINALLY!
I'M LOOKING FOR PEPPINO!
YOU FRIEND PEPPINO?
YES!! I WANT TO HELP THE REBELS...
MAU BÁZIU. ROG BAZIRB PEPPINO ANIB. GO, GAMB DUN.
KEA!
HEY! COME DOWN WITH ROPE.
NOW YOU, BE GOOD, FOLLOW US.
YES, YES, I WILL BE GOOD.

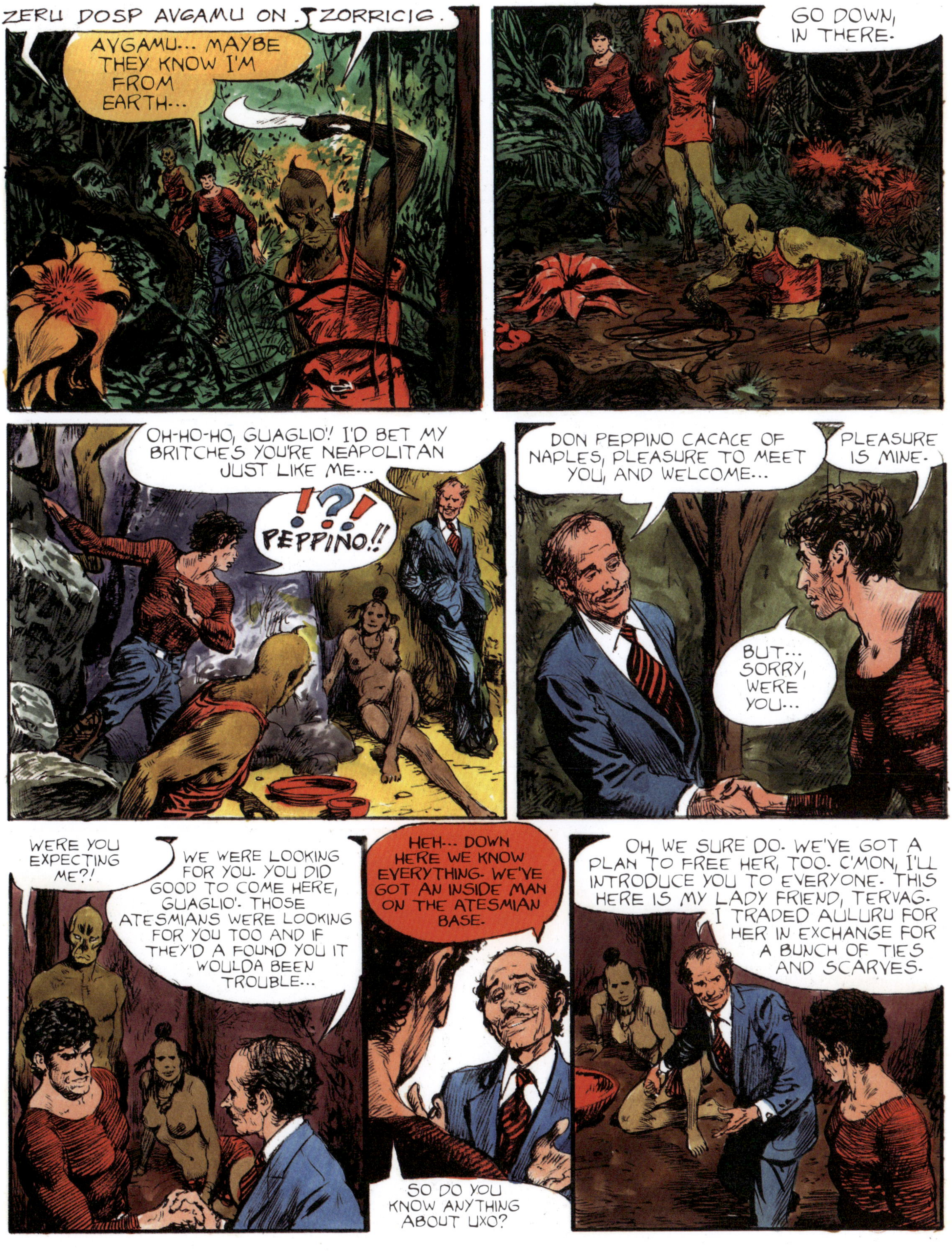
ZERU DOSP AVGAMU ON ZORRICIG.
AYGAMU... MAYBE THEY KNOW I'M FROM EARTH...
GO DOWN, IN THERE.
OH-HO-HO, GUAGLIO'! I'D BET MY BRITCHES YOU'RE NEAPOLITAN JUST LIKE ME...
!?!
PEPPINO!!
DON PEPPINO CACACE OF NAPLES, PLEASURE TO MEET YOU, AND WELCOME...
PLEASURE IS MINE.
BUT... SORRY, WERE YOU...
WERE YOU EXPECTING ME?!
WE WERE LOOKING FOR YOU. YOU DID GOOD TO COME HERE, GUAGLIO'. THOSE ATESMIANS WERE LOOKING FOR YOU TOO AND IF THEY'D A FOUND YOU IT WOULDA BEEN TROUBLE...
HEH... DOWN HERE WE KNOW EVERYTHING. WE'VE GOT AN INSIDE MAN ON THE ATESMIAN BASE.
SO DO YOU KNOW ANYTHING ABOUT UXO?
OH, WE SURE DO. WE'VE GOT A PLAN TO FREE HER, TOO. C'MON, I'LL INTRODUCE YOU TO EVERYONE. THIS HERE IS MY LADY FRIEND, TERVAG. I TRADED AULURU FOR HER IN EXCHANGE FOR A BUNCH OF TIES AND SCARVES.

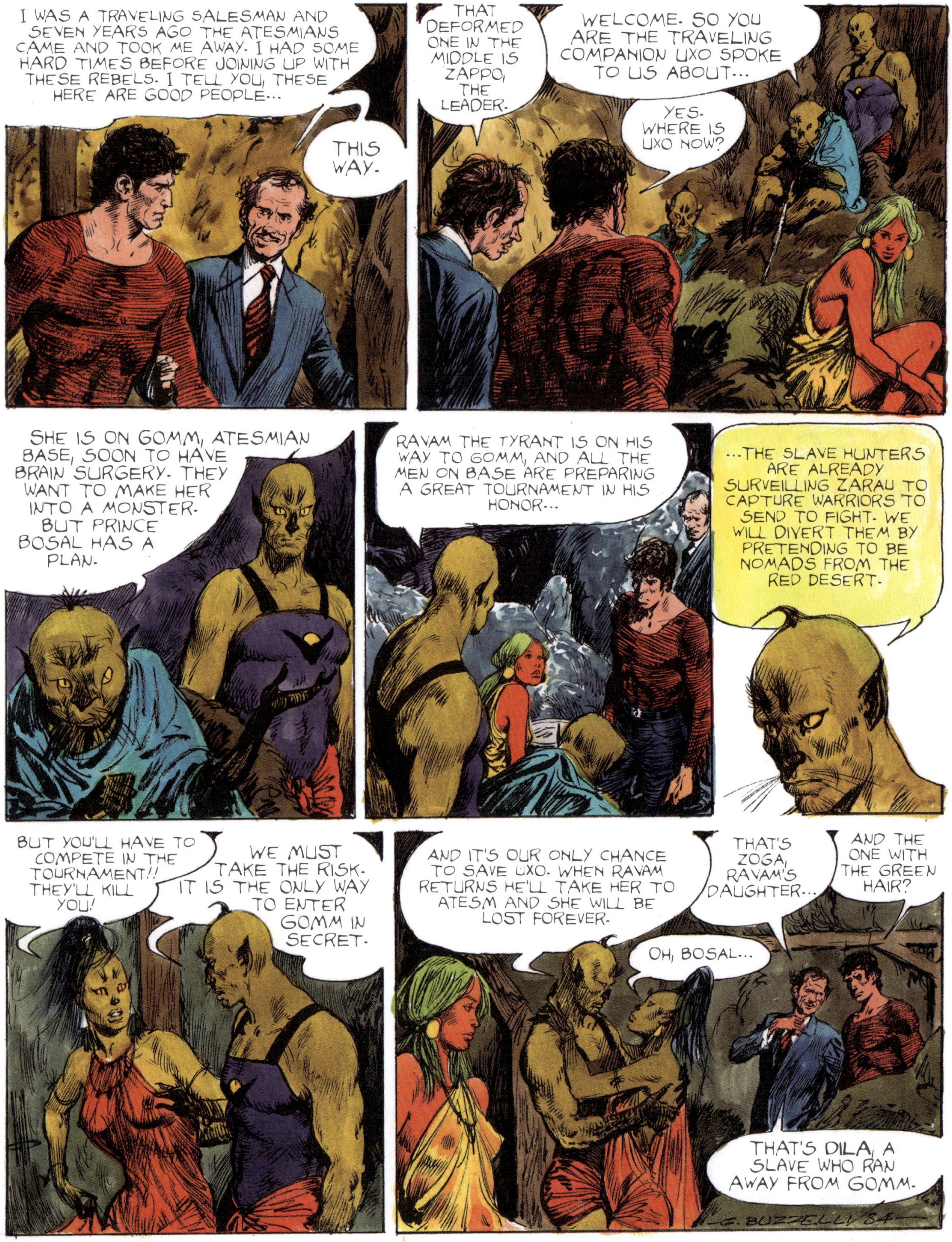
I WAS A TRAVELING SALESMAN AND SEVEN YEARS AGO THE ATESMIANS CAME AND TOOK ME AWAY. I HAD SOME HARD TIMES BEFORE JOINING UP WITH THESE REBELS. I TELL YOU, THESE HERE ARE GOOD PEOPLE...
THIS WAY.
THAT DEFORMED ONE IN THE MIDDLE IS ZAPPO, THE LEADER.
WELCOME. SO YOU ARE THE TRAVELING COMPANION UXO SPOKE TO US ABOUT...
YES. WHERE IS UXO NOW?
SHE IS ON GOMM, ATESMIAN BASE, SOON TO HAVE BRAIN SURGERY. THEY WANT TO MAKE HER INTO A MONSTER. BUT PRINCE BOSAL HAS A PLAN.
RAVAM THE TYRANT IS ON HIS WAY TO GOMM, AND ALL THE MEN ON BASE ARE PREPARING A GREAT TOURNAMENT IN HIS HONOR...
...THE SLAVE HUNTERS ARE ALREADY SURVEILLING ZARAU TO CAPTURE WARRIORS TO SEND TO FIGHT. WE WILL DIVERT THEM BY PRETENDING TO BE NOMADS FROM THE RED DESERT.
BUT YOU'LL HAVE TO COMPETE IN THE TOURNAMENT!! THEY'LL KILL YOU!
WE MUST TAKE THE RISK. IT IS THE ONLY WAY TO ENTER GOMM IN SECRET.
AND IT'S OUR ONLY CHANCE TO SAVE UXO. WHEN RAVAM RETURNS HE'LL TAKE HER TO ATESM AND SHE WILL BE LOST FOREVER.
OH, BOSAL...
THAT'S ZOGA, RAVAM'S DAUGHTER...
AND THE ONE WITH THE GREEN HAIR?
THAT'S DILA, A SLAVE WHO RAN AWAY FROM GOMM.
G. BUZZELLI '84

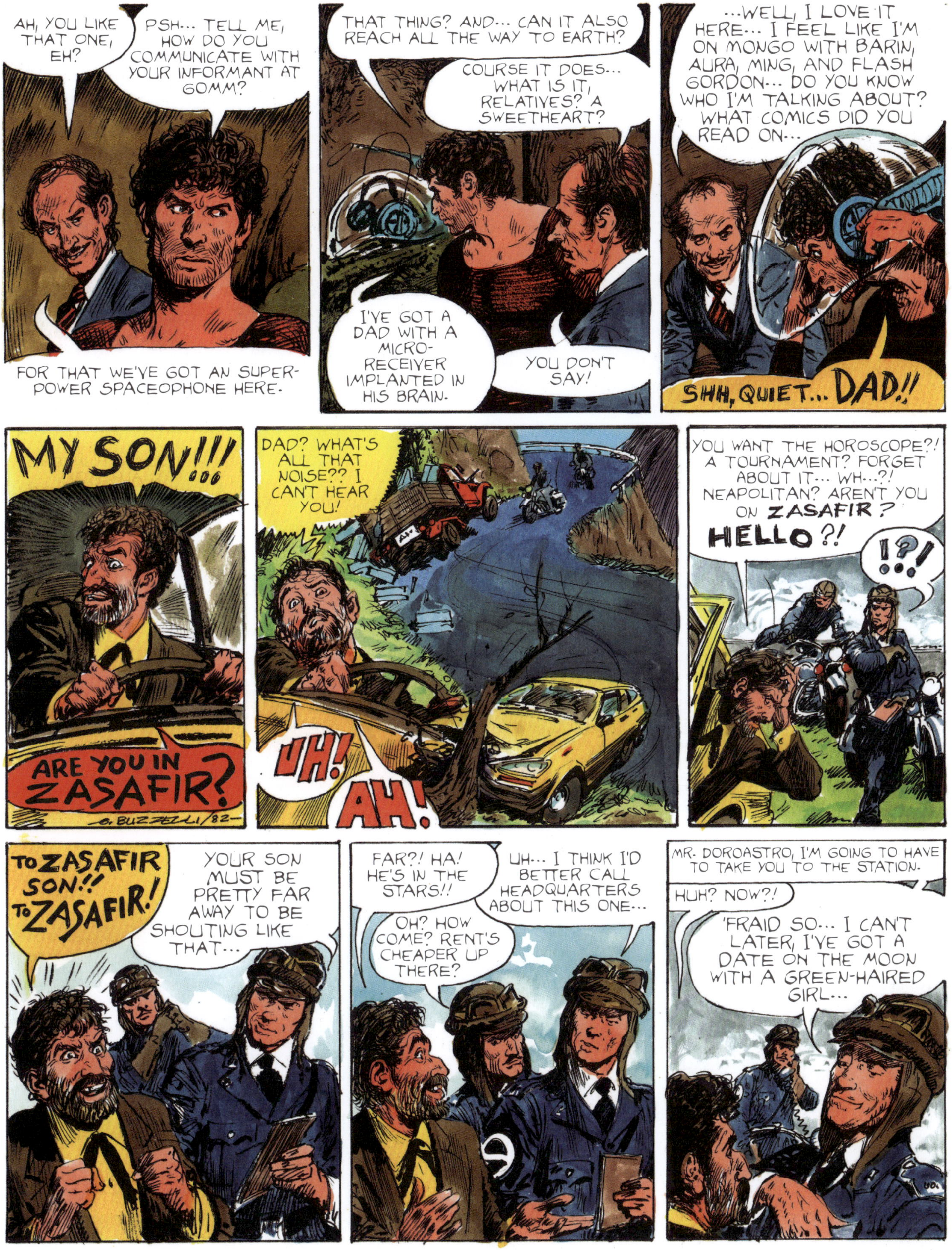
AH, YOU LIKE THAT ONE, EH?
PSH... TELL ME, HOW DO YOU COMMUNICATE WITH YOUR INFORMANT AT GOMM?
FOR THAT WE'VE GOT AN SUPER-POWER SPACEOPHONE HERE.
THAT THING? AND... CAN IT ALSO REACH ALL THE WAY TO EARTH?
COURSE IT DOES... WHAT IS IT, RELATIVES? A SWEETHEART?
I'VE GOT A DAD WITH A MICRO-RECEIVER IMPLANTED IN HIS BRAIN.
YOU DON'T SAY!
...WELL, I LOVE IT HERE... I FEEL LIKE I'M ON MONGO WITH BARIN, AURA, MING, AND FLASH GORDON... DO YOU KNOW WHO I'M TALKING ABOUT? WHAT COMICS DID YOU READ ON...
SHH, QUIET... DAD!!
MY SON!!!
ARE YOU IN ZASAFIR?
G. BUZZELLI /82
DAD? WHAT'S ALL THAT NOISE?? I CAN'T HEAR YOU!
UH! AH!
YOU WANT THE HOROSCOPE?! A TOURNAMENT? FORGET ABOUT IT... WH...?! NEAPOLITAN? AREN'T YOU ON ZASAFIR? HELLO?!
!?!
TO ZASAFIR SON!! TO ZASAFIR!
YOUR SON MUST BE PRETTY FAR AWAY TO BE SHOUTING LIKE THAT...
FAR?! HA! HE'S IN THE STARS!!
UH... I THINK I'D BETTER CALL HEADQUARTERS ABOUT THIS ONE...
OH? HOW COME? RENT'S CHEAPER UP THERE?
MR. DOROASTRO, I'M GOING TO HAVE TO TAKE YOU TO THE STATION.
HUH? NOW?!
'FRAID SO... I CAN'T LATER, I'VE GOT A DATE ON THE MOON WITH A GREEN-HAIRED GIRL...

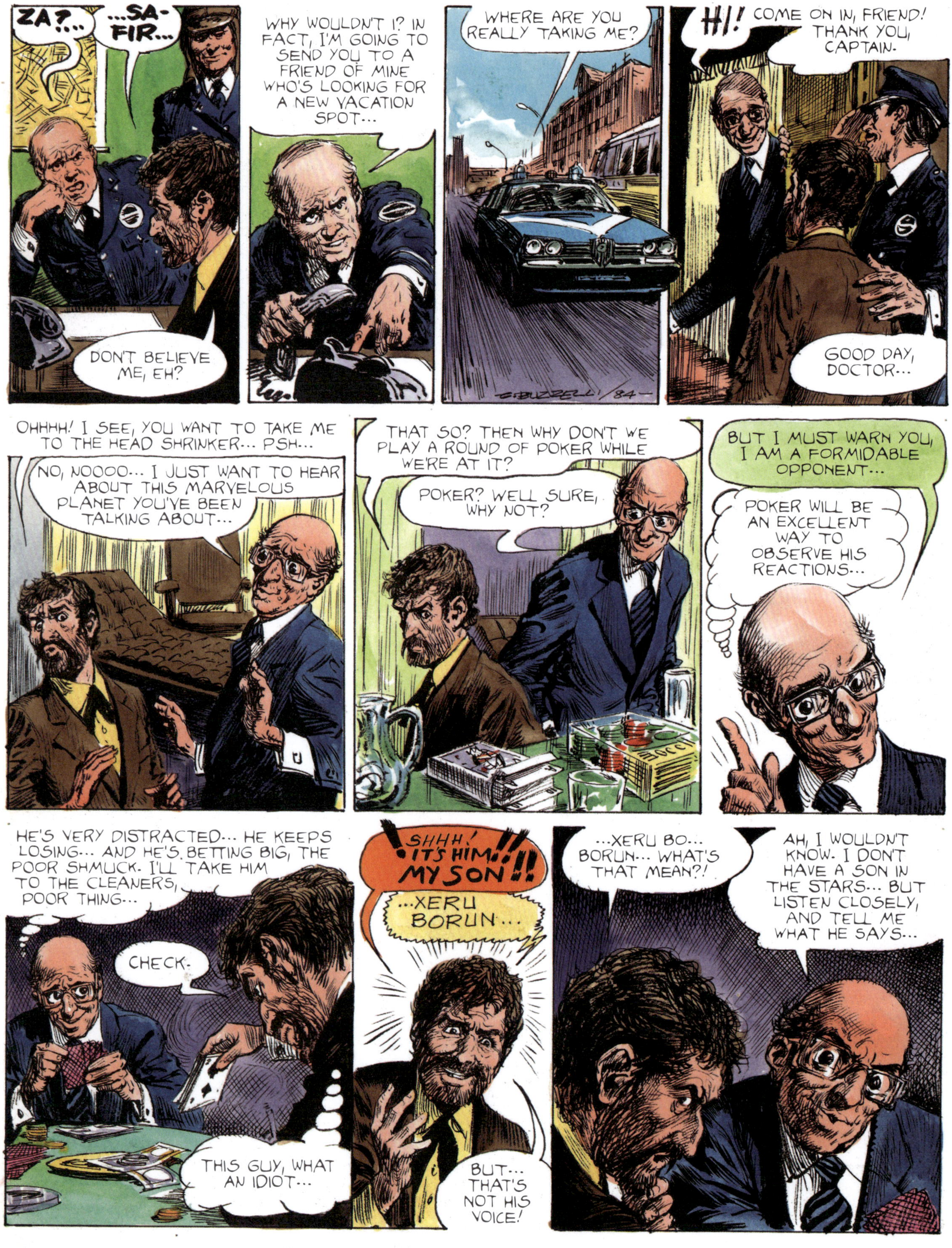
ZA?...
...SA-FIR...
DON'T BELIEVE ME, EH?
WHY WOULDN'T I? IN FACT, I'M GOING TO SEND YOU TO A FRIEND OF MINE WHO'S LOOKING FOR A NEW VACATION SPOT...
WHERE ARE YOU REALLY TAKING ME?
G. BUZZELLI /84
HI! COME ON IN, FRIEND! THANK YOU, CAPTAIN.
GOOD DAY, DOCTOR...
OHHHH! I SEE, YOU WANT TO TAKE ME TO THE HEAD SHRINKER... PSH...
NO, NOOOO... I JUST WANT TO HEAR ABOUT THIS MARVELOUS PLANET YOU'VE BEEN TALKING ABOUT...
THAT SO? THEN WHY DON'T WE PLAY A ROUND OF POKER WHILE WE'RE AT IT?
POKER? WELL SURE, WHY NOT?
BUT I MUST WARN YOU, I AM A FORMIDABLE OPPONENT...
POKER WILL BE AN EXCELLENT WAY TO OBSERVE HIS REACTIONS...
HE'S VERY DISTRACTED... HE KEEPS LOSING... AND HE'S BETTING BIG, THE POOR SHMUCK. I'LL TAKE HIM TO THE CLEANERS, POOR THING...
CHECK.
THIS GUY, WHAT AN IDIOT...
SHHH! IT'S HIM!! MY SON!!
...XERU BORUN...
BUT... THAT'S NOT HIS VOICE!
...XERU BO... BORUN... WHAT'S THAT MEAN?!
AH, I WOULDN'T KNOW. I DON'T HAVE A SON IN THE STARS... BUT LISTEN CLOSELY, AND TELL ME WHAT HE SAYS...

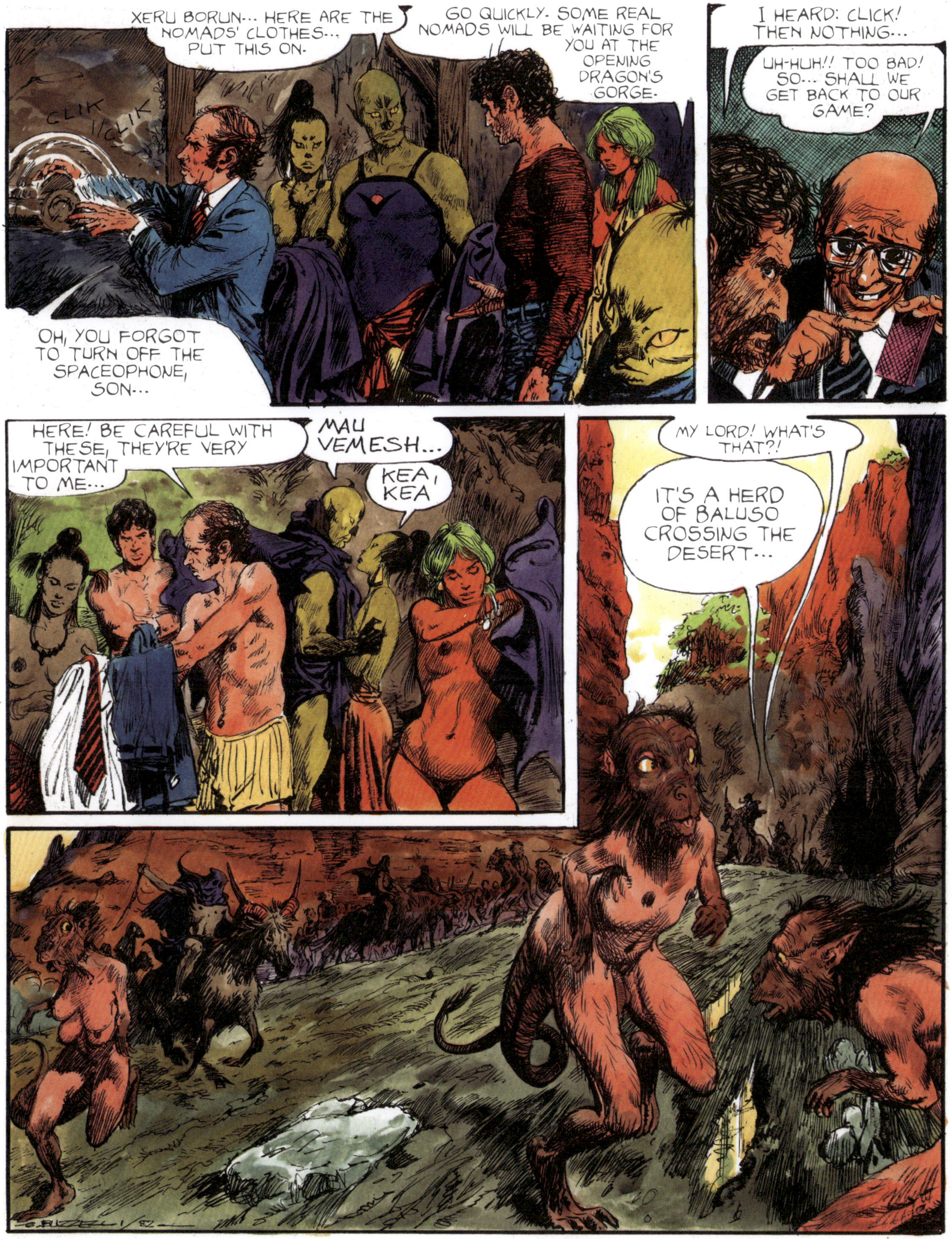
XERU BORUN... HERE ARE THE NOMADS' CLOTHES... PUT THIS ON.
GO QUICKLY. SOME REAL NOMADS WILL BE WAITING FOR YOU AT THE OPENING DRAGON'S GORGE.
CLIK CLIK
OH, YOU FORGOT TO TURN OFF THE SPACEOPHONE, SON...
I HEARD: CLICK! THEN NOTHING...
UH-HUH!! TOO BAD! SO... SHALL WE GET BACK TO OUR GAME?
HERE! BE CAREFUL WITH THESE, THEY'RE VERY IMPORTANT TO ME...
MAU VEMESH...
KEA, KEA
MY LORD! WHAT'S THAT?!
IT'S A HERD OF BALUSO CROSSING THE DESERT...

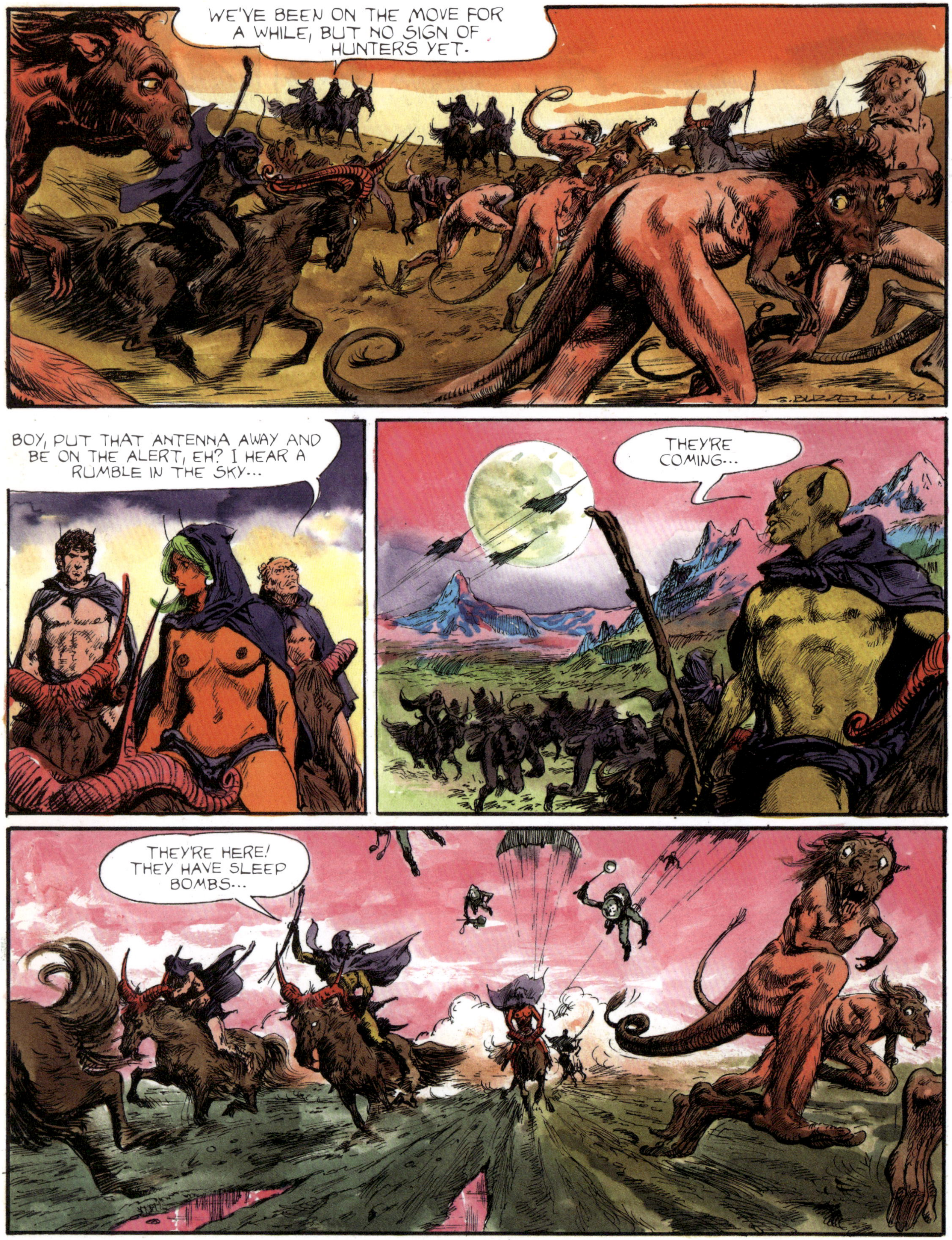
WE'VE BEEN ON THE MOVE FOR A WHILE, BUT NO SIGN OF HUNTERS YET.
BOY, PUT THAT ANTENNA AWAY AND BE ON THE ALERT, EH? I HEAR A RUMBLE IN THE SKY...
THEY'RE COMING...
THEY'RE HERE! THEY HAVE SLEEP BOMBS...

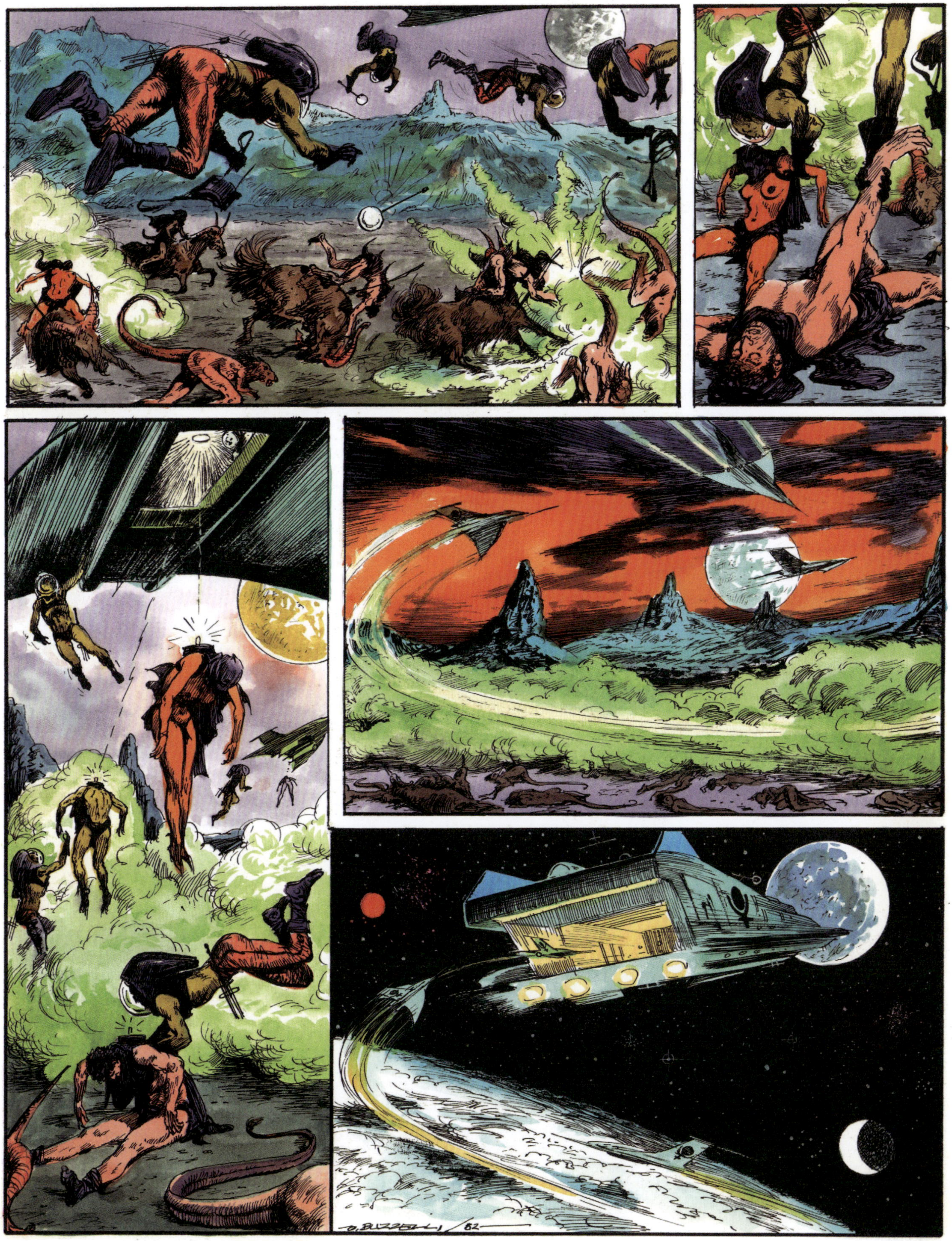
D. BUZZELLI /82

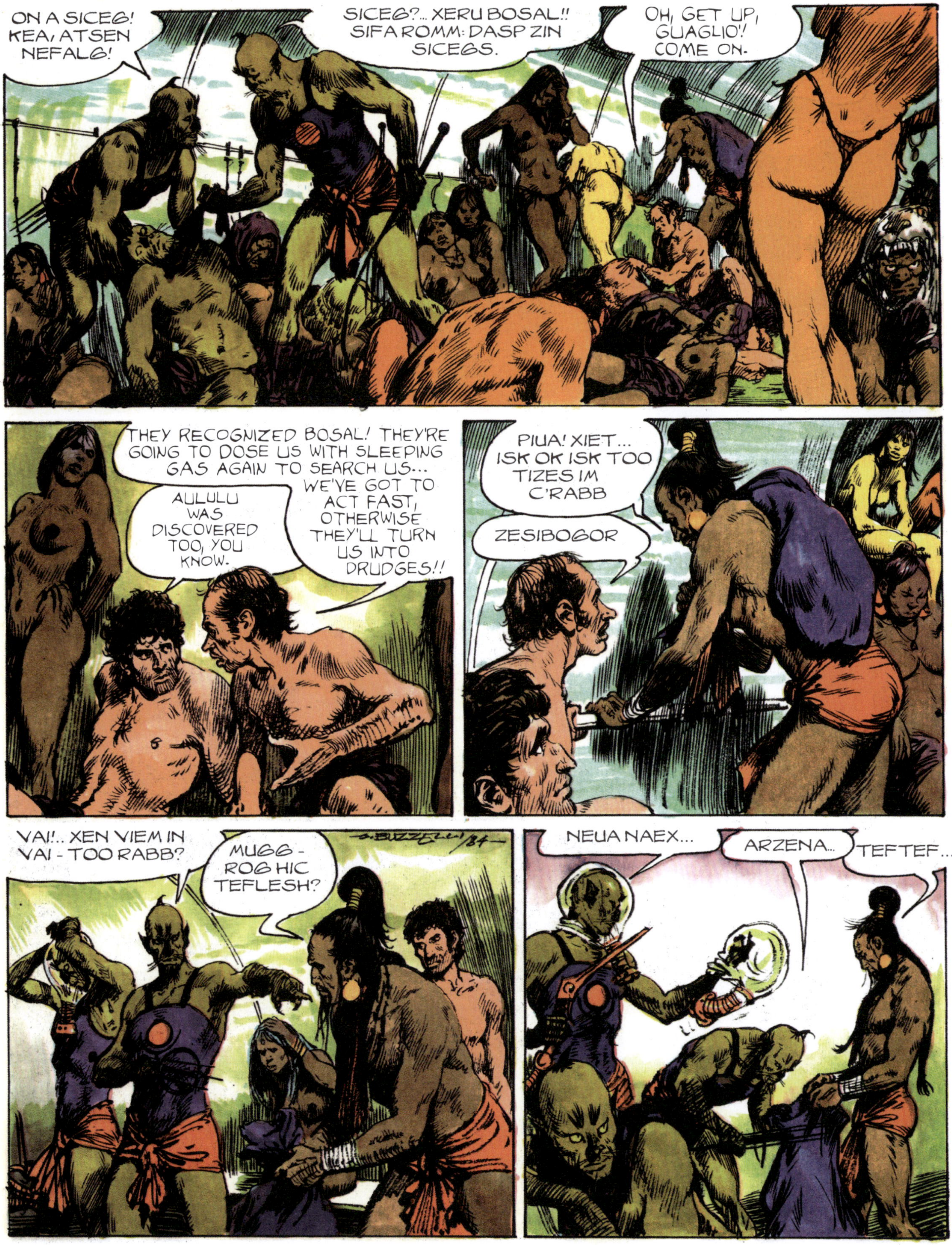

ON A SICEG! KEA, ATSEN NEFALG!
SICEG?... XERU BOSAL!! SIFA ROMM: DASP ZIN SICEGS.
OH, GET UP, GUAGLIO'! COME ON.
THEY RECOGNIZED BOSAL! THEY'RE GOING TO DOSE US WITH SLEEPING GAS AGAIN TO SEARCH US...
AULULU WAS DISCOVERED TOO, YOU KNOW.
WE'VE GOT TO ACT FAST, OTHERWISE THEY'LL TURN US INTO DRUDGES!!
PIUA! XIET... ISK OK ISK TOO TIZES IM C'RABB
ZESIBOGOR
VAI!.. XEN VIEM IN VAI - TOO RABB?
MUGG - ROG HIC TEFLESH?
NEUA NAEX...
ARZENA...
TEFTEF...

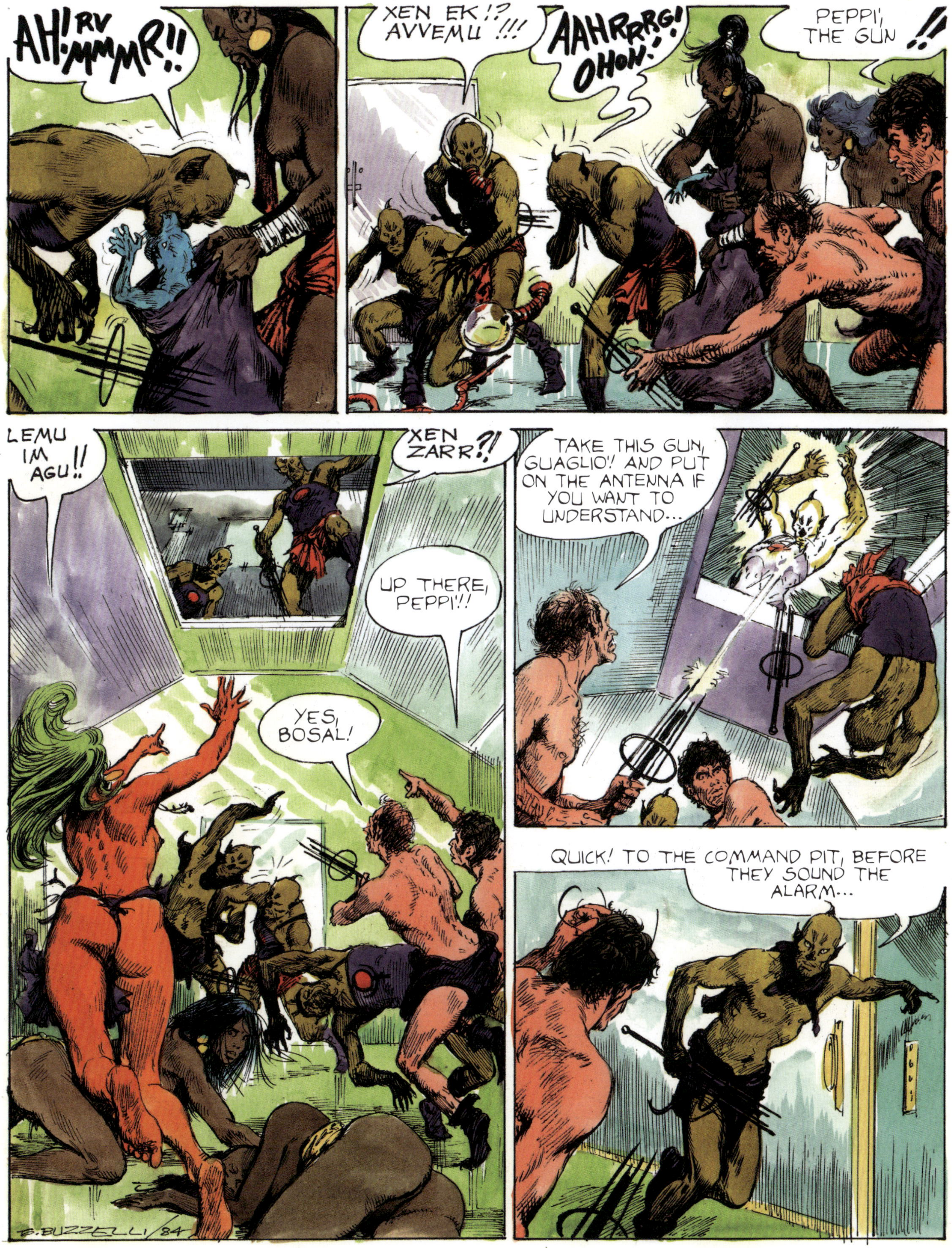
AH! RV MMMR!!
XEN EK!? AVVEMU!!!
AAHRRRG! OHON!!
PEPPI, THE GUN!!
LEMU IM AGU!!
XEN ZARR?!
TAKE THIS GUN, GUAGLIO'! AND PUT ON THE ANTENNA IF YOU WANT TO UNDERSTAND...
UP THERE, PEPPI!!
YES, BOSAL!
QUICK! TO THE COMMAND PIT, BEFORE THEY SOUND THE ALARM...
B. BUZZELLI/84

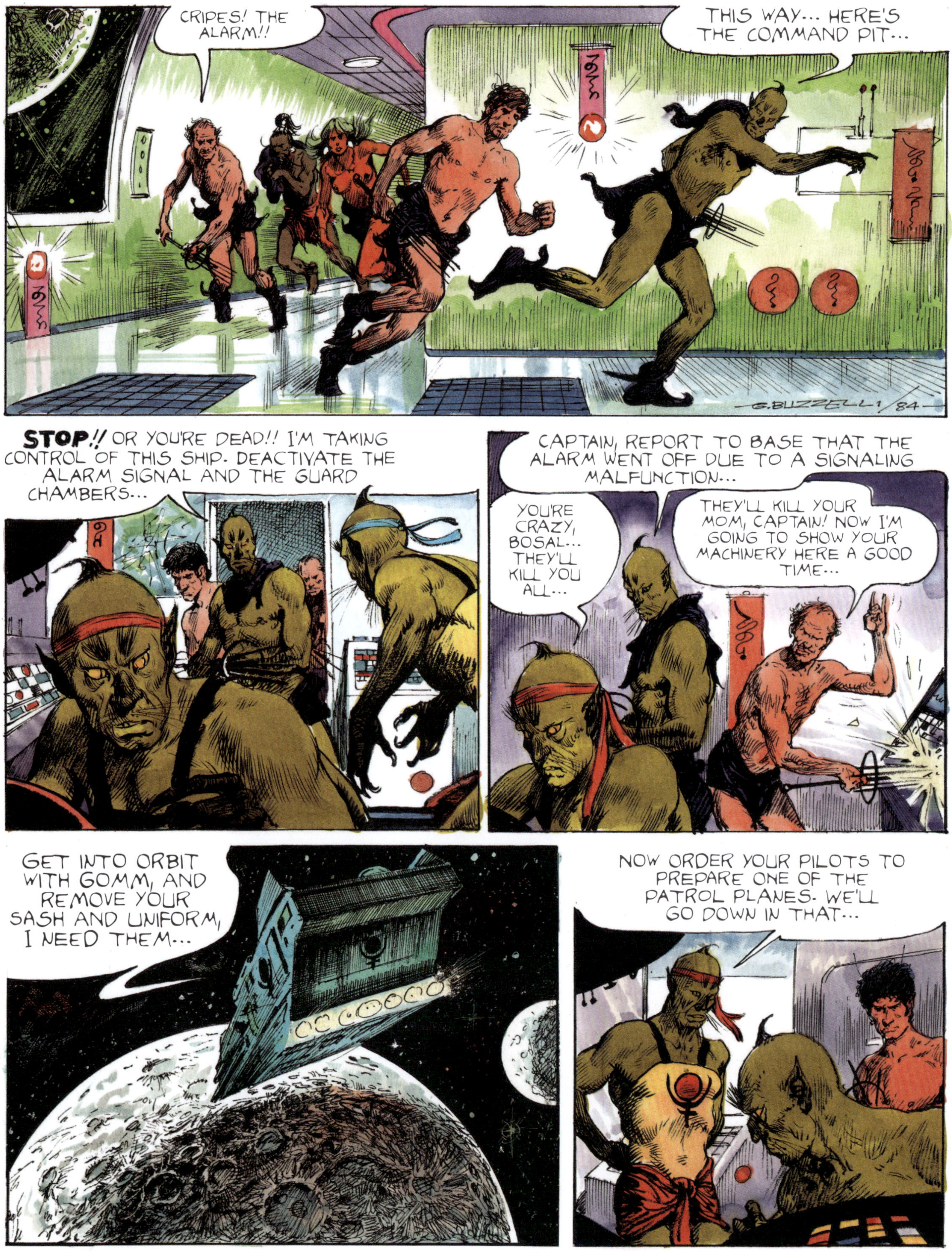
CRIPES! THE ALARM!!
THIS WAY... HERE'S THE COMMAND PIT...
G. BUZZELLI /84
STOP!! OR YOU'RE DEAD!! I'M TAKING CONTROL OF THIS SHIP. DEACTIVATE THE ALARM SIGNAL AND THE GUARD CHAMBERS...
CAPTAIN, REPORT TO BASE THAT THE ALARM WENT OFF DUE TO A SIGNALING MALFUNCTION...
YOU'RE CRAZY, BOSAL... THEY'LL KILL YOU ALL...
THEY'LL KILL YOUR MOM, CAPTAIN! NOW I'M GOING TO SHOW YOUR MACHINERY HERE A GOOD TIME...
GET INTO ORBIT WITH GOMM, AND REMOVE YOUR SASH AND UNIFORM, I NEED THEM...
NOW ORDER YOUR PILOTS TO PREPARE ONE OF THE PATROL PLANES. WE'LL GO DOWN IN THAT...

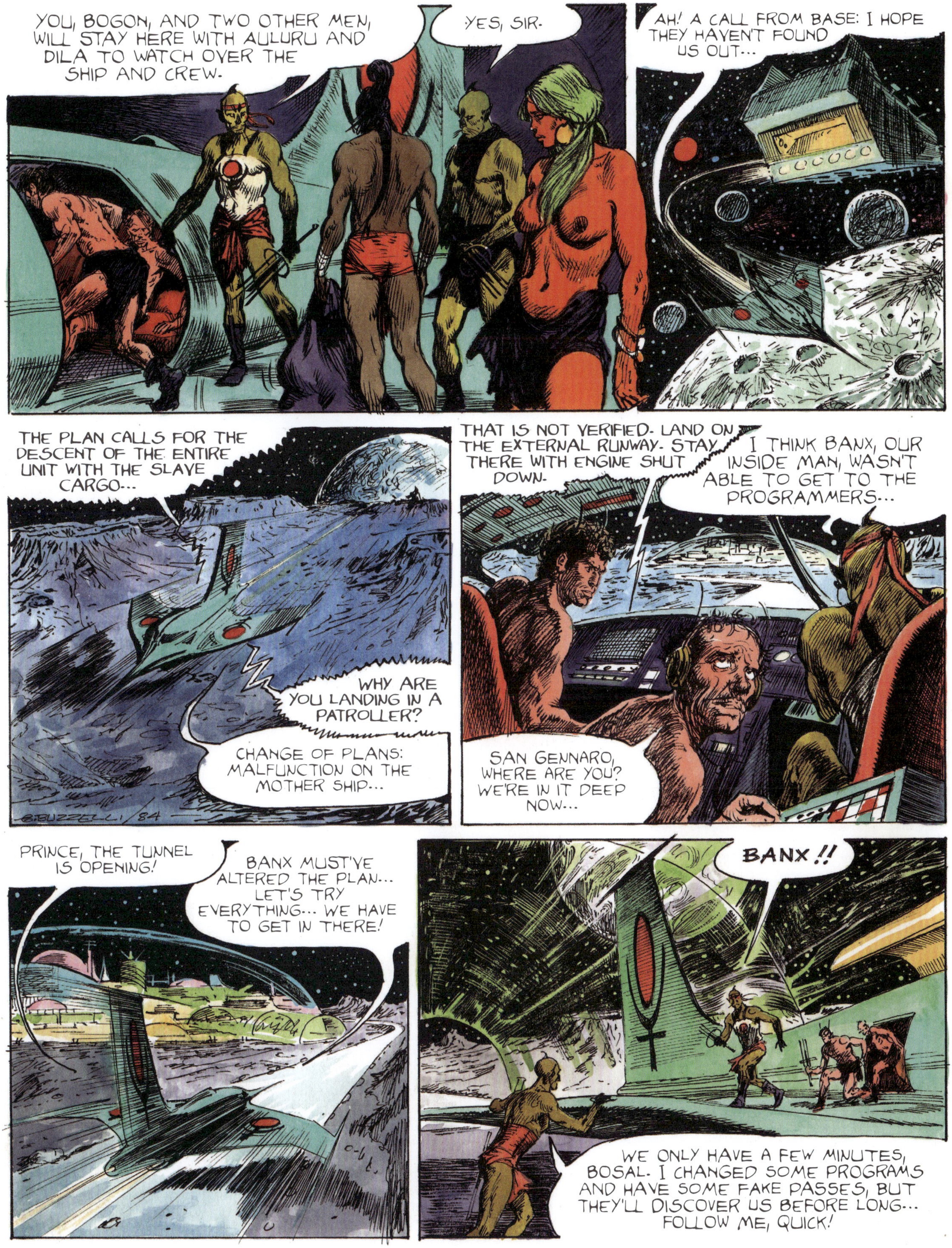
YOU, BOGON, AND TWO OTHER MEN, WILL STAY HERE WITH AULURU AND DILA TO WATCH OVER THE SHIP AND CREW.
YES, SIR.
AH! A CALL FROM BASE: I HOPE THEY HAVEN'T FOUND US OUT...
THE PLAN CALLS FOR THE DESCENT OF THE ENTIRE UNIT WITH THE SLAVE CARGO...
WHY ARE YOU LANDING IN A PATROLLER?
CHANGE OF PLANS: MALFUNCTION ON THE MOTHER SHIP...
G. BUZZELLI /84
THAT IS NOT VERIFIED. LAND ON THE EXTERNAL RUNWAY. STAY THERE WITH ENGINE SHUT DOWN.
I THINK BANX, OUR INSIDE MAN, WASN'T ABLE TO GET TO THE PROGRAMMERS...
SAN GENNARO, WHERE ARE YOU? WE'RE IN IT DEEP NOW...
PRINCE, THE TUNNEL IS OPENING!
BANX MUST'VE ALTERED THE PLAN... LET'S TRY EVERYTHING... WE HAVE TO GET IN THERE!
BANX!!
WE ONLY HAVE A FEW MINUTES, BOSAL. I CHANGED SOME PROGRAMS AND HAVE SOME FAKE PASSES, BUT THEY'LL DISCOVER US BEFORE LONG... FOLLOW ME, QUICK!

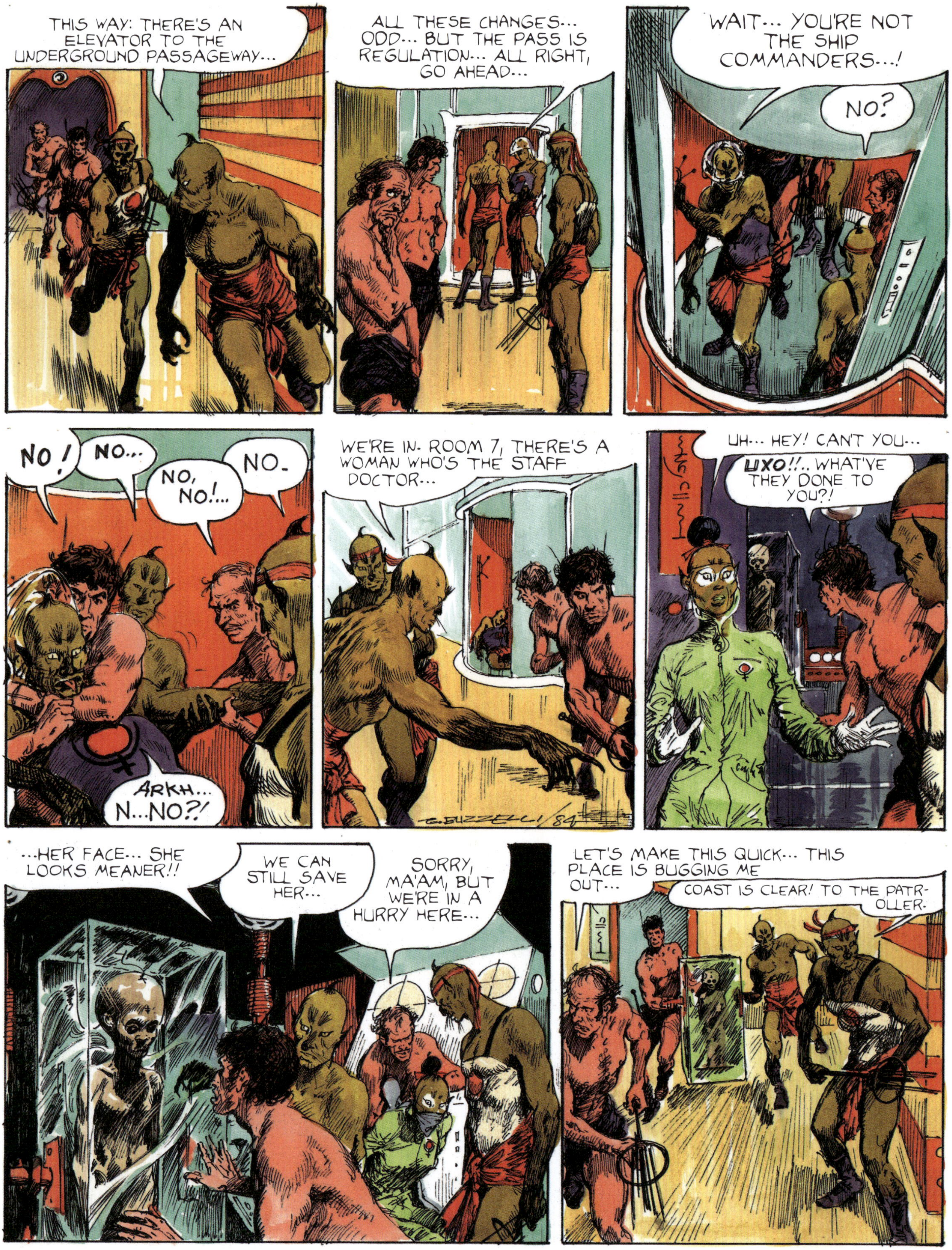
THIS WAY: THERE'S AN ELEVATOR TO THE UNDERGROUND PASSAGEWAY...
ALL THESE CHANGES... ODD... BUT THE PASS IS REGULATION... ALL RIGHT, GO AHEAD...
WAIT... YOU'RE NOT THE SHIP COMMANDERS...!
NO?
NO!
NO...
NO, NO!...
NO-
ARKH... N...NO?!
WE'RE IN ROOM 7, THERE'S A WOMAN WHO'S THE STAFF DOCTOR...
G. BUZZELLI '84
UH... HEY! CAN'T YOU...
UXO!!.. WHAT'VE THEY DONE TO YOU?!
...HER FACE... SHE LOOKS MEANER!!
WE CAN STILL SAVE HER...
SORRY, MA'AM, BUT WE'RE IN A HURRY HERE...
LET'S MAKE THIS QUICK... THIS PLACE IS BUGGING ME OUT...
COAST IS CLEAR! TO THE PATR-OLLER.

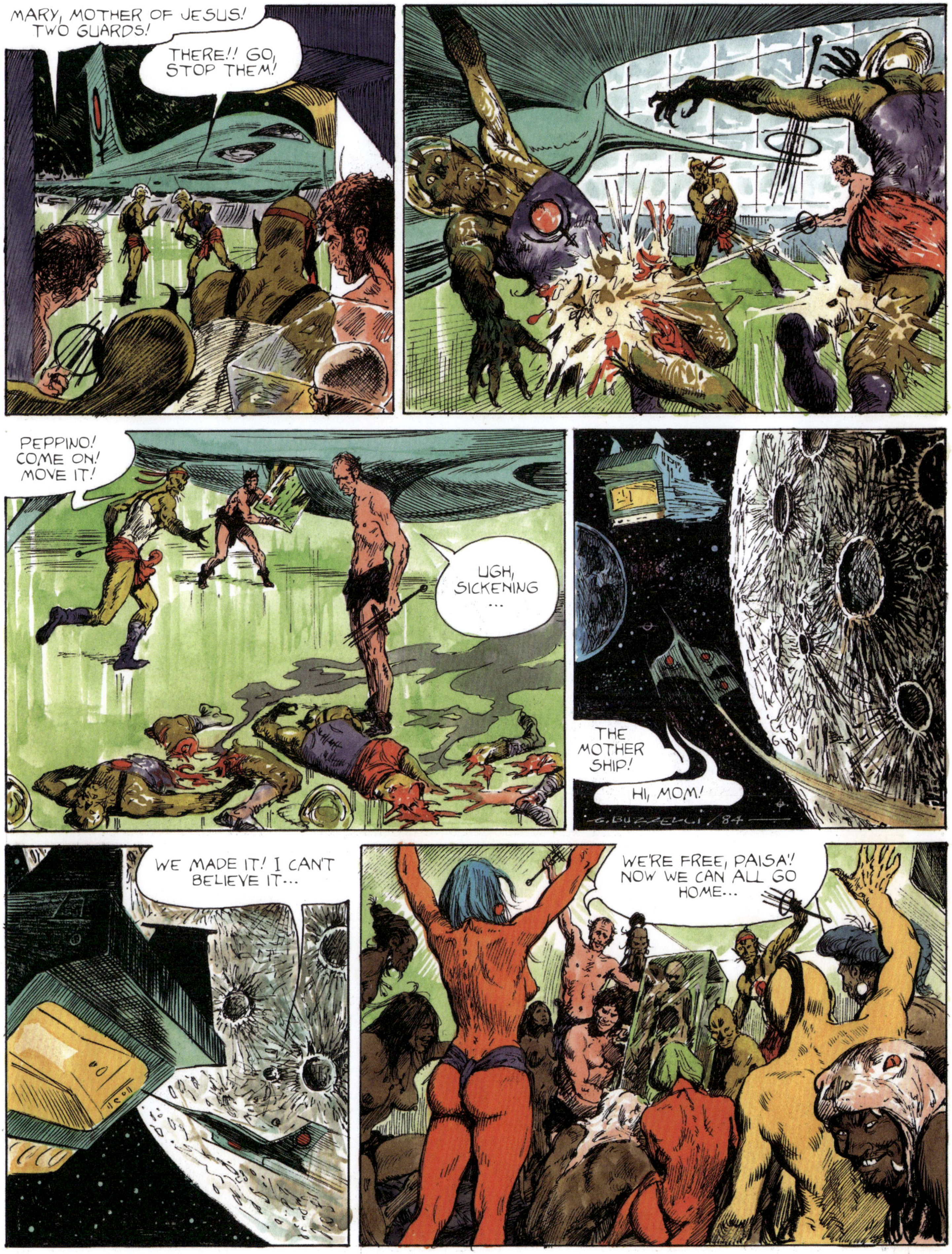
MARY, MOTHER OF JESUS! TWO GUARDS!
THERE!! GO, STOP THEM!
PEPPINO! COME ON! MOVE IT!
UGH, SICKENING ...
THE MOTHER SHIP!
HI, MOM!
G. BUZZELLI / 84
WE MADE IT! I CAN'T BELIEVE IT...
WE'RE FREE, PAISA'! NOW WE CAN ALL GO HOME...

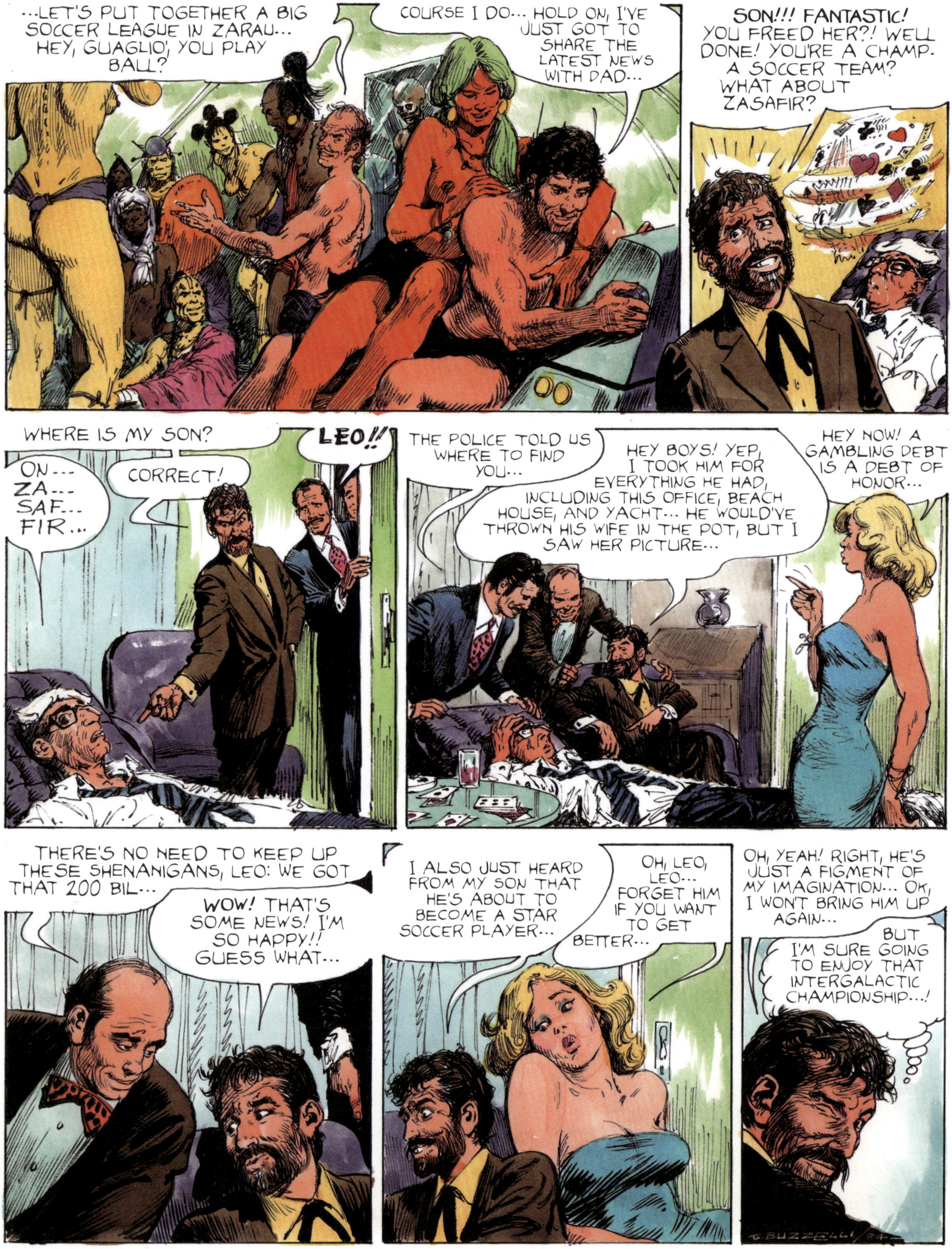
...LET'S PUT TOGETHER A BIG SOCCER LEAGUE IN ZARAU... HEY, GUAGLIO', YOU PLAY BALL?
COURSE I DO... HOLD ON, I'VE JUST GOT TO SHARE THE LATEST NEWS WITH DAD...
SON!!! FANTASTIC! YOU FREED HER?! WELL DONE! YOU'RE A CHAMP- A SOCCER TEAM? WHAT ABOUT ZASAFIR?
WHERE IS MY SON?
LEO!!
ON... ZA... SAF... FIR...
CORRECT!
THE POLICE TOLD US WHERE TO FIND YOU...
HEY BOYS! YEP, I TOOK HIM FOR EVERYTHING HE HAD, INCLUDING THIS OFFICE, BEACH HOUSE, AND YACHT... HE WOULD'VE THROWN HIS WIFE IN THE POT, BUT I SAW HER PICTURE...
HEY NOW! A GAMBLING DEBT IS A DEBT OF HONOR...
THERE'S NO NEED TO KEEP UP THESE SHENANIGANS, LEO: WE GOT THAT 200 BIL...
WOW! THAT'S SOME NEWS! I'M SO HAPPY!! GUESS WHAT...
I ALSO JUST HEARD FROM MY SON THAT HE'S ABOUT TO BECOME A STAR SOCCER PLAYER...
OH, LEO, LEO... FORGET HIM IF YOU WANT TO GET BETTER...
OH, YEAH! RIGHT, HE'S JUST A FIGMENT OF MY IMAGINATION... OK, I WON'T BRING HIM UP AGAIN...
BUT I'M SURE GOING TO ENJOY THAT INTERGALACTIC CHAMPIONSHIP...!
G. BUZZELLI / 84

The Incomplete Zasafir

(1984)

The following pages were recently rediscovered and published for the first time in Italy in 2017. They are a continuation of the previously published *Zasafir* story, which Buzzelli began working on in 1984.

The story, alas, remains unfinished.

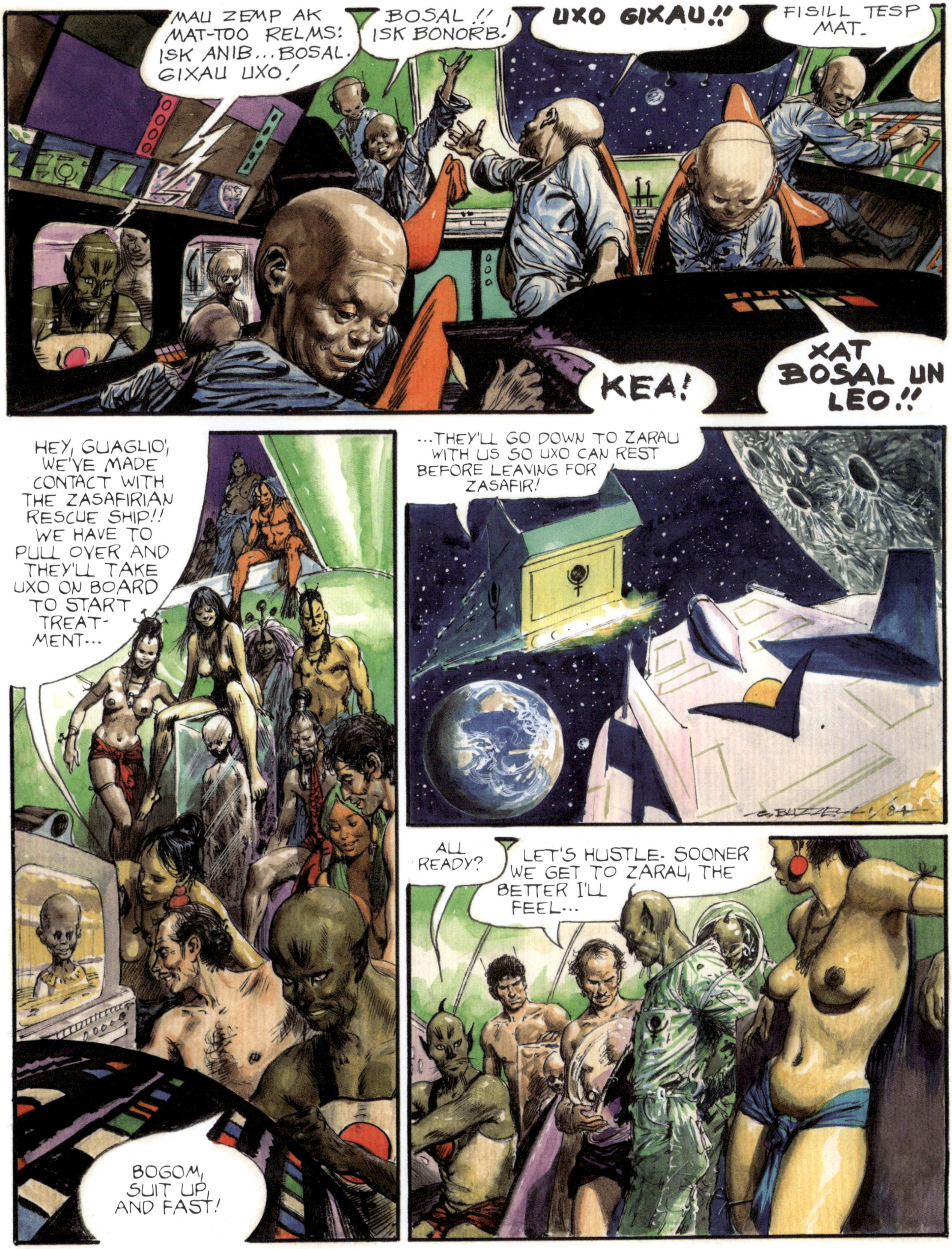
MAU ZEMP AK MAT-TOO RELMS: ISK ANIB... BOSAL. GIXAU UXO!
BOSAL!! ISK BONORB!
UXO GIXAU!!
FISILL TESP MAT.
KEA!
XAT BOSAL UN LEO!!
HEY, GUAGLIO', WE'VE MADE CONTACT WITH THE ZASAFIRIAN RESCUE SHIP!! WE HAVE TO PULL OVER AND THEY'LL TAKE UXO ON BOARD TO START TREAT-MENT...
BOGOM, SUIT UP, AND FAST!
...THEY'LL GO DOWN TO ZARAU WITH US SO UXO CAN REST BEFORE LEAVING FOR ZASAFIR!
ALL READY?
LET'S HUSTLE. SOONER WE GET TO ZARAU, THE BETTER I'LL FEEL...

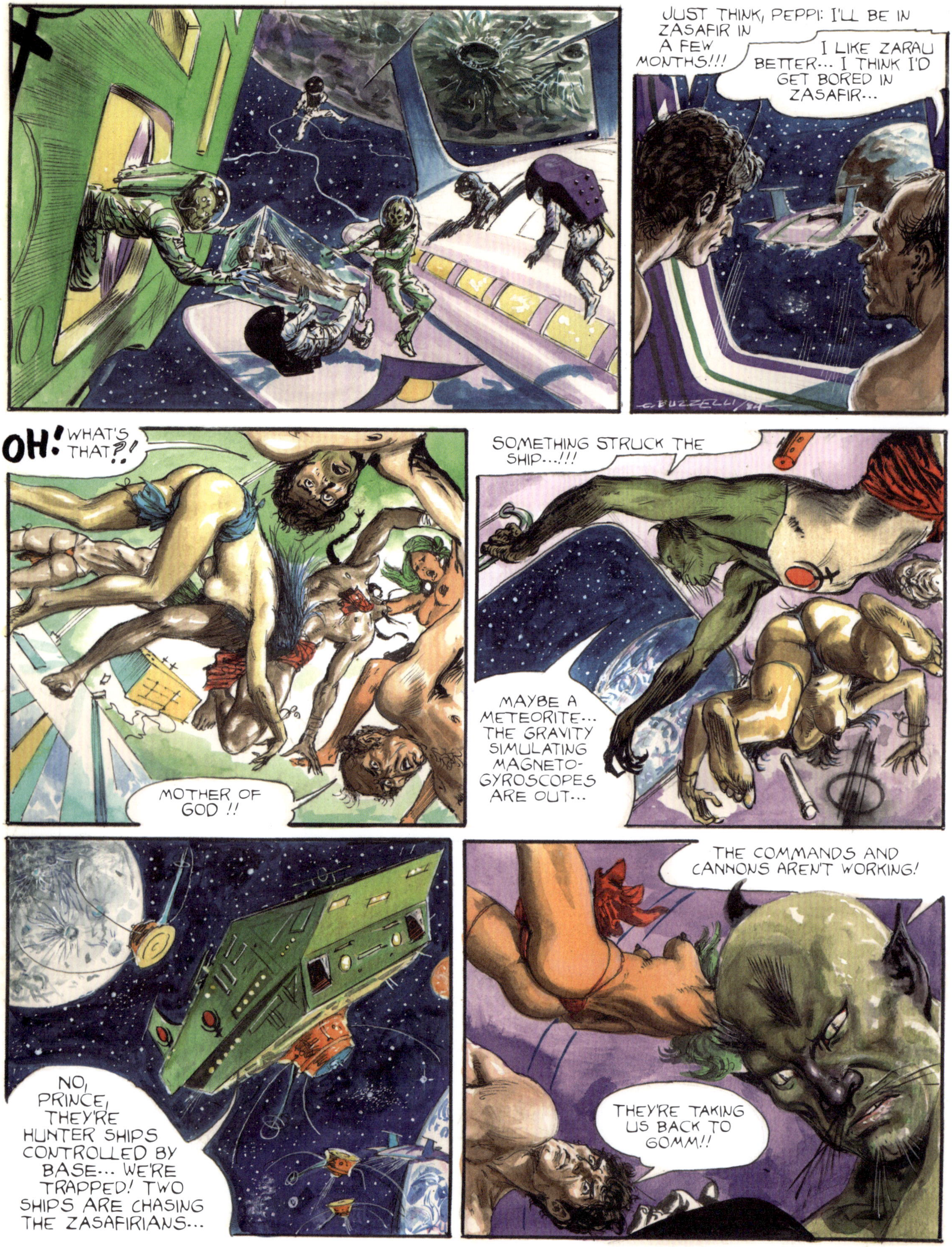

JUST THINK, PEPPI: I'LL BE IN ZASAFIR IN A FEW MONTHS!!!
I LIKE ZARAU BETTER... I THINK I'D GET BORED IN ZASAFIR...
G. BUZZELLI/84
OH! WHAT'S THAT?!
MOTHER OF GOD !!
SOMETHING STRUCK THE SHIP...!!!
MAYBE A METEORITE... THE GRAVITY SIMULATING MAGNETO-GYROSCOPES ARE OUT...
NO, PRINCE, THEY'RE HUNTER SHIPS CONTROLLED BY BASE... WE'RE TRAPPED! TWO SHIPS ARE CHASING THE ZASAFIRIANS...
THE COMMANDS AND CANNONS AREN'T WORKING!
THEY'RE TAKING US BACK TO GOMM!!

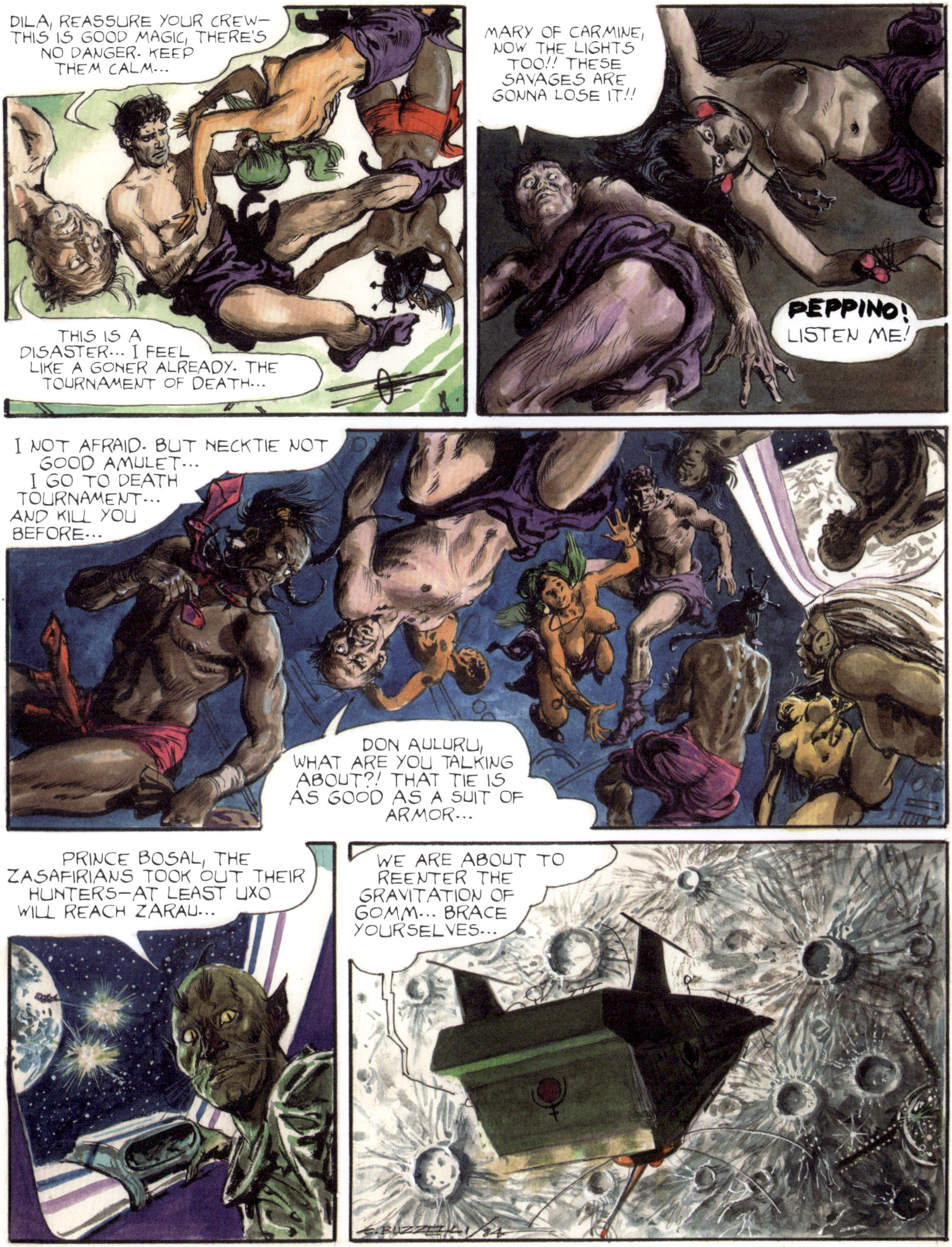

DILA, REASSURE YOUR CREW— THIS IS GOOD MAGIC, THERE'S NO DANGER. KEEP THEM CALM...
THIS IS A DISASTER... I FEEL LIKE A GONER ALREADY. THE TOURNAMENT OF DEATH...
MARY OF CARMINE, NOW THE LIGHTS TOO!! THESE SAVAGES ARE GONNA LOSE IT!!
PEPPINO! LISTEN ME!
I NOT AFRAID. BUT NECKTIE NOT GOOD AMULET... I GO TO DEATH TOURNAMENT... AND KILL YOU BEFORE...
DON AULURU, WHAT ARE YOU TALKING ABOUT?! THAT TIE IS AS GOOD AS A SUIT OF ARMOR...
PRINCE BOSAL, THE ZASAFIRIANS TOOK OUT THEIR HUNTERS—AT LEAST UXO WILL REACH ZARAU...
WE ARE ABOUT TO REENTER THE GRAVITATION OF GOMM... BRACE YOURSELVES...

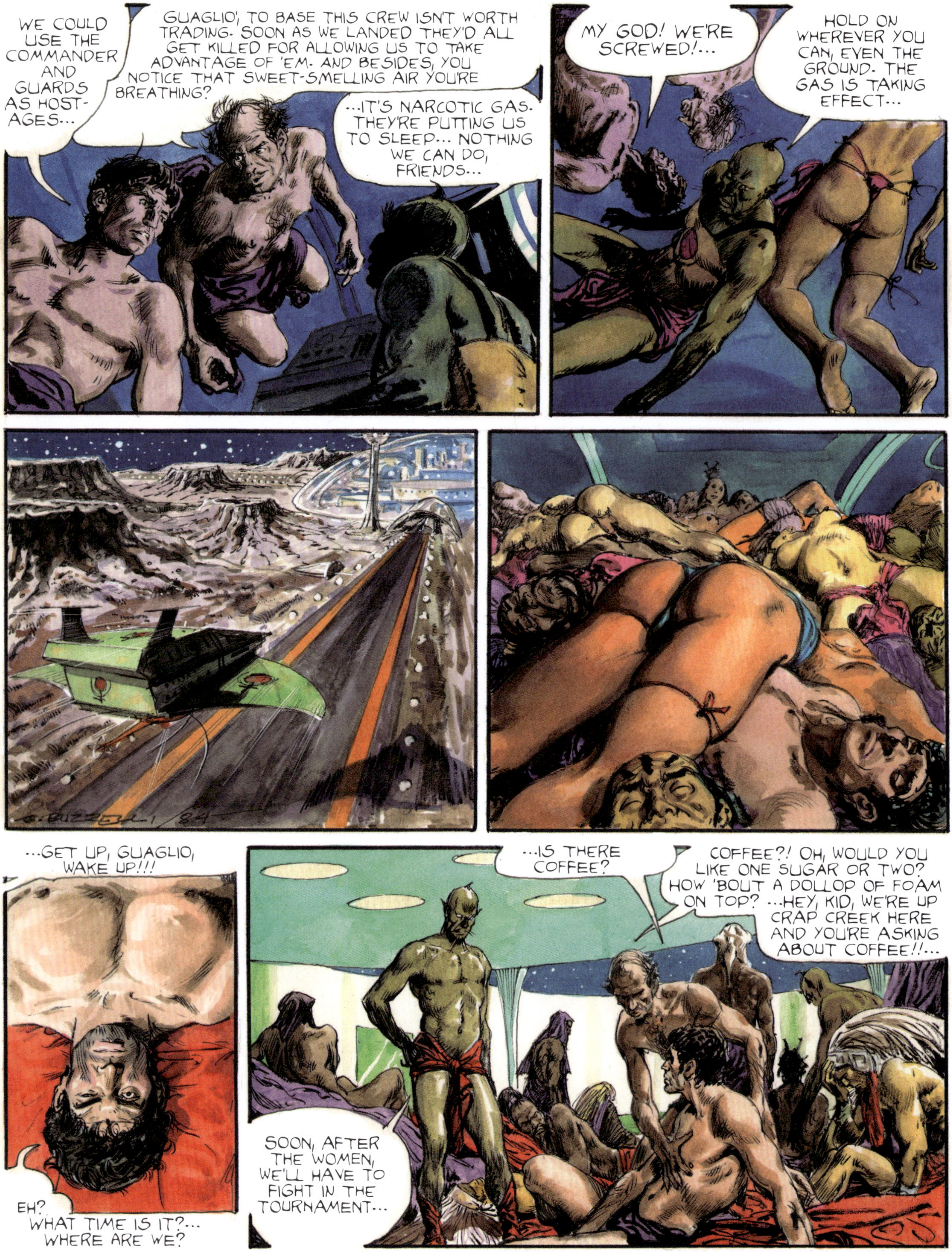
WE COULD USE THE COMMANDER AND GUARDS AS HOSTAGES...
GUAGLIO', TO BASE THIS CREW ISN'T WORTH TRADING. SOON AS WE LANDED THEY'D ALL GET KILLED FOR ALLOWING US TO TAKE ADVANTAGE OF 'EM. AND BESIDES, YOU NOTICE THAT SWEET-SMELLING AIR YOU'RE BREATHING?
...IT'S NARCOTIC GAS. THEY'RE PUTTING US TO SLEEP... NOTHING WE CAN DO, FRIENDS...
MY GOD! WE'RE SCREWED!...
HOLD ON WHEREVER YOU CAN, EVEN THE GROUND. THE GAS IS TAKING EFFECT...
G. BUZZELLI '84
...GET UP, GUAGLIO, WAKE UP!!!
EH? WHAT TIME IS IT?... WHERE ARE WE?
...IS THERE COFFEE?
COFFEE?! OH, WOULD YOU LIKE ONE SUGAR OR TWO? HOW 'BOUT A DOLLOP OF FOAM ON TOP? ...HEY, KID, WE'RE UP CRAP CREEK HERE AND YOU'RE ASKING ABOUT COFFEE!!...
SOON, AFTER THE WOMEN, WE'LL HAVE TO FIGHT IN THE TOURNAMENT...

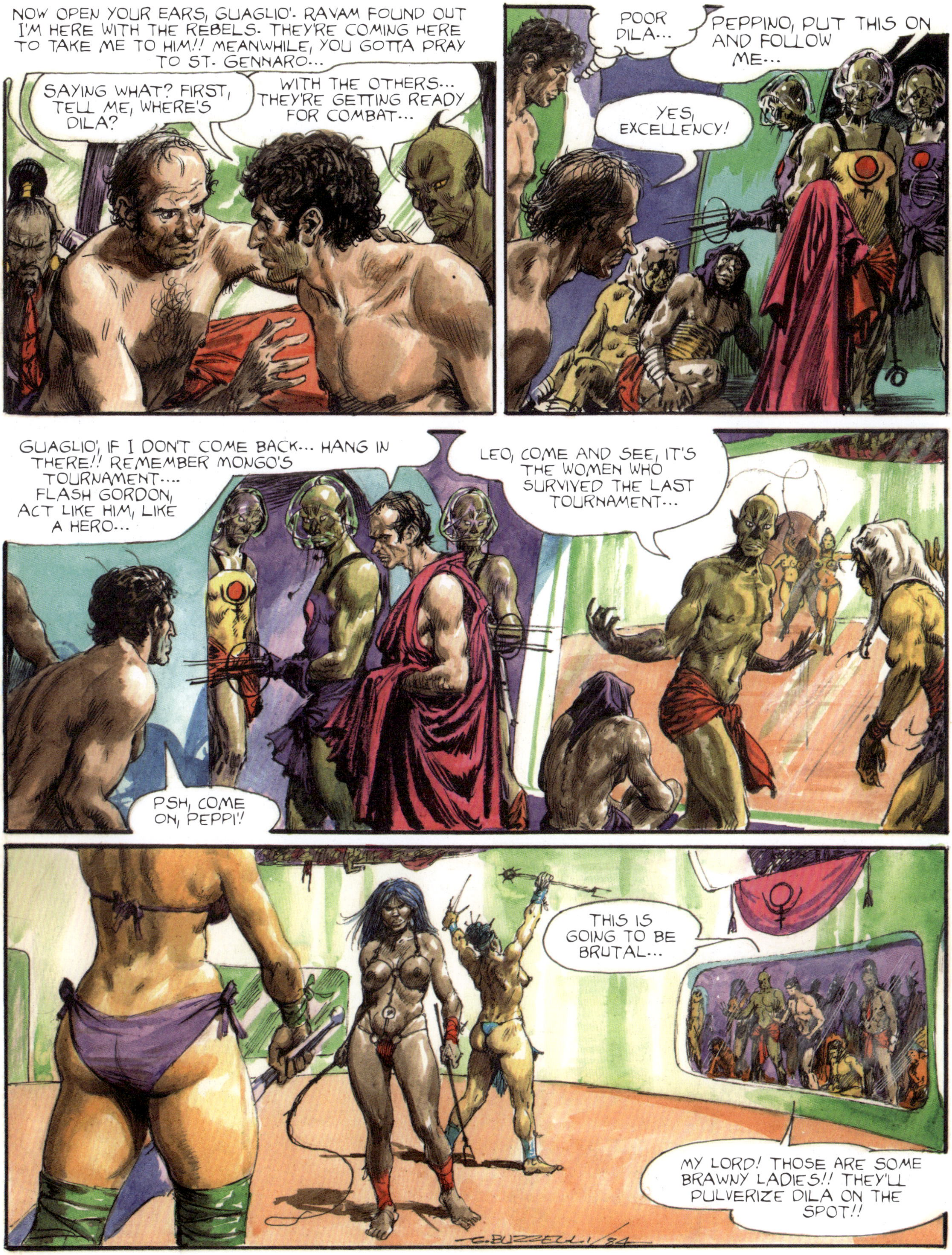
NOW OPEN YOUR EARS, GUAGLIO'. RAVAM FOUND OUT I'M HERE WITH THE REBELS. THEY'RE COMING HERE TO TAKE ME TO HIM!! MEANWHILE, YOU GOTTA PRAY TO ST. GENNARO...
SAYING WHAT? FIRST, TELL ME, WHERE'S DILA?
WITH THE OTHERS... THEY'RE GETTING READY FOR COMBAT...
POOR DILA...
PEPPINO, PUT THIS ON AND FOLLOW ME...
YES, EXCELLENCY!
GUAGLIO', IF I DON'T COME BACK... HANG IN THERE!! REMEMBER MONGO'S TOURNAMENT.... FLASH GORDON, ACT LIKE HIM, LIKE A HERO...
PSH, COME ON, PEPPI'!
LEO, COME AND SEE, IT'S THE WOMEN WHO SURVIVED THE LAST TOURNAMENT...
THIS IS GOING TO BE BRUTAL...
MY LORD! THOSE ARE SOME BRAWNY LADIES!! THEY'LL PULVERIZE DILA ON THE SPOT!!
G. BUZZELLI/84

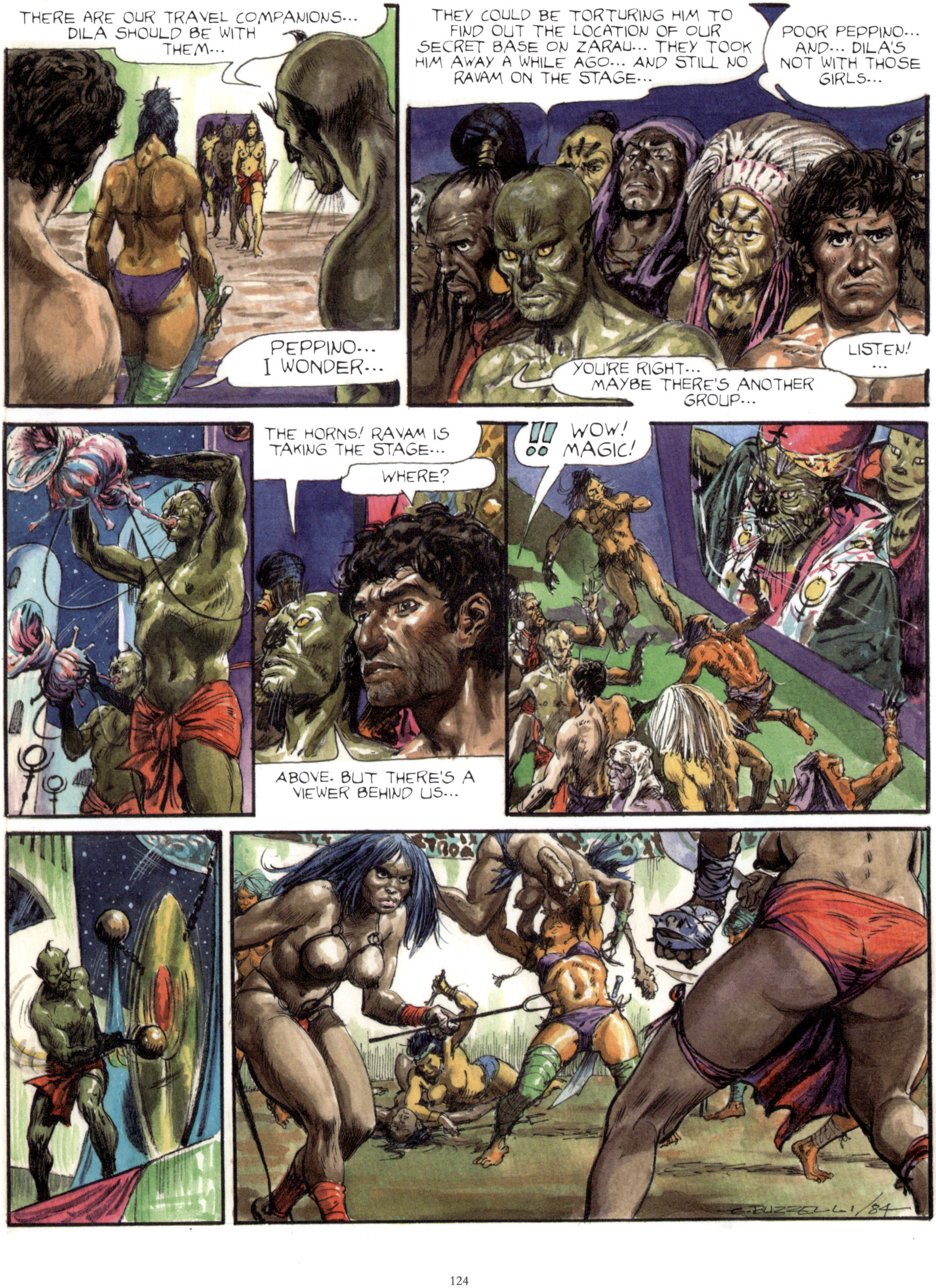
THERE ARE OUR TRAVEL COMPANIONS... DILA SHOULD BE WITH THEM...
PEPPINO... I WONDER...
THEY COULD BE TORTURING HIM TO FIND OUT THE LOCATION OF OUR SECRET BASE ON ZARAU... THEY TOOK HIM AWAY A WHILE AGO... AND STILL NO RAVAM ON THE STAGE...
POOR PEPPINO... AND... DILA'S NOT WITH THOSE GIRLS...
YOU'RE RIGHT... MAYBE THERE'S ANOTHER GROUP...
LISTEN! ...
THE HORNS! RAVAM IS TAKING THE STAGE...
WHERE?
ABOVE. BUT THERE'S A VIEWER BEHIND US...
!!
WOW! MAGIC!

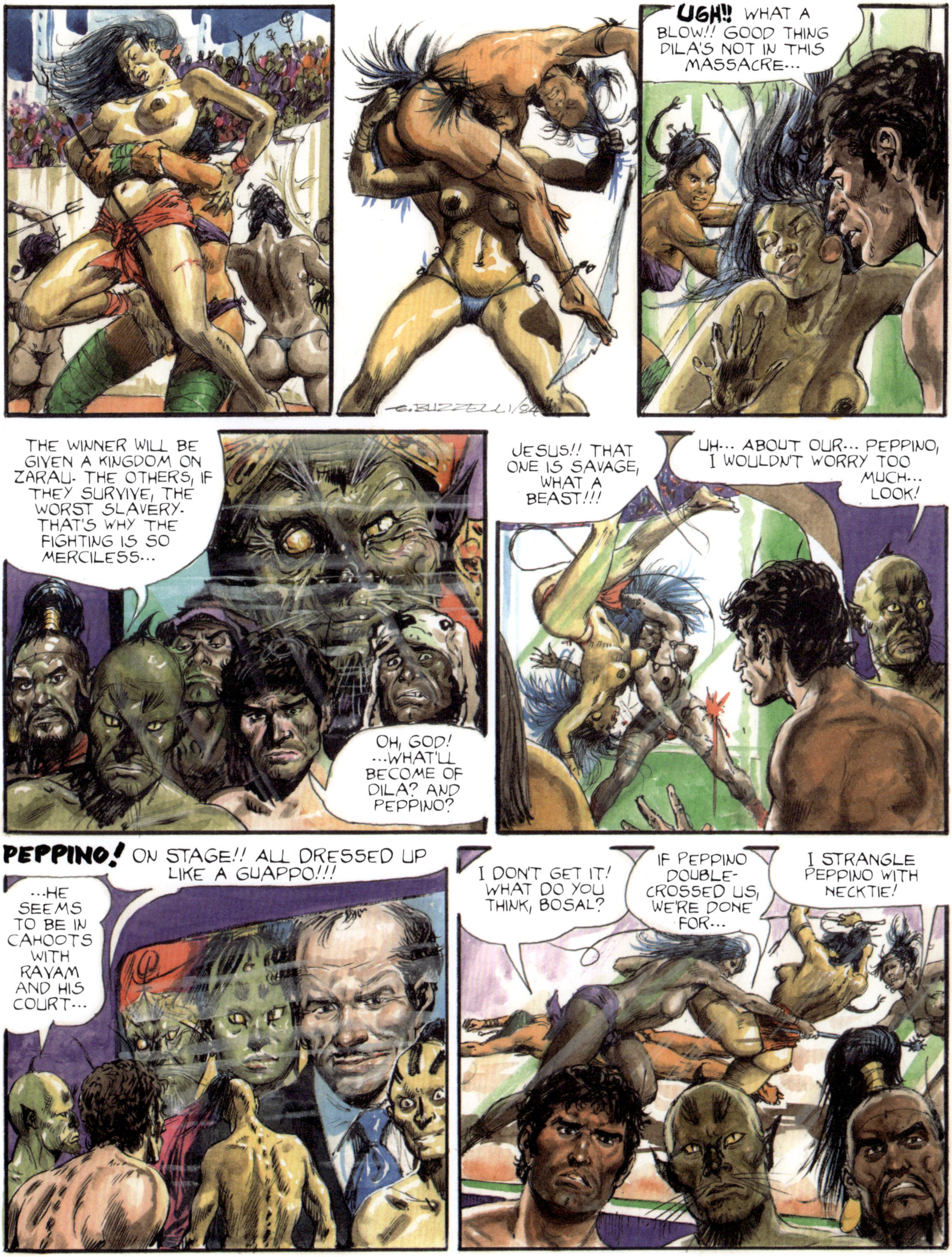
G.BUZZELLI/84
UGH!! WHAT A BLOW!! GOOD THING DILA'S NOT IN THIS MASSACRE...
THE WINNER WILL BE GIVEN A KINGDOM ON ZARAU. THE OTHERS, IF THEY SURVIVE, THE WORST SLAVERY. THAT'S WHY THE FIGHTING IS SO MERCILESS...
OH, GOD! ...WHAT'LL BECOME OF DILA? AND PEPPINO?
JESUS!! THAT ONE IS SAVAGE, WHAT A BEAST!!!
UH... ABOUT OUR... PEPPINO, I WOULDN'T WORRY TOO MUCH... LOOK!
PEPPINO! ON STAGE!! ALL DRESSED UP LIKE A GUAPPO!!!
...HE SEEMS TO BE IN CAHOOTS WITH RAYAM AND HIS COURT...
I DON'T GET IT! WHAT DO YOU THINK, BOSAL?
IF PEPPINO DOUBLE-CROSSED US, WE'RE DONE FOR...
I STRANGLE PEPPINO WITH NECKTIE!

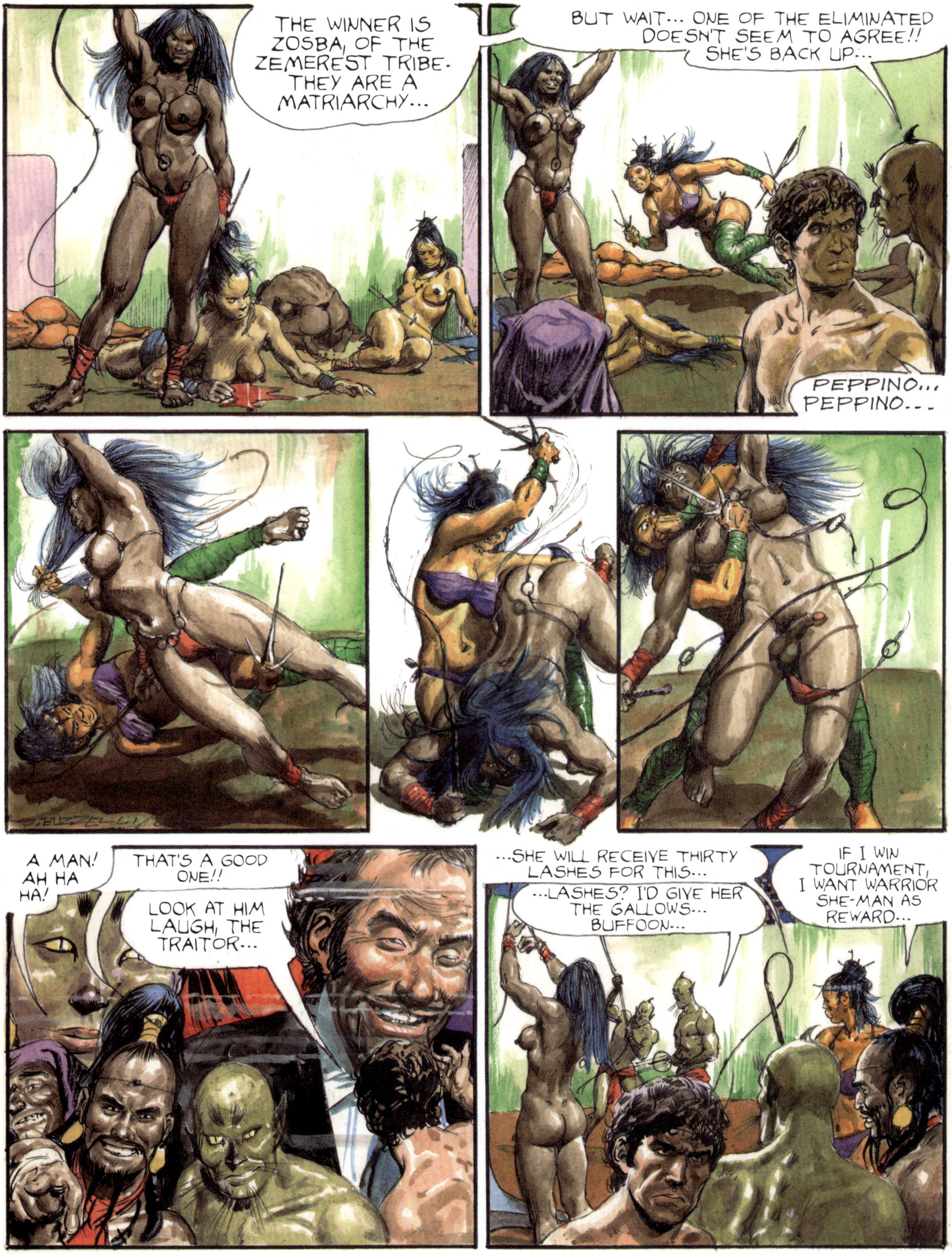
THE WINNER IS ZOSBA, OF THE ZEMEREST TRIBE. THEY ARE A MATRIARCHY...
BUT WAIT... ONE OF THE ELIMINATED DOESN'T SEEM TO AGREE!! SHE'S BACK UP...
PEPPINO... PEPPINO...
A MAN! AH HA HA!
THAT'S A GOOD ONE!!
LOOK AT HIM LAUGH, THE TRAITOR...
...SHE WILL RECEIVE THIRTY LASHES FOR THIS...
...LASHES? I'D GIVE HER THE GALLOWS... BUFFOON...
IF I WIN TOURNAMENT, I WANT WARRIOR SHE-MAN AS REWARD...

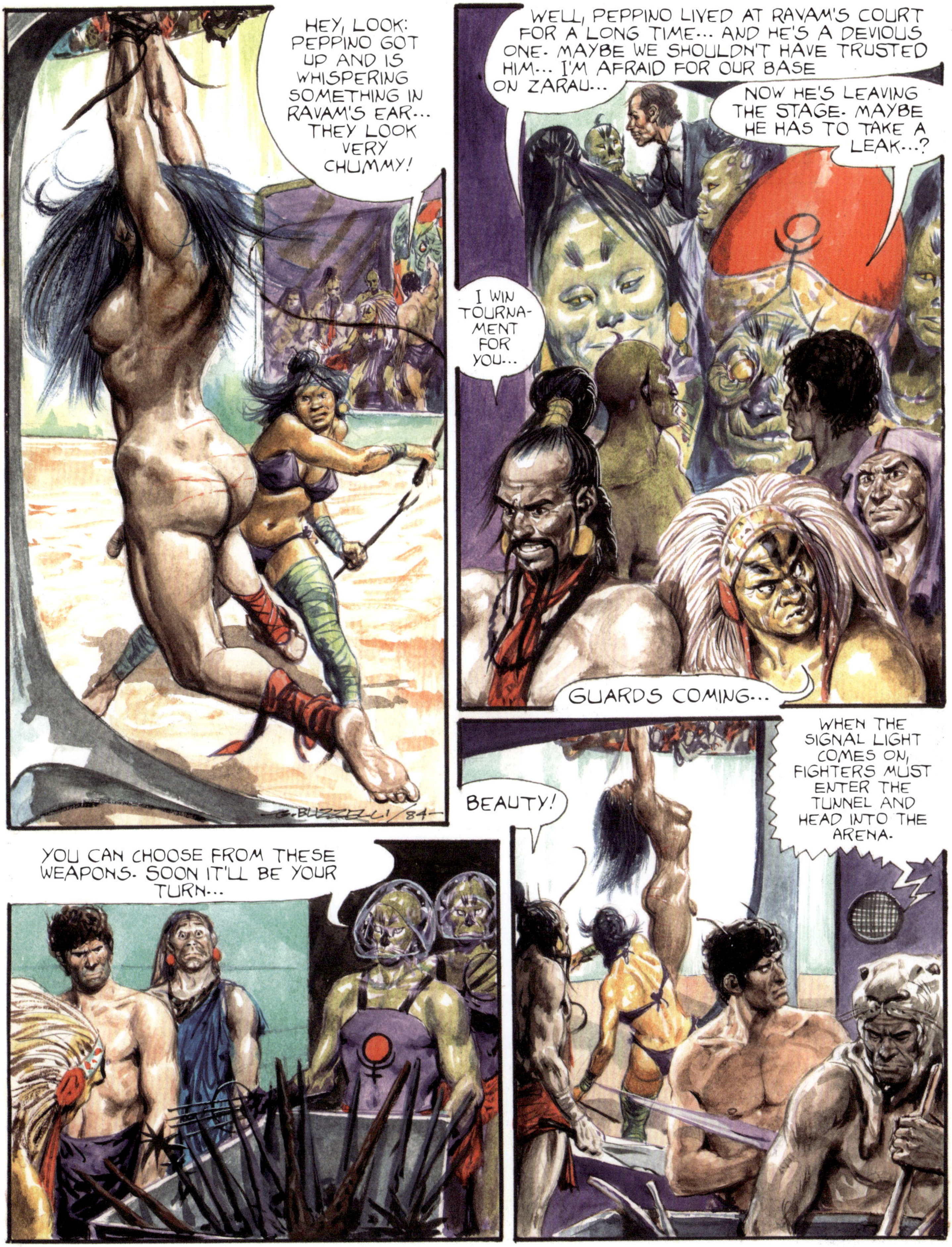
HEY, LOOK: PEPPINO GOT UP AND IS WHISPERING SOMETHING IN RAVAM'S EAR... THEY LOOK VERY CHUMMY!
B. BUZZELLI/84
WELL, PEPPINO LIVED AT RAVAM'S COURT FOR A LONG TIME... AND HE'S A DEVIOUS ONE. MAYBE WE SHOULDN'T HAVE TRUSTED HIM... I'M AFRAID FOR OUR BASE ON ZARAU...
NOW HE'S LEAVING THE STAGE. MAYBE HE HAS TO TAKE A LEAK...?
I WIN TOURNAMENT FOR YOU...
GUARDS COMING...
YOU CAN CHOOSE FROM THESE WEAPONS. SOON IT'LL BE YOUR TURN...
BEAUTY!
WHEN THE SIGNAL LIGHT COMES ON, FIGHTERS MUST ENTER THE TUNNEL AND HEAD INTO THE ARENA.

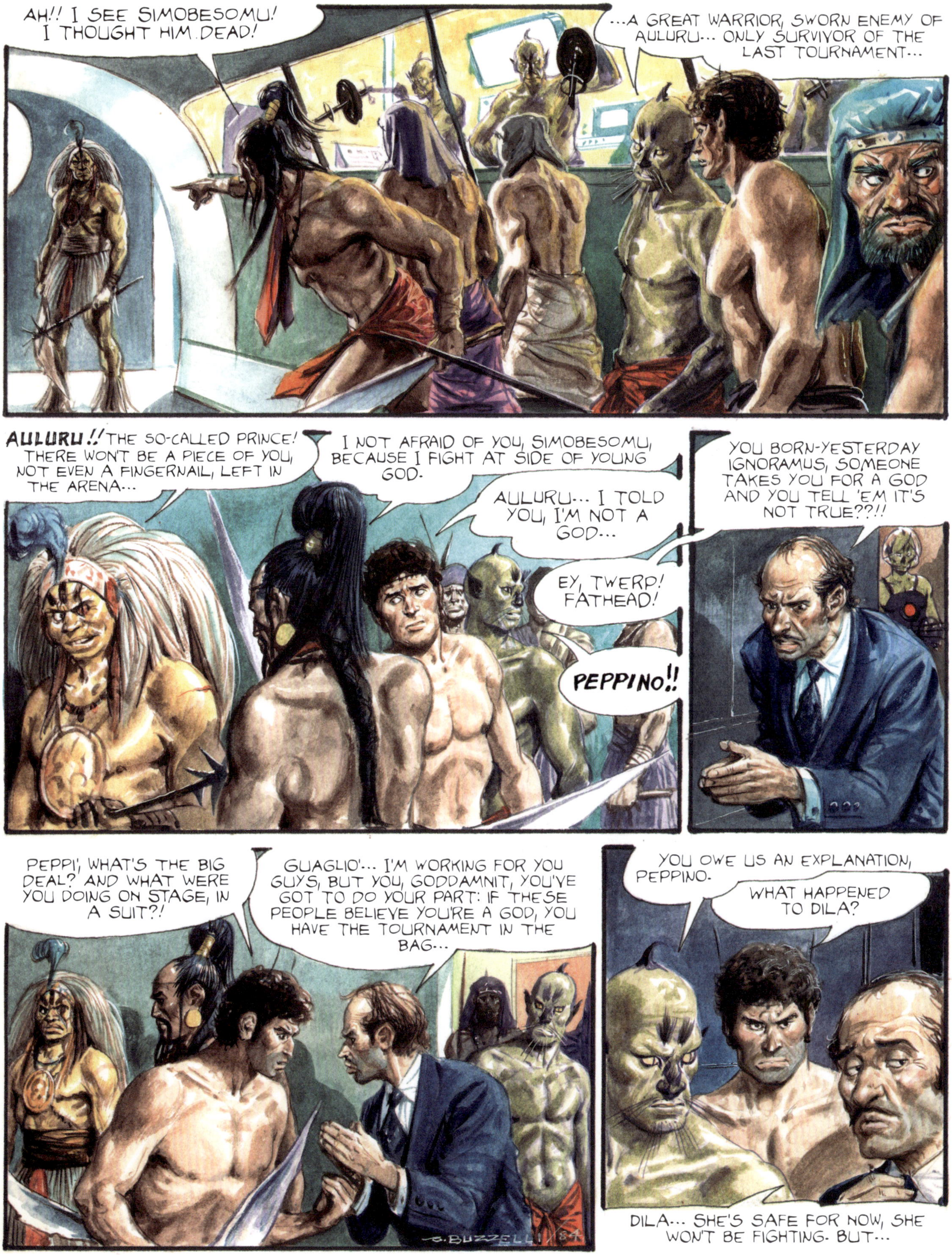
AH!! I SEE SIMOBESOMU! I THOUGHT HIM DEAD!
...A GREAT WARRIOR, SWORN ENEMY OF AULURU... ONLY SURVIVOR OF THE LAST TOURNAMENT...
AULURU!! THE SO-CALLED PRINCE! THERE WON'T BE A PIECE OF YOU, NOT EVEN A FINGERNAIL, LEFT IN THE ARENA...
I NOT AFRAID OF YOU, SIMOBESOMU, BECAUSE I FIGHT AT SIDE OF YOUNG GOD.
AULURU... I TOLD YOU, I'M NOT A GOD...
EY, TWERP! FATHEAD!
PEPPINO!!
YOU BORN-YESTERDAY IGNORAMUS, SOMEONE TAKES YOU FOR A GOD AND YOU TELL 'EM IT'S NOT TRUE??!!
PEPPI', WHAT'S THE BIG DEAL? AND WHAT WERE YOU DOING ON STAGE, IN A SUIT?!
GUAGLIO'... I'M WORKING FOR YOU GUYS, BUT YOU, GODDAMNIT, YOU'VE GOT TO DO YOUR PART: IF THESE PEOPLE BELIEVE YOU'RE A GOD, YOU HAVE THE TOURNAMENT IN THE BAG...
G. BUZZELLI '84
YOU OWE US AN EXPLANATION, PEPPINO.
WHAT HAPPENED TO DILA?
DILA... SHE'S SAFE FOR NOW, SHE WON'T BE FIGHTING. BUT...

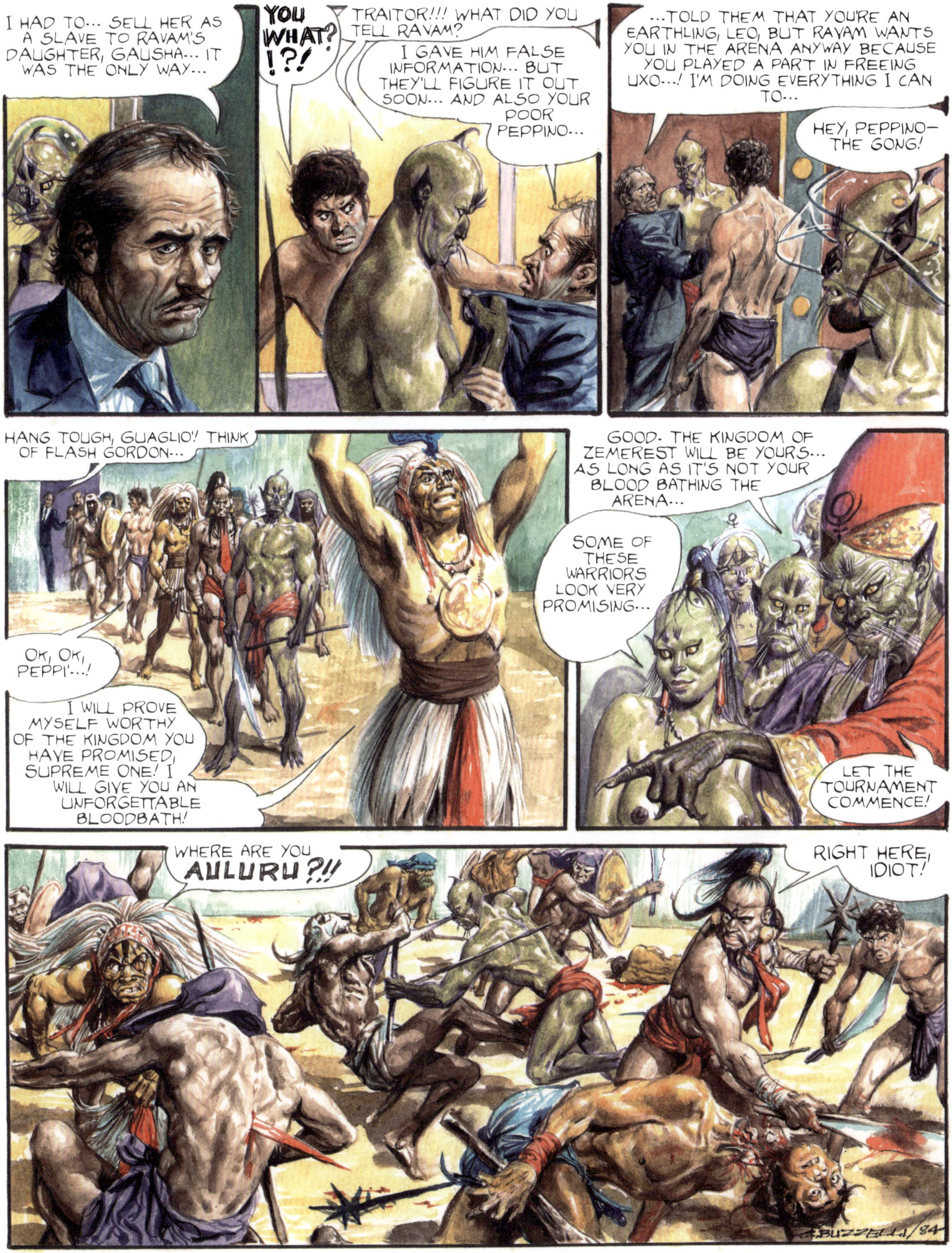

I HAD TO... SELL HER AS A SLAVE TO RAVAM'S DAUGHTER, GAUSHA... IT WAS THE ONLY WAY...
YOU WHAT? !?!
TRAITOR!!! WHAT DID YOU TELL RAVAM?
I GAVE HIM FALSE INFORMATION... BUT THEY'LL FIGURE IT OUT SOON... AND ALSO YOUR POOR PEPPINO...
...TOLD THEM THAT YOU'RE AN EARTHLING, LEO, BUT RAVAM WANTS YOU IN THE ARENA ANYWAY BECAUSE YOU PLAYED A PART IN FREEING UXO...! I'M DOING EVERYTHING I CAN TO...
HEY, PEPPINO— THE GONG!
HANG TOUGH, GUAGLIO'! THINK OF FLASH GORDON...
OK, OK, PEPPI'...!
I WILL PROVE MYSELF WORTHY OF THE KINGDOM YOU HAVE PROMISED, SUPREME ONE! I WILL GIVE YOU AN UNFORGETTABLE BLOODBATH!
GOOD. THE KINGDOM OF ZEMEREST WILL BE YOURS... AS LONG AS IT'S NOT YOUR BLOOD BATHING THE ARENA...
SOME OF THESE WARRIORS LOOK VERY PROMISING...
LET THE TOURNAMENT COMMENCE!
WHERE ARE YOU AULURU?!!
RIGHT HERE, IDIOT!
G. BUZZELLI/84

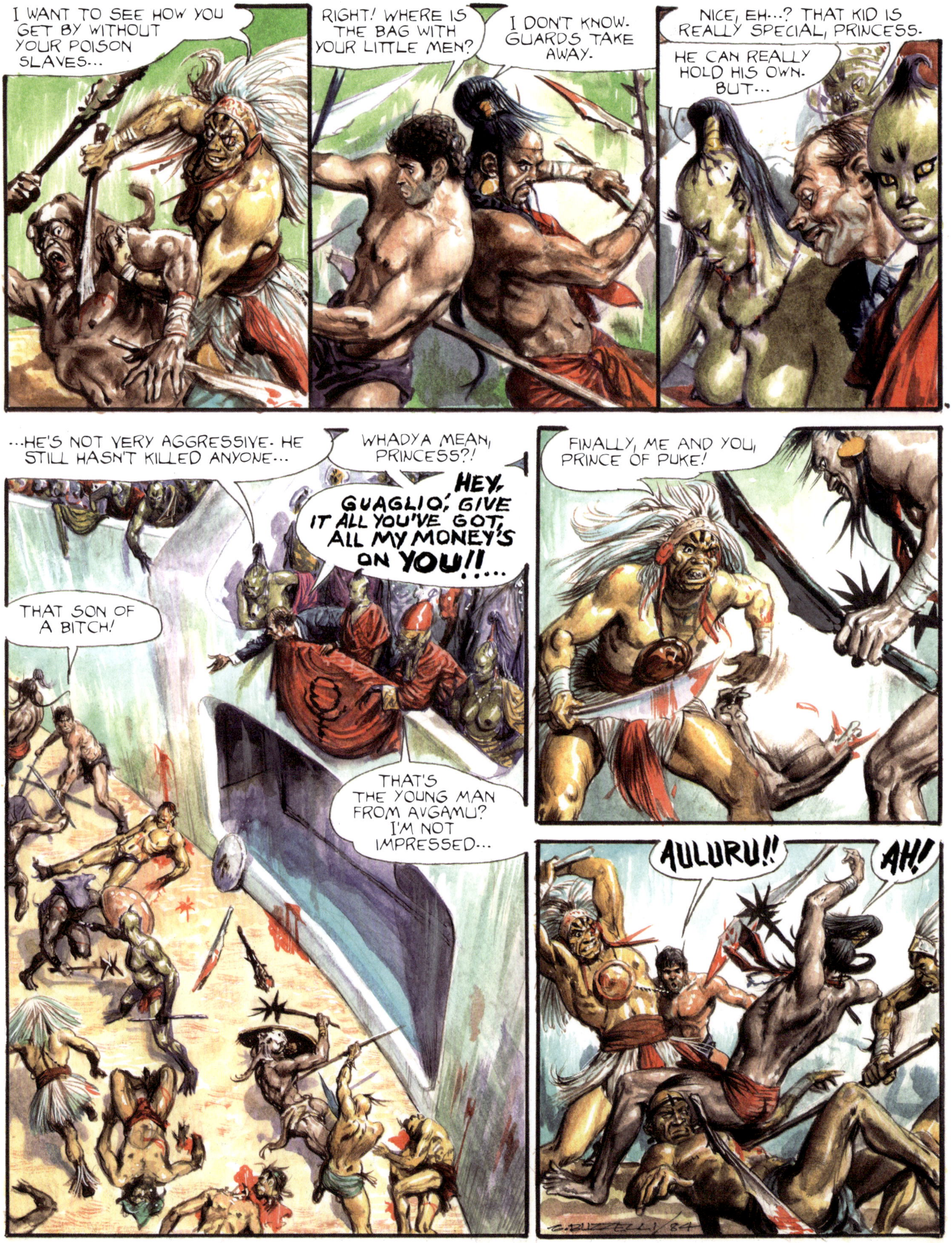
I WANT TO SEE HOW YOU GET BY WITHOUT YOUR POISON SLAVES...
RIGHT! WHERE IS THE BAG WITH YOUR LITTLE MEN?
I DON'T KNOW. GUARDS TAKE AWAY.
NICE, EH...? THAT KID IS REALLY SPECIAL, PRINCESS.
HE CAN REALLY HOLD HIS OWN. BUT...
...HE'S NOT VERY AGGRESSIVE. HE STILL HASN'T KILLED ANYONE...
WHADYA MEAN, PRINCESS?!
HEY, GUAGLIO', GIVE IT ALL YOU'VE GOT, ALL MY MONEY'S ON YOU!!...
THAT SON OF A BITCH!
THAT'S THE YOUNG MAN FROM AVGAMU? I'M NOT IMPRESSED...
FINALLY, ME AND YOU, PRINCE OF PUKE!
AULURU!!
AH!
C. RIZZELLI / 84

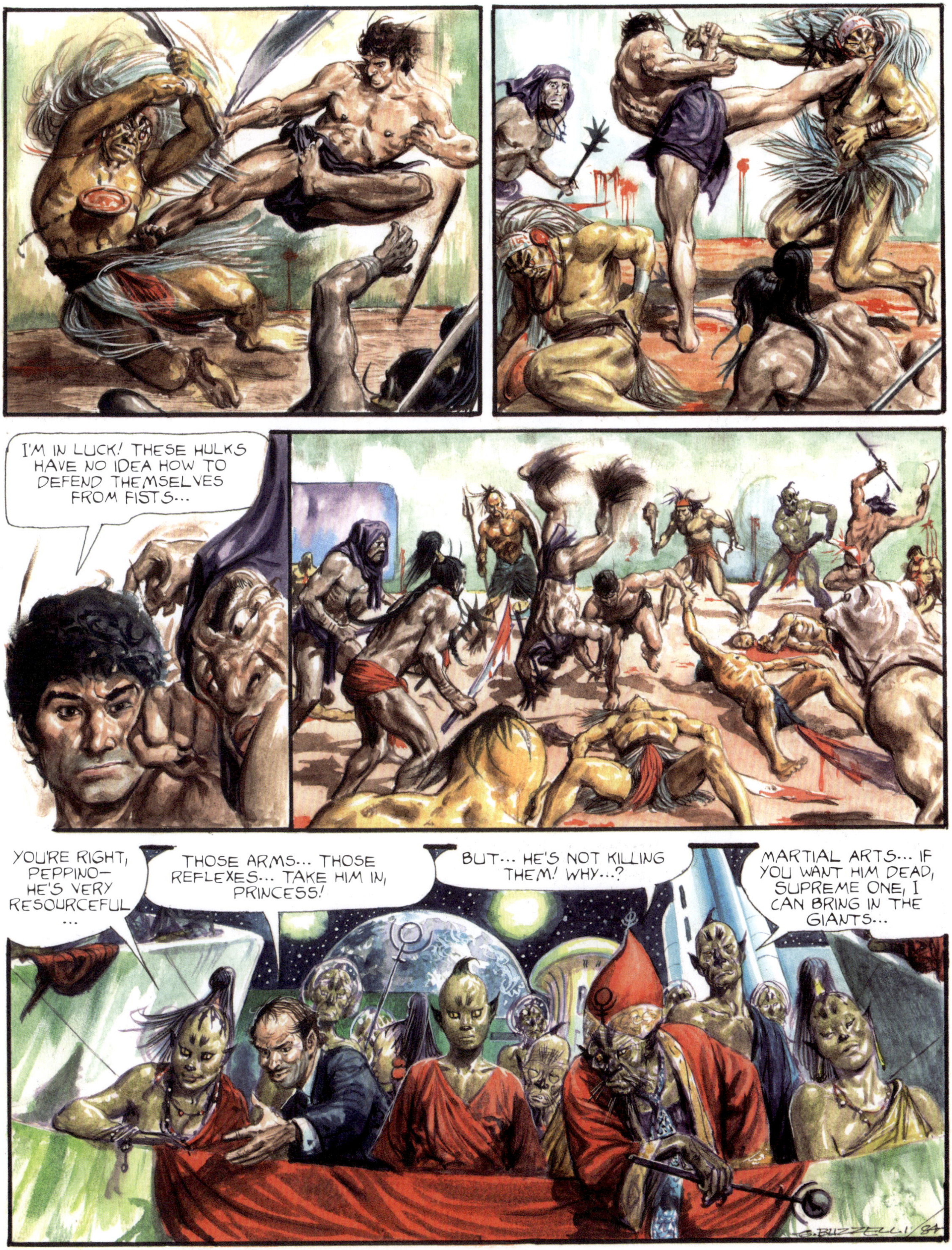
I'M IN LUCK! THESE HULKS HAVE NO IDEA HOW TO DEFEND THEMSELVES FROM FISTS...
YOU'RE RIGHT, PEPPINO— HE'S VERY RESOURCEFUL ...
THOSE ARMS... THOSE REFLEXES... TAKE HIM IN, PRINCESS!
BUT... HE'S NOT KILLING THEM! WHY...?
MARTIAL ARTS... IF YOU WANT HIM DEAD, SUPREME ONE, I CAN BRING IN THE GIANTS...
G. BUZZELLI '84

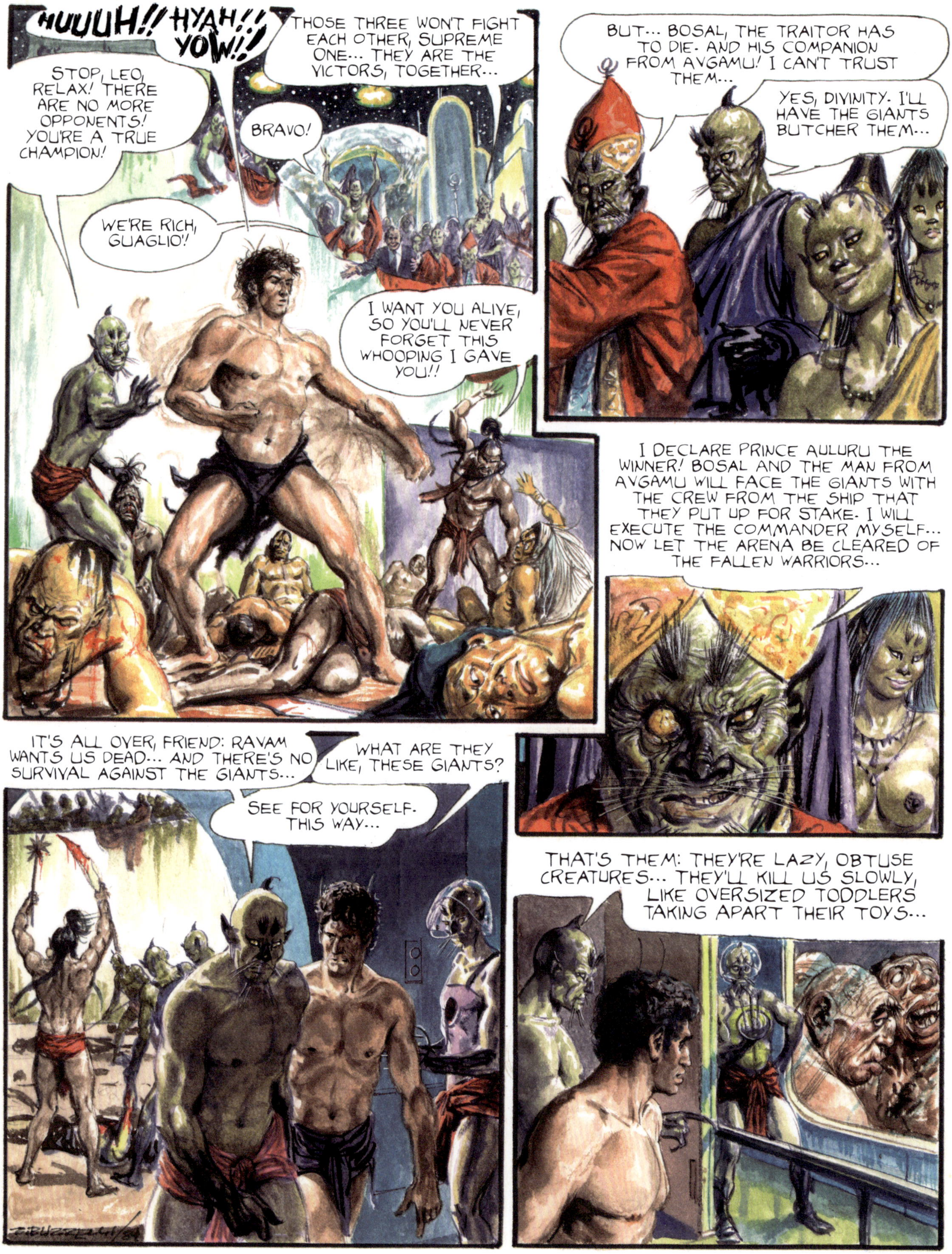
HUUUH!! HYAH!! YOW!!
THOSE THREE WON'T FIGHT EACH OTHER, SUPREME ONE... THEY ARE THE VICTORS, TOGETHER...
STOP, LEO, RELAX! THERE ARE NO MORE OPPONENTS! YOU'RE A TRUE CHAMPION!
BRAVO!
WE'RE RICH, GUAGLIO'!
I WANT YOU ALIVE, SO YOU'LL NEVER FORGET THIS WHOOPING I GAVE YOU!!
BUT... BOSAL, THE TRAITOR HAS TO DIE. AND HIS COMPANION FROM AVGAMU! I CAN'T TRUST THEM...
YES, DIVINITY. I'LL HAVE THE GIANTS BUTCHER THEM...
I DECLARE PRINCE AULURU THE WINNER! BOSAL AND THE MAN FROM AVGAMU WILL FACE THE GIANTS WITH THE CREW FROM THE SHIP THAT THEY PUT UP FOR STAKE. I WILL EXECUTE THE COMMANDER MYSELF... NOW LET THE ARENA BE CLEARED OF THE FALLEN WARRIORS...
IT'S ALL OVER, FRIEND: RAVAM WANTS US DEAD... AND THERE'S NO SURVIVAL AGAINST THE GIANTS...
WHAT ARE THEY LIKE, THESE GIANTS?
SEE FOR YOURSELF. THIS WAY...
THAT'S THEM: THEY'RE LAZY, OBTUSE CREATURES... THEY'LL KILL US SLOWLY, LIKE OVERSIZED TODDLERS TAKING APART THEIR TOYS...

THEY'LL MAIM US UNTIL WE DIE... THE HEIGHT OF ENTERTAINMENT FOR RAVAM AND HIS DEPRAVED COURT...
JESUS GOD!!!!!
GUAGLIO'!...
WHAT'S WRONG? YOU'RE AS WHITE AS A SHEET OF PAPER!! THE GIANTS...? DON'T BE AFRAID, GUAGLIO'. THANKS TO YOUR PAL PEPPINO, YOU WON'T END UP IN THE HANDS OF THESE BRUTES... COME ON...
PRINCESS GAUSHA WANTS A WORD WITH YOU... THERE'S A GARMENT YOU HAVE TO WEAR... COME IN HERE...
?!
WHAT ARE THOSE THINGS?
DRAGON EGGS. I'M MAKING YOU A ZABAIONE, YOU'LL NEED IT...
OH, BROTHER! UGH. I DON'T WANT IT. FIND ME A SPACEOPHONE INSTEAD...
OK, OK, GO AND CALL YOUR PAPA BUT AT LEAST SHAVE AFTERWARDS, THAT LADY IS A PRINCESS!
PAPA!

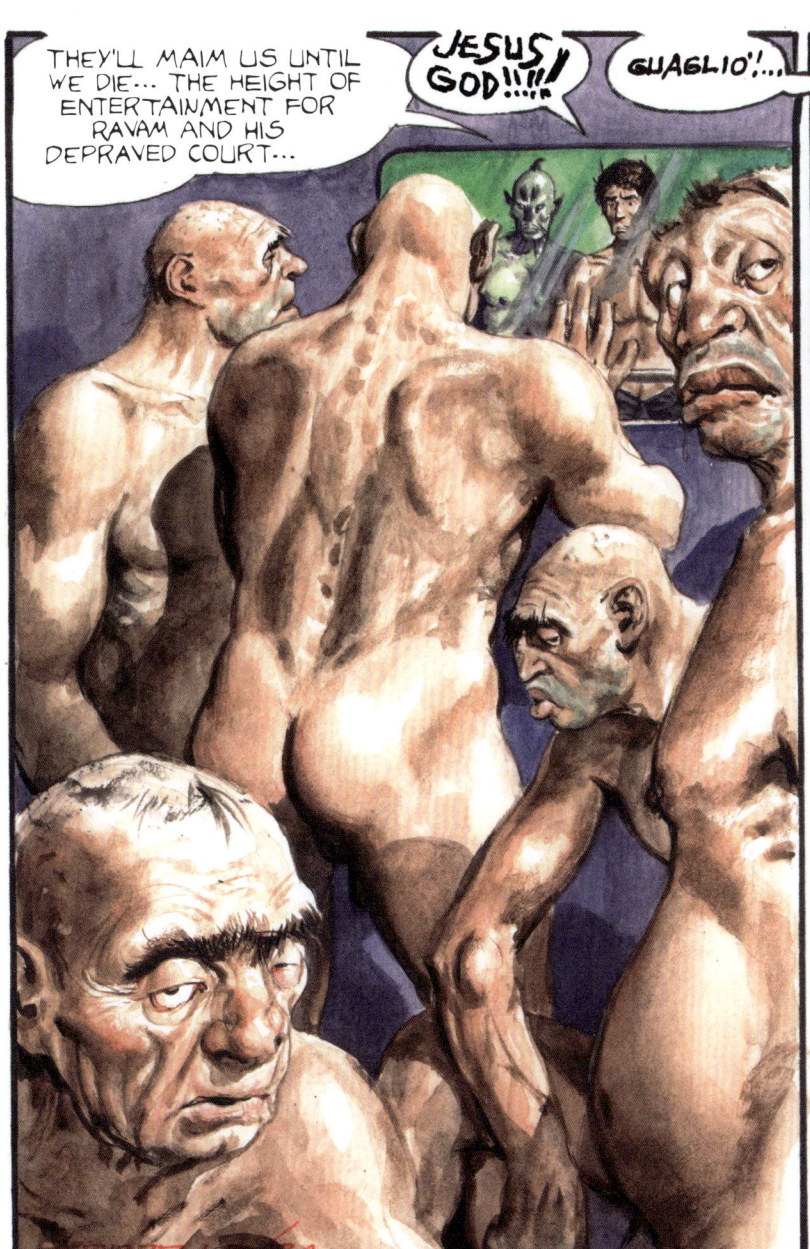

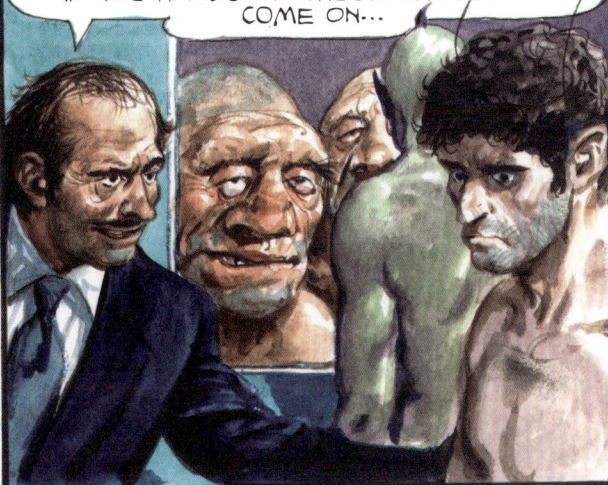

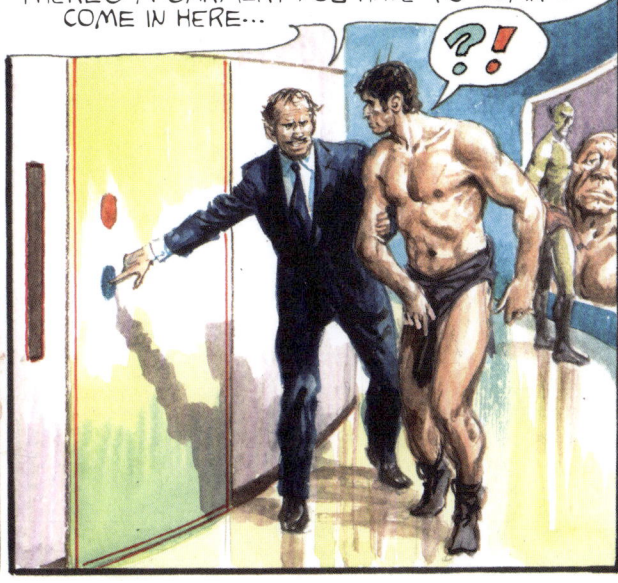

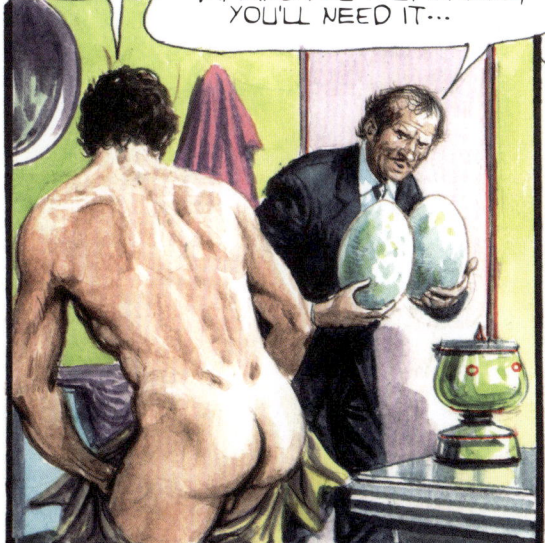

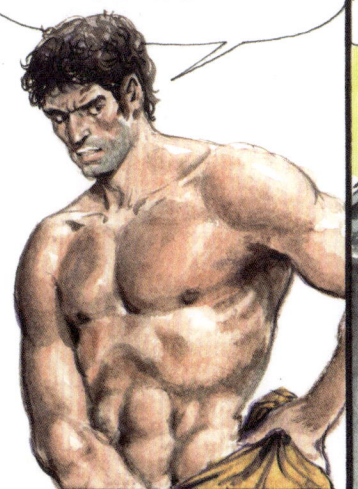

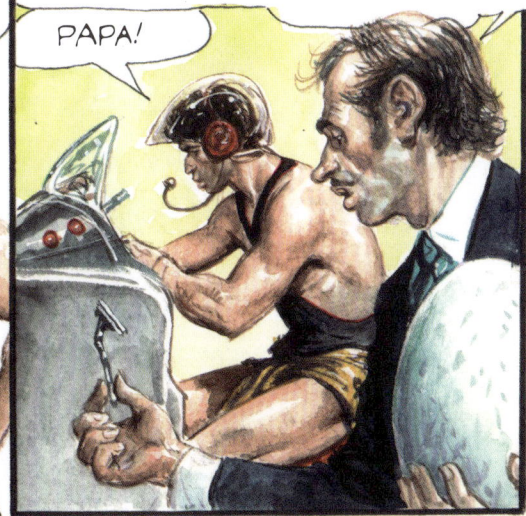

SON!!! FINALLY! HOW ARE YOU? ZASAFIR? HUH? THE STARS?
BUBU?! WHAT'S WITH YOU?
...THEY SAID YOU'RE GOING TO MEET A BAD WOMAN WHO MAY CAUSE YOU TROUBLE... WHAT? YOU HEAR VOICES? WHO'S THERE WITH ME?!
WHO ARE YOU TALKING TO?!!
AH, YES... THAT'S CHARLOTTE AND MARION... EH, MY FRIENDS SENT THEM HERE TO DISTRACT ME...
THEY WANT TO GET MY MIND OFF YOU.. YOU KNOW, THEY THINK YOU'RE JUST A FIGMENT OF MY IMAGINATION... BEAUTIFUL GIRLS, THOUGH... I LIKE THEM A LOT...
PAPA!! AT YOUR AGE?! COME ON... YOUR BALLS ARE GONNA BURST!
WORRY ABOUT YOUR OWN BALLS!! YOU, YOUR TOURNAMENTS, YOUR STUPID PRINCESSES!! UGH!! ...... THIS KID IS NEVER GOING TO MAKE IT TO ZASAFIR... I HAVE TO DO SOME-THING... I HAVE TO GET TO HIM!
POOR PAPA... HE'S LOSING IT... ZASAFIR, ZASAFIR!! AS IF HE COULD JUST ZIP OVER THERE... WHAT DOES HE THINK...
GUAGLIO', YOUR ZABAIONE. TAKE IT. ATESMIAN WOMEN ARE TREMENDOUS...
PSH... I DON'T NEED IT! COME ON, LET'S GO...
SO MUCH FOR MY SPECIAL CONCOCTION... BYE BYE...
G. BUZZELLI /84

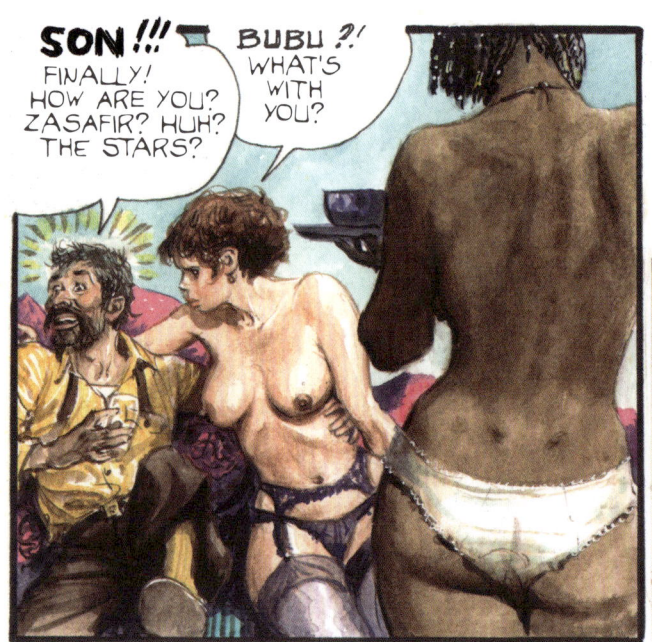

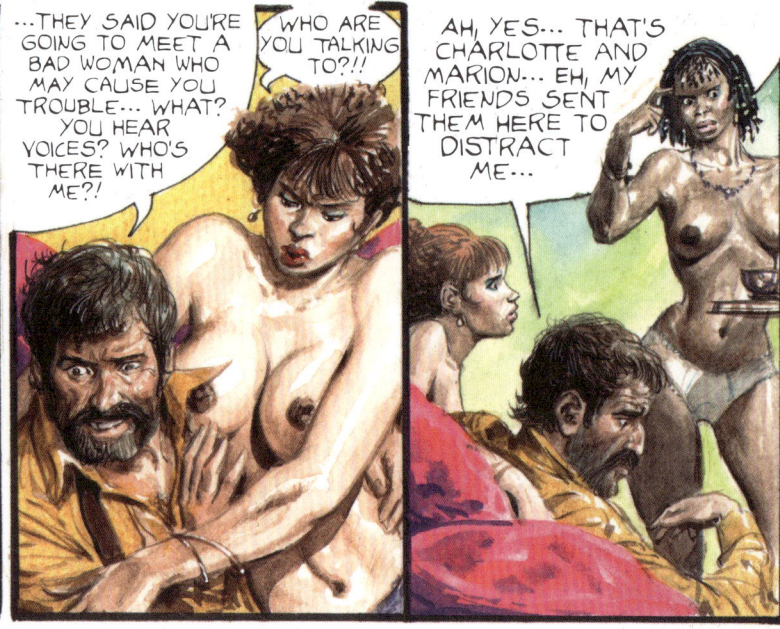

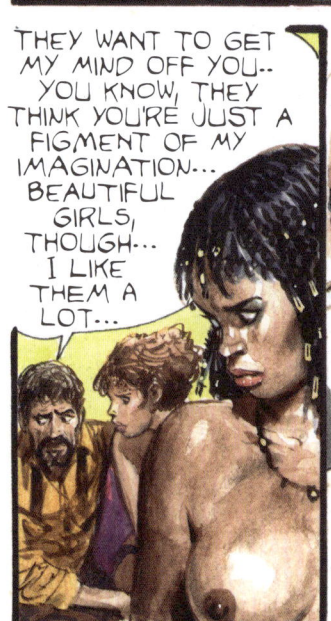

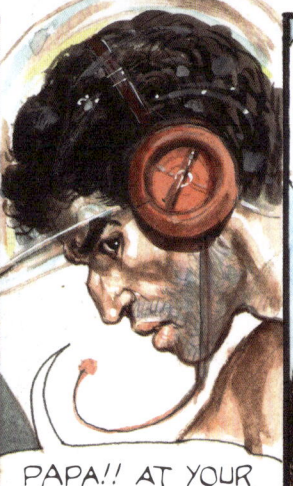

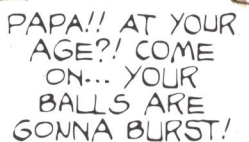

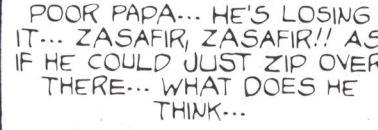

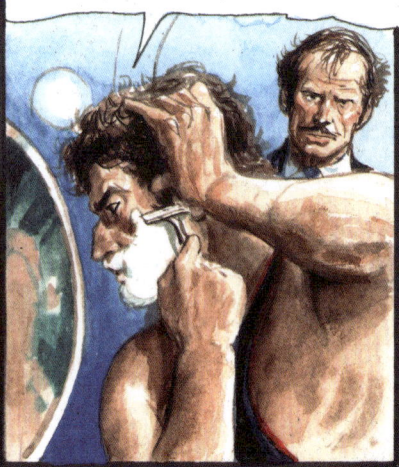

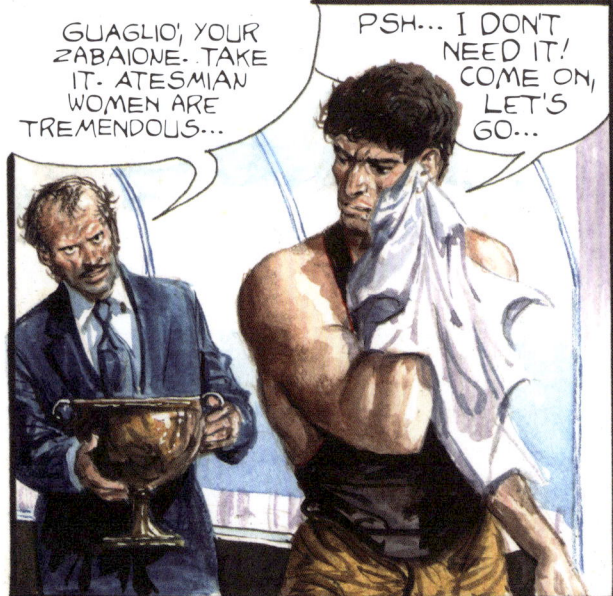

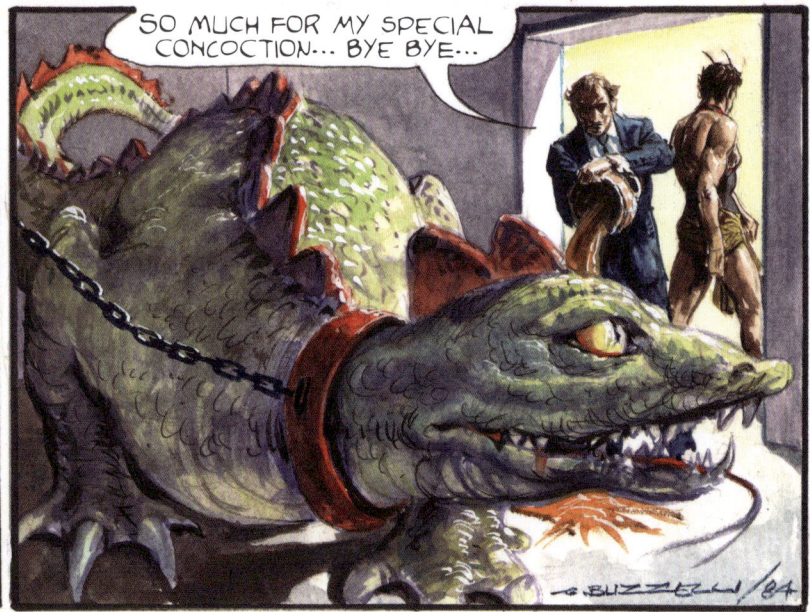

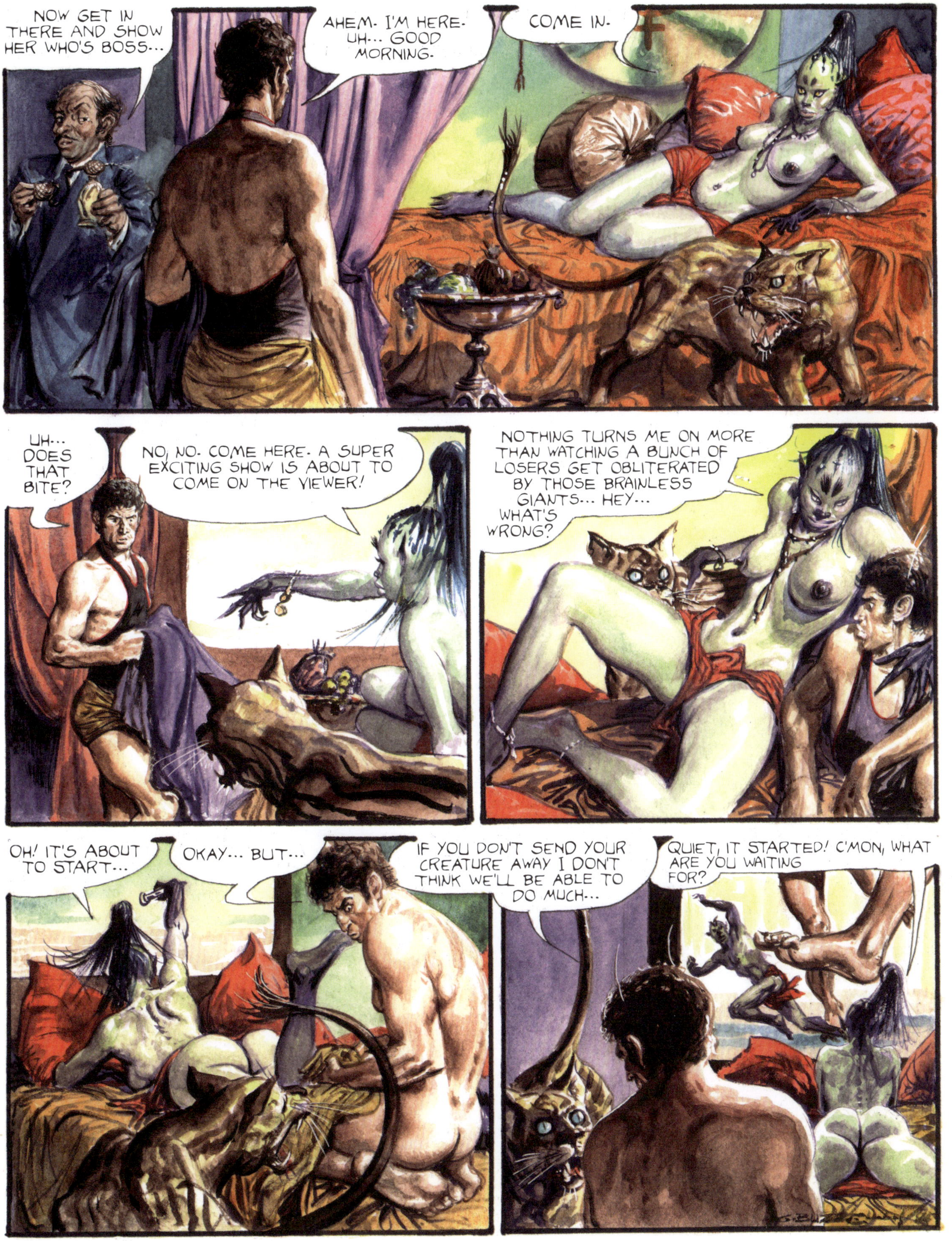
NOW GET IN THERE AND SHOW HER WHO'S BOSS...
AHEM. I'M HERE. UH... GOOD MORNING.
COME IN.
UH... DOES THAT BITE?
NO, NO. COME HERE. A SUPER EXCITING SHOW IS ABOUT TO COME ON THE VIEWER!
NOTHING TURNS ME ON MORE THAN WATCHING A BUNCH OF LOSERS GET OBLITERATED BY THOSE BRAINLESS GIANTS... HEY... WHAT'S WRONG?
OH! IT'S ABOUT TO START...
OKAY... BUT...
IF YOU DON'T SEND YOUR CREATURE AWAY I DON'T THINK WE'LL BE ABLE TO DO MUCH...
QUIET, IT STARTED! C'MON, WHAT ARE YOU WAITING FOR?

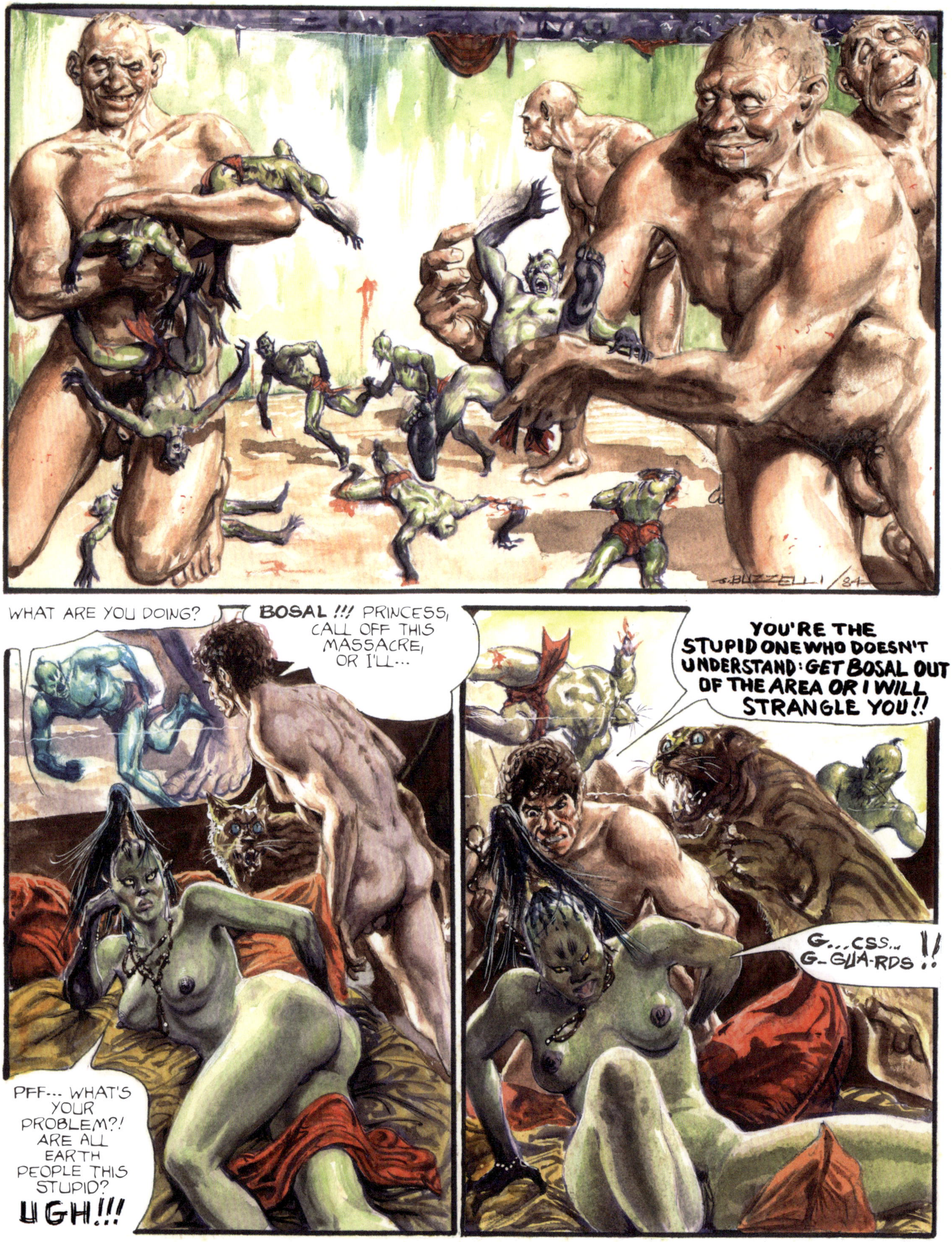

BUZZELLI /84
WHAT ARE YOU DOING?
BOSAL !!! PRINCESS, CALL OFF THIS MASSACRE, OR I'LL...
PFF... WHAT'S YOUR PROBLEM?! ARE ALL EARTH PEOPLE THIS STUPID? UGH!!!
YOU'RE THE STUPID ONE WHO DOESN'T UNDERSTAND: GET BOSAL OUT OF THE AREA OR I WILL STRANGLE YOU!!
G...CSS.. G-GUA-RDS !!

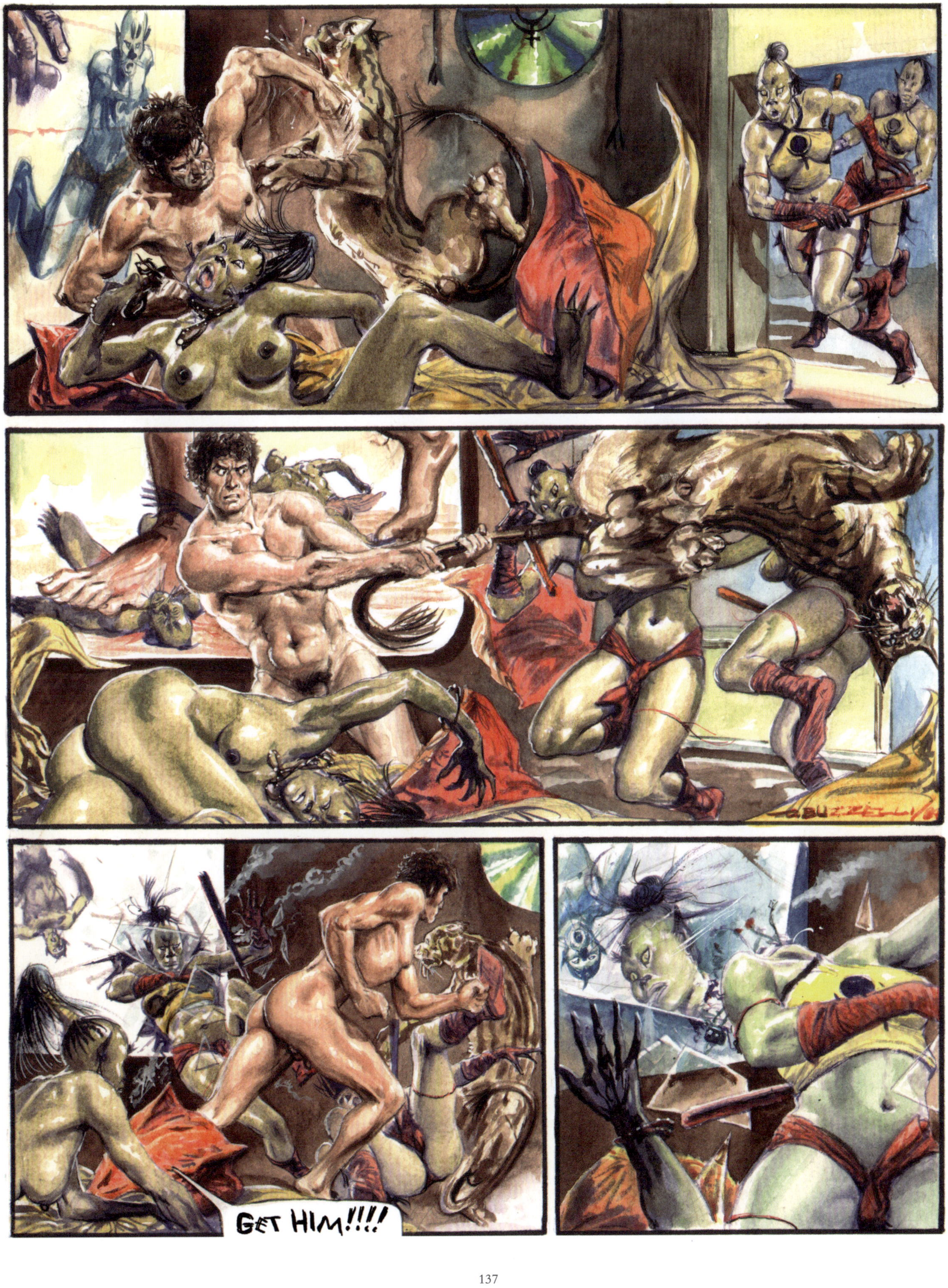
GET HIM!!!!

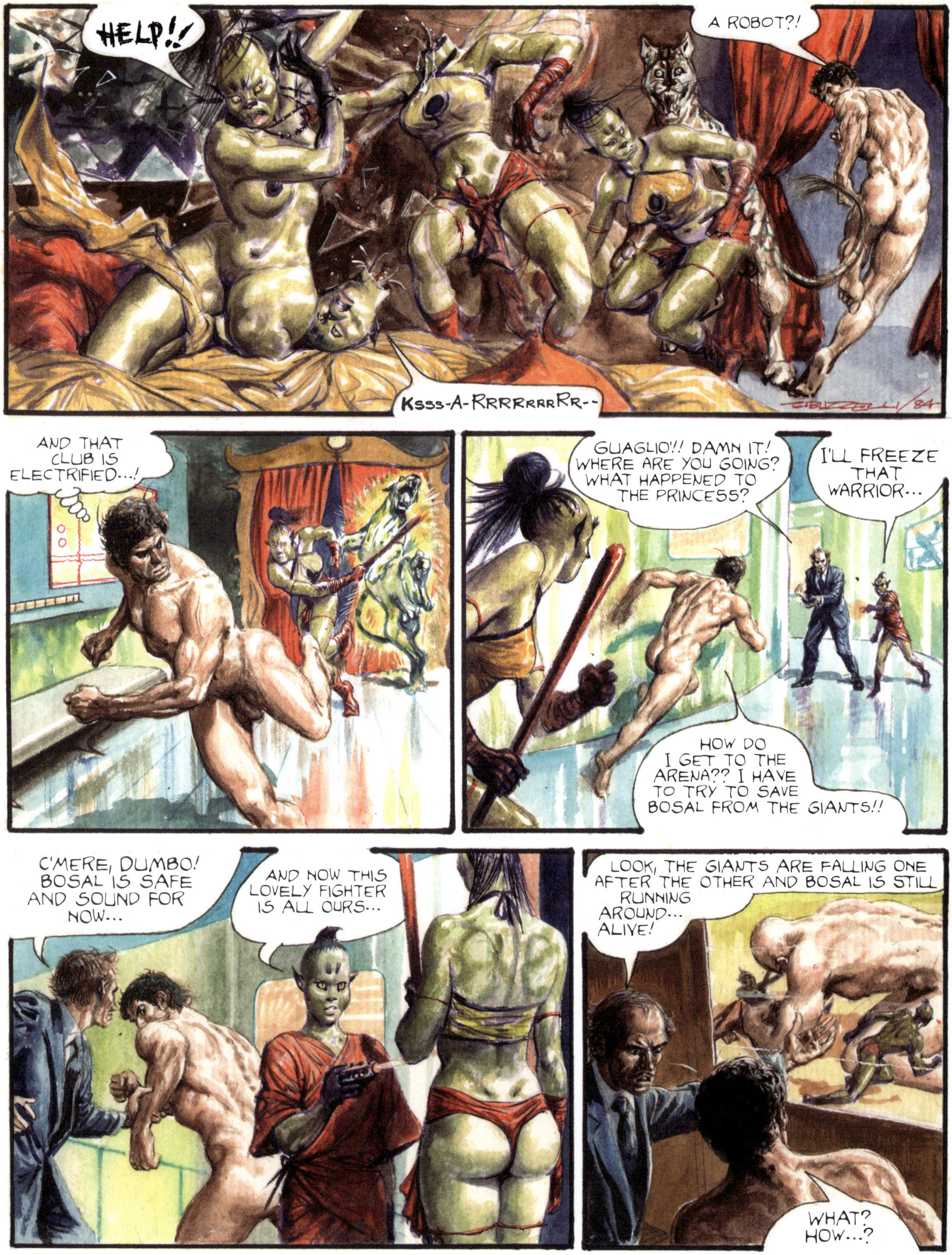
HELP!!
A ROBOT?!
Ksss-A-RRRRRRRRR--
AND THAT CLUB IS ELECTRIFIED...!
GUAGLIO!! DAMN IT! WHERE ARE YOU GOING? WHAT HAPPENED TO THE PRINCESS?
I'LL FREEZE THAT WARRIOR...
HOW DO I GET TO THE ARENA?? I HAVE TO TRY TO SAVE BOSAL FROM THE GIANTS!!
C'MERE, DUMBO! BOSAL IS SAFE AND SOUND FOR NOW...
AND NOW THIS LOVELY FIGHTER IS ALL OURS...
LOOK, THE GIANTS ARE FALLING ONE AFTER THE OTHER AND BOSAL IS STILL RUNNING AROUND... ALIVE!
WHAT? HOW...?

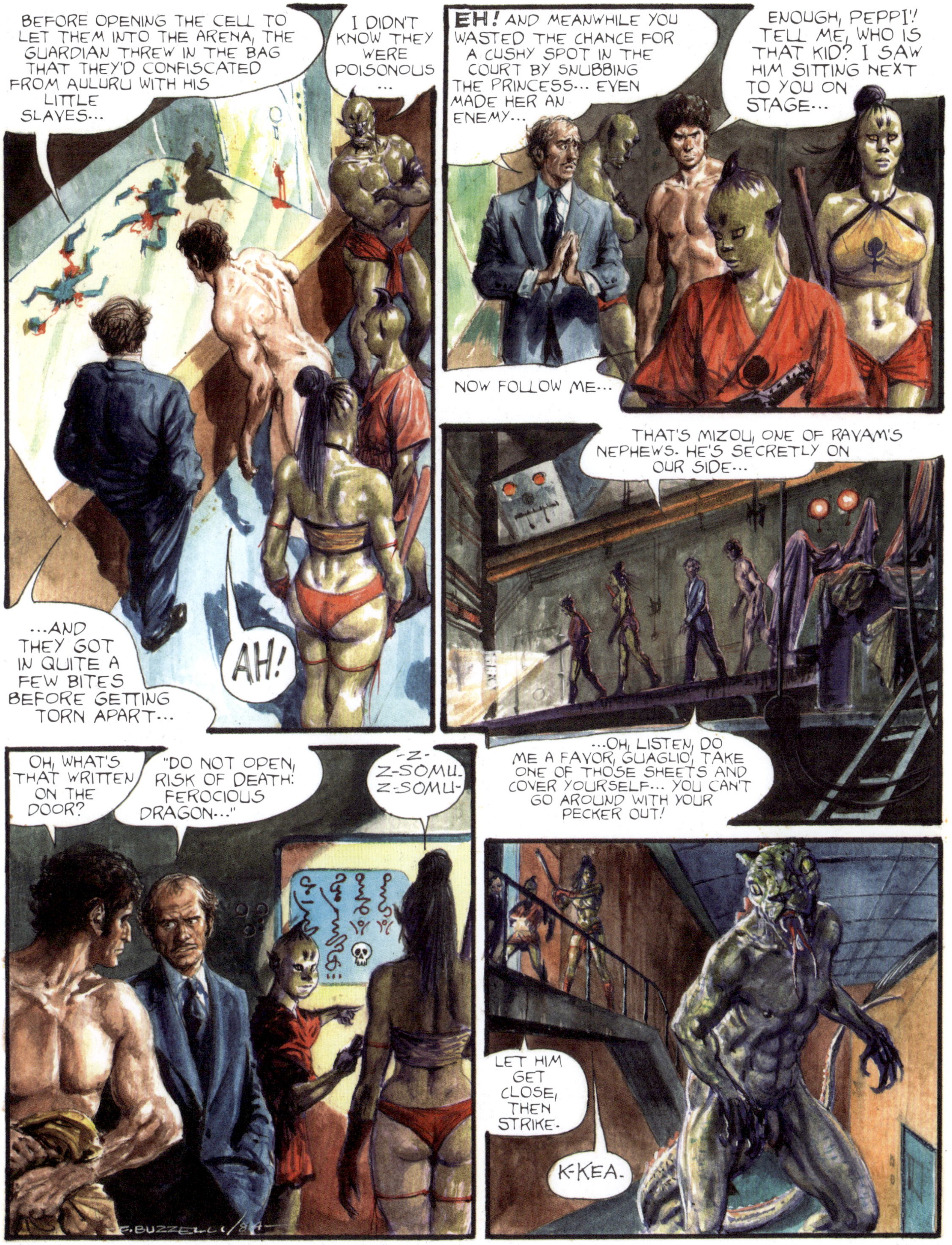
BEFORE OPENING THE CELL TO LET THEM INTO THE ARENA, THE GUARDIAN THREW IN THE BAG THAT THEY'D CONFISCATED FROM AULURU WITH HIS LITTLE SLAVES...
I DIDN'T KNOW THEY WERE POISONOUS ...
...AND THEY GOT IN QUITE A FEW BITES BEFORE GETTING TORN APART...
AH!
EH! AND MEANWHILE YOU WASTED THE CHANCE FOR A CUSHY SPOT IN THE COURT BY SNUBBING THE PRINCESS... EVEN MADE HER AN ENEMY...
ENOUGH, PEPPI! TELL ME, WHO IS THAT KID? I SAW HIM SITTING NEXT TO YOU ON STAGE...
NOW FOLLOW ME...
THAT'S MIZOU, ONE OF RAYAM'S NEPHEWS. HE'S SECRETLY ON OUR SIDE...
...OH, LISTEN, DO ME A FAVOR, GUAGLIO, TAKE ONE OF THOSE SHEETS AND COVER YOURSELF... YOU CAN'T GO AROUND WITH YOUR PECKER OUT!
OH, WHAT'S THAT WRITTEN ON THE DOOR?
"DO NOT OPEN, RISK OF DEATH: FEROCIOUS DRAGON..."
-Z- Z-SOMU. Z-SOMU-
LET HIM GET CLOSE, THEN STRIKE.
K-KEA.

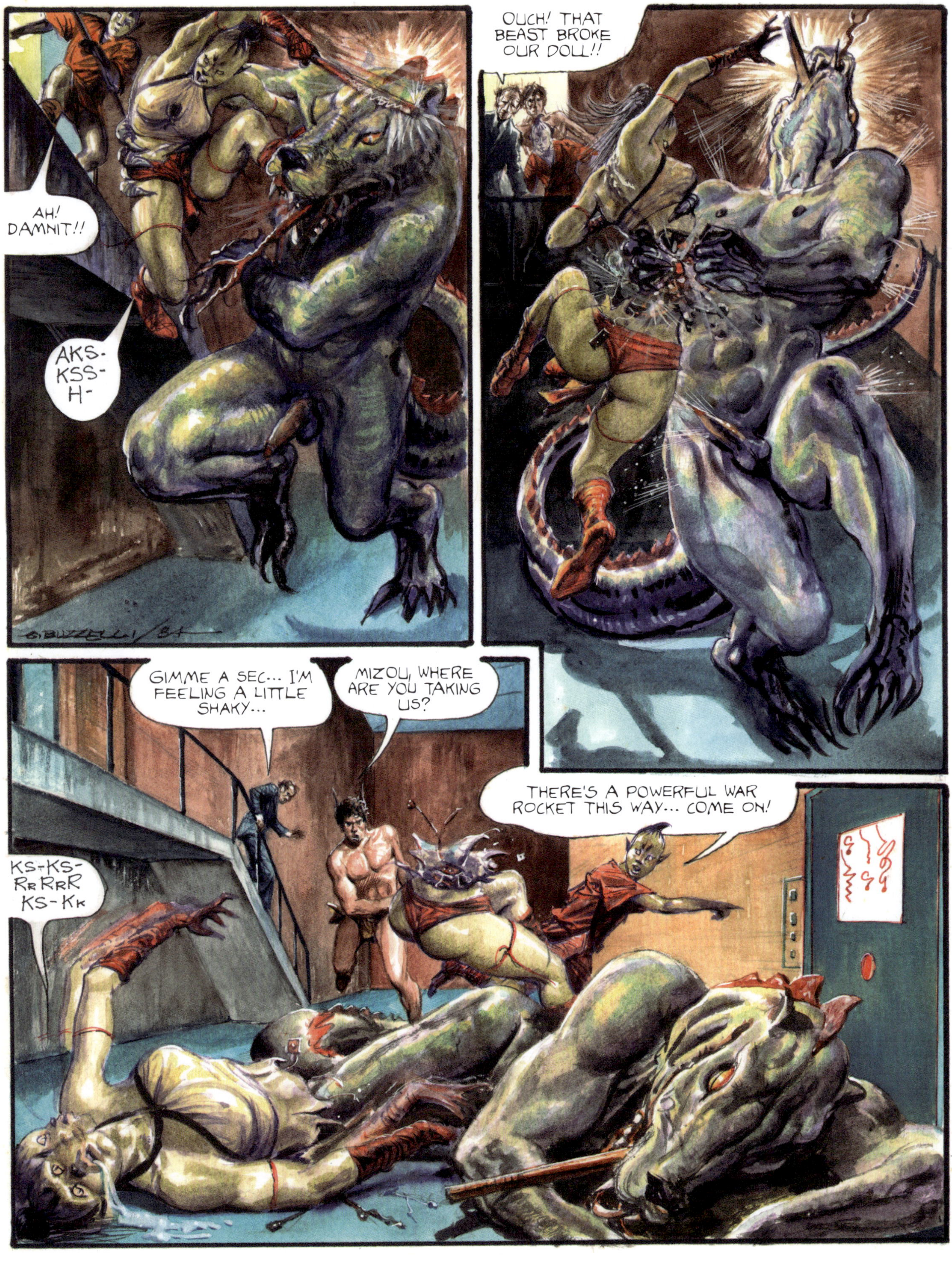
AH! DAMNIT!!
AKS-KSS-H-
OUCH! THAT BEAST BROKE OUR DOLL!!
GIMME A SEC... I'M FEELING A LITTLE SHAKY...
MIZOU, WHERE ARE YOU TAKING US?
THERE'S A POWERFUL WAR ROCKET THIS WAY... COME ON!
KS-KS-RRRRR KS-KK

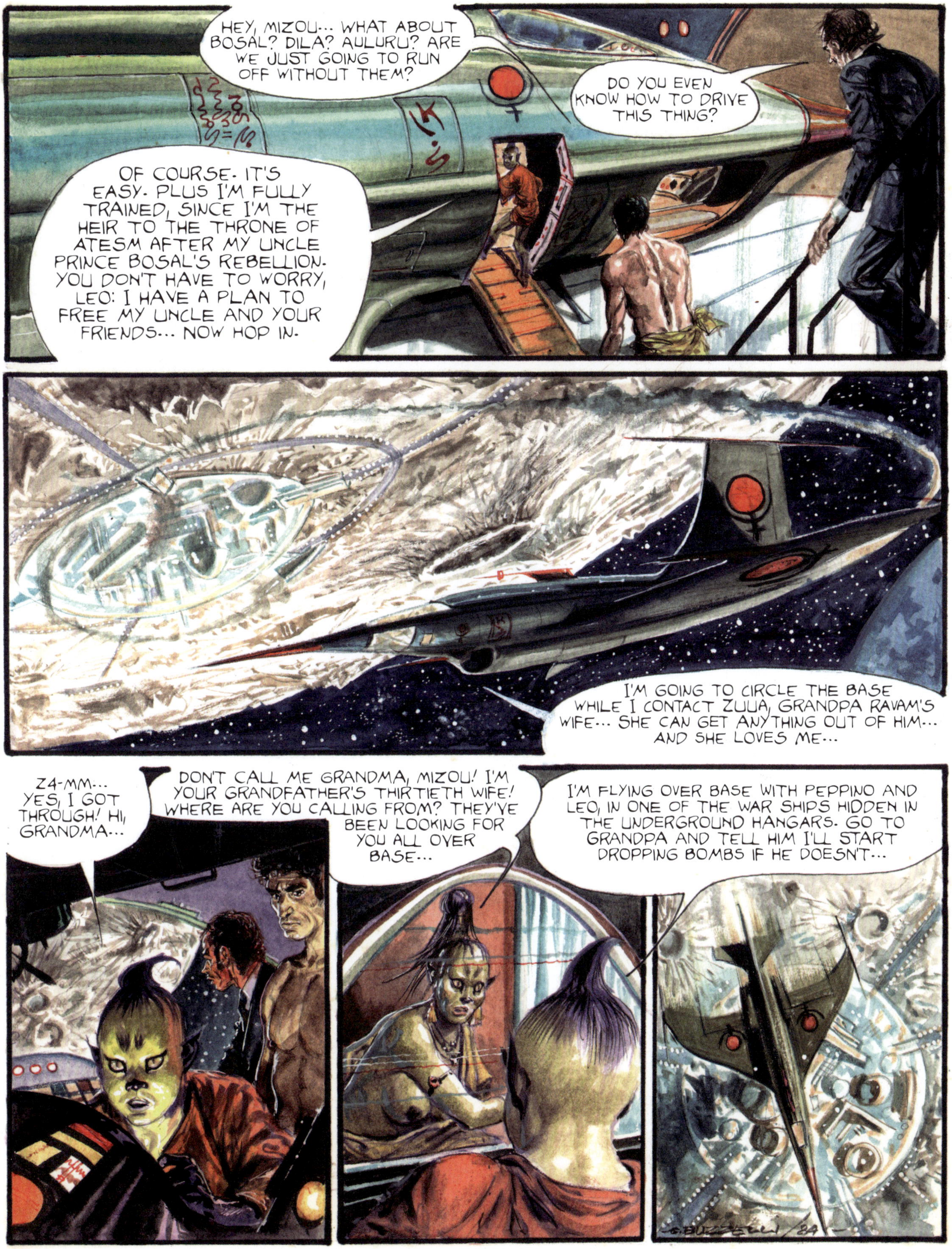
HEY, MIZOU... WHAT ABOUT BOSAL? DILA? AULURU? ARE WE JUST GOING TO RUN OFF WITHOUT THEM?
DO YOU EVEN KNOW HOW TO DRIVE THIS THING?
OF COURSE. IT'S EASY. PLUS I'M FULLY TRAINED, SINCE I'M THE HEIR TO THE THRONE OF ATESM AFTER MY UNCLE PRINCE BOSAL'S REBELLION. YOU DON'T HAVE TO WORRY, LEO: I HAVE A PLAN TO FREE MY UNCLE AND YOUR FRIENDS... NOW HOP IN.
I'M GOING TO CIRCLE THE BASE WHILE I CONTACT ZUUA, GRANDPA RAVAM'S WIFE... SHE CAN GET ANYTHING OUT OF HIM... AND SHE LOVES ME...
Z4-MM... YES, I GOT THROUGH! HI, GRANDMA...
DON'T CALL ME GRANDMA, MIZOU! I'M YOUR GRANDFATHER'S THIRTIETH WIFE! WHERE ARE YOU CALLING FROM? THEY'VE BEEN LOOKING FOR YOU ALL OVER BASE...
I'M FLYING OVER BASE WITH PEPPINO AND LEO, IN ONE OF THE WAR SHIPS HIDDEN IN THE UNDERGROUND HANGARS. GO TO GRANDPA AND TELL HIM I'LL START DROPPING BOMBS IF HE DOESN'T...

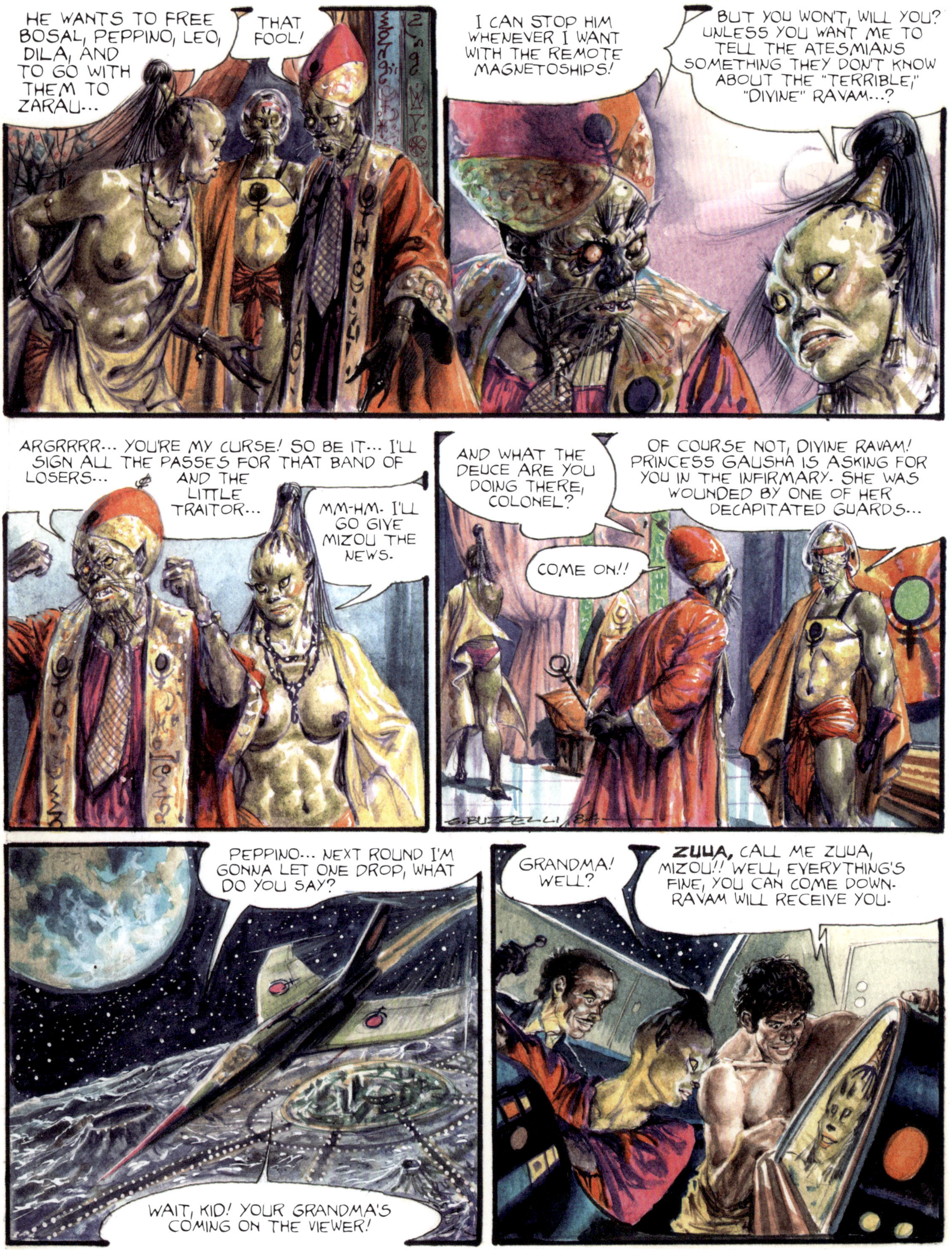
HE WANTS TO FREE BOSAL, PEPPINO, LEO, DILA, AND TO GO WITH THEM TO ZARAU...
THAT FOOL!
I CAN STOP HIM WHENEVER I WANT WITH THE REMOTE MAGNETOSHIPS!
BUT YOU WON'T, WILL YOU? UNLESS YOU WANT ME TO TELL THE ATESMIANS SOMETHING THEY DON'T KNOW ABOUT THE "TERRIBLE," "DIVINE" RAVAM...?
ARGRRRR... YOU'RE MY CURSE! SO BE IT... I'LL SIGN ALL THE PASSES FOR THAT BAND OF LOSERS...
AND THE LITTLE TRAITOR...
MM-HM. I'LL GO GIVE MIZOU THE NEWS.
AND WHAT THE DEUCE ARE YOU DOING THERE, COLONEL?
OF COURSE NOT, DIVINE RAVAM! PRINCESS GAUSHA IS ASKING FOR YOU IN THE INFIRMARY. SHE WAS WOUNDED BY ONE OF HER DECAPITATED GUARDS...
COME ON!!
G. BUZZELLI /84
PEPPINO... NEXT ROUND I'M GONNA LET ONE DROP, WHAT DO YOU SAY?
WAIT, KID! YOUR GRANDMA'S COMING ON THE VIEWER!
GRANDMA! WELL?
ZUUA, CALL ME ZUUA, MIZOU!! WELL, EVERYTHING'S FINE, YOU CAN COME DOWN. RAVAM WILL RECEIVE YOU.

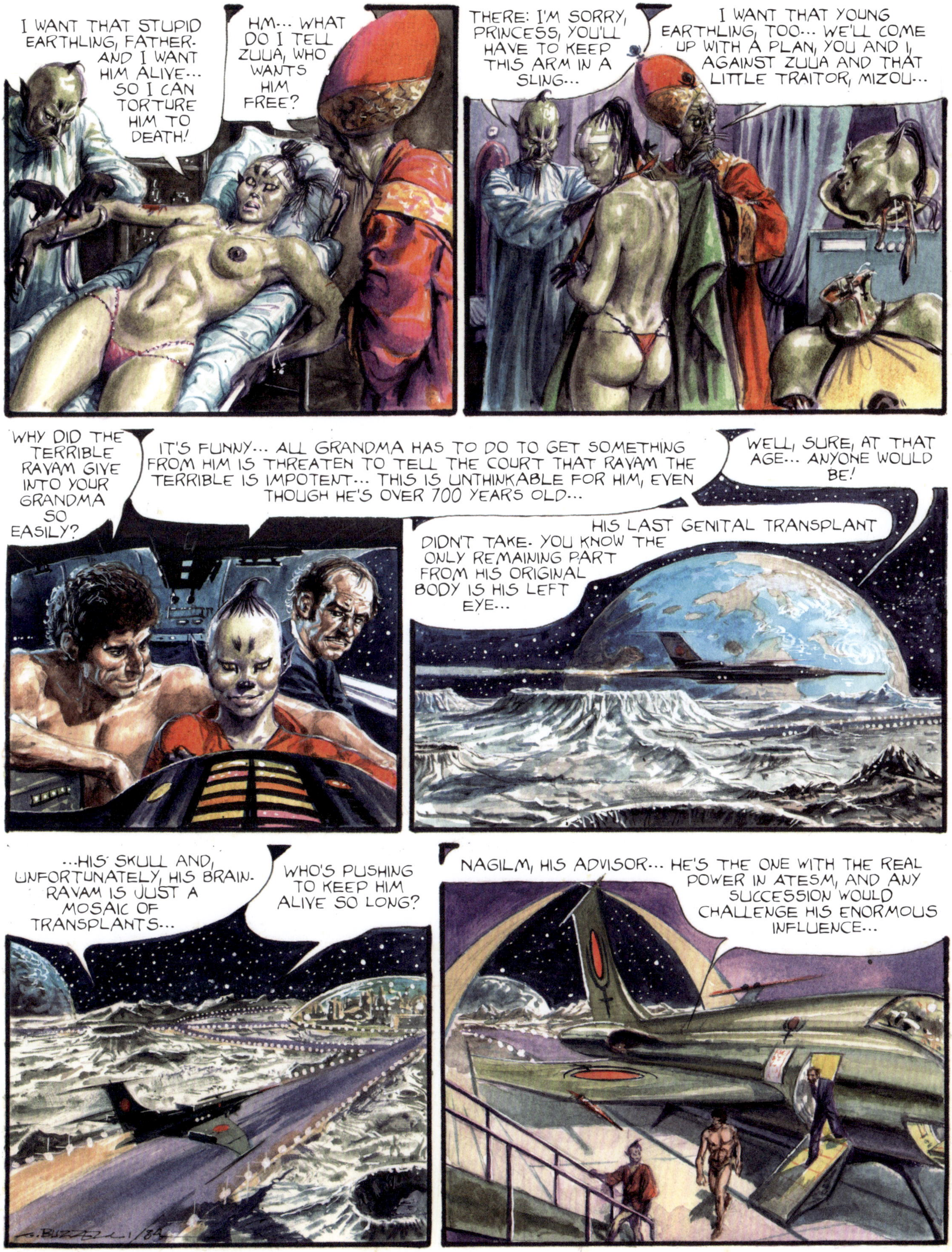

I WANT THAT STUPID EARTHLING, FATHER- AND I WANT HIM ALIVE... SO I CAN TORTURE HIM TO DEATH!
HM... WHAT DO I TELL ZUUA, WHO WANTS HIM FREE?
THERE: I'M SORRY, PRINCESS, YOU'LL HAVE TO KEEP THIS ARM IN A SLING...
I WANT THAT YOUNG EARTHLING, TOO... WE'LL COME UP WITH A PLAN, YOU AND I, AGAINST ZUUA AND THAT LITTLE TRAITOR, MIZOU...
WHY DID THE TERRIBLE RAVAM GIVE INTO YOUR GRANDMA SO EASILY?
IT'S FUNNY... ALL GRANDMA HAS TO DO TO GET SOMETHING FROM HIM IS THREATEN TO TELL THE COURT THAT RAVAM THE TERRIBLE IS IMPOTENT... THIS IS UNTHINKABLE FOR HIM, EVEN THOUGH HE'S OVER 700 YEARS OLD...
WELL, SURE, AT THAT AGE... ANYONE WOULD BE!
HIS LAST GENITAL TRANSPLANT DIDN'T TAKE. YOU KNOW THE ONLY REMAINING PART FROM HIS ORIGINAL BODY IS HIS LEFT EYE...
...HIS SKULL AND, UNFORTUNATELY, HIS BRAIN. RAVAM IS JUST A MOSAIC OF TRANSPLANTS...
WHO'S PUSHING TO KEEP HIM ALIVE SO LONG?
NAGILM, HIS ADVISOR... HE'S THE ONE WITH THE REAL POWER IN ATESM, AND ANY SUCCESSION WOULD CHALLENGE HIS ENORMOUS INFLUENCE...

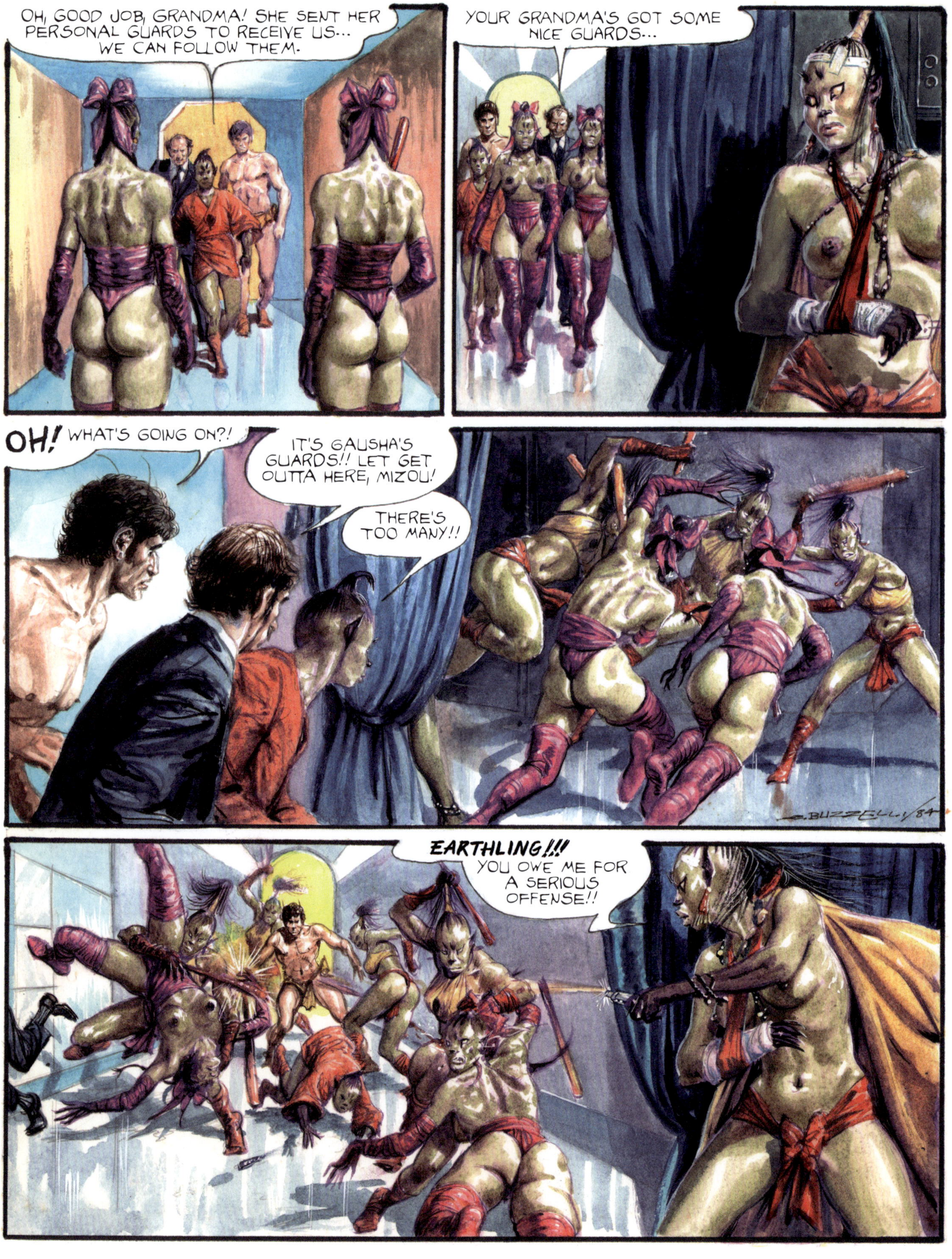
OH, GOOD JOB, GRANDMA! SHE SENT HER PERSONAL GUARDS TO RECEIVE US... WE CAN FOLLOW THEM.
YOUR GRANDMA'S GOT SOME NICE GUARDS...
OH! WHAT'S GOING ON?!
IT'S GAUSHA'S GUARDS!! LET GET OUTTA HERE, MIZOU!
THERE'S TOO MANY!!
BUZZELLI '84
EARTHLING!!! YOU OWE ME FOR A SERIOUS OFFENSE!!

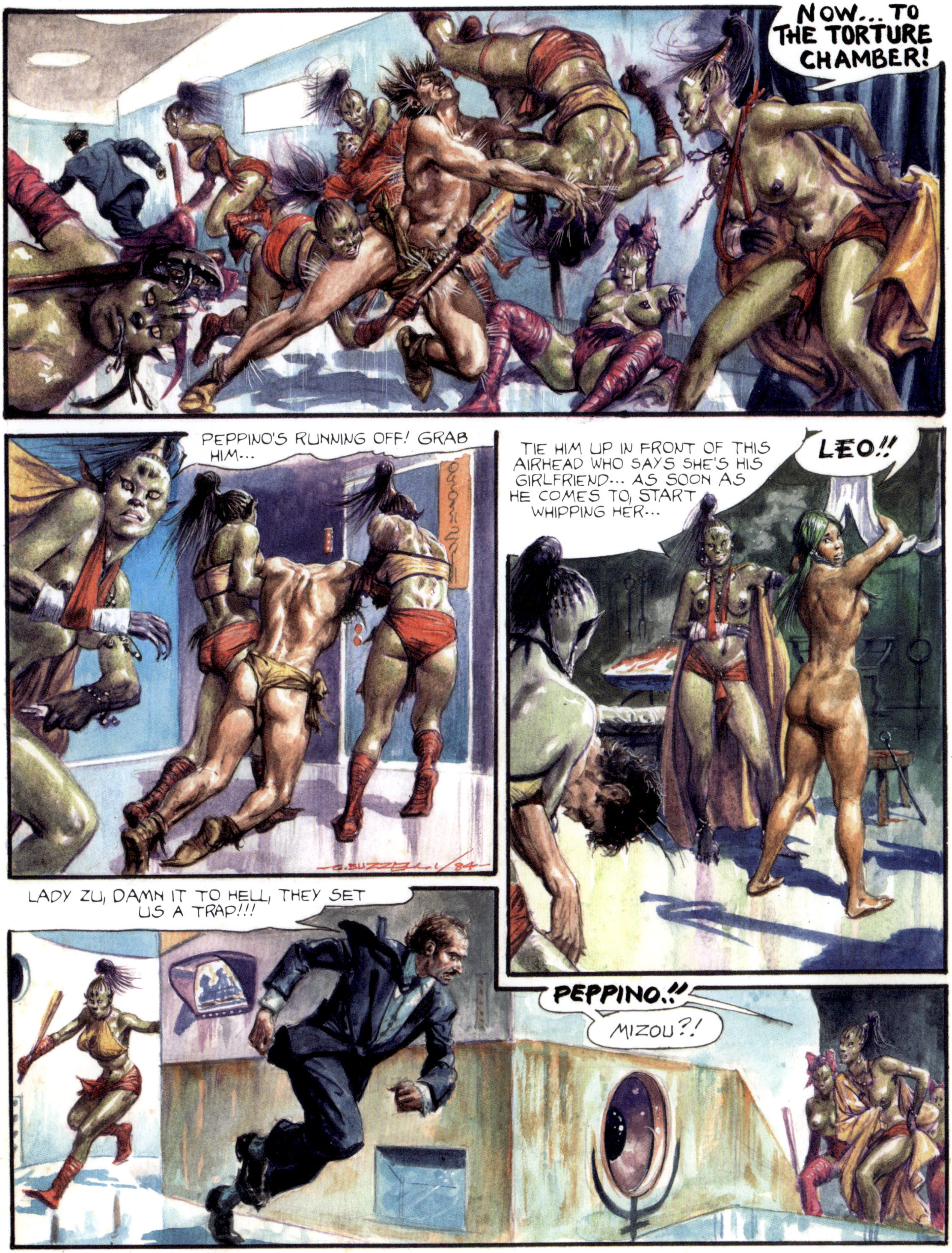
NOW... TO THE TORTURE CHAMBER!
PEPPINO'S RUNNING OFF! GRAB HIM...
TIE HIM UP IN FRONT OF THIS AIRHEAD WHO SAYS SHE'S HIS GIRLFRIEND... AS SOON AS HE COMES TO, START WHIPPING HER...
LEO!!
LADY ZU, DAMN IT TO HELL, THEY SET US A TRAP!!!
PEPPINO.!!
MIZOU?!

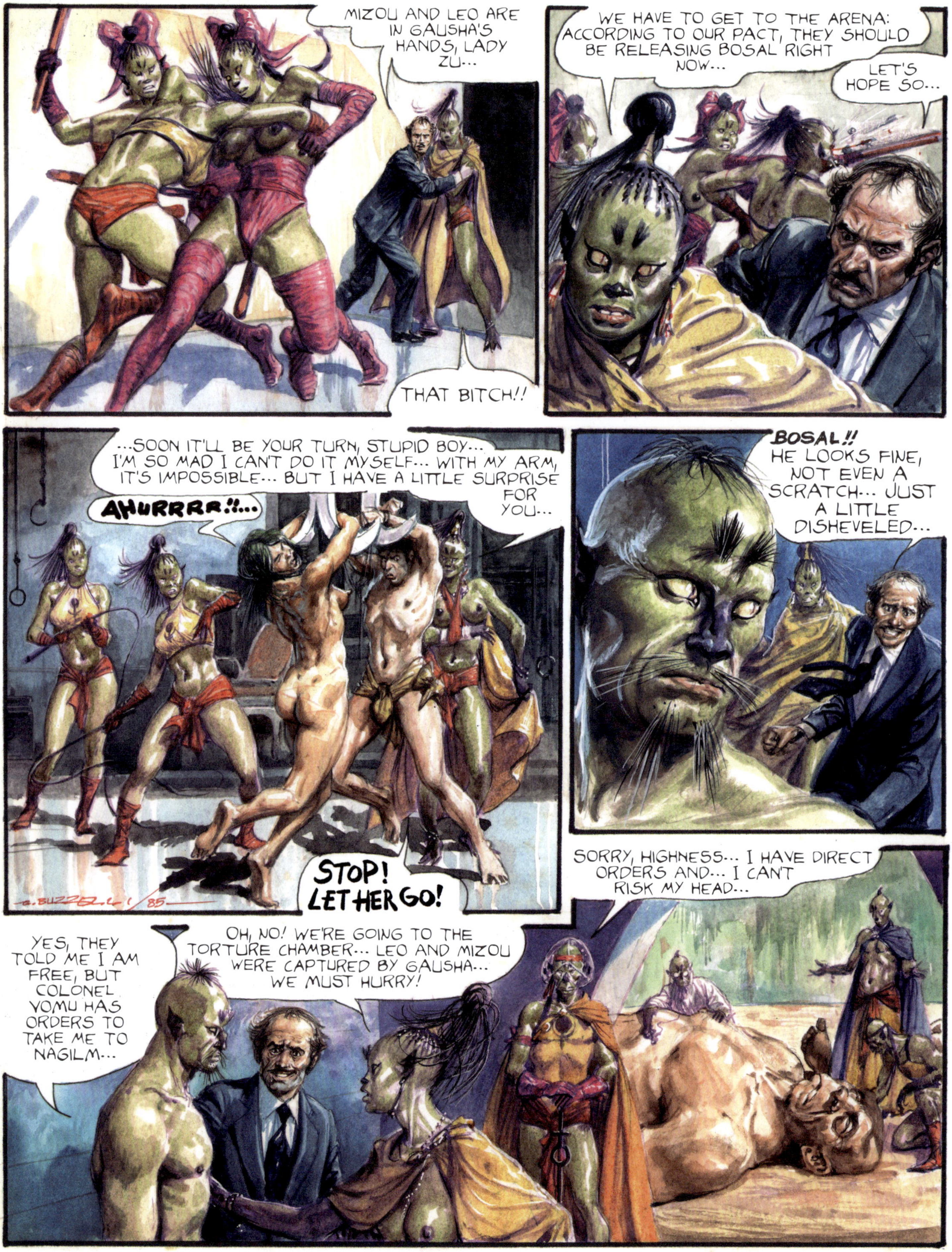
MIZOU AND LEO ARE IN GAUSHA'S HANDS, LADY ZU...
THAT BITCH!!
WE HAVE TO GET TO THE ARENA: ACCORDING TO OUR PACT, THEY SHOULD BE RELEASING BOSAL RIGHT NOW...
LET'S HOPE SO...
...SOON IT'LL BE YOUR TURN, STUPID BOY... I'M SO MAD I CAN'T DO IT MYSELF... WITH MY ARM, IT'S IMPOSSIBLE... BUT I HAVE A LITTLE SURPRISE FOR YOU...
AHURRRR!!...
STOP! LET HER GO!
BOSAL!!
HE LOOKS FINE, NOT EVEN A SCRATCH... JUST A LITTLE DISHEVELED...
SORRY, HIGHNESS... I HAVE DIRECT ORDERS AND... I CAN'T RISK MY HEAD...
YES, THEY TOLD ME I AM FREE, BUT COLONEL YOMU HAS ORDERS TO TAKE ME TO NAGILM...
OH, NO! WE'RE GOING TO THE TORTURE CHAMBER... LEO AND MIZOU WERE CAPTURED BY GAUSHA... WE MUST HURRY!

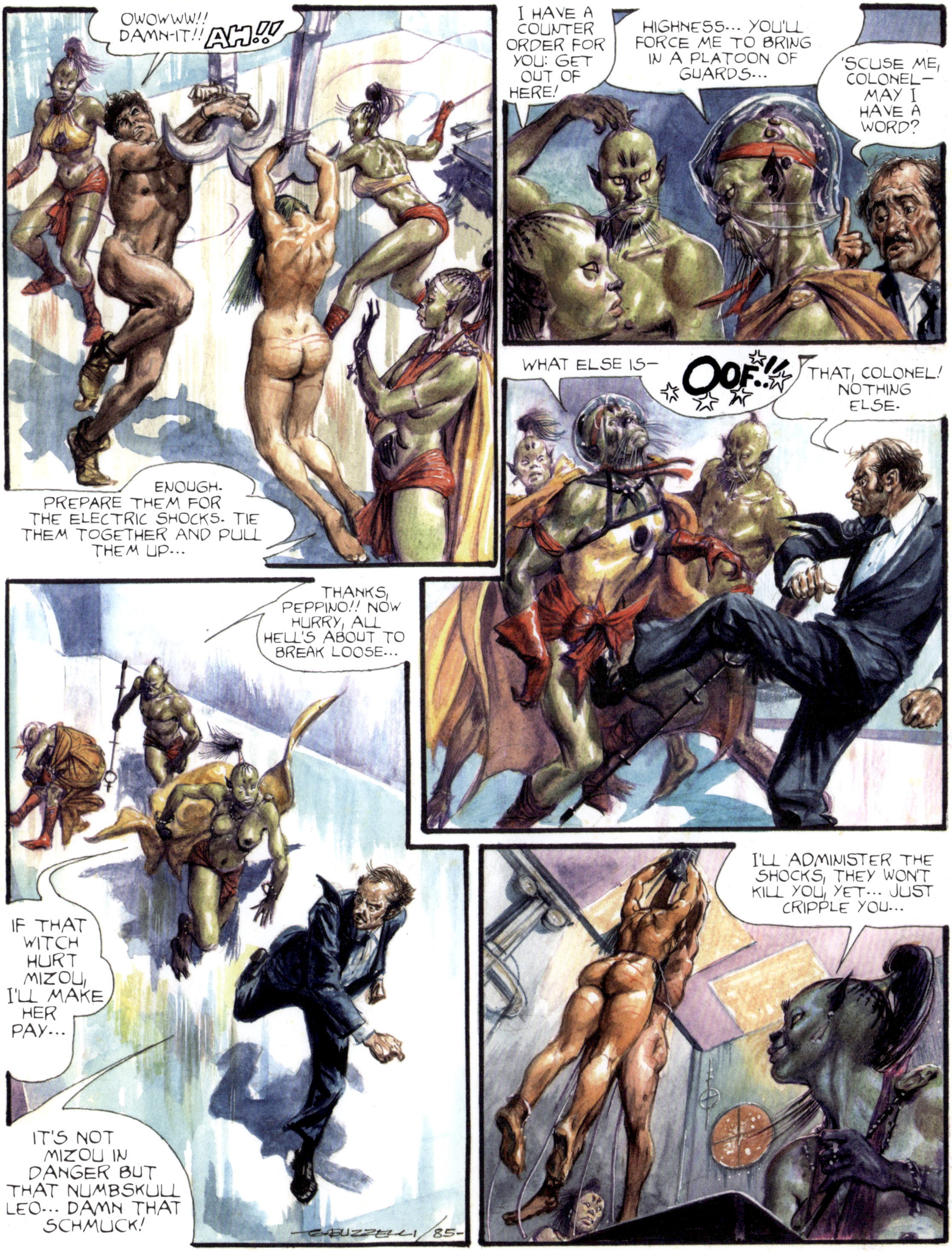
OWOWWW!! DAMN-IT!! AH!!
ENOUGH. PREPARE THEM FOR THE ELECTRIC SHOCKS. TIE THEM TOGETHER AND PULL THEM UP...
I HAVE A COUNTER ORDER FOR YOU: GET OUT OF HERE!
HIGHNESS... YOU'LL FORCE ME TO BRING IN A PLATOON OF GUARDS...
'SCUSE ME, COLONEL— MAY I HAVE A WORD?
WHAT ELSE IS—
OOF!!
THAT, COLONEL! NOTHING ELSE.
THANKS, PEPPINO!! NOW HURRY, ALL HELL'S ABOUT TO BREAK LOOSE...
IF THAT WITCH HURT MIZOU, I'LL MAKE HER PAY...
IT'S NOT MIZOU IN DANGER BUT THAT NUMBSKULL LEO... DAMN THAT SCHMUCK!
I'LL ADMINISTER THE SHOCKS, THEY WON'T KILL YOU, YET... JUST CRIPPLE YOU...

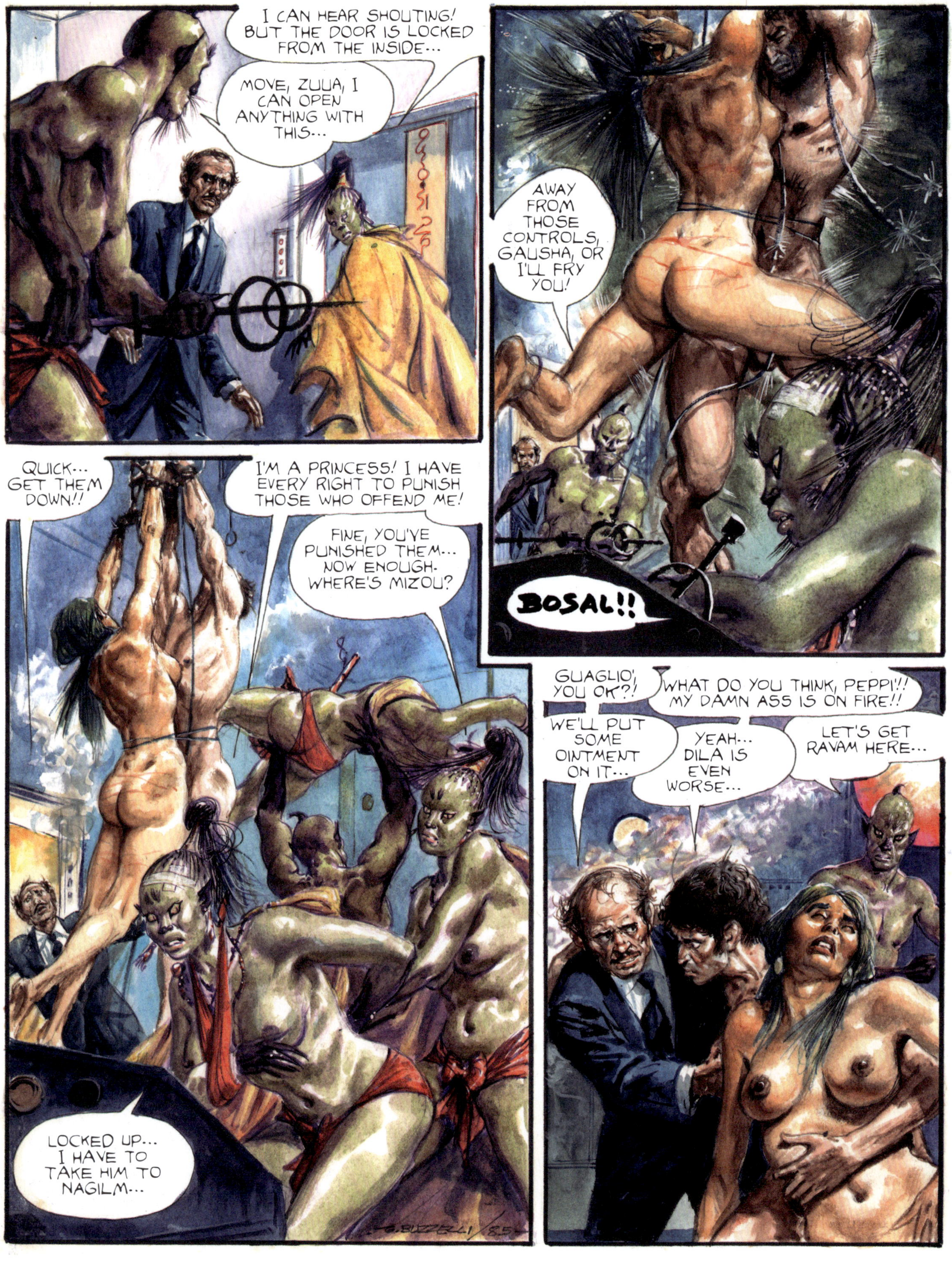
I CAN HEAR SHOUTING! BUT THE DOOR IS LOCKED FROM THE INSIDE...
MOVE, ZULA, I CAN OPEN ANYTHING WITH THIS...
AWAY FROM THOSE CONTROLS, GAUSHA, OR I'LL FRY YOU!
BOSAL!!
QUICK... GET THEM DOWN!!
I'M A PRINCESS! I HAVE EVERY RIGHT TO PUNISH THOSE WHO OFFEND ME!
FINE, YOU'VE PUNISHED THEM... NOW ENOUGH. WHERE'S MIZOU?
LOCKED UP... I HAVE TO TAKE HIM TO NAGILM...
GUAGLIO', YOU OK?!
WHAT DO YOU THINK, PEPPI!! MY DAMN ASS IS ON FIRE!!
WE'LL PUT SOME OINTMENT ON IT...
YEAH... DILA IS EVEN WORSE...
LET'S GET RAVAM HERE...

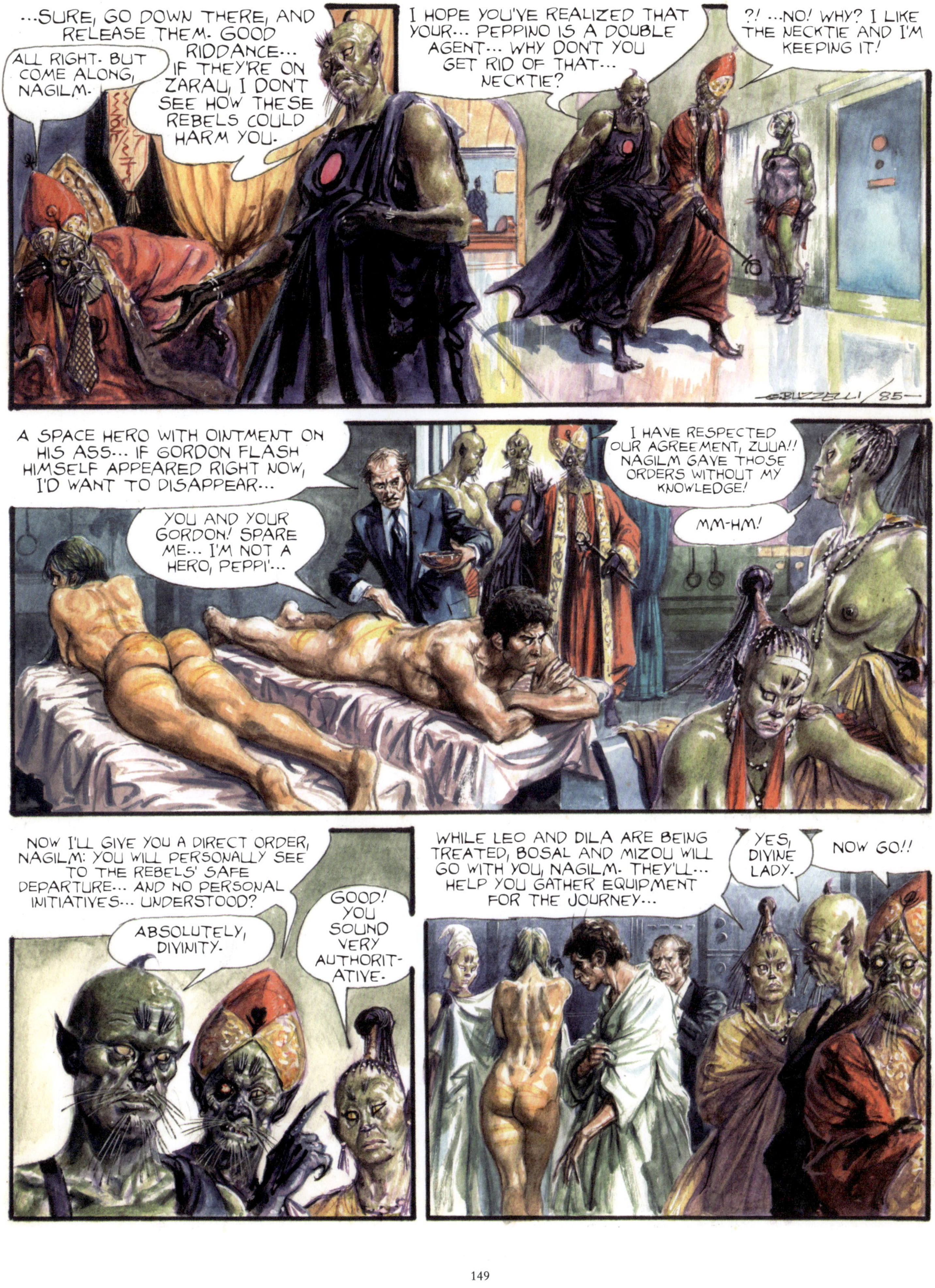
...SURE, GO DOWN THERE, AND RELEASE THEM. GOOD RIDDANCE... IF THEY'RE ON ZARAU, I DON'T SEE HOW THESE REBELS COULD HARM YOU.
ALL RIGHT. BUT COME ALONG, NAGILM.
I HOPE YOU'VE REALIZED THAT YOUR... PEPPINO IS A DOUBLE AGENT... WHY DON'T YOU GET RID OF THAT... NECKTIE?
?! ...NO! WHY? I LIKE THE NECKTIE AND I'M KEEPING IT!
G. BUZZELLI /85
A SPACE HERO WITH OINTMENT ON HIS ASS... IF GORDON FLASH HIMSELF APPEARED RIGHT NOW, I'D WANT TO DISAPPEAR...
YOU AND YOUR GORDON! SPARE ME... I'M NOT A HERO, PEPPI'...
I HAVE RESPECTED OUR AGREEMENT, ZUUA!! NAGILM GAVE THOSE ORDERS WITHOUT MY KNOWLEDGE!
MM-HM!
NOW I'LL GIVE YOU A DIRECT ORDER, NAGILM: YOU WILL PERSONALLY SEE TO THE REBELS' SAFE DEPARTURE... AND NO PERSONAL INITIATIVES... UNDERSTOOD?
ABSOLUTELY, DIVINITY.
GOOD! YOU SOUND VERY AUTHORITATIVE.
WHILE LEO AND DILA ARE BEING TREATED, BOSAL AND MIZOU WILL GO WITH YOU, NAGILM. THEY'LL... HELP YOU GATHER EQUIPMENT FOR THE JOURNEY...
YES, DIVINE LADY.
NOW GO!!

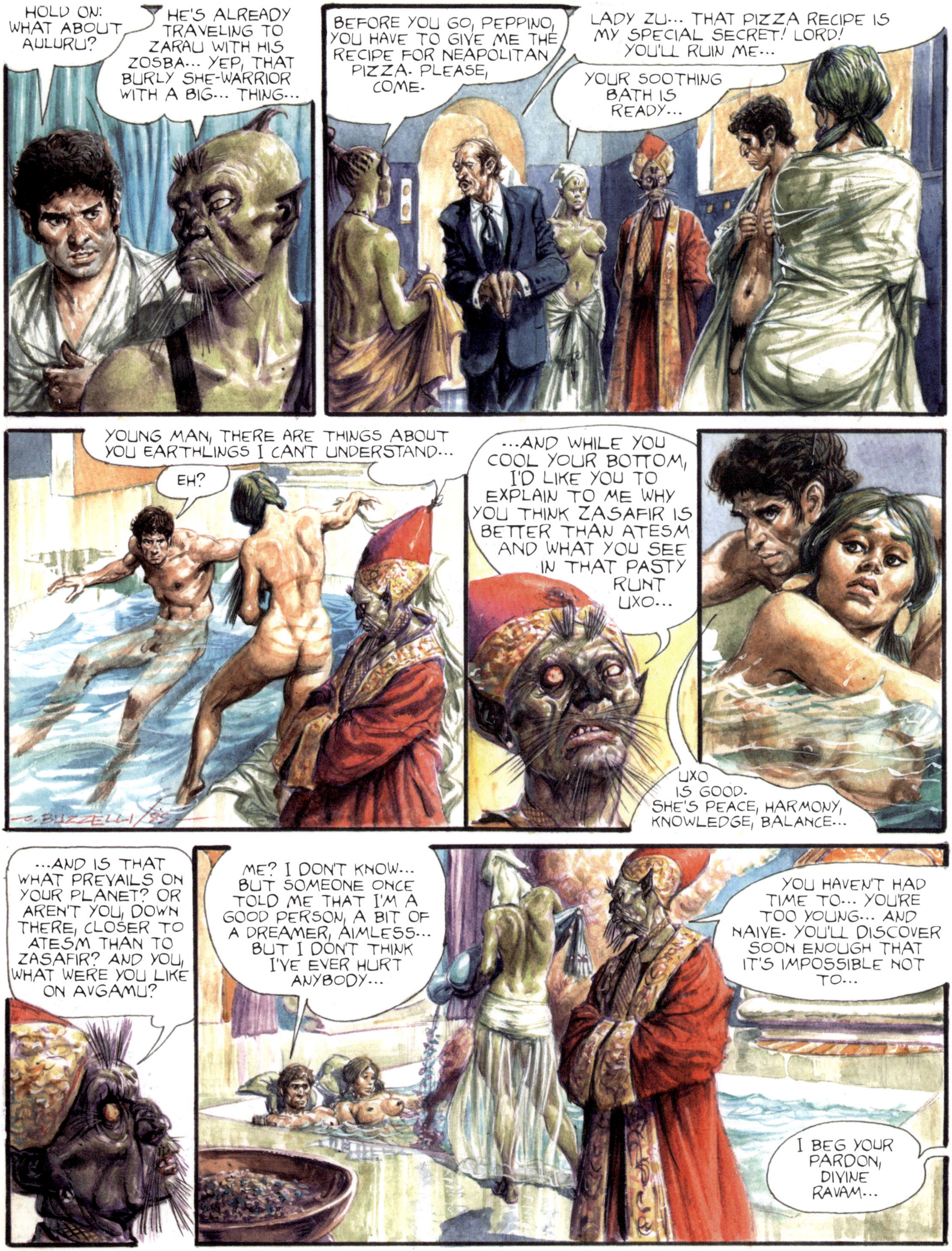
HOLD ON: WHAT ABOUT AULURU?
HE'S ALREADY TRAVELING TO ZARAU WITH HIS ZOSBA... YEP, THAT BURLY SHE-WARRIOR WITH A BIG... THING...
BEFORE YOU GO, PEPPINO, YOU HAVE TO GIVE ME THE RECIPE FOR NEAPOLITAN PIZZA. PLEASE, COME.
LADY ZU... THAT PIZZA RECIPE IS MY SPECIAL SECRET! LORD! YOU'LL RUIN ME...
YOUR SOOTHING BATH IS READY...
YOUNG MAN, THERE ARE THINGS ABOUT YOU EARTHLINGS I CAN'T UNDERSTAND...
EH?
G. BUZZELLI/85
...AND WHILE YOU COOL YOUR BOTTOM, I'D LIKE YOU TO EXPLAIN TO ME WHY YOU THINK ZASAFIR IS BETTER THAN ATESM AND WHAT YOU SEE IN THAT PASTY RUNT UXO...
UXO IS GOOD. SHE'S PEACE, HARMONY, KNOWLEDGE, BALANCE...
...AND IS THAT WHAT PREVAILS ON YOUR PLANET? OR AREN'T YOU, DOWN THERE, CLOSER TO ATESM THAN TO ZASAFIR? AND YOU, WHAT WERE YOU LIKE ON AVGAMU?
ME? I DON'T KNOW... BUT SOMEONE ONCE TOLD ME THAT I'M A GOOD PERSON, A BIT OF A DREAMER, AIMLESS... BUT I DON'T THINK I'VE EVER HURT ANYBODY...
YOU HAVEN'T HAD TIME TO... YOU'RE TOO YOUNG... AND NAIVE. YOU'LL DISCOVER SOON ENOUGH THAT IT'S IMPOSSIBLE NOT TO...
I BEG YOUR PARDON, DIVINE RAVAM...

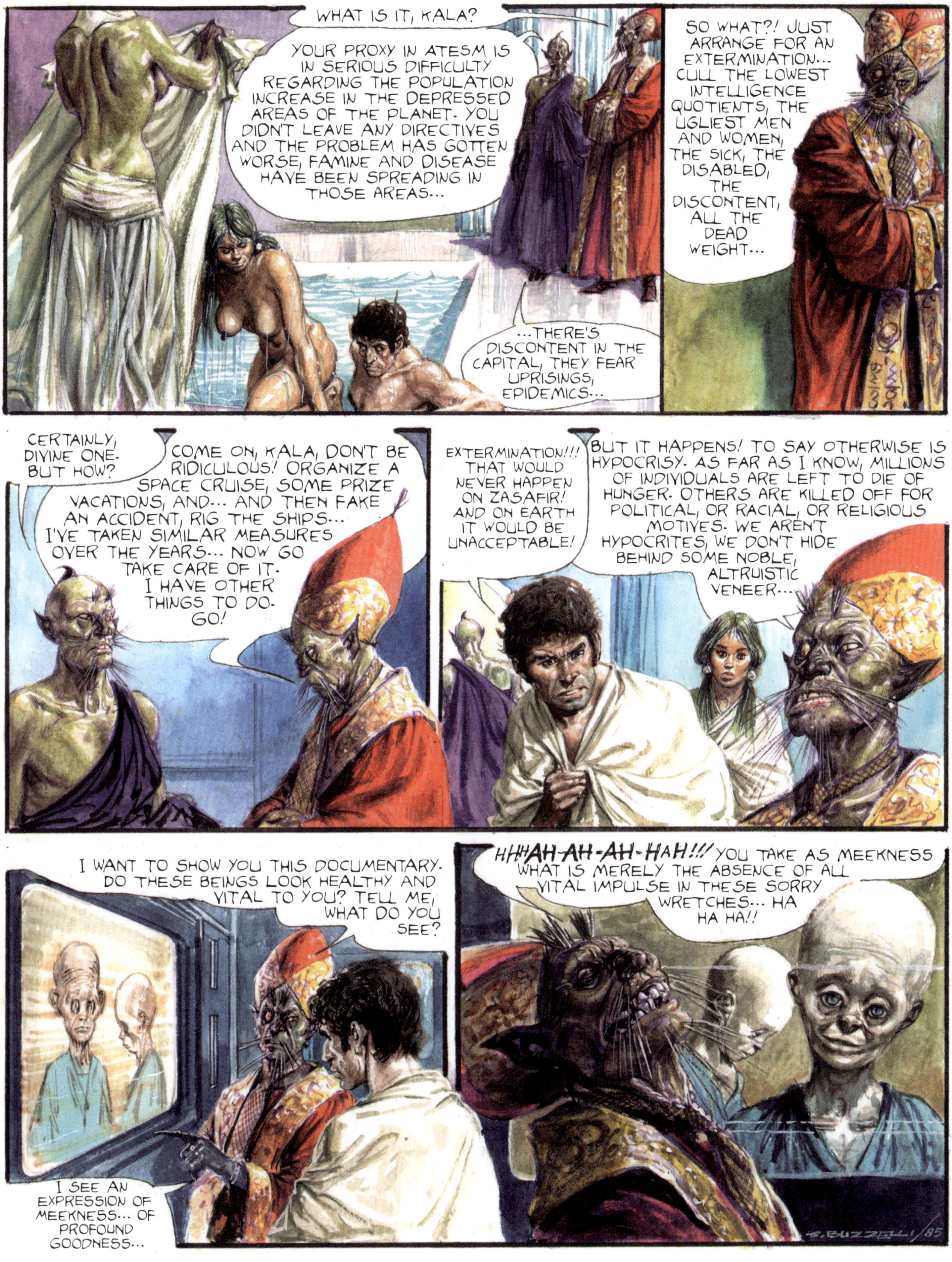
WHAT IS IT, KALA?
YOUR PROXY IN ATESM IS IN SERIOUS DIFFICULTY REGARDING THE POPULATION INCREASE IN THE DEPRESSED AREAS OF THE PLANET. YOU DIDN'T LEAVE ANY DIRECTIVES AND THE PROBLEM HAS GOTTEN WORSE, FAMINE AND DISEASE HAVE BEEN SPREADING IN THOSE AREAS...
...THERE'S DISCONTENT IN THE CAPITAL, THEY FEAR UPRISINGS, EPIDEMICS...
SO WHAT?! JUST ARRANGE FOR AN EXTERMINATION... CULL THE LOWEST INTELLIGENCE QUOTIENTS, THE UGLIEST MEN AND WOMEN, THE SICK, THE DISABLED, THE DISCONTENT, ALL THE DEAD WEIGHT...
CERTAINLY, DIVINE ONE. BUT HOW?
COME ON, KALA, DON'T BE RIDICULOUS! ORGANIZE A SPACE CRUISE, SOME PRIZE VACATIONS, AND... AND THEN FAKE AN ACCIDENT, RIG THE SHIPS... I'VE TAKEN SIMILAR MEASURES OVER THE YEARS... NOW GO TAKE CARE OF IT. I HAVE OTHER THINGS TO DO. GO!
EXTERMINATION!!! THAT WOULD NEVER HAPPEN ON ZASAFIR! AND ON EARTH IT WOULD BE UNACCEPTABLE!
BUT IT HAPPENS! TO SAY OTHERWISE IS HYPOCRISY. AS FAR AS I KNOW, MILLIONS OF INDIVIDUALS ARE LEFT TO DIE OF HUNGER. OTHERS ARE KILLED OFF FOR POLITICAL, OR RACIAL, OR RELIGIOUS MOTIVES. WE AREN'T HYPOCRITES, WE DON'T HIDE BEHIND SOME NOBLE, ALTRUISTIC VENEER...
I WANT TO SHOW YOU THIS DOCUMENTARY. DO THESE BEINGS LOOK HEALTHY AND VITAL TO YOU? TELL ME, WHAT DO YOU SEE?
I SEE AN EXPRESSION OF MEEKNESS... OF PROFOUND GOODNESS...
HHHAH-AH-AH-HAH!!! YOU TAKE AS MEEKNESS WHAT IS MERELY THE ABSENCE OF ALL VITAL IMPULSE IN THESE SORRY WRETCHES... HA HA HA!!
G. BUZZELLI/85

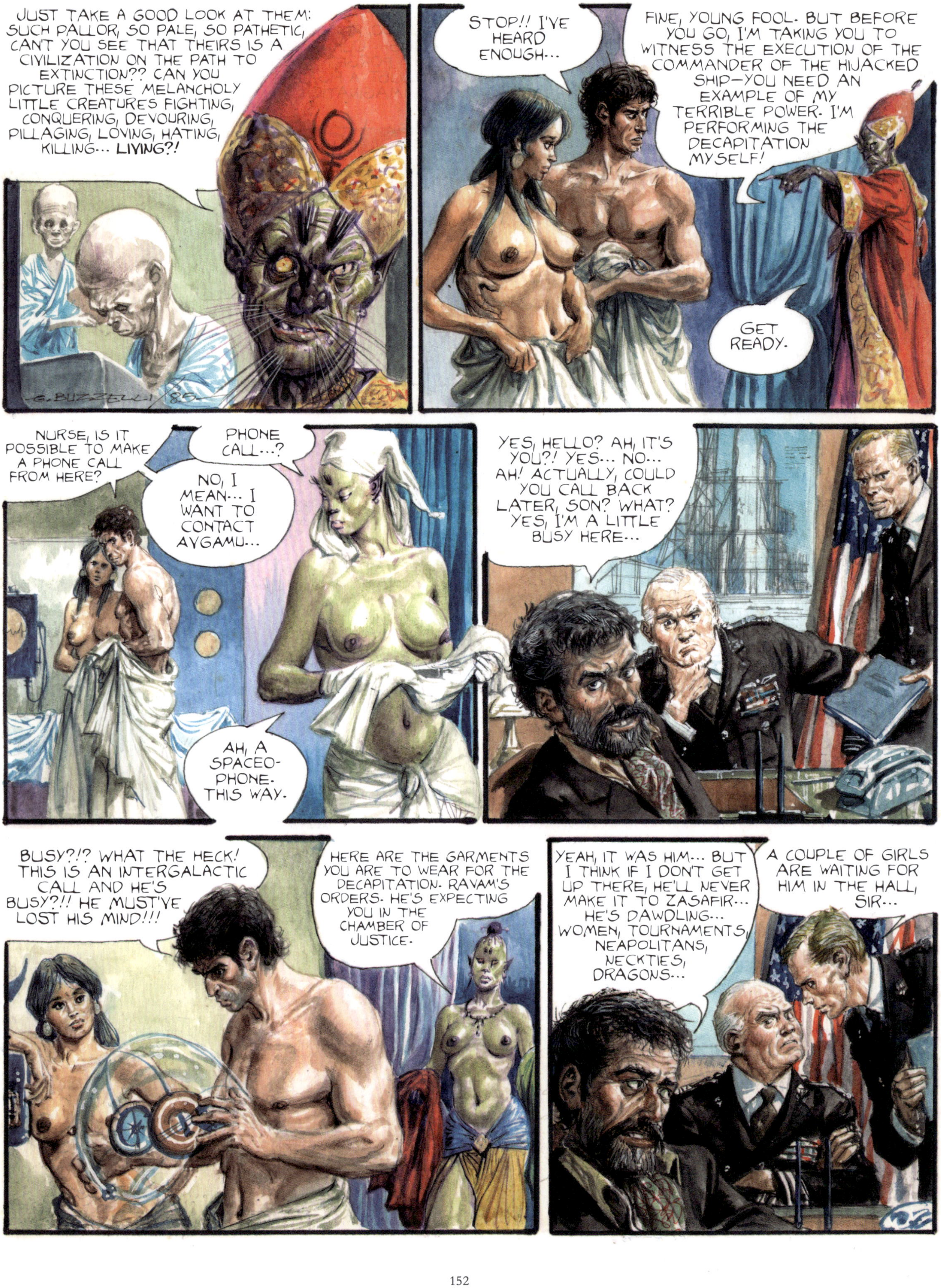
JUST TAKE A GOOD LOOK AT THEM: SUCH PALLOR, SO PALE, SO PATHETIC, CAN'T YOU SEE THAT THEIRS IS A CIVILIZATION ON THE PATH TO EXTINCTION?? CAN YOU PICTURE THESE MELANCHOLY LITTLE CREATURES FIGHTING, CONQUERING, DEVOURING, PILLAGING, LOVING, HATING, KILLING... LIVING?!
G. BUZZELLI '85
STOP!! I'VE HEARD ENOUGH...
FINE, YOUNG FOOL. BUT BEFORE YOU GO, I'M TAKING YOU TO WITNESS THE EXECUTION OF THE COMMANDER OF THE HIJACKED SHIP—YOU NEED AN EXAMPLE OF MY TERRIBLE POWER. I'M PERFORMING THE DECAPITATION MYSELF!
GET READY.
NURSE, IS IT POSSIBLE TO MAKE A PHONE CALL FROM HERE?
PHONE CALL...?
NO, I MEAN... I WANT TO CONTACT AYGAMU...
AH, A SPACEO-PHONE. THIS WAY.
YES, HELLO? AH, IT'S YOU?! YES... NO... AH! ACTUALLY, COULD YOU CALL BACK LATER, SON? WHAT? YES, I'M A LITTLE BUSY HERE...
BUSY?!? WHAT THE HECK! THIS IS AN INTERGALACTIC CALL AND HE'S BUSY?!! HE MUST'VE LOST HIS MIND!!!
HERE ARE THE GARMENTS YOU ARE TO WEAR FOR THE DECAPITATION. RAVAM'S ORDERS. HE'S EXPECTING YOU IN THE CHAMBER OF JUSTICE.
YEAH, IT WAS HIM... BUT I THINK IF I DON'T GET UP THERE, HE'LL NEVER MAKE IT TO ZASAFIR... HE'S DAWDLING... WOMEN, TOURNAMENTS, NEAPOLITANS, NECKTIES, DRAGONS...
A COUPLE OF GIRLS ARE WAITING FOR HIM IN THE HALL, SIR...

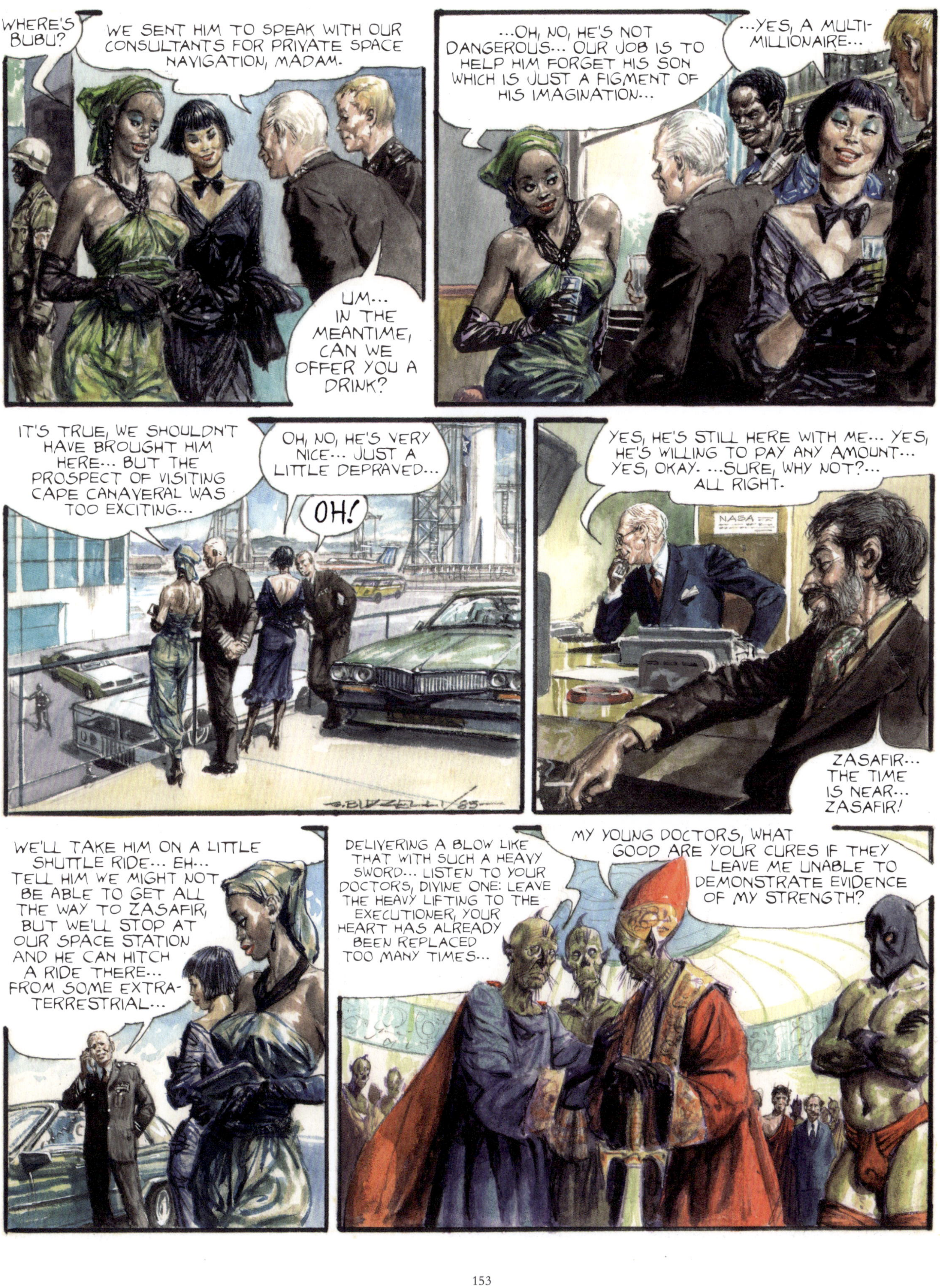
WHERE'S BUBU?
WE SENT HIM TO SPEAK WITH OUR CONSULTANTS FOR PRIVATE SPACE NAVIGATION, MADAM.
UM... IN THE MEANTIME, CAN WE OFFER YOU A DRINK?
...OH, NO, HE'S NOT DANGEROUS... OUR JOB IS TO HELP HIM FORGET HIS SON WHICH IS JUST A FIGMENT OF HIS IMAGINATION...
...YES, A MULTI-MILLIONAIRE...
IT'S TRUE, WE SHOULDN'T HAVE BROUGHT HIM HERE... BUT THE PROSPECT OF VISITING CAPE CANAVERAL WAS TOO EXCITING...
OH, NO, HE'S VERY NICE... JUST A LITTLE DEPRAVED...
OH!
YES, HE'S STILL HERE WITH ME... YES, HE'S WILLING TO PAY ANY AMOUNT... YES, OKAY. ...SURE, WHY NOT?... ALL RIGHT.
NASA
ZASAFIR... THE TIME IS NEAR... ZASAFIR!
WE'LL TAKE HIM ON A LITTLE SHUTTLE RIDE... EH... TELL HIM WE MIGHT NOT BE ABLE TO GET ALL THE WAY TO ZASAFIR, BUT WE'LL STOP AT OUR SPACE STATION AND HE CAN HITCH A RIDE THERE... FROM SOME EXTRA-TERRESTRIAL...
DELIVERING A BLOW LIKE THAT WITH SUCH A HEAVY SWORD... LISTEN TO YOUR DOCTORS, DIVINE ONE: LEAVE THE HEAVY LIFTING TO THE EXECUTIONER, YOUR HEART HAS ALREADY BEEN REPLACED TOO MANY TIMES...
MY YOUNG DOCTORS, WHAT GOOD ARE YOUR CURES IF THEY LEAVE ME UNABLE TO DEMONSTRATE EVIDENCE OF MY STRENGTH?

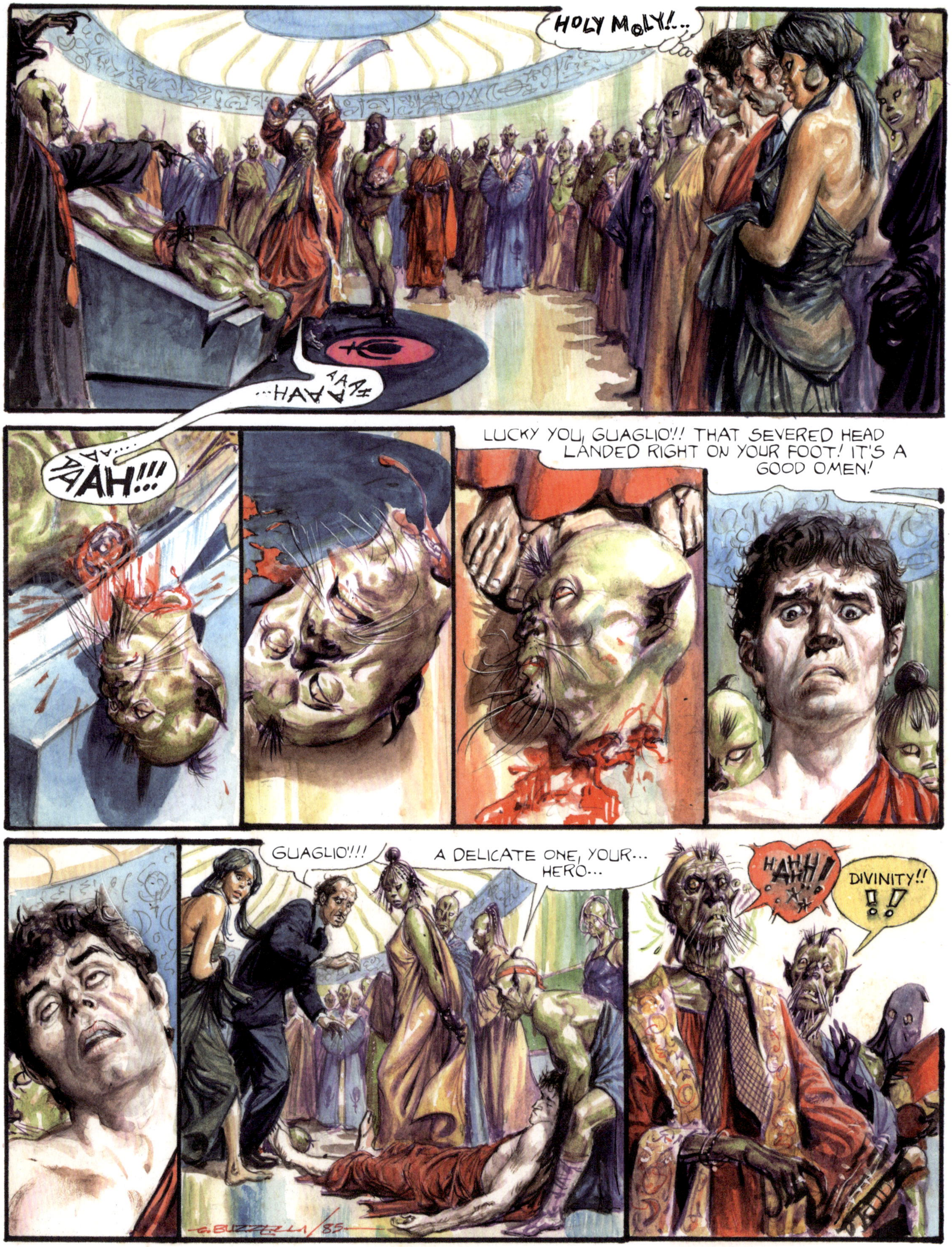
HOLY MOLY!..
AAAAH...
AAAH!!!
LUCKY YOU, GUAGLIO!! THAT SEVERED HEAD LANDED RIGHT ON YOUR FOOT! IT'S A GOOD OMEN!
GUAGLIO!!!
A DELICATE ONE, YOUR... HERO...
DIVINITY!! !!
G. BUZZELLI/85

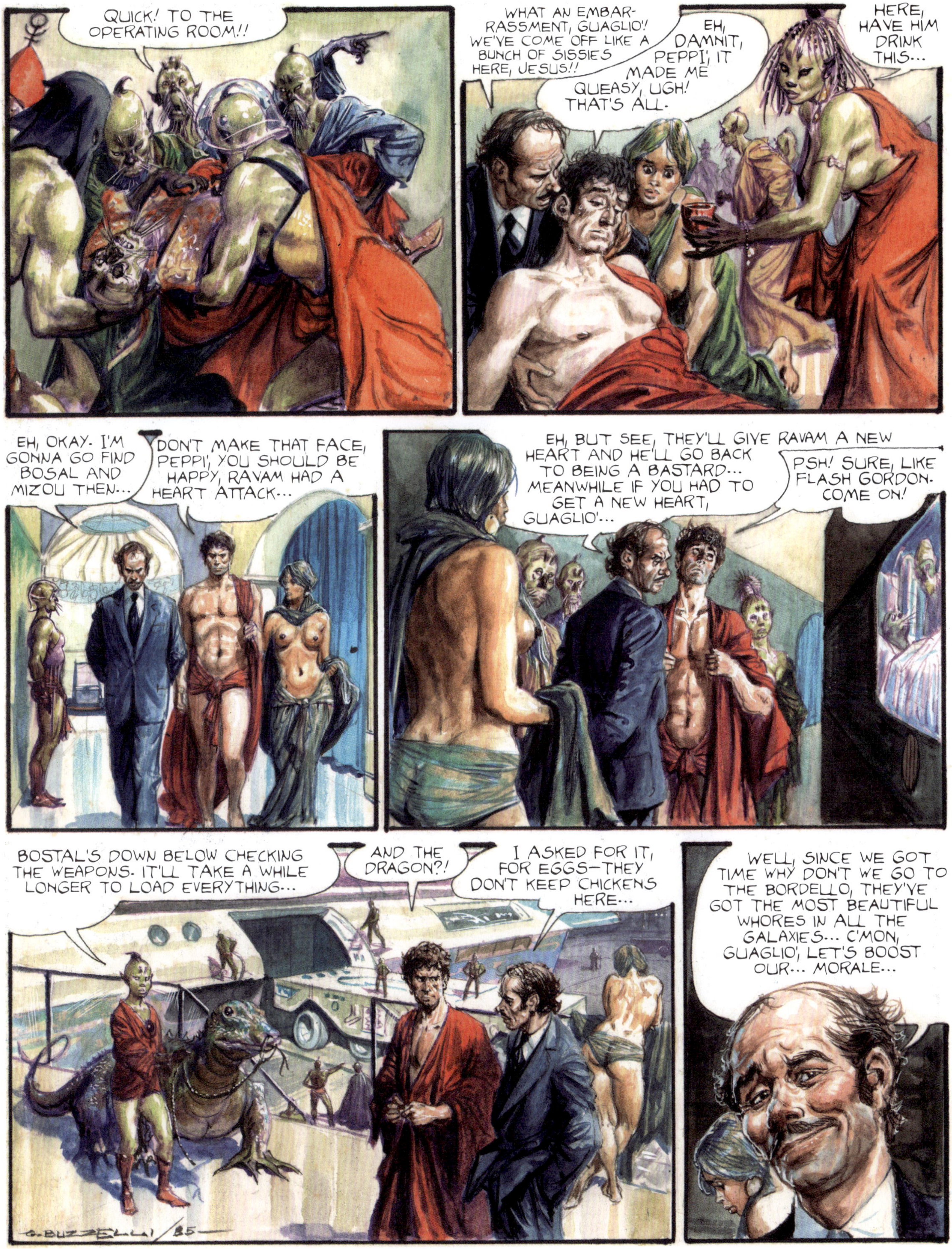
QUICK! TO THE OPERATING ROOM!!
WHAT AN EMBARRASSMENT, GUAGLIO'! WE'VE COME OFF LIKE A BUNCH OF SISSIES HERE, JESUS!!
EH, DAMNIT, PEPPI', IT MADE ME QUEASY, UGH! THAT'S ALL.
HERE, HAVE HIM DRINK THIS...
EH, OKAY. I'M GONNA GO FIND BOSAL AND MIZOU THEN...
DON'T MAKE THAT FACE, PEPPI', YOU SHOULD BE HAPPY, RAVAM HAD A HEART ATTACK...
EH, BUT SEE, THEY'LL GIVE RAVAM A NEW HEART AND HE'LL GO BACK TO BEING A BASTARD... MEANWHILE IF YOU HAD TO GET A NEW HEART, GUAGLIO'...
PSH! SURE, LIKE FLASH GORDON. COME ON!
BOSTAL'S DOWN BELOW CHECKING THE WEAPONS. IT'LL TAKE A WHILE LONGER TO LOAD EVERYTHING...
AND THE DRAGON?!
I ASKED FOR IT, FOR EGGS—THEY DON'T KEEP CHICKENS HERE...
WELL, SINCE WE GOT TIME WHY DON'T WE GO TO THE BORDELLO, THEY'VE GOT THE MOST BEAUTIFUL WHORES IN ALL THE GALAXIES... C'MON, GUAGLIO', LET'S BOOST OUR... MORALE...
G. BUZZELLI /85

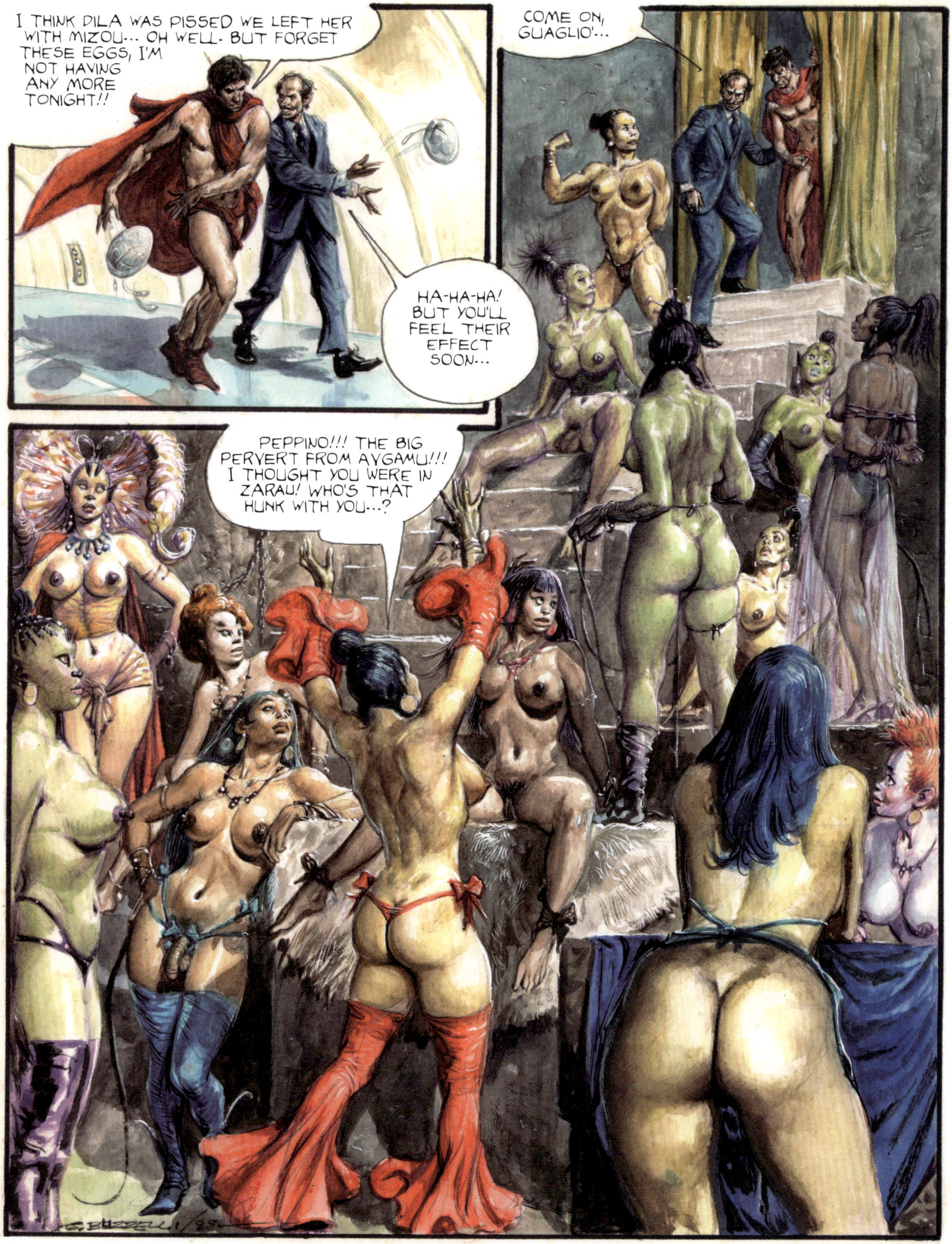
I THINK DILA WAS PISSED WE LEFT HER WITH MIZOU... OH WELL. BUT FORGET THESE EGGS, I'M NOT HAVING ANY MORE TONIGHT!!
HA-HA-HA! BUT YOU'LL FEEL THEIR EFFECT SOON...
COME ON, GUAGLIO'...
PEPPINO!!! THE BIG PERVERT FROM AYGAMU!!! I THOUGHT YOU WERE IN ZARAU! WHO'S THAT HUNK WITH YOU...?

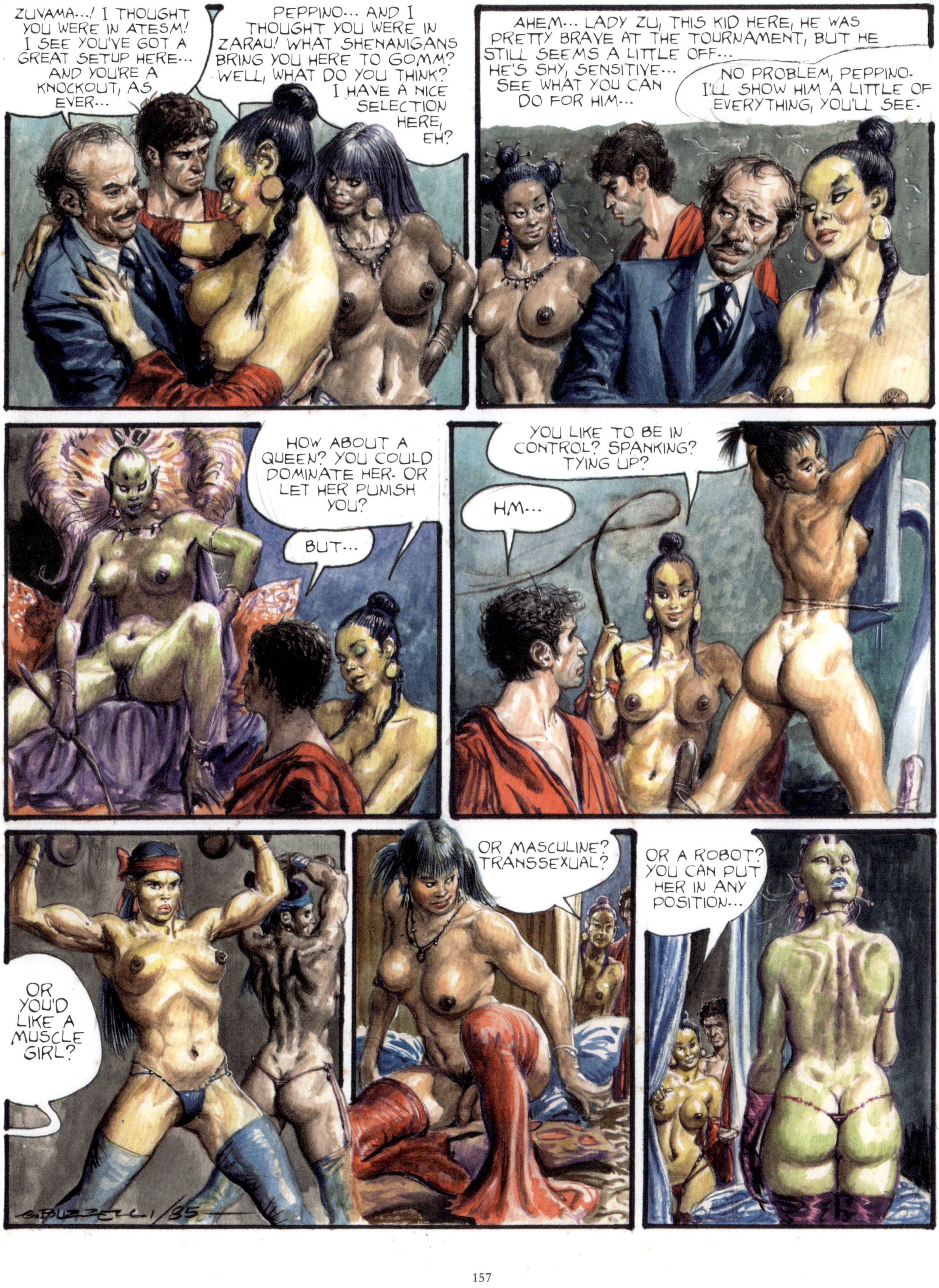
ZUVAMA...! I THOUGHT YOU WERE IN ATESM! I SEE YOU'VE GOT A GREAT SETUP HERE... AND YOU'RE A KNOCKOUT, AS EVER...
PEPPINO... AND I THOUGHT YOU WERE IN ZARAU! WHAT SHENANIGANS BRING YOU HERE TO GOMM? WELL, WHAT DO YOU THINK? I HAVE A NICE SELECTION HERE, EH?
AHEM... LADY ZU, THIS KID HERE, HE WAS PRETTY BRAVE AT THE TOURNAMENT, BUT HE STILL SEEMS A LITTLE OFF... HE'S SHY, SENSITIVE... SEE WHAT YOU CAN DO FOR HIM...
NO PROBLEM, PEPPINO. I'LL SHOW HIM A LITTLE OF EVERYTHING, YOU'LL SEE.
HOW ABOUT A QUEEN? YOU COULD DOMINATE HER. OR LET HER PUNISH YOU?
BUT...
YOU LIKE TO BE IN CONTROL? SPANKING? TYING UP?
HM...
OR YOU'D LIKE A MUSCLE GIRL?
G. BUZZELLI/85
OR MASCULINE? TRANSSEXUAL?
OR A ROBOT? YOU CAN PUT HER IN ANY POSITION...

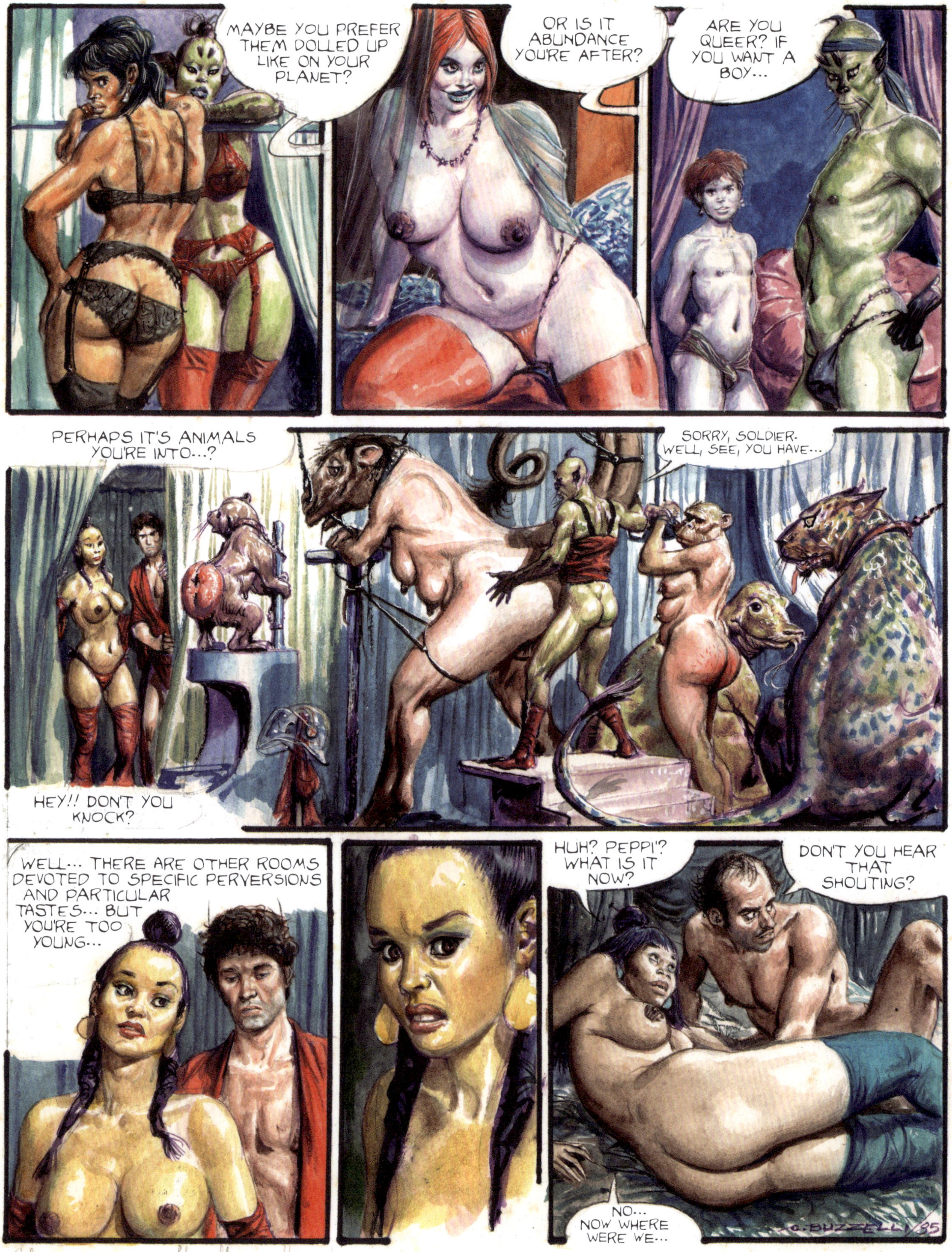
MAYBE YOU PREFER THEM DOLLED UP LIKE ON YOUR PLANET?
OR IS IT ABUNDANCE YOU'RE AFTER?
ARE YOU QUEER? IF YOU WANT A BOY...
PERHAPS IT'S ANIMALS YOU'RE INTO...?
SORRY, SOLDIER. WELL, SEE, YOU HAVE...
HEY!! DON'T YOU KNOCK?
WELL... THERE ARE OTHER ROOMS DEVOTED TO SPECIFIC PERVERSIONS AND PARTICULAR TASTES... BUT YOU'RE TOO YOUNG...
HUH? PEPPI'? WHAT IS IT NOW?
DON'T YOU HEAR THAT SHOUTING?
NO... NOW WHERE WERE WE...
G. BUZZELLI/85

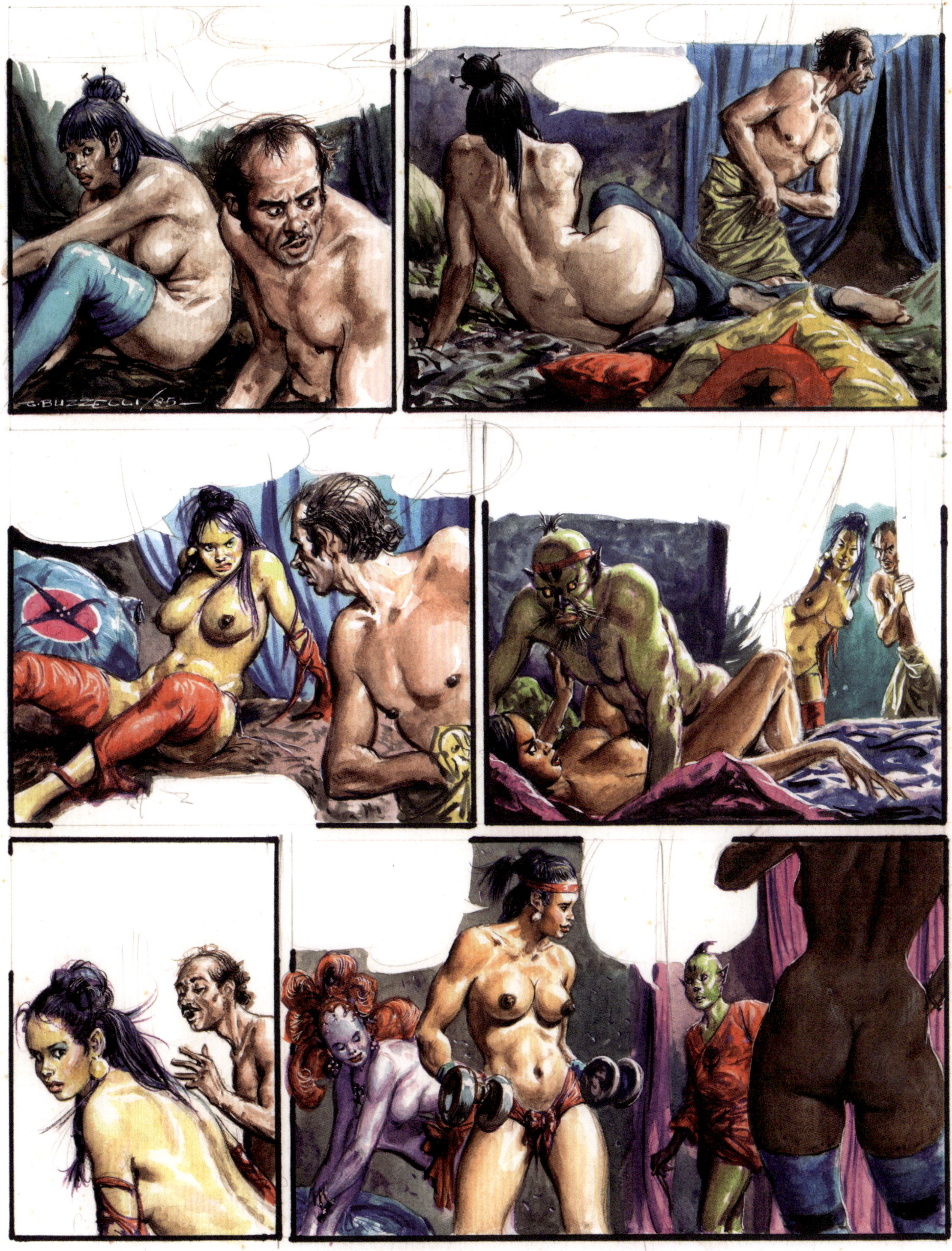
G.BUZZELLI/85

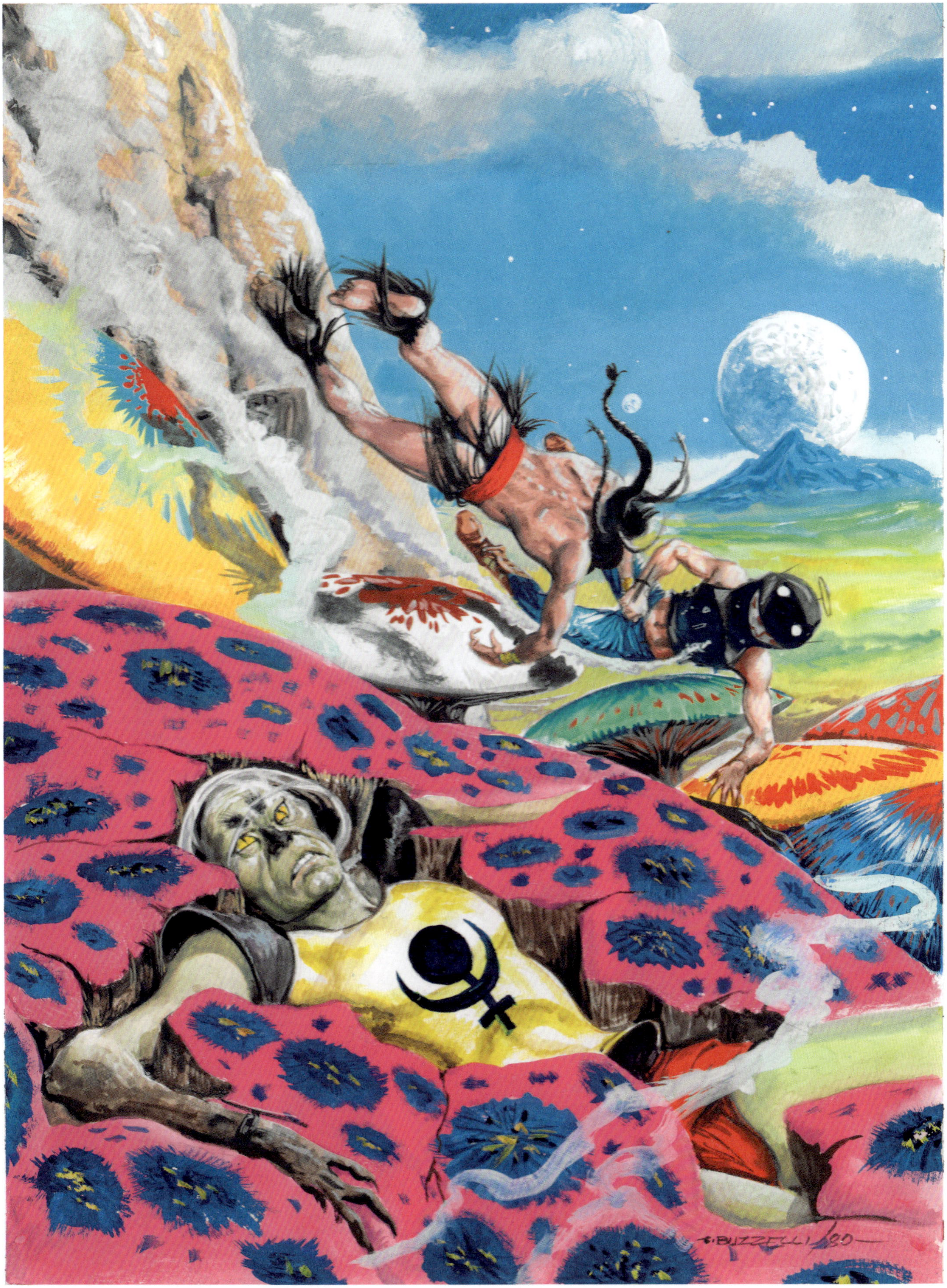
G. BUZZELLI /80

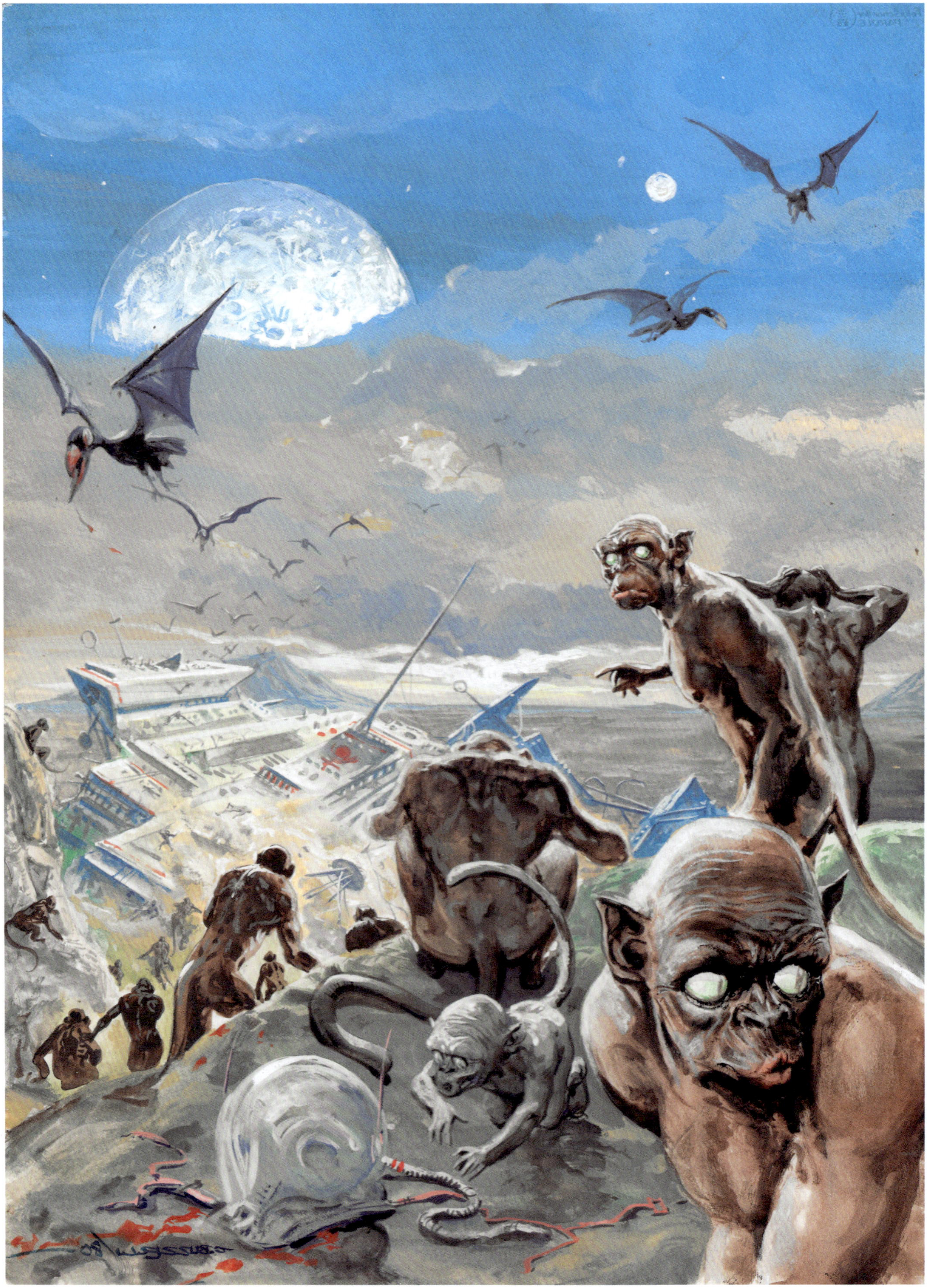

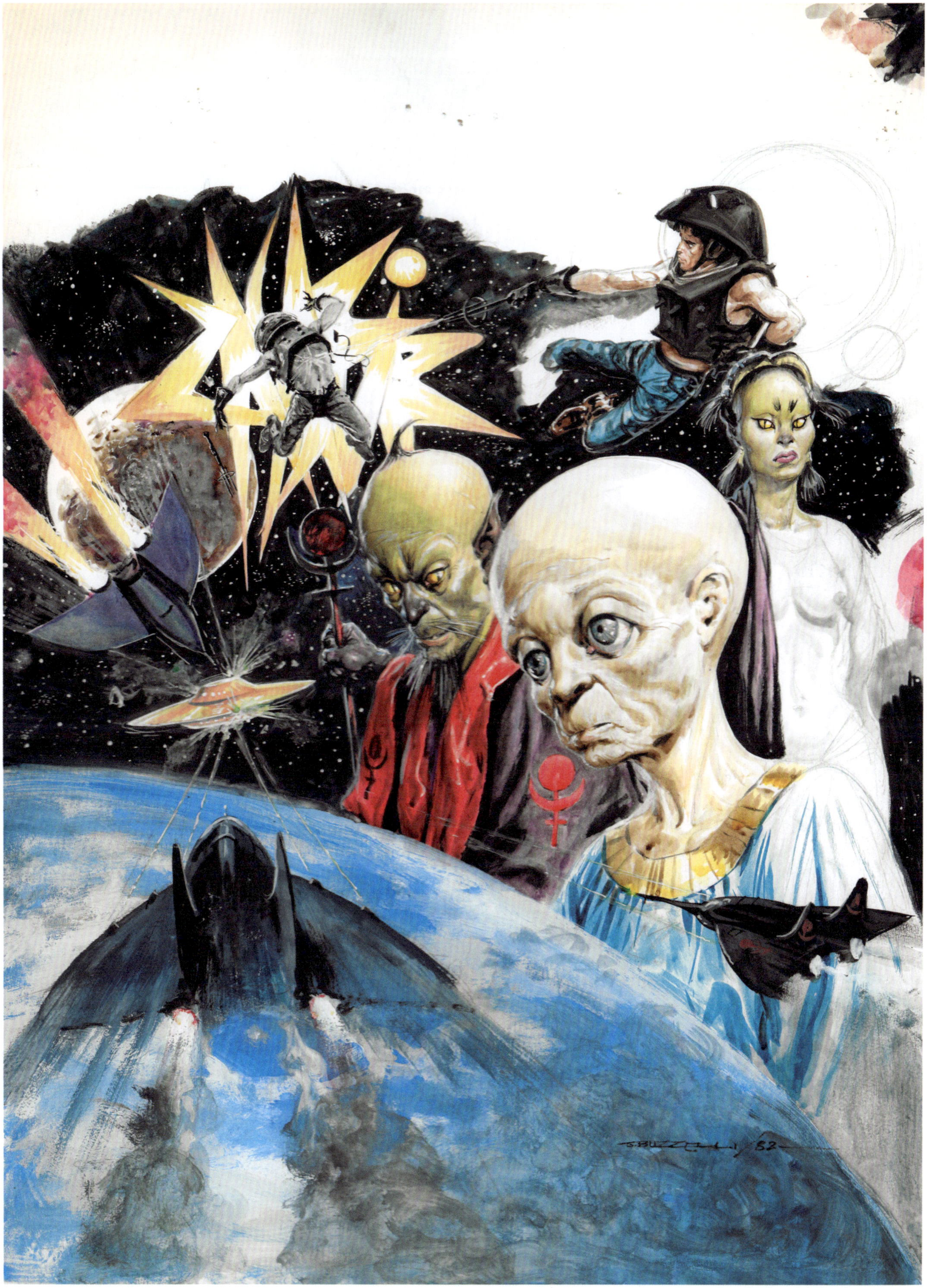

HAILED IN ITALY AND FRANCE, Buzzelli has been called "the Michelangelo of monsters," "the Goya of comics," "the patron saint of all Italian cartoonists." A pioneer active from the 1950s-1980s, today virtually unknown in English, Guido Buzzelli horrifies, fascinates, entertains, provokes, with his unique blend of surrealism and dynamism. Displaying a range of influences from Westerns and science fiction to Renaissance art and futurism, Buzzelli's stories are a delightful, quasi-postmodern mishmash of high and low, showing an intricate hand and stylish narrative skill.

What I admire most in his work is the evident impulse to exploit the full powers of the imagination, using fantasy to draw beyond what reality can produce. And yet all in the service of subtle but mordant social commentary: on our complicated relationship with technology, our so-called civilization and the notion of progress, our proclivity for barbarism and warfare. In short, Buzzelli depicts the monstrous in the human, and the human in the monstrous—and almost always with a more or less secret self-portrait, perhaps an artist painting in the background, or sometimes an alter-ego protagonist.

"Comics is theater in paper and ink, made for pockets and libraries, where the actors stand motionless waiting for someone to turn the pages and bring them to life," is how Buzzelli once described his idea of the graphic narrative art. A modern master, not to be missed.

—Jamie Richards

Buzzelli Collected Works Vol. 3
The Revolt of the Wretched

Entire contents copyright © by Grazia De Stefani Buzzelli, 2017. Translation copyright © by Jamie Richards, 2024.
This edition copyright © by Floating World Comics, 2024. © for the original Italian edition Coconino Press - Fandango, 2017.

This work was translated with support from the Center for Books and Reading of the Italian Ministry of Culture.

All rights reserved. No part of this book (except small portions for review purposes) may be reproduced in any form without written permission from Grazia De Stefani Buzzelli or Floating World Comics.

Translation made in arrangement with Am-Book (www.am-book.com).

Translated by Jamie Richards
Cover, book, and original typeface design by François Vigneault
Editing by Jason Leivian and Jamie Richards
Lettering by Jason Leivian
Hand lettering by Tim Goodyear
Original scans by Paolo Altibrandi

First edition: December 2024. Printed in China.

ISBN 978-1942801672 Published by Floating World Comics.